# BELIEVE

## STUDENT EDITION

LIVING THE STORY OF THE BIBLE
TO BECOME LIKE JESUS

SELECTIONS FROM THE NEW INTERNATIONAL VERSION

# BELIEVE
## STUDENT EDITION
### LIVING THE STORY OF THE BIBLE TO BECOME LIKE JESUS

GENERAL EDITOR
# RANDY FRAZEE

**ZONDERVAN®**

ZONDERVAN

This title is also available as a Zondervan ebook.

*Believe Student Edition*
Copyright © 2015 by Zondervan

Visit www.zondervan.com/ebooks.

Requests for information should be addressed to:
Zondervan, 3900 *Sparks Drive SE, Grand Rapids, Michigan,* 49546

ISBN: 978-0-310-74561-7

Cover design: *Extra Credit Projects*

*Printed in the United States of America*

15 16 17 18 19 20 21 22 23 24 25 /DCI/ 15 14 13 12 11 10 9 8 7 6 5 4 3 2 1

# Table of Contents

## BE

# Who Am I Becoming?

# Preface

From 1933 to 1945, under the leadership of Adolf Hitler, Nazi Germany engaged in a horrific act of persecution and genocide against the Jews of Europe. They sought to completely exterminate the Jewish people from the face of the earth. By 1945, when Hitler's regime was finally defeated, 6 million of the estimated 9 million Jews had been killed. Historians suggest that only a small percentage of the population participated in this holocaust, another small percentage tried to do something to stop it and the majority did nothing.

Among the few who tried to stop this catastrophe were a group of Christian students from the Netherlands. They formed a "resistance army" and partnered with Corrie ten Boom (who later authored *The Hiding Place*) and others to hide Jews from the Third Reich. From 1940 to 1945 they were responsible for saving the lives of 800 Jews. Many members of this student-led movement lost their lives in an effort to save others.

A rabbi who hid in the home of Ms. ten Boom asked young Hans Poley, a member of the teenage army, what persuaded him to get involved even though he knew he could lose his life for doing so. He responded, "I want to follow my Master who died for total strangers and even for those who hated him. He stood in the gap to take the violence upon himself." The rabbi then said, "Your religion really does mean so much to you doesn't it?" Hans spoke with conviction, "Actually, the Christian truth isn't a religion but a revolution against the kingdom of darkness."

What inspired and compelled these young men and women to engage in such an act of sacrifice?

In a nutshell — they BELIEVED.

They simply, by faith, believed the powerful truths taught in the Scriptures with their whole hearts. It changed them from the inside out. Their loving and courageous actions toward the Jewish people were merely outpourings of what was flowing from the inside.

This is not the first time teenagers were used by God to uphold justice, extend mercy and offer grace as willing participants. Throughout the pages of Scripture we are introduced to the lives of young men and women who simply said yes to God. They resisted evil, but they did not resist God.

- Joseph — At the young age of 17, Joseph received a dream from God on an important role he would play in the unfolding of God's grand plan. Eventually placing Joseph second in command in all of Egypt, God used him to save Israel from a famine.
- David — At the age of 15 or 16, David was secretly anointed to be the next king of Israel. After King Saul died about 15 years later, David ruled over Israel as a man after God's own heart until his death.
- Josiah — At the age of 8, Josiah was inaugurated as king of Judah during a very dark time in Israel's history. Under his 31-year reign he led the people through a godly reformation.
- Daniel — Likely as teenagers, Daniel and three friends were deported to Babylon to serve as leaders in the ever-expanding kingdom of Babylon. Daniel and his friends stood for God without compromise in a pagan land.
- Mary — God chose Mary (who almost certainly was a teenager) to carry Jesus in her womb and raise him for his mission ahead.
- Timothy — The apostle Paul chose this gifted young man to join him on his missionary journeys and to help him establish churches in the world of the first century.

What are the core truths these young people believed that so radically changed their lives for the good? This is the content of the book you now hold in your hand.

The first ten chapters of Believe: Student Edition explain the core beliefs of the Christian life. Together they answer the question, "What do I believe?"

The second ten chapters discuss the core practices of the Christian life. Together they answer the question, "What should I do?"

The final ten chapters contain the core *virtues* of the Christian life. Together they answer the question, "Who am I becoming?"

Remember, *believe* is an action word. God doesn't want you to just believe these truths in your head; he wants you to believe with your whole heart in his Word as the operating system for your life. He wants to transform your life for the good now and forever. He wants you to join his revolution to stand and promote what is good and right. He wants to put the "extra" in your "ordinary" so you can live an "extraordinary" life in Christ. What he did so radically in the lives of young people in the past he wants to do again today through you if you too BELIEVE.

It is my prayer for you that you will recognize in your heart that God knows you by name and loves you deeply — he always has and always will. May he give you the faith to believe with your whole heart so that your entire life (words, thoughts, actions and relationships) is powerfully affected. As you finish reading the last page of this book, may you shout to the world — I believe!

— Randy Frazee
*General Editor*

# Introduction

*All Scripture is God-breathed and is useful for teaching, rebuking, correcting and training in righteousness.*

*2 Timothy 3:16*

## Book Sections

As you journey through *Believe: Student Edition*, you will read three ten-chapter sections:

**THINK.** The first ten chapters of *Believe* detail the core **Beliefs** of the Christian life. Together they answer the question, "What do I believe?"

**ACT.** The second ten chapters discuss the core **Practices** of the Christian life. Together they answer the question, "What should I do?"

**BE.** The final ten chapters contain the core **Virtues** of the Christian life. Together they answer the question, "Who am I becoming?"

## Scripture

*Believe: Student Edition* includes the actual, God-breathed words of the Bible. This is not one person's or one church's words on these important, life-altering topics. The Bible text alone is our source of teaching on each of these truths. *Believe: Student Edition* contains portions of Scripture that were thoughtfully and carefully excerpted from the Bible because they speak directly to the core belief, practice or virtue. You will read an Old Testament story, a New Testament story and several supporting texts from throughout the Bible. The Scripture text used in *Believe* is taken from the New International Version (NIV).

## Chapter Structure

Each chapter contains several elements to guide you through your *Believe: Student Edition* journey.

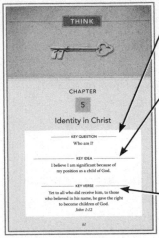

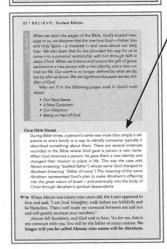

## The Keys

### Key Question

The key question poses the problem or issue that the chapter will grapple with.

### Key Idea

The key idea gives you words to use to express your beliefs. Try memorizing the key ideas so you "know that you know" what you believe!

### Key Verse

The key verse for each belief is the most important Scripture about that subject. The 30 key verses are also important to commit to memory, so you have the power of God's Word at the ready when you need it.

## Our Map

This section orients you to the belief, practice or virtue you are about to explore. You will get the big picture of what the chapter is about and see a preview of the topics to be covered.

## Transitions

The transition paragraphs between the Scripture text appear in *italic*. They were written to guide you through the chapter and connect the dots between each story. The transitions have been carefully crafted to avoid telling you what to believe; it is important that the Scripture itself be the driver of what you decide to believe. These segments aid you in digging into the meaning and significance of the Scripture.

## Key Stories

Look for key story symbols at the beginning and end of one Old Testament and one New Testament story in each chapter. The Bible characters in these stories best exemplify that belief, practice or virtue.

## Core Truths

As you read the Scripture, you will see core truths in **bold text**. The core truth is the essence of the message of that Scripture and helps you understand why that particular passage was selected to convey that truth.

## Reflection Questions

There are five reflection question sections embedded in each chapter. These questions and suggestions are there to help you get the most out of your reading. When you come to a question, pause and reflect. You will grow to understand the Bible better if you take the time to explore the issues raised by these questions. You can record your answers and observations in a journal or jot notes right in your book. Then talk about your discoveries with a friend or a group. Sharing your thoughts with others is a great way to dig deeper into what you've learned.

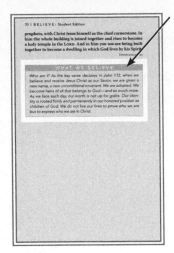

## What We Believe

At the conclusion of each chapter, the What We Believe section wraps it all up. The big ideas of the belief, practice or virtue are recapped in a helpful summary so you can recall everything you learned in the chapter and put it all together in a cohesive way.

## Back of the Book

At the back of the book, the epilogue gives you an idea of the global impact this story has had on the world. You'll also find the Chart of References, listing every Scripture passage in the book.

*Believe* is a full Bible-engagement campaign with resources for an entire church, school or group to experience together. Check out www.believethestory.com for more information.

# What Do I Believe?

*A good man brings good things out of the good stored up in his heart, and an evil man brings evil things out of the evil stored up in his heart. For the mouth speaks what the heart is full of.*
*Luke 6:45*

What we believe in our hearts defines who we become. God wants you to become like Jesus. This is who God created you to be. It is the most truthful and powerful way to live. And the journey to *becoming* like Jesus begins by *thinking* like Jesus.

The following ten chapters are about the key beliefs of the Christian life. These beliefs were not only taught by Jesus but also modeled by him when he walked this earth. Because we live from the heart, embracing these core truths in both our minds and our hearts is the first step to truly becoming like Jesus.

Each of the following chapters contains Scripture passages which focus on a particular belief. You are about to discover what God wants you to know and believe about these important topics. Begin each chapter with a passion to learn and understand. Then prayerfully ask, "What do *I* believe?"

Fully adopting these fantastic truths in your heart may not come by the end of reading each chapter. If you are honest, it may take a while, and that's okay. The Christian life is a journey. There are no shortcuts. As each of the key concepts takes up residence in your heart, they will, with the amazing help of God's presence in your life, change your life in a most positive way.

When you start *thinking* like Jesus, you are well on your way to *becoming* like Jesus.

# THINK

## CHAPTER

### 1

# God

———— KEY QUESTION ————

Who is God?

———— KEY IDEA ————

I believe the God of the Bible is the only true God —
Father, Son and Holy Spirit.

———— KEY VERSE ————

May the grace of the Lord Jesus Christ,
and the love of God, and the fellowship
of the Holy Spirit be with you all.
*2 Corinthians 13:14*

---

> Belief in God is the very foundation of the Christian faith. Christianity is the only spiritual belief system based on a Creator-God who had no beginning, who interacts with his creation as a plural being and who actively demonstrates his superiority over all other gods and beings.
>
> You will be reading Scripture passages in this chapter that describe how we know about God, the aspects of his character and what that means to us:
>
> - God Reveals Himself
> - The One True God
> - God in Three Persons: Father, Son and Holy Spirit
> - The Trinity in Our Lives

## GOD REVEALS HIMSELF

*Everything begins with God. The Bible never tries to defend the existence of God—it is just assumed. God has revealed himself so powerfully through his creation—both at the most grand and most microscopic ends of the scale—that at the end of the day, no one will have an excuse for not putting their trust in him.*

**In the beginning God created the heavens and the earth.**

GENESIS 1:1

The heavens declare the glory of God;
   the skies proclaim the work of his hands.
Day after day they pour forth speech;
   night after night they reveal knowledge.
They have no speech, they use no words;
   no sound is heard from them.
Yet their voice goes out into all the earth,
   their words to the ends of the world.
In the heavens God has pitched a tent for the sun.

PSALM 19:1–4

For since the creation of the world God's invisible qualities — his eternal power and divine nature — have been clearly seen, being understood from what has been made, so that people are without excuse.

ROMANS 1:20

---

In what ways do you see the invisible qualities
of God revealed in nature? In other words,
what does creation tell us about our Creator?

---

## THE ONE TRUE GOD

*From beginning to end, the Bible reveals that there is only one true God. But who is he? The book of Deuteronomy looks back at how Moses had led the Israelites out of slavery in Egypt. During that time God, through the ten plagues, had revealed himself as the one true, all-powerful God over Pharaoh. Now a new generation had grown up in the wilderness and was poised to inherit the land God had promised Abraham. Moses offered the second generation a series of farewell speeches to remind them to choose, worship and follow the one true God—the God of Abraham, Isaac and Jacob. If they did, all would go well for them.*

These are the commands, decrees and laws the LORD your God directed me to teach you to observe in the land that you are crossing the Jordan to possess, so that you, your children and their children after them may fear the LORD your God as long as you live by keeping all his decrees and commands that I give you, and so that you may enjoy long life. Hear, Israel, and be careful to obey so that it may go well with you and that you may increase greatly in a land flowing with milk and honey, just as the LORD, the God of your ancestors, promised you.

**Hear, O Israel: The LORD our God, the LORD is one.** Love the LORD your God with all your heart and with all your soul and with all your strength. These commandments that I give you today are to be on your hearts. Impress them on your children. Talk about them when you sit at home and when you walk along the road, when you lie down and when you get up. Tie them as symbols on your hands and bind them on your foreheads. Write them on the doorframes of your houses and on your gates.

DEUTERONOMY 6:1–9

What are some of God's requirements for his people?
Which of these requirements do you think
God would like you to improve on?

*After Moses died, Joshua became the next great leader of the Israelites. He was charged with leading the people into the promised land. God was with them and fought for them as they began conquering the land. Under Joshua's leadership, the Israelites remained steady in their devotion to God. Before Joshua died, he gathered the people together and issued them a stiff challenge to choose to serve the Lord, the one true God.*

Joshua said to all the people, "This is what the LORD, the God of Israel, says: 'Long ago your ancestors, including Terah the father of Abraham and Nahor, lived beyond the Euphrates River and worshiped other gods.'"                                          JOSHUA 24:2

"'When I brought your people out of Egypt, you came to the sea, and the Egyptians pursued them with chariots and horsemen as far as the Red Sea. But they cried to the LORD for help, and he put darkness between you and the Egyptians; he brought the sea over them and covered them. You saw with your own eyes what I did to the Egyptians. Then you lived in the wilderness for a long time.

"'I brought you to the land of the Amorites who lived east of the Jordan. They fought against you, but I gave them into your hands. I destroyed them from before you, and you took possession of their land. When Balak son of Zippor, the king of Moab, prepared to fight against Israel, he sent for Balaam son of Beor to put a curse on you. But I would not listen to Balaam, so he blessed you again and again, and I delivered you out of his hand.

"'Then you crossed the Jordan and came to Jericho. The citizens of Jericho fought against you, as did also the Amorites, Perizzites, Canaanites, Hittites, Girgashites, Hivites and Jebusites, but I gave them into your hands. I sent the hornet ahead of you, which drove them out before you — also the two Amorite kings. You did not do it with your own sword and bow. So I gave you a land on which you did not toil and cities you did not build; and you live in them and eat from vineyards and olive groves that you did not plant.'

**"Now fear the LORD and serve him with all faithfulness. Throw away the gods your ancestors worshiped beyond the Euphrates River and in Egypt, and serve the LORD."**

JOSHUA 24:6–14

*Unfortunately the Israelites failed to keep their promise to follow only God. Instead they followed the poor examples of their kings. King Ahab was a particularly wicked king, as he introduced Israel to the worship of the pagan god Baal. But God dramatically proved through the prophet Elijah that he, not Baal or any other "god," is the one true God.*

**Elijah went before the people and said, "How long will you waver between two opinions? If the LORD is God, follow him; but if Baal is God, follow him."**

But the people said nothing.

Then Elijah said to them, "I am the only one of the LORD's prophets left, but Baal has four hundred and fifty prophets. Get two bulls for us. Let Baal's prophets choose one for themselves, and let them cut it into pieces and put it on the wood but not set fire to it. I will prepare the other bull and put it on the wood but not set fire to it. Then you call on the name of your god, and I will call on the name of the LORD. The god who answers by fire — he is God."

Then all the people said, "What you say is good."

Elijah said to the prophets of Baal, "Choose one of the bulls and prepare it first, since there are so many of you. Call on the name of your god, but do not light the fire." So they took the bull given them and prepared it.

Then they called on the name of Baal from morning till noon. "Baal, answer us!" they shouted. But there was no response; no one answered. And they danced around the altar they had made.

At noon Elijah began to taunt them. "Shout louder!" he said. "Surely he is a god! Perhaps he is deep in thought, or busy, or traveling. Maybe he is sleeping and must be awakened." So they shouted louder and slashed themselves with swords and spears, as was their custom, until their blood flowed. Midday passed, and they continued their frantic prophesying until the time for the evening sacrifice. But there was no response, no one answered, no one paid attention.

Then Elijah said to all the people, "Come here to me." They came to him, and he repaired the altar of the LORD, which had been torn down. Elijah took twelve stones, one for each of the tribes descended from Jacob, to whom the word of the LORD had come, saying, "Your name shall be Israel." With the stones he built an altar in the name of the LORD, and he dug a trench around it large enough to hold two seahs of seed. He arranged the wood, cut the bull into pieces and laid it on the wood. Then he said to them, "Fill four large jars with water and pour it on the offering and on the wood."

"Do it again," he said, and they did it again.

"Do it a third time," he ordered, and they did it the third time. The water ran down around the altar and even filled the trench.

**At the time of sacrifice, the prophet Elijah stepped forward and prayed: "LORD, the God of Abraham, Isaac and Israel, let it be known today that you are God in Israel and that I am your servant and have done all these things at your command. Answer me, LORD, answer me, so these people will know that you, LORD, are God, and that you are turning their hearts back again."**

Then the fire of the LORD fell and burned up the sacrifice, the wood, the stones and the soil, and also licked up the water in the trench.

**When all the people saw this, they fell prostrate and cried, "The LORD — he is God! The LORD — he is God!"** 1 KINGS 18:21–39

---

Why did God have to prove over
and over that he is the one true God?
Do people today have the same
problem believing the proof they see
of God's existence?

---

## GOD IN THREE PERSONS: FATHER, SON AND HOLY SPIRIT

*Throughout the Old Testament, people were invited to worship the one true God, but what do we know about this amazing God of miracles and creative wonder? Christians believe God is actually three persons, a "Trinity." Though the word "Trinity" isn't found in the Bible, in the very beginning of God's story, the creation story, we see hints that God is plural. Genesis 1:26 says, "Then God said, 'Let **us** make mankind in **our** image, in **our** likeness.' " God is himself a mini-community.*

*The creation story tells us we were created in God's image. When he made the first human (Adam), God wanted him to experience the community and relationship that has eternally existed within the Trinity. That's why he made Eve. Notice that Adam and Eve were not two separate beings. Eve came out of Adam and they became two distinct persons who shared one being, like God. God is three distinct persons who share a single being.*

The LORD God took the man and put him in the Garden of Eden to work it and take care of it. And the LORD God commanded the man, "You are free to eat from any tree in the garden; but you must not eat from the tree of the knowledge of good and evil, for when you eat from it you will certainly die."

**The LORD God said, "It is not good for the man to be alone. I will make a helper suitable for him."**

Now the LORD God had formed out of the ground all the wild animals and all the birds in the sky. He brought them to the man to see what he would name them; and whatever the man called each living creature, that was its name. So the man gave names to all the livestock, the birds in the sky and all the wild animals.

But for Adam no suitable helper was found. So the LORD God caused the man to fall into a deep sleep; and while he was sleeping, he took one of the man's ribs and then closed up the place with flesh. **Then the LORD God made a woman from the rib he had taken out of the man, and he brought her to the man.**

The man said,

"This is now bone of my bones
    and flesh of my flesh;

> she shall be called 'woman,'
>    for she was taken out of man."

That is why a man leaves his father and mother and is united to his wife, and they become one flesh.     GENESIS 2:15–24

*Recalling Genesis 1:26, "Then God said, 'Let us make mankind in our image, in our likeness,' " God as a plural being is clearly evident from the very beginning of the Bible. But what are the identities of the individual persons of God, and how are they just one being? How do they interact? The opening words of John's gospel make the answer more clear.*

**In the beginning was the Word, and the Word was with God, and the Word was God. He was with God in the beginning.** Through him all things were made; without him nothing was made that has been made. In him was life, and that life was the light of all mankind. The light shines in the darkness, and the darkness has not overcome it.     JOHN 1:1–5

*The "Word" here refers to Jesus because he is God's way of communicating with us. John refers to him as "God," as divine. John also says Jesus was there in the beginning. Jesus, the divine Word, partnered with God to create all that we see and all that we have yet to see.*

*So who are the other members of the Trinity? The second sentence of the Bible tells us that the Holy Spirit was also present at creation: "The earth was formless and empty, darkness was over the surface of the deep, and the Spirit of God was hovering over the waters" (Genesis 1:2). Jesus and the Spirit were at the creation of the world, so these two persons are God. Is that it? Who else makes up the person of God? Fast-forward to the baptism of Jesus at the age of 30 to discover the answer. Look for the appearance of all three persons of the Trinity.*

The people were waiting expectantly and were all wondering in their hearts if John might possibly be the Messiah. John answered them all, "I baptize you with water. But one who is more powerful than I will come, the straps of whose sandals I am not worthy to untie. He will baptize you with the Holy Spirit and fire. His winnowing fork is in his hand to clear his threshing floor and to gather the wheat into his barn, but he will burn up the chaff with unquenchable fire." And with many other words John exhorted the people and proclaimed the good news to them.　LUKE 3:15–18

**When all the people were being baptized, Jesus was baptized too. And as he was praying, heaven was opened and the Holy Spirit descended on him in bodily form like a dove. And a voice came from heaven: "You are my Son, whom I love; with you I am well pleased."**　LUKE 3:21–22 ⚷

*Three distinct persons are fully revealed in Scripture to make up the identity of the one true God: the Father, the Son Jesus and the Spirit. And all three were involved at the baptism of Jesus — the Father spoke, the Son was baptized and the Holy Spirit descended on the Son. Throughout the centuries, followers of Jesus have come to call the one true God the Trinity, three persons who share one being. As difficult as this concept is to fully understand, it is relevant to our lives.*

---

In what ways have you experienced God as Father?
As Jesus the Son? As the Holy Spirit?

---

**THE TRINITY IN OUR LIVES**
*In short, here's how the triune God works: Because God the Father loves us so much, he sent God the Son to live and die for our sins. Now God the Holy Spirit lives in the hearts of all who believe in the death and resurrection of Jesus. That's good news!*
*There are many people in the Bible who devoted their lives to telling others about the good news of Jesus. The apostle Paul was one of those people. He traveled the ancient world telling all kinds of people about God. When he visited Greece, he noticed that the intellectual people who lived there created altars to many gods, including one dedicated "to an unknown God" in case they missed one and therefore offended him or her. Paul met with their council of elders, called the Areopa-*

*gus, and declares the identity of this God as the one who created everything in the beginning (see Genesis 1–2) and is now revealed in the second person of the Trinity, Jesus Christ. His words to the people of Athens are applicable to all those who believe — God is everywhere and there is nothing in this world that his hand has not touched. The Trinity is woven into every aspect of our lives.*

While Paul was waiting for [Silas and Timothy] in Athens, he was greatly distressed to see that the city was full of idols. So he reasoned in the synagogue with both Jews and God-fearing Greeks, as well as in the marketplace day by day with those who happened to be there. A group of Epicurean and Stoic philosophers began to debate with him. Some of them asked, "What is this babbler trying to say?" Others remarked, "He seems to be advocating foreign gods." They said this because Paul was preaching the good news about Jesus and the resurrection. Then they took him and brought him to a meeting of the Areopagus, where they said to him, "May we know what this new teaching is that you are presenting? You are bringing some strange ideas to our ears, and we would like to know what they mean." (All the Athenians and the foreigners who lived there spent their time doing nothing but talking about and listening to the latest ideas.)

Paul then stood up in the meeting of the Areopagus and said: "People of Athens! I see that in every way you are very religious. For as I walked around and looked carefully at your objects of worship, I even found an altar with this inscription: TO AN UNKNOWN GOD. So you are ignorant of the very thing you worship — and this is what I am going to proclaim to you.

**"The God who made the world and everything in it is the Lord of heaven and earth and does not live in temples built by human hands. And he is not served by human hands, as if he needed anything. Rather, he himself gives everyone life and breath and everything else.** From one man he made all the nations, that they should inhabit the whole earth; and he marked out their appointed times in history and the boundaries of their lands. God did this so that they would seek him and perhaps reach out for him and find him, though he is not far from any one of us.

'For in him we live and move and have our being.' As some of your own poets have said, 'We are his offspring.'

"Therefore since we are God's offspring, we should not think that the divine being is like gold or silver or stone — an image made by human design and skill. In the past God overlooked such ignorance, but now he commands all people everywhere to repent. For he has set a day when he will judge the world with justice by the man he has appointed. He has given proof of this to everyone by raising him from the dead."

When they heard about the resurrection of the dead, some of them sneered, but others said, "We want to hear you again on this subject." At that, Paul left the Council. Some of the people became followers of Paul and believed. Among them was Dionysius, a member of the Areopagus, also a woman named Damaris, and a number of others.                    ACTS 17:16–34

---

What do you think is meant by the phrase Paul quoted:
"For in him we live and move and have our being"?
How should this dependency on God affect our daily lives?

---

## WHAT WE BELIEVE

*The Bible never tries to prove the existence of God — his existence is simply an assumed fact. God has clearly revealed himself through creation, in events such as Jesus' baptism and in our own consciences, leaving everyone without excuse in the end. The key question we asked at the beginning of this chapter comes down to the declaration of who the one true God is. The God who protected Israel and demonstrated power over false gods declares, "I AM!"*

*The journey of faith begins with our belief in God. Like the Israelites of the Old Testament and the early Christians of the New Testament, we too are called to make a personal declaration. Do we believe in the one true God? Do we accept the Bible as it reveals that God exists in three persons?*

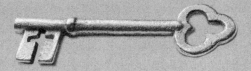

**THINK**

CHAPTER

## 2

# Personal God

―――――― KEY QUESTION ――――――

Does God care about me?

―――――――― KEY IDEA ――――――――

I believe God is involved in and cares
about my daily life.

―――――――― KEY VERSE ――――――――

I lift up my eyes to the mountains —
where does my help come from?
My help comes from the LORD,
the Maker of heaven and earth.
*Psalm 121:1–2*

28

OUR MAP

*The God of the Bible is the only true God—Father, Son and Holy Spirit. He is the one all-powerful, all-knowing eternal God. But is he good? Is he involved in his creation? Does he love us? Does he have a plan for us? Is he interceding and intervening to move the events of our life and world toward his intended purpose?*

*Consider these questions as you read the Scriptures in this chapter that explore three ways God shows us he is a personal God:*

- *God Is Good*
- *God Has a Plan*
- *God Cares for Us*

## GOD IS GOOD

*Abraham and Sarah—the great ancestors of the Israelite people—were first named Abram and Sarai. God had promised Abraham that he would be the father of a great nation, but how can you father a whole nation when you have no children?*

---

As you read the story of Abraham, Sarah and Hagar, look for some ways in which God showed his goodness to them. What impact did this have on them?

---

Now Sarai, Abram's wife, had borne him no children. But she had an Egyptian slave named Hagar; so she said to Abram, "The LORD has kept me from having children. Go, sleep with my slave; perhaps I can build a family through her."

Abram agreed to what Sarai said. So after Abram had been living in Canaan ten years, Sarai his wife took her Egyptian slave Hagar and gave her to her husband to be his wife. He slept with Hagar, and she conceived.

When she knew she was pregnant, she began to despise her mistress. Then Sarai said to Abram, "You are responsible for the wrong I am suffering. I put my slave in your arms, and now that she knows she is pregnant, she despises me. May the LORD judge between you and me."

"Your slave is in your hands," Abram said. "Do with her whatever you think best." Then Sarai mistreated Hagar; so she fled from her.

The angel of the LORD found Hagar near a spring in the desert; it was the spring that is beside the road to Shur. And he said, "Hagar, slave of Sarai, where have you come from, and where are you going?"

"I'm running away from my mistress Sarai," she answered.

Then the angel of the LORD told her, "Go back to your mistress and submit to her." The angel added, "I will increase your descendants so much that they will be too numerous to count."

The angel of the LORD also said to her:

> "You are now pregnant
>     and you will give birth to a son.
> You shall name him Ishmael,
>     for the LORD has heard of your misery.
> He will be a wild donkey of a man;
>     his hand will be against everyone
>     and everyone's hand against him,
> and he will live in hostility
>     toward all his brothers."

**She gave this name to the LORD who spoke to her: "You are the God who sees me," for she said, "I have now seen the One who sees me."** That is why the well was called Beer Lahai Roi; it is still there, between Kadesh and Bered.

So Hagar bore Abram a son, and Abram gave the name Ishmael to the son she had borne. Abram was eighty-six years old when Hagar bore him Ishmael.                    GENESIS 16:1–16

*Abraham and Sarah tried to "help God out" by having Abraham father a child with Hagar. The result was a big, fat mess for everybody. But even in this story, we see the beginning of a pattern—God takes our messes and turns them into something good. Hagar experienced the painful consequences of Abraham and*

*Sarah's lack of faith. Yet God heard her cries and helped her. The story continues ...*

**Now the LORD was gracious to Sarah as he had said, and the LORD did for Sarah what he had promised. Sarah became pregnant and bore a son to Abraham in his old age, at the very time God had promised him.** Abraham gave the name Isaac to the son Sarah bore him. When his son Isaac was eight days old, Abraham circumcised him, as God commanded him. Abraham was a hundred years old when his son Isaac was born to him.

**Sarah said, "God has brought me laughter, and everyone who hears about this will laugh with me."** And she added, "Who would have said to Abraham that Sarah would nurse children? Yet I have borne him a son in his old age."

The child grew and was weaned, and on the day Isaac was weaned Abraham held a great feast. But Sarah saw that the son whom Hagar the Egyptian had borne to Abraham was mocking, and she said to Abraham, "Get rid of that slave woman and her son, for that woman's son will never share in the inheritance with my son Isaac."

The matter distressed Abraham greatly because it concerned his son. But God said to him, "Do not be so distressed about the boy and your slave woman. Listen to whatever Sarah tells you, because it is through Isaac that your offspring will be reckoned. I will make the son of the slave into a nation also, because he is your offspring."

Early the next morning Abraham took some food and a skin of water and gave them to Hagar. He set them on her shoulders and then sent her off with the boy. She went on her way and wandered in the Desert of Beersheba.

When the water in the skin was gone, she put the boy under one of the bushes. Then she went off and sat down about a bowshot away, for she thought, "I cannot watch the boy die." And as she sat there, she began to sob.

**God heard the boy crying, and the angel of God called to Hagar from heaven and said to her, "What is the matter, Hagar? Do not be afraid; God has heard the boy crying as he**

**lies there. Lift the boy up and take him by the hand, for I will make him into a great nation."**

Then God opened her eyes and she saw a well of water. So she went and filled the skin with water and gave the boy a drink.

God was with the boy as he grew up. He lived in the desert and became an archer. While he was living in the Desert of Paran, his mother got a wife for him from Egypt.                    GENESIS 21:1–21

*Even though Hagar and Ishmael aren't the main characters of the biblical storyline, God still provided for them and promised to bless their descendants. He did this because he is a compassionate and personal God.*

*Another biblical character in whose life we see how much God is involved and cares about his people is David, the poet, singer, shepherd, warrior and king, who wrote and sang from a deep well of emotion as he journeyed through life and encountered the one true God. David composed many of the psalms found in our Bible. David wrote as a shepherd boy while gazing at the billions of stars God created; he wrote while being chased down by King Saul; he wrote while he was king of Israel; and he wrote as he was coming to the end of his life on earth. The songs that David and the other psalmists wrote express their personal and intimate relationship with God.*

**The LORD is my shepherd, I lack nothing.**
   **He makes me lie down in green pastures,**
**he leads me beside quiet waters,**
   **he refreshes my soul.**
**He guides me along the right paths**
   **for his name's sake.**
**Even though I walk**
   **through the darkest valley,**
**I will fear no evil,**
   **for you are with me;**
**your rod and your staff,**
   **they comfort me.**

**You prepare a table before me**
   **in the presence of my enemies.**

**You anoint my head with oil;**
**my cup overflows.**
**Surely your goodness and love will follow me**
**all the days of my life,**
**and I will dwell in the house of the LORD**
**forever.** PSALM 23:1–6

---

How have you experienced God's personal knowledge of you?
When have you known he was searching your heart?
What was the result?

---

## GOD HAS A PLAN

*Out of all the kings who followed David, only a handful of them were good. One of them was Hezekiah. He courageously obeyed the Lord even when it wasn't popular.*

*Then when he was about 38 years old, Hezekiah became ill and was about to die. He was afraid and pleaded with the Lord for mercy. In response, the Lord came to him with a shocking message and a tender change of plan.*

*We know from the Bible that God has a plan for our individual lives—he even has the days of each of our lives numbered. This story shows how God will hear our prayers and see our tears. He may not answer us in the way we desire, but at our request he will sometimes alter the plan he has for us.*

In those days Hezekiah became ill and was at the point of death. The prophet Isaiah son of Amoz went to him and said, "This is what the LORD says: Put your house in order, because you are going to die; you will not recover."

Hezekiah turned his face to the wall and prayed to the LORD, "Remember, LORD, how I have walked before you faithfully and with wholehearted devotion and have done what is good in your eyes." And Hezekiah wept bitterly.

Before Isaiah had left the middle court, the word of the LORD came to him: **"Go back and tell Hezekiah, the ruler of my people, 'This is what the LORD, the God of your father David, says: I have heard your prayer and seen your tears; I will heal** you. **On the third day from now you will go up to the temple of the LORD. I will add fifteen years to your life.** And I will deliver you and this city from the hand of the king of Assyria. I will defend this city for my sake and for the sake of my servant David.'"

Then Isaiah said, "Prepare a poultice of figs." They did so and applied it to the boil, and he recovered. 2 KINGS 20:1–7

*While Hezekiah's story focuses on the length of his life, Jeremiah's story goes all the way back before he was born. Jeremiah was a prophet who lived in the time of the divided kingdom. He lived in the southern kingdom of Judah and prophesied to the people that the Babylonians were coming to conquer the land and take away the people. In the lives of both Hezekiah and Jeremiah, God was not distant or careless, but near and loving. Notice how specific and detailed God's warnings were and yet how he assured Jeremiah of his intervention and protection.*

The word of the LORD came to me, saying,

> **"Before I formed you in the womb I knew you,**
> **before you were born I set you apart;**
> **I appointed you as a prophet to the nations."**

"Alas, Sovereign LORD," I said, "I do not know how to speak; I am too young."

But the LORD said to me, "Do not say, 'I am too young.' You must go to everyone I send you to and say whatever I command you. Do not be afraid of them, for I am with you and will rescue you," declares the LORD.

Then the LORD reached out his hand and touched my mouth and said to me, "I have put my words in your mouth. See, today I appoint you over nations and kingdoms to uproot and tear down, to destroy and overthrow, to build and to plant." JEREMIAH 1:4–10

"Get yourself ready! Stand up and say to them whatever I command you. Do not be terrified by them, or I will terrify you before them. Today I have made you a fortified city, an iron pillar and a bronze wall to stand against the whole land — against the kings of

Judah, its officials, its priests and the people of the land. They will fight against you but will not overcome you, for I am with you and will rescue you," declares the LORD.                           JEREMIAH 1:17–19

*Jeremiah's calling was very specific and very difficult—warn the southern kingdom of Judah about their unfaithfulness and wickedness and God's impending discipline. He knew up front that they would not listen, but his task was simply to be faithful and courageous and to deliver the message from God anyway.*

*Three times the dreaded Babylonians attacked Jerusalem and carried away some of the people to Babylon. In 597 BC, after the second deportation, God gave Jeremiah the assignment of writing a letter to those exiles to remind them that, as Jeremiah had experienced personally, God had a grand and good plan for their lives.*

This is the text of the letter that the prophet Jeremiah sent from Jerusalem to the surviving elders among the exiles and to the priests, the prophets and all the other people Nebuchadnezzar had carried into exile from Jerusalem to Babylon.          JEREMIAH 29:1

This is what the LORD says: "When seventy years are completed for Babylon, I will come to you and fulfill my good promise to bring you back to this place. **For I know the plans I have for you," declares the LORD, "plans to prosper you and not to harm you, plans to give you hope and a future.** Then you will call on me and come and pray to me, and I will listen to you. You will seek me and find me when you seek me with all your heart. I will be found by you," declares the LORD, "and will bring you back from captivity. I will gather you from all the nations and places where I have banished you," declares the LORD, "and will bring you back to the place from which I carried you into exile."          JEREMIAH 29:10–14

---

How did God show the captives
in Babylon that he still cared for them
and wanted the best for them? How has
God comforted you in difficult times?

---

## God Cares for Us

*Jesus, the Son of God, came to earth. He was born as a human baby and lived among us. His arrival removes any doubt about the nearness of God in our lives. Jesus is Immanuel, "God with us."*

*When a large crowd assembled on a hillside by the Sea of Galilee, Jesus taught this weary and worn bunch about the detailed involvement of God in their lives.*

"Therefore I tell you, do not worry about your life, what you will eat or drink; or about your body, what you will wear. Is not life more than food, and the body more than clothes? Look at the birds of the air; they do not sow or reap or store away in barns, and yet your heavenly Father feeds them. Are you not much more valuable than they? Can any one of you by worrying add a single hour to your life?

"And why do you worry about clothes? See how the flowers of the field grow. They do not labor or spin. Yet I tell you that not even Solomon in all his splendor was dressed like one of these. If that is how God clothes the grass of the field, which is here today and tomorrow is thrown into the fire, will he not much more clothe you — you of little faith? **So do not worry, saying, 'What shall we eat?' or 'What shall we drink?' or 'What shall we wear?' For the pagans run after all these things, and your heavenly Father knows that you need them.** But seek first his kingdom and his righteousness, and all these things will be given to you as well. Therefore do not worry about tomorrow, for tomorrow will worry about itself. Each day has enough trouble of its own."

MATTHEW 6:25–34

---

Why does Jesus want us to not worry?
What is something you are currently worrying about?
What promise of God can you hold onto
for strength and confidence?

---

*After Jesus died on the cross and rose from the grave, he ascended to heaven to be with the Father. Now he sends the Holy Spirit into the hearts of all who believe in him. God used to dwell in temples built by humans, but now he lives in human hearts. The Holy Spirit changes us from the inside out by direct-ing, challenging, affirming, comforting and empowering us. The book of Romans, written by the apostle Paul, tells us about the Holy Spirit's power in people's lives.*

The Spirit helps us in our weakness. We do not know what we ought to pray for, but the Spirit himself intercedes for us through wordless groans. And he who searches our hearts knows the mind of the Spirit, because the Spirit intercedes for God's people in ac-cordance with the will of God.

**And we know that in all things God works for the good of those who love him, who have been called according to his purpose.** ROMANS 8:26–28

**For I am convinced that neither death nor life, neither an-gels nor demons, neither the present nor the future, nor any powers, neither height nor depth, nor anything else in all cre-ation, will be able to separate us from the love of God that is in Christ Jesus our Lord.** ROMANS 8:38–39

*What amazing love God has for his people! In the spirit of this love, James, the half brother of Jesus, wrote a practical letter to Jesus' early disciples. He reminded them that God is involved in and cares about their daily lives—although they too had a role to play. In the good times and even in the hard times, God is always there and always cares. We can seek God and ask him for wisdom. We must also be careful not to blame God for our trials and temptations and instead thank him for every good gift he gives us.*

---

As you read the Scriptures below ask yourself,
how does God show his care and concern for us
when we go through difficult experiences in life?

---

Consider it pure joy, my brothers and sisters, whenever you face trials of many kinds, because you know that the testing of your

faith produces perseverance. Let perseverance finish its work so
that you may be mature and complete, not lacking anything. If any
of you lacks wisdom, you should ask God, who gives generously to
all without finding fault, and it will be given to you.      JAMES 1:2–5

When tempted, no one should say, "God is tempting me." For
God cannot be tempted by evil, nor does he tempt anyone; but
each person is tempted when they are dragged away by their own
evil desire and enticed. Then, after desire has conceived, it gives
birth to sin; and sin, when it is full-grown, gives birth to death.
**Don't be deceived, my dear brothers and sisters. Every good
and perfect gift is from above, coming down from the Father of
the heavenly lights, who does not change like shifting shadows.**
He chose to give us birth through the word of truth, that we might
be a kind of firstfruits of all he created.      JAMES 1:13–18

## WHAT WE BELIEVE

*The God of the Bible is the only true God and is all-powerful
and all-knowing. As we read the pages of the Bible, we discover
over and over again that God is good. His heart and desire for
us is always for what is right, just and good. God also is working out his good and grand plan to restore his original vision
to be with us, in community. He is involved in the details of our
individual lives. His plan for us offers us hope, prosperity and a
future. Bottom line … God cares for us. When we grasp these
key beliefs not only in our minds but also in our hearts, we can
walk through each day with joy, hope and great confidence.*

# CHAPTER

## 3

# Salvation

---

**KEY QUESTION**

How do I have a relationship with God?

---

**KEY IDEA**

I believe a person comes into a right relationship
with God by God's grace through faith in Jesus Christ.

---

**KEY VERSE**

For it is by grace you have been saved, through faith —
and this is not from yourselves, it is the gift of God —
not by works, so that no one can boast.
*Ephesians 2:8–9*

OUR MAP

*We have discovered so far that the God of the Bible is the one true God—Father, Son and Holy Spirit. We have also discovered he is not a distant being uninterested in our world and our lives; he is personal and near. He is utterly good. He has a plan and purpose for our lives. He cares deeply for us. Now we turn to what may be the most important question of all, "How do I come into a relationship with God?"*

*In this chapter you will be reading a collection of Scripture passages about salvation that has all the makings of the greatest love story ever told:*

- *The Problem: We are not born into a relationship with God.*
- *The Solution: There is only one solution, and our good God provided it.*
- *The Outcome: We can have a lasting relationship with our loving God.*

## THE PROBLEM

*Satan, the great deceiver, clothed himself as a serpent, one of God's good creatures, and set out to trick Adam and Eve into disobeying their gracious God. After creating Adam and Eve, God told them not to eat of the fruit of a certain tree in the Garden of Eden. But Satan suggested that God wasn't being honest when he warned of the results of eating the forbidden fruit. The deceiver's ploy succeeded, and Adam and Eve rejected God and his promise of life together in the garden.*

*The consequences of Adam and Eve's rebellion were passed on to their children and then again and again to every generation since. The Bible calls it sin. Every human receives this "virus" at conception and then acts out of this sinful nature throughout their life. It causes death—both the physical death of our bodies and the spiritual death of separation from God.*

Now the LORD God had planted a garden in the east, in Eden; and there he put the man he had formed. The LORD God made all kinds of trees grow out of the ground—trees that were pleasing to the eye and good for food. In the middle of the garden were the tree of life and the tree of the knowledge of good and evil.

GENESIS 2:8–9

**The LORD God took the man and put him in the Garden of Eden to work it and take care of it. And the LORD God commanded the man, "You are free to eat from any tree in the garden; but you must not eat from the tree of the knowledge of good and evil, for when you eat from it you will certainly die."**

GENESIS 2:15–17

Now the serpent was more crafty than any of the wild animals the LORD God had made. He said to the woman, "Did God really say, 'You must not eat from any tree in the garden'?"

The woman said to the serpent, "We may eat fruit from the trees in the garden, but God did say, 'You must not eat fruit from the tree that is in the middle of the garden, and you must not touch it, or you will die.'"

"You will not certainly die," the serpent said to the woman. "For God knows that when you eat from it your eyes will be opened, and you will be like God, knowing good and evil."

**When the woman saw that the fruit of the tree was good for food and pleasing to the eye, and also desirable for gaining wisdom, she took some and ate it. She also gave some to her husband, who was with her, and he ate it.** GENESIS 3:1–6

Then the LORD God said to the woman, "What is this you have done?"

The woman said, "The serpent deceived me, and I ate."

So the LORD God said to the serpent, "Because you have done this,

> "Cursed are you above all livestock
>   and all wild animals!
> You will crawl on your belly
>   and you will eat dust
>   all the days of your life.

> And I will put enmity
> > between you and the woman,
> > and between your offspring and hers;
> he will crush your head,
> > and you will strike his heel." Genesis 3:13–15

The Lord God made garments of skin for Adam and his wife and clothed them. And the Lord God said, "The man has now become like one of us, knowing good and evil. He must not be allowed to reach out his hand and take also from the tree of life and eat, and live forever." **So the Lord God banished him from the Garden of Eden to work the ground from which he had been taken. After he drove the man out, he placed on the east side of the Garden of Eden cherubim and a flaming sword flashing back and forth to guard the way to the tree of life.**

Genesis 3:21–24 ⚷

---

How would you describe Adam and Eve's life in the garden with God before they disobeyed him? What was life like for them afterward? How does your life change when you disobey God?

---

## The Solution

*When Adam and Eve sinned, God set into motion his plan to get people back into a relationship with him. When he replaced their clothes of fig leaves with the skins of animals, he signaled something important—it would take the blood of another to cover the sins of humankind.*

*One of the earliest examples of this "blood covering" took place as God was preparing to deliver Israel from 400 years of captivity in Egypt. God chose Moses as his messenger to Pharaoh to demand that he release God's people from slavery and let them take possession of the promised land. But Pharaoh was hardhearted and would not let the people leave. To make Pharaoh understand and believe in God's power, God issued ten brutal plagues on Egypt and its people. The tenth and final plague foreshadows the ultimate solution of deliverance from humankind's slavery to sin—the Lamb of God, Jesus Christ.*

**Then Moses summoned all the elders of Israel and said to them, "Go at once and select the animals for your families and slaughter the Passover lamb. Take a bunch of hyssop, dip it into the blood in the basin and put some of the blood on the top and on both sides of the doorframe. None of you shall go out of the door of your house until morning. When the LORD goes through the land to strike down the Egyptians, he will see the blood on the top and sides of the doorframe and will pass over that doorway, and he will not permit the destroyer to enter your houses and strike you down.**

"Obey these instructions as a lasting ordinance for you and your descendants. When you enter the land that the LORD will give you as he promised, observe this ceremony. And when your children ask you, 'What does this ceremony mean to you?' then tell them, 'It is the Passover sacrifice to the LORD, who passed over the houses of the Israelites in Egypt and spared our homes when he struck down the Egyptians.'" Then the people bowed down and worshiped. The Israelites did just what the LORD commanded Moses and Aaron.

At midnight the LORD struck down all the firstborn in Egypt, from the firstborn of Pharaoh, who sat on the throne, to the firstborn of the prisoner, who was in the dungeon, and the firstborn of all the livestock as well. Pharaoh and all his officials and all the Egyptians got up during the night, and there was loud wailing in Egypt, for there was not a house without someone dead.

During the night Pharaoh summoned Moses and Aaron and said, "Up! Leave my people, you and the Israelites! Go, worship the LORD as you have requested."                    EXODUS 12:21–31

---

What are the similarities between the sacrificed lamb
and the sacrifice of Jesus? What type of "Passover" has been
caused by Jesus' blood applied to our lives?

---

*About 700 years after the exodus and 700 years before the birth of Jesus, God inspired the prophet Isaiah to speak on his behalf. The following prophecy about the Lord's "suffering servant" takes the concept of blood sacrifice and the Passover lamb to a new level. This Scripture, which is quoted more often in the New Testament than any other Old Testament passage, also foretells the mission of the One who will provide the way for our sins to be forgiven.*

---

Recalling the details of Jesus' time on earth,
look for similarities between Jesus' life and
Isaiah's prophecy of the "suffering servant."

---

He grew up before him like a tender shoot,
    and like a root out of dry ground.
He had no beauty or majesty to attract us to him,
    nothing in his appearance that we should desire him.
He was despised and rejected by mankind,
    a man of suffering, and familiar with pain.
Like one from whom people hide their faces
    he was despised, and we held him in low esteem.

Surely he took up our pain
    and bore our suffering,
yet we considered him punished by God,
    stricken by him, and afflicted.
**But he was pierced for our transgressions,**
    **he was crushed for our iniquities;**
**the punishment that brought us peace was on him,**
    **and by his wounds we are healed.**
We all, like sheep, have gone astray,
    each of us has turned to our own way;
and the LORD has laid on him
    the iniquity of us all.

He was oppressed and afflicted,
    yet he did not open his mouth;
he was led like a lamb to the slaughter,
    and as a sheep before its shearers is silent,
    so he did not open his mouth.
By oppression and judgment he was taken away.
    Yet who of his generation protested?

For he was cut off from the land of the living;
    for the transgression of my people he was punished.
He was assigned a grave with the wicked,
    and with the rich in his death,
though he had done no violence,
    nor was any deceit in his mouth.         Isaiah 53:2–9

*God's solution to our problem of separation from him was predicted and demonstrated throughout Jewish history. When God spared the Israelites through the sacrifice of their Passover lambs, his point was clear. When Isaiah foresaw one who would be "pierced for our transgressions and crushed for our iniquities," the identity of the suffering servant was undeniable. The ritual and the prophecy were fulfilled when the Messiah Jesus was crucified on a cross for the sins of humankind. God's plan, set into motion in the Garden of Eden, was at long last finished.*

Those who passed by hurled insults at him, shaking their heads and saying, "You who are going to destroy the temple and build it in three days, save yourself! Come down from the cross, if you are the Son of God!" In the same way the chief priests, the teachers of the law and the elders mocked him. "He saved others," they said, "but he can't save himself! He's the king of Israel! Let him come down now from the cross, and we will believe in him. He trusts in God. Let God rescue him now if he wants him, for he said, 'I am the Son of God.'" In the same way the rebels who were crucified with him also heaped insults on him.

From noon until three in the afternoon darkness came over all the land. About three in the afternoon Jesus cried out in a loud voice, *"Eli, Eli, lema sabachthani?"* (which means "My God, my God, why have you forsaken me?").

When some of those standing there heard this, they said, "He's calling Elijah."

Immediately one of them ran and got a sponge. He filled it with wine vinegar, put it on a staff, and offered it to Jesus to drink. The rest said, "Now leave him alone. Let's see if Elijah comes to save him."

**And when Jesus had cried out again in a loud voice, he gave up his spirit.**

At that moment the curtain of the temple was torn in two from top to bottom. The earth shook, the rocks split and the tombs broke open. The bodies of many holy people who had died were raised to life. They came out of the tombs after Jesus' resurrection and went into the holy city and appeared to many people.

When the centurion and those with him who were guarding Jesus saw the earthquake and all that had happened, they were terrified, and exclaimed, "Surely he was the Son of God!"

MATTHEW 27:39–54

*Jesus was buried and sealed behind a stone in a tomb with Roman guards protecting the body from being stolen. But on the third day, no sealed tomb or guard could keep Jesus in the grave.*

After the Sabbath, at dawn on the first day of the week, Mary Magdalene and the other Mary went to look at the tomb.

There was a violent earthquake, for an angel of the Lord came down from heaven and, going to the tomb, rolled back the stone and sat on it. His appearance was like lightning, and his clothes were white as snow. The guards were so afraid of him that they shook and became like dead men.

The angel said to the women, "Do not be afraid, for I know that you are looking for Jesus, who was crucified. He is not here; he has risen, just as he said. Come and see the place where he lay. Then go quickly and tell his disciples: 'He has risen from the dead and is going ahead of you into Galilee. There you will see him.' Now I have told you."

So the women hurried away from the tomb, afraid yet filled with joy, and ran to tell his disciples. Suddenly Jesus met them. "Greetings," he said. They came to him, clasped his feet and worshiped him. Then Jesus said to them, "Do not be afraid. Go and tell my brothers to go to Galilee; there they will see me."

MATTHEW 28:1–10

Can you pinpoint a moment in time when you realized
that Christ died for you? Describe your thought process.
What were you feeling?

## THE OUTCOME

*Even with all the incredible stories connecting the dots from the promised Messiah to the person Jesus, most Jews didn't recognize or accept Jesus as the Savior of the world. They didn't recognize the One who would provide the way for our sin to be forgiven so we could enter into a personal relationship with God, overcome death and have eternal life. John tells the story of one Jewish religious leader who approached Jesus at night to ask questions about Jesus' true identity and mission.*

Now there was a Pharisee, a man named Nicodemus who was a member of the Jewish ruling council. He came to Jesus at night and said, "Rabbi, we know that you are a teacher who has come from God. For no one could perform the signs you are doing if God were not with him."

Jesus replied, "Very truly I tell you, no one can see the kingdom of God unless they are born again."

"How can someone be born when they are old?" Nicodemus asked. "Surely they cannot enter a second time into their mother's womb to be born!"

Jesus answered, "Very truly I tell you, no one can enter the kingdom of God unless they are born of water and the Spirit. Flesh gives birth to flesh, but the Spirit gives birth to spirit. You should not be surprised at my saying, 'You must be born again.' The wind blows wherever it pleases. You hear its sound, but you cannot tell where it comes from or where it is going. So it is with everyone born of the Spirit."

"How can this be?" Nicodemus asked.

"You are Israel's teacher," said Jesus, "and do you not understand these things? Very truly I tell you, we speak of what we know, and we testify to what we have seen, but still you people do not accept our testimony. I have spoken to you of earthly things and you do not believe; how then will you believe if I speak of heavenly things? No one has ever gone into heaven except the one who came from heaven — the Son of Man. Just as Moses lifted up the snake in the wilderness, so the Son of Man must be lifted up, that everyone who believes may have eternal life in him."

**For God so loved the world that he gave his one and only Son, that whoever believes in him shall not perish but have eternal life.** For God did not send his Son into the world to condemn the world, but to save the world through him. Whoever believes in him is not condemned, but whoever does not believe stands condemned already because they have not believed in the name of God's one and only Son. JOHN 3:1–18

*In his letter to the church in Rome, the apostle Paul—who was called by God to share this Good News with the rest of the world—reminds us what we must do to receive this gift of grace, the salvation of our souls.*

Therefore, just as sin entered the world through one man, and death through sin, and in this way death came to all people, because all sinned. ROMANS 5:12

But the gift is not like the trespass. For if the many died by the trespass of the one man, how much more did God's grace and the gift that came by the grace of the one man, Jesus Christ, overflow to the many! Nor can the gift of God be compared with the result of one man's sin: The judgment followed one sin and brought condemnation, but the gift followed many trespasses and brought justification. **For if, by the trespass of the one man, death reigned through that one man, how much more will those who receive God's abundant provision of grace and of the gift of righteousness reign in life through the one man, Jesus Christ!**

Consequently, just as one trespass resulted in condemnation for all people, so also one righteous act resulted in justification and life for all people. For just as through the disobedience of the one man the many were made sinners, so also through the obedience of the one man the many will be made righteous. ROMANS 5:15–19

**If you declare with your mouth, "Jesus is Lord," and believe in your heart that God raised him from the dead, you will be saved. For it is with your heart that you believe and are justified, and it is with your mouth that you profess your faith and are saved.** ROMANS 10:9–10

Why is it important to both believe in our hearts and
profess with our mouths that Jesus is Lord?
What happens if you do one without the other?

## WHAT WE BELIEVE

*Before the creation of the world, God had a Plan B in place for humanity to be in relationship with him. Sure enough, Plan B became necessary when Adam and Eve ate the forbidden fruit, ushering in sin and death to all. But thanks to the sacrifice of the second person of the Trinity—the Son—the way was provided to come back to God through faith in Jesus Christ. If we believe this truth, not only in our heads but also in our hearts, and publicly confess it for the world to hear, we will be saved.*

## CHAPTER

4

# The Bible

───── KEY QUESTION ─────

How do I know God and his will for my life?

───── KEY IDEA ─────

I believe the Bible is the inspired Word of God
that guides my beliefs and actions.

───── KEY VERSE ─────

All Scripture is God-breathed and is useful for teaching,
rebuking, correcting and training in righteousness,
so that the servant of God may be thoroughly
equipped for every good work.
*2 Timothy 3:16–17*

OUR MAP

*How do we know God? How do we understand and see the world we live in? How do we grasp where we came from and why we are here? How do we know where this story is ultimately heading? The answer is profound—God reveals himself and his grand plan to us. Our job is to listen and believe.*

*By simply looking at nature and the world around us we can conclude there is a God. But how do we learn about this God? How do we come into a full relationship with God? What are his plans and purposes for us? What are the principles he wants us to live by to guide us into his truth? The answer to all of these questions is found in God's revelation to us—the Bible.*

*In this chapter we will read some of God's messages in Scripture that clearly convey his will, and we will discover why the Bible holds such power for Christians:*

- *God Speaks*
- *The Authority of Scripture*
- *The Purpose of Scripture*

## GOD SPEAKS

*On many occasions in the Bible, God communicated specific messages to his people. In some cases, such as with Moses at the burning bush, God spoke out loud. In other instances he spoke through dreams, visions or less direct impressions. But the words of the Lord were always given to his people to reveal his plan for them and then recorded in the Scriptures for the benefit of all humanity. God spelled out his story in the Bible because he loves us.*

**Now Moses was tending the flock of Jethro his father-in-law, the priest of Midian, and he led the flock to the far side of the wilderness and came to Horeb, the mountain of God. There the angel of the LORD appeared to him in flames of fire from within a bush. Moses saw that though the bush was on fire it did not burn up. So Moses thought, "I will go over and see this strange sight — why the bush does not burn up."**

When the LORD saw that he had gone over to look, God called to him from within the bush, "Moses! Moses!"

And Moses said, "Here I am."

"Do not come any closer," God said. "Take off your sandals, for the place where you are standing is holy ground." Then he said, "I am the God of your father, the God of Abraham, the God of Isaac and the God of Jacob." At this, Moses hid his face, because he was afraid to look at God.

The LORD said, "I have indeed seen the misery of my people in Egypt. I have heard them crying out because of their slave drivers, and I am concerned about their suffering. So I have come down to rescue them from the hand of the Egyptians and to bring them up out of that land into a good and spacious land, a land flowing with milk and honey — the home of the Canaanites, Hittites, Amorites, Perizzites, Hivites and Jebusites. And now the cry of the Israelites has reached me, and I have seen the way the Egyptians are oppressing them. So now, go. I am sending you to Pharaoh to bring my people the Israelites out of Egypt."

But Moses said to God, "Who am I that I should go to Pharaoh and bring the Israelites out of Egypt?"

And God said, "I will be with you. And this will be the sign to you that it is I who have sent you: When you have brought the people out of Egypt, you will worship God on this mountain."

Moses said to God, "Suppose I go to the Israelites and say to them, 'The God of your fathers has sent me to you,' and they ask me, 'What is his name?' Then what shall I tell them?"

God said to Moses, "I AM WHO I AM. This is what you are to say to the Israelites: 'I AM has sent me to you.'"     EXODUS 3:1–14

---

What can we learn about the character of God
from the story of Moses and the burning bush?
How did Moses react to this direct communication from God?
How would you respond if you were in that situation?

---

*The Lord spoke mostly through prophets in the Old Testament and through Jesus and the apostles in the New Testament. After Jesus' death on the cross and miraculous resurrection, two of his followers were walking on the road from Jerusalem to Emmaus. Jesus came up and started walking with them and talking about his identity, though they were kept from recognizing him at first. Soon after, Jesus appeared to them again once they rejoined the disciples. It is significant that in order to prove to them he is the Messiah, he draws from the Law and the Prophets and the Psalms in the Old Testament. Jesus obviously understood these writings to be inspired by God.*

**Beginning with Moses and all the Prophets, [Jesus] explained to them what was said in all the Scriptures concerning himself.**

As they approached the village to which they were going, Jesus continued on as if he were going farther. But they urged him strongly, "Stay with us, for it is nearly evening; the day is almost over." So he went in to stay with them.

When he was at the table with them, he took bread, gave thanks, broke it and began to give it to them. Then their eyes were opened and they recognized him, and he disappeared from their sight. **They asked each other, "Were not our hearts burning within us while he talked with us on the road and opened the Scriptures to us?"**

They got up and returned at once to Jerusalem. There they found the Eleven and those with them, assembled together and saying, "It is true! The Lord has risen and has appeared to Simon." Then the two told what had happened on the way, and how Jesus was recognized by them when he broke the bread.

While they were still talking about this, Jesus himself stood among them and said to them, "Peace be with you."

They were startled and frightened, thinking they saw a ghost. He said to them, "Why are you troubled, and why do doubts rise in your minds? Look at my hands and my feet. It is I myself! Touch me and see; a ghost does not have flesh and bones, as you see I have."

When he had said this, he showed them his hands and feet. And while they still did not believe it because of joy and amazement, he asked them, "Do you have anything here to eat?" They gave him a piece of broiled fish, and he took it and ate it in their presence.

**He said to them, "This is what I told you while I was still with you: Everything must be fulfilled that is written about me in the Law of Moses, the Prophets and the Psalms."**

**Then he opened their minds so they could understand the Scriptures.** He told them, "This is what is written: The Messiah will suffer and rise from the dead on the third day, and repentance for the forgiveness of sins will be preached in his name to all nations, beginning at Jerusalem. You are witnesses of these things. I am going to send you what my Father has promised; but stay in the city until you have been clothed with power from on high."

LUKE 24:27–49

---

How did Jesus help his disciples understand
who he was and why he came?

---

*Before appearing to the eleven disciples in Jerusalem, Jesus appeared to Simon Peter who, after denying Jesus, went on to become a faithful follower of Christ and a key leader in the early church.*

*Like other leaders of the church, Peter sent letters to the early believers; those letters are preserved in the Bible in the New Testament. He wrote his second letter to one of the churches because false teaching had begun creeping into the church and causing people to stray from God's Word. Peter wrote to guide them back to the truth. He explained how God directs the writing of Scripture and how followers can use it to guide their lives.*

---

As you read Peter's message below, think about how the
Bible helps us understand the identity and purpose of Jesus.
How would you describe who Jesus is and why he came?

---

Simon Peter, a servant and apostle of Jesus Christ,

To those who through the righteousness of our God and Savior Jesus Christ have received a faith as precious as ours:

Grace and peace be yours in abundance through the knowledge of God and of Jesus our Lord.

His divine power has given us everything we need for a godly life through our knowledge of him who called us by his own glory and goodness. Through these he has given us his very great and precious promises, so that through them you may participate in the divine nature, having escaped the corruption in the world caused by evil desires.

For this very reason, make every effort to add to your faith goodness; and to goodness, knowledge; and to knowledge, self-control; and to self-control, perseverance; and to perseverance, godliness; and to godliness, mutual affection; and to mutual affection, love. For if you possess these qualities in increasing measure, they will keep you from being ineffective and unproductive in your knowledge of our Lord Jesus Christ. But whoever does not have them is nearsighted and blind, forgetting that they have been cleansed from their past sins.

Therefore, my brothers and sisters, make every effort to confirm your calling and election. For if you do these things, you will never stumble, and you will receive a rich welcome into the eternal kingdom of our Lord and Savior Jesus Christ.

So I will always remind you of these things, even though you know them and are firmly established in the truth you now have. I think it is right to refresh your memory as long as I live in the tent of this body, because I know that I will soon put it aside, as our LORD Jesus Christ has made clear to me. And I will make every effort to see that after my departure you will always be able to remember these things.

For we did not follow cleverly devised stories when we told you about the coming of our Lord Jesus Christ in power, but we were eyewitnesses of his majesty. He received honor and glory from God the Father when the voice came to him from the Majestic Glory, saying, "This is my Son, whom I love; with him I am well pleased." We ourselves heard this voice that came from heaven when we were with him on the sacred mountain.

We also have the prophetic message as something completely reliable, and you will do well to pay attention to it, as to a light shining in a dark place, until the day dawns and the morning star rises in your hearts. **Above all, you must understand that no prophecy of Scripture came about by the prophet's own interpretation of things. For prophecy never had its origin in the human will, but prophets, though human, spoke from God as they were carried along by the Holy Spirit.** 2 PETER 1:1–21

## THE AUTHORITY OF SCRIPTURE

*To understand how powerful Scripture is and why it carried so much authority in the lives of the Jews, we must go back to the early days of Israel. With a mighty hand God led the Israelites out of slavery in Egypt. In the wilderness God made preparations for them to enter into the land of Canaan that he had promised to Abraham 600 years earlier. Then God descended from the heavens to the foot of Mount Sinai to meet with his servant Moses and the people and proclaim to them the Ten Commandments. These laws, spoken directly from God to Moses, had the authority to guide the values and behavior of the Israelites for thousands of years.*

⚷ **And God spoke all these words:**

"I am the LORD your God, who brought you out of Egypt, out of the land of slavery.

"You shall have no other gods before me.

"You shall not make for yourself an image in the form of anything in heaven above or on the earth beneath or in the waters below. You shall not bow down to them or worship them; for I, the LORD your God, am a jealous God, punishing the children for the sin of the parents to the third and fourth generation of those who hate me, but showing love to a thousand generations of those who love me and keep my commandments.

"You shall not misuse the name of the LORD your God, for the LORD will not hold anyone guiltless who misuses his name.

"Remember the Sabbath day by keeping it holy. Six days you shall labor and do all your work, but the seventh day is a sabbath to the LORD your God. On it you shall not do any work, neither you, nor your son or daughter, nor your male or female servant, nor your animals, nor any foreigner residing in your towns. For in six days the LORD made the heavens and the earth, the sea, and all that is in them, but he rested on the seventh day. Therefore the LORD blessed the Sabbath day and made it holy.

"Honor your father and your mother, so that you may live long in the land the LORD your God is giving you.

"You shall not murder.

"You shall not commit adultery.

"You shall not steal.

"You shall not give false testimony against your neighbor.

"You shall not covet your neighbor's house. You shall not covet your neighbor's wife, or his male or female servant, his ox or donkey, or anything that belongs to your neighbor."

EXODUS 20:1–17

---

Are the Ten Commandments still relevant for us today? Which of the commandments are most difficult for you personally?

---

*God's words in the Bible carry so much authority because it is God who is speaking them. Examples of the authority of Scripture are found throughout the Bible, in both the New and Old Testaments. For instance, immediately after John baptized Jesus, the Spirit led Jesus into the wilderness where Satan tried to take advantage of Jesus' isolation, hunger and physical exhaustion. But the power of God's Word was revealed in Jesus' interactions with Satan; Jesus quoted Scripture three times—twice from Deuteronomy and once from Psalms—as his authority to overcome each temptation. Despite facing genuine temptations at a time when he was vulnerable, Jesus remained rooted in the truth of God's Word.*

Then Jesus was led by the Spirit into the wilderness to be tempted by the devil. After fasting forty days and forty nights, he was hungry. The tempter came to him and said, "If you are the Son of God, tell these stones to become bread."

**Jesus answered, "It is written: 'Man shall not live on bread alone, but on every word that comes from the mouth of God.'"**

Then the devil took him to the holy city and had him stand on the highest point of the temple. "If you are the Son of God," he said, "throw yourself down. For it is written:

> "'He will command his angels concerning you,
>> and they will lift you up in their hands,
>> so that you will not strike your foot against a stone.'"

**Jesus answered him, "It is also written: 'Do not put the Lord your God to the test.'"**

Again, the devil took him to a very high mountain and showed him all the kingdoms of the world and their splendor. "All this I will give you," he said, "if you will bow down and worship me."

**Jesus said to him, "Away from me, Satan! For it is written: 'Worship the Lord your God, and serve him only.'"**

Then the devil left him, and angels came and attended him.

MATTHEW 4:1–11 ⚷

## THE PURPOSE OF SCRIPTURE

*Jesus himself relied on Scripture, and he passed his dependence on God's Word to his followers. One faithful follower, the apostle Paul, was in a dungeon in Rome waiting to die. Despite his suffering, he found a way to send letters encouraging young pastor Timothy to step up and be a good leader. It is interesting to see that Paul's advice about leading well involves reading well — reading the Scriptures and depending on them because they contain tools that equip leaders for every good work.*

But as for you, continue in what you have learned and have become convinced of, because you know those from whom you learned it, and how from infancy you have known the Holy Scriptures, which are able to make you wise for salvation through faith in Christ Jesus. All Scripture is God-breathed and is useful for teaching, rebuking, correcting and training in righteousness, so that the servant of God may be thoroughly equipped for every good work.

2 TIMOTHY 3:14–17

*The writer of the book of Hebrews builds on the idea that God breathed life into things — including the words of the Bible.*

*Scripture is dynamic and alive and has a way of "getting under our skin."*

For the word of God is alive and active. Sharper than any double-edged sword, it penetrates even to dividing soul and spirit, joints and marrow; it judges the thoughts and attitudes of the heart.                                                                    HEBREWS 4:12

---

In what practical ways have you experienced the Word
of God as "alive and active" in your own spiritual life?

---

*Throughout the Bible the writers warned readers that they should not add to or take away from God's Word. God has given us the Bible and preserved it for us so we can rely on it to guide our lives. Therefore, Christians trust the Bible and affirm its right and authority to command our beliefs and actions.*

*Moses writes,*

Now, Israel, hear the decrees and laws I am about to teach you. Follow them so that you may live and may go in and take possession of the land the LORD, the God of your ancestors, is giving you. Do not add to what I command you and do not subtract from it, but keep the commands of the LORD your God that I give you.

DEUTERONOMY 4:1–2

*In the book of Proverbs, Agur declares,*

> "Every word of God is flawless;
>     he is a shield to those who take refuge in him.
> Do not add to his words,
>     or he will rebuke you and prove you a liar." PROVERBS 30:5–6

*John, the author of Revelation, writes,*

I warn everyone who hears the words of the prophecy of this scroll: If anyone adds anything to them, God will add to that person the plagues described in this scroll. And if anyone takes words away from this scroll of prophecy, God will take away from that person any share in the tree of life and in the Holy City, which are described in this scroll. REVELATION 22:18–19

## WHAT WE BELIEVE

*How do we know God and his will for our lives? The loving, personal, one true God speaks to us. Throughout history God has spoken through dreams, visions and even a burning bush. The primary way God reveals himself and his truth to us today is through the Bible. Because these words are from God, we can give the Bible the rightful authority to guide our lives. Whatever God promises in his Word will come to pass and accomplish his purposes. Do you believe the Bible is the Word of God and has the right to command your beliefs and actions?*

# CHAPTER

## 5

# Identity in Christ

--- KEY QUESTION ---

Who am I?

--- KEY IDEA ---

I believe I am significant because of
my position as a child of God.

--- KEY VERSE ---

Yet to all who did receive him, to those
who believed in his name, he gave the right
to become children of God.
*John 1:12*

OUR MAP

*When we open the pages of the Bible, God's trusted message to us, we discover that the one true God—Father, Son and Holy Spirit—is involved in and cares about our daily lives. We also learn that he has provided the way for us to come into a personal relationship with him through faith in Jesus Christ. When we believe and receive this gift of grace, we become a new person with a new identity and a new outlook on life. Our worth is no longer defined by what we do, but by who we know. We are significant because we are children of God.*

*Who am I? In the following pages soak in God's truth about:*

- *Our New Name*
- *A New Covenant*
- *Our Adoption*
- *Being an Heir of God*

## OUR NEW NAME

*During Bible times, a person's name was more than simply a reference to one's family or a way to identify someone; typically it described something about them. There are several instances recorded in the Bible where God gave a person a new name. When God renamed a person, he gave them a new identity and changed their mission or place in life. This was the case with Abram (meaning "exalted father") whose name God changed to Abraham (meaning "father of many"). The meaning of the name Abraham represented God's plan to make Abraham's offspring into the great nation of Israel—and eventually into the body of Christ through Abraham's spiritual descendants.*

When Abram was ninety-nine years old, the LORD appeared to him and said, "I am God Almighty; walk before me faithfully and be blameless. Then I will make my covenant between me and you and will greatly increase your numbers."

Abram fell facedown, and God said to him, "As for me, this is my covenant with you: You will be the father of many nations. **No longer will you be called Abram; your name will be Abraham,**

**for I have made you a father of many nations.** I will make you very fruitful; I will make nations of you, and kings will come from you. I will establish my covenant as an everlasting covenant between me and you and your descendants after you for the generations to come, to be your God and the God of your descendants after you."

GENESIS 17:1–7

---

God gave Abraham and Sarah new names to represent
their new identity and their covenant with God.
Looking back on the time since you first encountered God,
what would your new name be if you could pick one? Why?

---

## A NEW COVENANT

*In Old Testament times, God gave his people a promise which we call the old covenant. This covenant included his directions to his people under Moses' leadership. A covenant is a binding agreement between two parties, in this case God and Israel, which lays out what each side promises to do. The prophet Jeremiah, however, spoke of a new covenant—a new deal God had in the works—that would redefine the identity of God's people. This time it involved more than just a name change. The old covenant changed God's people from the outside in; the new covenant changes us from the inside out.*

> **"The days are coming," declares the LORD,**
> **"when I will make a new covenant**
> **with the people of Israel**
> **and with the people of Judah.**
> It will not be like the covenant
> I made with their ancestors
> when I took them by the hand
> to lead them out of Egypt,
> because they broke my covenant,
> though I was a husband to them,"
> declares the LORD.
> "This is the covenant I will make with the people of Israel
> after that time," declares the LORD.

"I will put my law in their minds
 and write it on their hearts.
I will be their God,
 and they will be my people.
No longer will they teach their neighbor,
 or say to one another, 'Know the LORD,'
because they will all know me,
 from the least of them to the greatest,"
 declares the LORD.
**"For I will forgive their wickedness
and will remember their sins no more."** JEREMIAH 31:31–34

---

What are the main points of God's new covenant? What effect does the new covenant have on our identity—on how God sees us?

---

*Jesus Christ fulfilled the requirements of the old covenant God made with Moses and ushered in a new season of amazing grace. Those who embrace this new covenant and turn from their sins will have their sins wiped away and will receive a new identity.*

The true light that gives light to everyone was coming into the world. He was in the world, and though the world was made through him, the world did not recognize him. He came to that which was his own, but his own did not receive him. **Yet to all who did receive him, to those who believed in his name, he gave the right to become children of God** — children born not of natural descent, nor of human decision or a husband's will, but born of God. JOHN 1:9–13

## OUR ADOPTION

*The beautiful thing about God's kingdom is that all those who welcome Jesus as their Lord are given a new identity through him. This is illustrated poignantly through the story of a crooked tax collector named Zacchaeus. Tax collectors were some of the most despised people in Israel because they chose to work for Rome and were making themselves rich by overcharging their fellow Jews. But the story of Zacchaeus shows that even the outcast can be adopted by God and made new.*

---

Before reading this section on spiritual adoption,
think about what it means to be adopted.
What does adoption tell us about the one doing the adopting?
What can the idea that God adopted us teach us about ourselves?

---

⚷ Jesus entered Jericho and was passing through. A man was there by the name of Zacchaeus; he was a chief tax collector and was wealthy. He wanted to see who Jesus was, but because he was short he could not see over the crowd. So he ran ahead and climbed a sycamore-fig tree to see him, since Jesus was coming that way.

When Jesus reached the spot, he looked up and said to him, "Zacchaeus, come down immediately. I must stay at your house today." So he came down at once and welcomed him gladly.

All the people saw this and began to mutter, "He has gone to be the guest of a sinner."

But Zacchaeus stood up and said to the Lord, "Look, Lord! Here and now I give half of my possessions to the poor, and if I have cheated anybody out of anything, I will pay back four times the amount."

**Jesus said to him, "Today salvation has come to this house, because this man, too, is a son of Abraham."** Luke 19:1–9 ⚷

*The people in the early church were living examples of the changes that resulted from following Jesus. The letter to the Romans was written by the apostle Paul to present the full scope of the transaction of the new covenant—its cost, the payment exacted for it and the promise it holds for those who agree to it. Follow along as Paul starts with our position in sin and the payment required, and then finishes with a glorious description of how our adoption into God's family gives us a new identity.*

As it is written:

"There is no one righteous, not even one;
    there is no one who understands;
    there is no one who seeks God.

All have turned away,
    they have together become worthless;
there is no one who does good,
    not even one."
"Their throats are open graves;
    their tongues practice deceit."
"The poison of vipers is on their lips."
    "Their mouths are full of cursing and bitterness."
"Their feet are swift to shed blood;
    ruin and misery mark their ways,
and the way of peace they do not know."
    "There is no fear of God before their eyes."

Now we know that whatever the law says, it says to those who are under the law, so that every mouth may be silenced and the whole world held accountable to God. Therefore no one will be declared righteous in God's sight by the works of the law; rather, through the law we become conscious of our sin.

But now apart from the law the righteousness of God has been made known, to which the Law and the Prophets testify. This righteousness is given through faith in Jesus Christ to all who believe. There is no difference between Jew and Gentile, for all have sinned and fall short of the glory of God, and all are justified freely by his grace through the redemption that came by Christ Jesus. God presented Christ as a sacrifice of atonement, through the shedding of his blood — to be received by faith. He did this to demonstrate his righteousness, because in his forbearance he had left the sins committed beforehand unpunished — he did it to demonstrate his righteousness at the present time, so as to be just and the one who justifies those who have faith in Jesus.     Romans 3:10–26

You see, at just the right time, when we were still powerless, Christ died for the ungodly. Very rarely will anyone die for a righteous person, though for a good person someone might possibly dare to die. But God demonstrates his own love for us in this: While we were still sinners, Christ died for us.

Since we have now been justified by his blood, how much more shall we be saved from God's wrath through him! For if, while we were God's enemies, we were reconciled to him through the death of his Son, how much more, having been reconciled, shall we be saved through his life! Not only is this so, but we also boast in God through our Lord Jesus Christ, through whom we have now received reconciliation. ROMANS 5:6–11

What shall we say, then? Shall we go on sinning so that grace may increase? By no means! We are those who have died to sin; how can we live in it any longer? Or don't you know that all of us who were baptized into Christ Jesus were baptized into his death? We were therefore buried with him through baptism into death in order that, just as Christ was raised from the dead through the glory of the Father, we too may live a new life.

For if we have been united with him in a death like his, we will certainly also be united with him in a resurrection like his. **For we know that our old self was crucified with him so that the body ruled by sin might be done away with, that we should no longer be slaves to sin — because anyone who has died has been set free from sin.** ROMANS 6:1–7

---

As you read the writings of Paul below from Romans 8, look for what God gives to those who find their identity in Jesus Christ.

---

Therefore, there is now no condemnation for those who are in Christ Jesus, because through Christ Jesus the law of the Spirit who gives life has set you free from the law of sin and death.

ROMANS 8:1–2

If Christ is in you, then even though your body is subject to death because of sin, the Spirit gives life because of righteousness. And if the Spirit of him who raised Jesus from the dead is living in you, he who raised Christ from the dead will also give life to your mortal bodies because of his Spirit who lives in you.

Therefore, brothers and sisters, we have an obligation — but it is not to the flesh, to live according to it. For if you live according to the flesh, you will die; but if by the Spirit you put to death the misdeeds of the body, you will live.

For those who are led by the Spirit of God are the children of God. **The Spirit you received does not make you slaves, so that you live in fear again; rather, the Spirit you received brought about your adoption to sonship. And by him we cry, "*Abba*, Father." The Spirit himself testifies with our spirit that we are God's children. Now if we are children, then we are heirs — heirs of God and co-heirs with Christ, if indeed we share in his sufferings in order that we may also share in his glory.**

I consider that our present sufferings are not worth comparing with the glory that will be revealed in us. For the creation waits in eager expectation for the children of God to be revealed. For the creation was subjected to frustration, not by its own choice, but by the will of the one who subjected it, in hope that the creation itself will be liberated from its bondage to decay and brought into the freedom and glory of the children of God.

**We know that the whole creation has been groaning as in the pains of childbirth right up to the present time. Not only so, but we ourselves, who have the firstfruits of the Spirit, groan inwardly as we wait eagerly for our adoption to sonship, the redemption of our bodies.** For in this hope we were saved. But hope that is seen is no hope at all. Who hopes for what they already have? But if we hope for what we do not yet have, we wait for it patiently.                                    ROMANS 8:10–25

## BEING AN HEIR OF GOD

*One of Paul's favorite themes throughout his writings was our identity in Christ. He wrote to the Romans in the previous passages about how the Father adopted us and gave us a new identity. In this next passage, he lays out for the Ephesians the incredible reality that as his adopted children we inherit everything his Son (Jesus) inherits! All this is made possible by God's great love.*

As you read this chapter from the Book of Ephesians, highlight or underline all the phrases that talk about our new identity in Christ.

As for you, you were dead in your transgressions and sins, in which you used to live when you followed the ways of this world and of the ruler of the kingdom of the air, the spirit who is now at work in those who are disobedient. All of us also lived among them at one time, gratifying the cravings of our flesh and following its desires and thoughts. Like the rest, we were by nature deserving of wrath. But because of his great love for us, God, who is rich in mercy, made us alive with Christ even when we were dead in transgressions — it is by grace you have been saved. And God raised us up with Christ and seated us with him in the heavenly realms in Christ Jesus, in order that in the coming ages he might show the incomparable riches of his grace, expressed in his kindness to us in Christ Jesus. For it is by grace you have been saved, through faith — and this is not from yourselves, it is the gift of God — not by works, so that no one can boast. **For we are God's handiwork, created in Christ Jesus to do good works, which God prepared in advance for us to do.**

Therefore, remember that formerly you who are Gentiles by birth and called "uncircumcised" by those who call themselves "the circumcision" (which is done in the body by human hands) — remember that at that time you were separate from Christ, excluded from citizenship in Israel and foreigners to the covenants of the promise, without hope and without God in the world. But now in Christ Jesus you who once were far away have been brought near by the blood of Christ.

For he himself is our peace, who has made the two groups one and has destroyed the barrier, the dividing wall of hostility, by setting aside in his flesh the law with its commands and regulations. His purpose was to create in himself one new humanity out of the two, thus making peace, and in one body to reconcile both of them to God through the cross, by which he put to death their hostility. He came and preached peace to you who were far away and peace to those who were near. For through him we both have access to the Father by one Spirit.

**Consequently, you are no longer foreigners and strangers, but fellow citizens with God's people and also members of his household, built on the foundation of the apostles and prophets, with Christ Jesus himself as the chief cornerstone. In**

him the whole building is joined together and rises to become a holy temple in the Lord. And in him you too are being built together to become a dwelling in which God lives by his Spirit.

EPHESIANS 2:1–22

## WHAT WE BELIEVE

*Who am I? As the key verse declares in John 1:12, when we believe and receive Jesus Christ as our Savior, we are given a new name, a new unconditional covenant. We are adopted. We become heirs of all that belongs to God—and so much more. As we face each day, our worth is not up for grabs. Our identity is rooted firmly and permanently in our honored position as children of God. We do not live our lives to prove who we are but to express who we are in Christ.*

CHAPTER

6

# Church

——— KEY QUESTION ———

How will God accomplish his plan?

——— KEY IDEA ———

I believe the church is God's primary way
to accomplish his purposes on earth.

——— KEY VERSE ———

Speaking the truth in love, we will grow
to become in every respect the mature body of him
who is the head, that is, Christ.
*Ephesians 4:15*

OUR MAP

*The first five key beliefs we have read about so far are mostly vertical in nature—they deal with our relationship with God. The God of the Bible is the one true God who is involved in and cares about our daily lives. This God has provided the way for us to come into a relationship with him through faith in Jesus Christ. God revealed this to us along with a roadmap (the Bible) for our lives. This special book is from God and therefore has the right to command our beliefs and actions. We who embrace these beliefs and receive Jesus as our Savior from sin are given a new identity. From that moment on we can find our significance not in our performance but in our position as children of God.*

*The final set of five beliefs is more horizontal in nature— they deal with our relationship with others. Out of our relationship with God we engage our world in a purposeful and fruitful way. How will God accomplish the plan for humanity he has laid out in the Bible? God has chosen to use two communities he created—the ancient nation of Israel and the church—to accomplish his purposes on earth. If you are a Christian, you are a part of this community.*

*In this chapter you will explore:*

- *Founding of the Church*
- *Expansion of the Church*
- *Purpose of the Church*

## FOUNDING OF THE CHURCH

*From the very beginning, God had a vision to be with his people in perfect community. When the first two humans—Adam and Eve—rejected this vision and were escorted from the Garden of Eden, God began to unveil a plan to provide the way back to him.*

*God's plan consisted of making Abraham's offspring into a great nation. From this single nation would come the solution for all people of all nations to come back into a relationship with the one true God. From here on, the story of Israel pointed people to Abraham's descendent Jesus, who was God's plan to restore a relationship with his people.*

*Again we return to the story of Abraham (Abram) to observe the beginnings of God's covenant with a people who came to be known as Israel. When we are introduced to Abram in the book of Genesis, the first thing we get to observe is God's call to Abram and Abram's amazing response of complete faith and trust.*

**The LORD had said to Abram, "Go from your country, your people and your father's household to the land I will show you.**

> **"I will make you into a great nation,**
> **and I will bless you;**
> **I will make your name great,**
> **and you will be a blessing.**
> **I will bless those who bless you,**
> **and whoever curses you I will curse;**
> **and all peoples on earth**
> **will be blessed through you."**

So Abram went, as the LORD had told him; and Lot went with him. Abram was seventy-five years old when he set out from Harran. GENESIS 12:1–4

After this, the word of the LORD came to Abram in a vision:

> "Do not be afraid, Abram.
> I am your shield,
> your very great reward."

But Abram said, "Sovereign LORD, what can you give me since I remain childless and the one who will inherit my estate is Eliezer of Damascus?" And Abram said, "You have given me no children; so a servant in my household will be my heir."

Then the word of the LORD came to him: "This man will not be your heir, but a son who is your own flesh and blood will be your heir." He took him outside and said, "Look up at the sky and count the stars — if indeed you can count them." Then he said to him, "So shall your offspring be."

Abram believed the LORD, and he credited it to him as righteousness. GENESIS 15:1–6

*Israel was Abraham's biological offspring (they had the same blood line as he did); the church is Abraham's spiritual descendants (those who have the same faith as he did). Jesus was both the biological and spiritual descendent of Abraham. He was the physical fulfillment of God's covenant with Abraham, and he was the spiritual founder of God's new covenant family, the church.*

*Jesus prepared his disciples for their role in accomplishing God's plan for the coming kingdom. In this conversation Jesus speaks of the founding of a new community—the church.*

When Jesus came to the region of Caesarea Philippi, he asked his disciples, "Who do people say the Son of Man is?"

They replied, "Some say John the Baptist; others say Elijah; and still others, Jeremiah or one of the prophets."

"But what about you?" he asked. "Who do you say I am?"

Simon Peter answered, "You are the Messiah, the Son of the living God."

**Jesus replied, "Blessed are you, Simon son of Jonah, for this was not revealed to you by flesh and blood, but by my Father in heaven. And I tell you that you are Peter, and on this rock I will build my church, and the gates of Hades will not overcome it."**

MATTHEW 16:13–18

---

Look back over the last two stories of Abraham and Peter. What was Abraham's response that was "credited to him as righteousness"? How did Peter respond when Jesus asked, "Who do you say I am"? How are these responses related?

---

*After the resurrection and ascension of Jesus, God formed this community led by his disciples called the church. The story of the church points people of all nations to the second coming of Christ when he will fully restore God's original vision.*

*Forty days after Jesus' resurrection and just before his ascension to the Father, Jesus visited with his disciples and gave them his final instructions. (Luke, who also wrote the gospel bearing his name, recorded the incident in the book of Acts.) The result? The church was born!*

On one occasion, while he was eating with them, he gave them this command: "Do not leave Jerusalem, but wait for the gift my Father promised, which you have heard me speak about. For John baptized with water, but in a few days you will be baptized with the Holy Spirit."

ACTS 1:4–5

**"You will receive power when the Holy Spirit comes on you; and you will be my witnesses in Jerusalem, and in all Judea and Samaria, and to the ends of the earth."**

After he said this, he was taken up before their very eyes, and a cloud hid him from their sight.

ACTS 1:8–9

---

How did God equip the early church to carry out the mission to spread the gospel of Jesus Christ?
What mission has God given you? How has God equipped you to carry out your mission?

---

*For the next ten days, Jesus' followers—about 120 men and women—met together. They constantly prayed together, anticipating what was about to happen. After they became filled with the Holy Spirit, Peter used the "keys of the kingdom" that Jesus had mentioned earlier. He announced that the door of the kingdom had been unlocked by Jesus.*

When the day of Pentecost came, they were all together in one place. Suddenly a sound like the blowing of a violent wind came from heaven and filled the whole house where they were sitting. They saw what seemed to be tongues of fire that separated and came to rest on each of them. All of them were filled with the Holy Spirit and began to speak in other tongues as the Spirit enabled them.

Now there were staying in Jerusalem God-fearing Jews from every nation under heaven. When they heard this sound, a crowd came together in bewilderment, because each one heard their own language being spoken. Utterly amazed, they asked: "Aren't all these who are speaking Galileans? Then how is it that each of us hears them in our native language? Parthians, Medes and

Elamites; residents of Mesopotamia, Judea and Cappadocia, Pontus and Asia, Phrygia and Pamphylia, Egypt and the parts of Libya near Cyrene; visitors from Rome (both Jews and converts to Judaism); Cretans and Arabs — we hear them declaring the wonders of God in our own tongues!" Amazed and perplexed, they asked one another, "What does this mean?"

Some, however, made fun of them and said, "They have had too much wine."

Then Peter stood up with the Eleven, raised his voice and addressed the crowd: "Fellow Jews and all of you who live in Jerusalem, let me explain this to you; listen carefully to what I say. These people are not drunk, as you suppose. It's only nine in the morning! No, this is what was spoken by the prophet Joel:

"'In the last days, God says,
    I will pour out my Spirit on all people.
Your sons and daughters will prophesy,
    your young men will see visions,
    your old men will dream dreams.
Even on my servants, both men and women,
    I will pour out my Spirit in those days,
    and they will prophesy.
I will show wonders in the heavens above
    and signs on the earth below,
    blood and fire and billows of smoke.
The sun will be turned to darkness
    and the moon to blood
    before the coming of the great and glorious day
        of the Lord.
And everyone who calls
    on the name of the Lord will be saved.'

"Fellow Israelites, listen to this: Jesus of Nazareth was a man accredited by God to you by miracles, wonders and signs, which God did among you through him, as you yourselves know. This man was handed over to you by God's deliberate plan and foreknowledge; and you, with the help of wicked men, put him to death by nailing him to the cross. But God raised him from the dead, freeing him from the agony of death, because it was impossible for death to keep its hold on him." ACTS 2:1–24

"Therefore let all Israel be assured of this: God has made this Jesus, whom you crucified, both Lord and Messiah."

**When the people heard this, they were cut to the heart and said to Peter and the other apostles, "Brothers, what shall we do?"**

**Peter replied, "Repent and be baptized, every one of you, in the name of Jesus Christ for the forgiveness of your sins. And you will receive the gift of the Holy Spirit. The promise is for you and your children and for all who are far off — for all whom the Lord our God will call."**

With many other words he warned them; and he pleaded with them, "Save yourselves from this corrupt generation." Those who accepted his message were baptized, and about three thousand were added to their number that day. ACTS 2:36–41

## EXPANSION OF THE CHURCH

*The book of Acts records how Peter and the other apostles went out to share the Good News, now that they were empowered by the Holy Spirit. At first they focused their efforts primarily on Jews, teaching in the local synagogues in every town to which they traveled. Although the church was building gradually as more and more Jews were baptized, God began making it clear that the Good News was for everyone, Jews and Gentiles alike.*

*In this next passage, we see the apostle Paul and his companions in the Greek city of Antioch. As was their typical practice, they went first to the Jewish synagogue where Paul stood up and gave a powerful sermon similar to Peter's on the day of Pentecost. Paul told them the story of the Jews in chronological order beginning with Israel of the Old Testament. We pick up at the end of his message, where Paul boldly extends an invitation to them to receive this Good News. Notice then the shift in focus away from the Jews, based on their rejection.*

**"Therefore, my friends, I want you to know that through Jesus the forgiveness of sins is proclaimed to you. Through him**

everyone who believes is set free from every sin, a justification you were not able to obtain under the law of Moses." ACTS 13:38–39

On the next Sabbath almost the whole city gathered to hear the word of the Lord. When the Jews saw the crowds, they were filled with jealousy. They began to contradict what Paul was saying and heaped abuse on him.

**Then Paul and Barnabas answered them boldly: "We had to speak the word of God to you first. Since you reject it and do not consider yourselves worthy of eternal life, we now turn to the Gentiles. For this is what the Lord has commanded us:**

**" 'I have made you a light for the Gentiles,
    that you may bring salvation to the ends of the earth.' "**

When the Gentiles heard this, they were glad and honored the word of the Lord; and all who were appointed for eternal life believed. ACTS 13:44–48

---

Identify how the abuse Paul and the apostles experienced from the Jews actually helped the early church spread the gospel. Describe a time in your own life when God has turned a tough situation into a good thing.

---

*After this persecution by the Jews, Paul's attention turned to spreading the gospel and building the church in a world dominated by Gentiles. One of the churches close to Paul's heart was the one at Ephesus. During his third missionary journey, he spent a few years there building the church and training its leaders.*

*A couple of years later, around AD 57, Paul was in a hurry to get to Jerusalem. Concerned that he might never make it back to Ephesus, he asked the leaders of the church to meet him on his way to Jerusalem. He wanted to have one last meeting with them to build up the fledgling church he had sacrificed so much to launch.*

From Miletus, Paul sent to Ephesus for the elders of the church. When they arrived, he said to them: "You know how I lived the whole time I was with you, from the first day I came into the province of Asia. I served the Lord with great humility and with tears and in the midst of severe testing by the plots of my Jewish opponents. You know that I have not hesitated to preach anything that would be helpful to you but have taught you publicly and from house to house. I have declared to both Jews and Greeks that they must turn to God in repentance and have faith in our Lord Jesus.

"And now, compelled by the Spirit, I am going to Jerusalem, not knowing what will happen to me there. I only know that in every city the Holy Spirit warns me that prison and hardships are facing me. **However, I consider my life worth nothing to me; my only aim is to finish the race and complete the task the Lord Jesus has given me — the task of testifying to the good news of God's grace.**

"Now I know that none of you among whom I have gone about preaching the kingdom will ever see me again. Therefore, I declare to you today that I am innocent of the blood of any of you. For I have not hesitated to proclaim to you the whole will of God. **Keep watch over yourselves and all the flock of which the Holy Spirit has made you overseers. Be shepherds of the church of God, which he bought with his own blood.** I know that after I leave, savage wolves will come in among you and will not spare the flock. Even from your own number men will arise and distort the truth in order to draw away disciples after them. So be on your guard! Remember that for three years I never stopped warning each of you night and day with tears." Acts 20:17–31

## Purpose of the Church

*Prison and hardship awaited Paul when he arrived in Jerusalem. While under house arrest in Rome a few years later, around AD 60, Paul wrote a letter to the church at Ephesus. Paul explained God's great plan for the church, the new community of followers of Jesus. Along with reconciling individuals to himself, God has also reconciled them to another. Through his death, Christ has broken down all kinds of social, racial and relational barriers. The church community is now invited to live up to the calling they have in Jesus Christ.*

As you read these Scriptures, try to zero in on the
main purpose of the church. Why do you go to church?
What can you do to make your time with your
church group more meaningful?

As a prisoner for the Lord, then, I urge you to live a life worthy of the calling you have received. Be completely humble and gentle; be patient, bearing with one another in love. Make every effort to keep the unity of the Spirit through the bond of peace. There is one body and one Spirit, just as you were called to one hope when you were called; one Lord, one faith, one baptism; one God and Father of all, who is over all and through all and in all.

EPHESIANS 4:1–6

**So Christ himself gave the apostles, the prophets, the evangelists, the pastors and teachers, to equip his people for works of service, so that the body of Christ may be built up until we all reach unity in the faith and in the knowledge of the Son of God and become mature, attaining to the whole measure of the fullness of Christ.**

Then we will no longer be infants, tossed back and forth by the waves, and blown here and there by every wind of teaching and by the cunning and craftiness of people in their deceitful scheming. Instead, speaking the truth in love, we will grow to become in every respect the mature body of him who is the head, that is, Christ. From him the whole body, joined and held together by every supporting ligament, grows and builds itself up in love, as each part does its work.

EPHESIANS 4:11–16

Nowhere in the Scripture passages in this chapter
do you see the word "building" used to describe
the church. Going back through this chapter,
what words were used to define the church, and
how do those words explain the purpose of the
church better than the word "building"?

## WHAT WE BELIEVE

*God used both Israel and the church to accomplish his grand plan to redeem and restore us to a right relationship with him. God's plan for Israel was to bring us Jesus, who would provide the only way back to God. It took a little more than 2,000 years for this divine plan to be fulfilled.*

*After Jesus' resurrection and ascension to the Father, God created the church. Empowered by the Holy Spirit, the church has existed for approximately 2,000 years. God's primary plan for the church is to spread the good news of Jesus Christ to all nations until Jesus comes again. Today there are an estimated 2.2 billion Christians in the world. If you have received and accepted the grace of Christ you are a member of the body of Christ. And remember you are an important part of his plan— God placed you into his church family to accomplish his great and wonderful purposes!*

## THINK

# CHAPTER

### 7

# Humanity

―――――― KEY QUESTION ――――――

How does God see us?

―――――― KEY IDEA ――――――

I believe all people are loved by God
and need Jesus Christ as their Savior.

―――――― KEY VERSE ――――――

For God so loved the world
that he gave his one and only Son,
that whoever believes in him shall not perish
but have eternal life.
*John 3:16*

*OUR MAP*

*God created everything, but the pinnacle of creation was the making of human beings—creatures crafted in the image of God. Humanity is special, and the Bible is the record of the love story between Creator and created, between God and humans. From the very beginning of time to the era of the modern-day church, God has loved and pursued his people in order to restore his image within and among them.*

*In this chapter you will read Bible passages on:*

- *Origins—A reminder of how we began*
- *The Devastating Human Condition—How we got in the position we are in*
- *God's Love—Why we have a way out*
- *All and Whoever—Who is included in the extent of God's love*
- *Seeing People as God Sees Them*

## ORIGINS

*God is the origin of all life. The creation account describes how he spoke into existence the planets and light, water and land, plants and trees, fish and birds and animals. After all that magnificent handiwork, God created his ultimate masterpiece: us.*

Then God said, "Let us make mankind in our image, in our likeness, so that they may rule over the fish in the sea and the birds in the sky, over the livestock and all the wild animals, and over all the creatures that move along the ground."

So God created mankind in his own image,
in the image of God he created them;
male and female he created them.

God blessed them and said to them, "Be fruitful and increase in number; fill the earth and subdue it. Rule over the fish in the sea and the birds in the sky and over every living creature that moves on the ground."

Then God said, "I give you every seed-bearing plant on the face of the whole earth and every tree that has fruit with seed in it.

They will be yours for food. And to all the beasts of the earth and all the birds in the sky and all the creatures that move along the ground — everything that has the breath of life in it — I give every green plant for food." And it was so.

God saw all that he had made, and it was very good. And there was evening, and there was morning — the sixth day. Genesis 1:26–31

---

Describe in your own words God's original purpose
for the human race.

---

## THE DEVASTATING HUMAN CONDITION

*God created the world and everything in it. He wanted to be in a perfect and harmonious relationship with his people, but when Adam and Eve sinned, that made them unfit for community with a holy God. After their rebellion in the garden, sin became part of our spiritual "DNA" — we all have the virus. Sin not only breaks our relationship with God, it also affects the way we treat each other — even those we love.*

---

What are some of the results of human sin you can see in the
Scripture text in this section? What are some practical
consequences of sin you have experienced in your own life?

---

Adam made love to his wife Eve, and she became pregnant and gave birth to Cain. She said, "With the help of the Lord I have brought forth a man." Later she gave birth to his brother Abel.

Now Abel kept flocks, and Cain worked the soil. In the course of time Cain brought some of the fruits of the soil as an offering to the Lord. And Abel also brought an offering — fat portions from some of the firstborn of his flock. The Lord looked with favor on Abel and his offering, but on Cain and his offering he did not look with favor. So Cain was very angry, and his face was downcast.

Genesis 4:1–5

*Here we vividly see the results of Adam and Eve's sinful choices. We know from other places in Scripture that God rejected Cain's offering and accepted Abel's offering because of the faith of the two men. The Bible doesn't tell us exactly why God rejected Cain's offering, but it had something to do with Cain's bad attitude toward God.*

Then the LORD said to Cain, "Why are you angry? Why is your face downcast? **If you do what is right, will you not be accepted? But if you do not do what is right, sin is crouching at your door; it desires to have you, but you must rule over it."**

Now Cain said to his brother Abel, "Let's go out to the field." While they were in the field, Cain attacked his brother Abel and killed him.

Then the LORD said to Cain, "Where is your brother Abel?"

"I don't know," he replied. "Am I my brother's keeper?"

The LORD said, "What have you done? Listen! Your brother's blood cries out to me from the ground. Now you are under a curse and driven from the ground, which opened its mouth to receive your brother's blood from your hand. When you work the ground, it will no longer yield its crops for you. You will be a restless wanderer on the earth."

**Cain said to the LORD, "My punishment is more than I can bear. Today you are driving me from the land, and I will be hidden from your presence;** I will be a restless wanderer on the earth, and whoever finds me will kill me."

But the LORD said to him, "Not so; anyone who kills Cain will suffer vengeance seven times over." Then the LORD put a mark on Cain so that no one who found him would kill him. So Cain went out from the LORD's presence and lived in the land of Nod, east of Eden.                    GENESIS 4:6–16

## GOD'S LOVE

*Adam and Eve had more children, but their offspring continued inheriting and passing on a fallen, sinful nature. Yet, throughout history, God shows his love for humankind by pursuing a relationship with us, even though we don't deserve it. In the book of Hosea, God described his relationship with Israel in terms of an unfaithful wife and a rebellious son. He helped the Israelites even when, like a rebellious son, they didn't value his presence.*

*Out of love he rescued them from slavery in Egypt. Now Israel,
often referred to as Ephraim (Israel's largest tribe), was about to
go into slavery yet again. This time the mighty nation of Assyria
was going to take the people captive. They would experience
discipline for walking away from God, but he declared yet again
that he would redeem them out of slavery. This is the same kind
of unending, persistent, merciful love God has for us.*

---

As you read, look for God's discipline and punishment as well
as his compassion and kindness. How does his discipline
and punishment fit with your concept of God as a God of love?

---

"When Israel was a child, I loved him,
    and out of Egypt I called my son.
But the more they were called,
    the more they went away from me.
They sacrificed to the Baals
    and they burned incense to images.
It was I who taught Ephraim to walk,
    taking them by the arms;
but they did not realize
    it was I who healed them.
I led them with cords of human kindness,
    with ties of love.
To them I was like one who lifts
    a little child to the cheek,
    and I bent down to feed them.

"Will they not return to Egypt
    and will not Assyria rule over them
    because they refuse to repent?
A sword will flash in their cities;
    it will devour their false prophets
    and put an end to their plans.
My people are determined to turn from me.
    Even though they call me God Most High,
    I will by no means exalt them.

> **"How can I give you up, Ephraim?**
>> **How can I hand you over, Israel?**
> **How can I treat you like Admah?**
>> **How can I make you like Zeboyim?**
> **My heart is changed within me;**
>> **all my compassion is aroused.**
> I will not carry out my fierce anger,
>> nor will I devastate Ephraim again.
> For I am God, and not a man—
>> the Holy One among you.
>> I will not come against their cities.
> They will follow the LORD;
>> he will roar like a lion.
> When he roars,
>> his children will come trembling from the west.
> They will come from Egypt,
>> trembling like sparrows,
>> from Assyria, fluttering like doves.
> I will settle them in their homes,"
>> declares the LORD.          HOSEA 11:1–11

## ALL AND WHOEVER

*One of the special assignments John took on in his gospel was to share that Jesus' offer of forgiveness and restoration to God for eternity is for everyone. Throughout his gospel, John uses the words "all" and "whoever." As you read this collection of powerful declarations, keep in mind that we are included in the "all" and "whoever"; therefore God extends his offer of love to us. He "so loves us."*

---

Try reading these verses out loud, and wherever you see "all" or "whoever" or "the world," replace it with your own name. Then, pause and thank God that he "so loved you!"

---

In [the Word, Jesus Christ] was life, and that life was the light of **all mankind.**          JOHN 1:4

[John the Baptist] came as a witness to testify concerning that light, so that through him **all** might believe.                        JOHN 1:7

For God so loved **the world** that he gave his one and only Son, that **whoever** believes in him shall not perish but have eternal life.
                                                                    JOHN 3:16

**Whoever** believes in the Son has eternal life, but **whoever** rejects the Son will not see life, for God's wrath remains on them.
                                                                    JOHN 3:36

"**Whoever** drinks the water I give them will never thirst. Indeed, the water I give them will become in them a spring of water welling up to eternal life."                                     JOHN 4:14

"Very truly I tell you, **whoever** hears my word and believes him who sent me has eternal life and will not be judged but has crossed over from death to life."                                        JOHN 5:24

"All those the Father gives me will come to me, and **whoever** comes to me I will never drive away."                           JOHN 6:37

"I am the living bread that came down from heaven. **Whoever** eats this bread will live forever. This bread is my flesh, which I will give for the life of **the world**."                            JOHN 6:51

When Jesus spoke again to the people, he said, "I am the light of **the world. Whoever** follows me will never walk in darkness, but will have the light of life."                                JOHN 8:12

"Very truly I tell you, **whoever** obeys my word will never see death."                                                           JOHN 8:51

"I am the gate; **whoever** enters through me will be saved. They will come in and go out, and find pasture."                 JOHN 10:9

"**Whoever** lives by believing in me will never die."     JOHN 11:26A

## SEEING PEOPLE AS GOD SEES THEM

*As the parable of the wandering sheep illustrates, God loves us deeply and personally—as if each of us was the only person on earth. He wants us to treat each other with this same sense of high value and worth.*

"What do you think? If a man owns a hundred sheep, and one of them wanders away, will he not leave the ninety-nine on the hills and go to look for the one that wandered off? And if he finds it, truly I tell you, he is happier about that one sheep than about the ninety-nine that did not wander off. In the same way your Father in heaven is not willing that any of these little ones should perish."

MATTHEW 18:12–14

*In the early season of his ministry, Jesus spoke to a large crowd of people who gathered to be healed by him and to hear what he had to say. In this setting, Jesus taught that we are to see and treat people the way God sees and treats us. Our heavenly Father provides the supreme example to follow.*

"But to you who are listening I say: Love your enemies, do good to those who hate you, bless those who curse you, pray for those who mistreat you. If someone slaps you on one cheek, turn to them the other also. If someone takes your coat, do not withhold your shirt from them. Give to everyone who asks you, and if anyone takes what belongs to you, do not demand it back. Do to others as you would have them do to you.

"If you love those who love you, what credit is that to you? Even sinners love those who love them. And if you do good to those who are good to you, what credit is that to you? Even sinners do that. And if you lend to those from whom you expect repayment, what credit is that to you? Even sinners lend to sinners, expecting to be repaid in full. **But love your enemies, do good to them, and lend to them without expecting to get anything back. Then your reward will be great, and you will be children of the Most High, because he is kind to the ungrateful and wicked. Be merciful, just as your Father is merciful."** LUKE 6:27–36

*The new reality in Christ is this: There is no more division between Jews and Gentiles, men and women, masters and slaves. We all belong to Christ equally. The apostle Paul had an opportunity to demonstrate this in the latter years of his life. His good friend Philemon had a slave—named Onesimus—who evidently stole from Philemon and then ran away (a crime punishable by death). Amazingly, while Paul was in Rome he met Onesimus, who then became a Christian. Paul wrote Philemon a letter with the personal request to welcome Onesimus back, not as a slave but as a brother in Christ. God gives us today the same challenge: to welcome every believer as a family member, no matter their race, gender or background.*

Paul, a prisoner of Christ Jesus, and Timothy our brother,

To Philemon our dear friend and fellow worker — also to Apphia our sister and Archippus our fellow soldier — and to the church that meets in your home:

Grace and peace to you from God our Father and the Lord Jesus Christ.

I always thank my God as I remember you in my prayers, because I hear about your love for all his holy people and your faith in the Lord Jesus. I pray that your partnership with us in the faith may be effective in deepening your understanding of every good thing we share for the sake of Christ. Your love has given me great joy and encouragement, because you, brother, have refreshed the hearts of the Lord's people.

Therefore, although in Christ I could be bold and order you to do what you ought to do, yet I prefer to appeal to you on the basis of love. It is as none other than Paul — an old man and now also a prisoner of Christ Jesus — that I appeal to you for my son Onesimus, who became my son while I was in chains. Formerly he was useless to you, but now he has become useful both to you and to me.

I am sending him — who is my very heart — back to you. I would have liked to keep him with me so that he could take your place in helping me while I am in chains for the gospel. But I did not want to do anything without your consent, so that any favor you do would not seem forced but would be voluntary. **Perhaps the reason he was separated from you for a little while was that you might have him back forever — no longer as a slave, but better than a slave, as a dear brother. He is very dear to me but even dearer to you, both as a fellow man and as a brother in the Lord.**

So if you consider me a partner, welcome him as you would welcome me. If he has done you any wrong or owes you anything, charge it to me. I, Paul, am writing this with my own hand. I will pay it back — not to mention that you owe me your very self. I do wish, brother, that I may have some benefit from you in the Lord; refresh my heart in Christ. Confident of your obedience, I write to you, knowing that you will do even more than I ask.

And one thing more: Prepare a guest room for me, because I hope to be restored to you in answer to your prayers.

Epaphras, my fellow prisoner in Christ Jesus, sends you greetings. And so do Mark, Aristarchus, Demas and Luke, my fellow workers.

The grace of the Lord Jesus Christ be with your spirit.

PHILEMON 1–25

---

How do the passages in this chapter highlight God's
loving persistence in bringing people into a
right relationship with him and one another?
Which phrases speak to you personally?

---

## WHAT WE BELIEVE

*It cannot be denied. We are the crowning achievement of God's creation. We were made in the very image of God with the purpose of living in perfect community with God on earth. But the first two people rejected God's vision, introducing death and separation from God into the human race. We see clearly in the story of Cain and Abel, throughout human history and even in our own stories that this sin nature has been passed down and all people fall victim to it. But God loves us and wants us back. "All of his compassion is aroused" (see Hosea 11:8) when he thinks of us. God's love knows no boundaries. Forgiveness and salvation are available to "all" and "whoever" will receive it in Christ Jesus. God calls all Christians to see people the same way he does. What would happen in our world if we would do just that?*

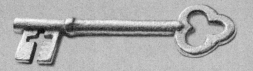

CHAPTER

8

# Compassion

───── KEY QUESTION ─────

What about the poor and injustice?

───── KEY IDEA ─────

I believe God calls all Christians to show
compassion to people in need.

───── KEY VERSE ─────

Defend the weak and the fatherless;
uphold the cause of the poor and the oppressed.
Rescue the weak and the needy;
deliver them from the hand of the wicked.
*Psalm 82:3–4*

**OUR MAP**

*All humans are valuable to God, and he calls us to see people as he sees them. Compassion goes a step further by compelling us to feel their pain. Compassion literally means "suffer with." God calls us to come alongside people who are suffering. It doesn't mean we can fix their problems, but it does mean we can enter into their pain. Before we practice this belief, we must believe it is God's call on the life of all Christ followers. When we believe this in our hearts, we will show compassion to all people, especially to those in need. This is not a "do as I say, not as I do" command from the Lord. God himself is merciful and full of compassion. This is where our journey into compassion starts.*

*In this chapter you will read about:*

- *God: Full of Justice AND Compassion*
- *Israel: Called to Compassion*
- *Jesus: Model of Compassion*
- *Believers: The Ongoing Call to Compassion*

## GOD: FULL OF JUSTICE AND COMPASSION

*Throughout their history, the Israelites struggled to stay true to God. Sometimes they followed God, but those periods of faithfulness were always followed by times of sin and rebellion. Even then, God's love for his people was evident. He offered his people relief from the trouble they were in, even though it was caused by their sinful decisions. In this passage, the Israelites are recalling some of their many cycles of faithfulness/rebellion/judgment/rescue.*

As you read this account from the book of Nehemiah, look for some of the ways God showed both compassion and justice to the Israelites. What are some ways God has shown compassion to you?

"They captured fortified cities and fertile land; they took possession of houses filled with all kinds of good things, wells already dug, vineyards, olive groves and fruit trees in abundance. They ate to the full and were well-nourished; they reveled in your great goodness.

"But they were disobedient and rebelled against you; they turned their backs on your law. They killed your prophets, who had warned them in order to turn them back to you; they committed awful blasphemies. So you delivered them into the hands of their enemies, who oppressed them. But when they were oppressed they cried out to you. **From heaven you heard them, and in your great compassion you gave them deliverers, who rescued them from the hand of their enemies.**

"But as soon as they were at rest, they again did what was evil in your sight. Then you abandoned them to the hand of their enemies so that they ruled over them. **And when they cried out to you again, you heard from heaven, and in your compassion you delivered them time after time."** NEHEMIAH 9:25–28

*The ultimate demonstration of God's compassion was the sacrifice of his one and only Son, Jesus Christ, on the cross for us. This one act of God not only showcased his mercy but also his justice. You see, because God is a holy and just God, sin had to be "paid for" (that's what "atonement" means), but because God is also a merciful God, he decided to pay for it himself. On the cross, Jesus suffered and paid for our sins, so that God's justice AND mercy could be satisfied. Jesus got what we deserved, and it is a perfect picture of God's compassion and justice working together. He died so we could live!*

All have sinned and fall short of the glory of God, and all are justified freely by his grace through the redemption that came by Christ Jesus. **God presented Christ as a sacrifice of atonement, through the shedding of his blood — to be received by faith. He did this to demonstrate his righteousness, because in his forbearance he had left the sins committed beforehand unpunished — he did it to demonstrate his righteousness at the present time, so as to be just and the one who justifies those who have faith in Jesus.** ROMANS 3:23–26

This is how God showed his love among us: He sent his one and only Son into the world that we might live through him. **This is love: not that we loved God, but that he loved us and sent his Son as an atoning sacrifice for our sins.** 1 JOHN 4:9–10

## ISRAEL: CALLED TO COMPASSION

*God wanted compassion to be the trademark of his people; God's people are compassionate people. That's why the laws he gave to Moses and the Israelites have so many instructions on how to help and support those in need.*

---

As you read these selected passages from the book of Deuteronomy, think about the possible reasons for having such laws about how to treat others. How would you summarize those laws into one main idea?

---

When you make a loan of any kind to your neighbor, do not go into their house to get what is offered to you as a pledge. Stay outside and let the neighbor to whom you are making the loan bring the pledge out to you. If the neighbor is poor, do not go to sleep with their pledge in your possession. Return their cloak by sunset so that your neighbor may sleep in it. Then they will thank you, and it will be regarded as a righteous act in the sight of the LORD your God.

Do not take advantage of a hired worker who is poor and needy, whether that worker is a fellow Israelite or a foreigner residing in one of your towns. Pay them their wages each day before sunset, because they are poor and are counting on it. Otherwise they may cry to the LORD against you, and you will be guilty of sin.

DEUTERONOMY 24:10–15

Do not deprive the foreigner or the fatherless of justice, or take the cloak of the widow as a pledge. Remember that you were slaves in Egypt and the LORD your God redeemed you from there. That is why I command you to do this.

**When you are harvesting in your field and you overlook a sheaf, do not go back to get it. Leave it for the foreigner, the**

**fatherless and the widow, so that the LORD your God may bless you in all the work of your hands.** When you beat the olives from your trees, do not go over the branches a second time. Leave what remains for the foreigner, the fatherless and the widow. When you harvest the grapes in your vineyard, do not go over the vines again. Leave what remains for the foreigner, the fatherless and the widow. Remember that you were slaves in Egypt. That is why I command you to do this. DEUTERONOMY 24:17–22

*Moses gave the above laws in the 1400s BC while the Israelites were still wandering in the wilderness. A couple of hundred years later, during the time of the judges, several of the laws about caring for widows were demonstrated in the story of Ruth.*

*Because of famine, Naomi and Elimelek and their two children left for the land of Moab. While there, the two sons married Moabite women, but over the years Elimelek and his sons died. Naomi and one of her daughters-in-law, Ruth, made their way back to Naomi's hometown of Bethlehem in Israel. Without husbands or children, Naomi and Ruth were forced to live a life of poverty.*

*One day, Ruth went out to glean (pick up leftovers) after the harvesters in order to provide food for herself and Naomi. The landowner, Boaz, was fulfilling the law of leaving grain behind for the foreigner, fatherless and widow that we just read about in Deuteronomy. When Ruth came home after a successful day of gleaning, her mother-in-law asked her in whose field she had worked. The rest of the story beautifully demonstrates another law—that of ensuring the widow has descendants and an inheritance by giving her a guardian-redeemer.*

Now Naomi had a relative on her husband's side, a man of standing from the clan of Elimelek, whose name was Boaz.

And Ruth the Moabite said to Naomi, "Let me go to the fields and pick up the leftover grain behind anyone in whose eyes I find favor."

Naomi said to her, "Go ahead, my daughter." So she went out, entered a field and began to glean behind the harvesters. As it turned out, she was working in a field belonging to Boaz, who was from the clan of Elimelek.

Just then Boaz arrived from Bethlehem and greeted the harvesters, "The LORD be with you!"

"The LORD bless you!" they answered.

Boaz asked the overseer of his harvesters, "Who does that young woman belong to?"

The overseer replied, "She is the Moabite who came back from Moab with Naomi. She said, 'Please let me glean and gather among the sheaves behind the harvesters.' She came into the field and has remained here from morning till now, except for a short rest in the shelter."

So Boaz said to Ruth, "My daughter, listen to me. Don't go and glean in another field and don't go away from here. Stay here with the women who work for me. Watch the field where the men are harvesting, and follow along after the women. I have told the men not to lay a hand on you. And whenever you are thirsty, go and get a drink from the water jars the men have filled."

At this, she bowed down with her face to the ground. She asked him, "Why have I found such favor in your eyes that you notice me — a foreigner?"

Boaz replied, "I've been told all about what you have done for your mother-in-law since the death of your husband — how you left your father and mother and your homeland and came to live with a people you did not know before. May the LORD repay you for what you have done. May you be richly rewarded by the LORD, the God of Israel, under whose wings you have come to take refuge."

"May I continue to find favor in your eyes, my Lord," she said. "You have put me at ease by speaking kindly to your servant — though I do not have the standing of one of your servants."

RUTH 2:1–13

Her mother-in-law asked her, "Where did you glean today? Where did you work? Blessed be the man who took notice of you!"

Then Ruth told her mother-in-law about the one at whose place she had been working. "The name of the man I worked with today is Boaz," she said.

**"The LORD bless him!" Naomi said to her daughter-in-law. "He has not stopped showing his kindness to the living and the**

**dead." She added, "That man is our close relative; he is one of our guardian-redeemers."** RUTH 2:19–20

Boaz announced to the elders and all the people, "Today you are witnesses that I have bought from Naomi all the property of Elimelek, Kilion and Mahlon. I have also acquired Ruth the Moabite, Mahlon's widow, as my wife, in order to maintain the name of the dead with his property, so that his name will not disappear from among his family or from his hometown. Today you are witnesses!"

Then the elders and all the people at the gate said, "We are witnesses. May the LORD make the woman who is coming into your home like Rachel and Leah, who together built up the family of Israel. May you have standing in Ephrathah and be famous in Bethlehem. Through the offspring the LORD gives you by this young woman, may your family be like that of Perez, whom Tamar bore to Judah."

So Boaz took Ruth and she became his wife. When he made love to her, the LORD enabled her to conceive, and she gave birth to a son. The women said to Naomi: "Praise be to the LORD, who this day has not left you without a guardian-redeemer. May he become famous throughout Israel! He will renew your life and sustain you in your old age. For your daughter-in-law, who loves you and who is better to you than seven sons, has given him birth."

Then Naomi took the child in her arms and cared for him. The women living there said, "Naomi has a son!" And they named him Obed. He was the father of Jesse, the father of David. RUTH 4:9–17

*What an amazing story of human compassion. But the blessings did not stop with Naomi and her family. Through Boaz's act of compassion, a child was born. From this child would come David, and from David would ultimately come Jesus, our compassionate Savior. A single act of compassion can live on for generations to come!*

---

How did Boaz express his faith when he helped Ruth and Naomi?
Has anyone ever been a "Boaz" for you (helping you through
a difficult time)? Have you ever been a "Boaz" for someone else?

## JESUS: MODEL OF COMPASSION

*Jesus, the very model of compassion, tells a beautiful story we call the Parable of the Good Samaritan. The telling of the story was prompted by an exchange that zeroed in on one of two chief laws of the Old Testament: to love our neighbor as ourselves. Through this classic story, Jesus made the startling point that his most mature follower is not necessarily the priest or the pastor but the one who actually lives out the commandment.*

On one occasion an expert in the law stood up to test Jesus. "Teacher," he asked, "what must I do to inherit eternal life?"

"What is written in the Law?" he replied. "How do you read it?"

He answered, "'Love the Lord your God with all your heart and with all your soul and with all your strength and with all your mind'; and, 'Love your neighbor as yourself.'"

"You have answered correctly," Jesus replied. "Do this and you will live."

But he wanted to justify himself, so he asked Jesus, "And who is my neighbor?"

In reply Jesus said: "A man was going down from Jerusalem to Jericho, when he was attacked by robbers. They stripped him of his clothes, beat him and went away, leaving him half dead. A priest happened to be going down the same road, and when he saw the man, he passed by on the other side. So too, a Levite, when he came to the place and saw him, passed by on the other side. But a Samaritan, as he traveled, came where the man was; and when he saw him, he took pity on him. He went to him and bandaged his wounds, pouring on oil and wine. Then he put the man on his own donkey, brought him to an inn and took care of him. The next day he took out two denarii and gave them to the innkeeper. 'Look after him,' he said, 'and when I return, I will reimburse you for any extra expense you may have.'

**"Which of these three do you think was a neighbor to the man who fell into the hands of robbers?"**

**The expert in the law replied, "The one who had mercy on him."**

**Jesus told him, "Go and do likewise."** LUKE 10:25–37

*Throughout his teaching ministry, Jesus instructed his followers to show compassion to people in need as the ultimate fulfillment of the Law of Moses. Toward the very end of his life on earth, Jesus provided his disciples with insight into the ministry of compassion to the poor and needy. He tells them their present acts of compassion have eternal consequences. When Jesus returns, he will separate the obedient followers from the unbelievers. The way we treat hurting people is closely related to the way we treat Jesus; what we do (or don't do) for them is what we do (or don't do) for Jesus.*

"The King will say to those on his right, 'Come, you who are blessed by my Father; take your inheritance, the kingdom prepared for you since the creation of the world. For I was hungry and you gave me something to eat, I was thirsty and you gave me something to drink, I was a stranger and you invited me in, I needed clothes and you clothed me, I was sick and you looked after me, I was in prison and you came to visit me.'

"Then the righteous will answer him, 'Lord, when did we see you hungry and feed you, or thirsty and give you something to drink? When did we see you a stranger and invite you in, or needing clothes and clothe you? When did we see you sick or in prison and go to visit you?'

**"The King will reply, 'Truly I tell you, whatever you did for one of the least of these brothers and sisters of mine, you did for me.'"**                    MATTHEW 25:34–40

---

In your own words, describe how love
for God and love for others are related.
Which one seems more difficult for you to live out?
Why do you think that is?

---

## BELIEVERS: THE ONGOING CALL TO COMPASSION

*The same principles of compassion God gave to the Israelites in the Old Testament are also given to the Christians of the New Testament. After the death and resurrection of Jesus, his half-brother (James) became a leader of the church in Jerusalem and wrote a letter to all the churches. This letter, which we call the book of James, gives practical instruction for how to live like Jesus. These same principles given to the early Christian believers also apply to us.*

**Do not merely listen to the word, and so deceive yourselves. Do what it says.** Anyone who listens to the word but does not do what it says is like someone who looks at his face in a mirror and, after looking at himself, goes away and immediately forgets what he looks like. But whoever looks intently into the perfect law that gives freedom, and continues in it — not forgetting what they have heard, but doing it — they will be blessed in what they do.

Those who consider themselves religious and yet do not keep a tight rein on their tongues deceive themselves, and their religion is worthless. **Religion that God our Father accepts as pure and faultless is this: to look after orphans and widows in their distress and to keep oneself from being polluted by the world.**

My brothers and sisters, believers in our glorious Lord Jesus Christ must not show favoritism. Suppose a man comes into your meeting wearing a gold ring and fine clothes, and a poor man in filthy old clothes also comes in. If you show special attention to the man wearing fine clothes and say, "Here's a good seat for you," but say to the poor man, "You stand there" or "Sit on the floor by my feet," have you not discriminated among yourselves and become judges with evil thoughts?             JAMES 1:22—2:4

Speak and act as those who are going to be judged by the law that gives freedom, because judgment without mercy will be shown to anyone who has not been merciful. Mercy triumphs over judgment.             JAMES 2:12–13

---

What are the kinds of attitudes that James
teaches us to have? How can you adopt
those attitudes? What is the relationship between
your attitudes and your actions?

## WHAT WE BELIEVE

*What about poverty and injustice? We begin by taking our cue from God himself. He showed the ultimate compassion toward humanity by sending Jesus as a sacrifice for sin when we did not deserve it. Throughout Israel's history, time and time again, God showed amazing compassion to rescue his people and provide for their needs. When we look back on our own lives, we will see the same pattern.*

*Israel was given laws to govern them regarding how to show compassion to each other and to strangers. The story of Ruth provides a beautiful example of the spirit of these laws lived out. And Jesus, the ultimate example of one who suffered for our sake, calls believers to a life of compassion not because the law demands it but because God's love in us compels us. Living life begins when we embrace the belief in our heads and our hearts that God calls all Christians to show compassion to those in need.*

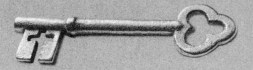

# CHAPTER

## 9

# Stewardship

---
**KEY QUESTION**
---

What is God's call on my life?

---
**KEY IDEA**
---

I believe everything I am and
everything I own belong to God.

---
**KEY VERSE**
---

The earth is the LORD's, and everything in it,
the world, and all who live in it;
for he founded it on the seas and
established it on the waters.
*Psalm 24:1–2*

**OUR MAP**

In Chapter 7 we learned to see people the way God sees them—through eyes of love. Then in Chapter 8 we were challenged to treat people the way God does—with compassion. And now Chapter 9 declares that everything we own belongs to God. These three beliefs are linked together. People devoted to thinking like Jesus believe they are to take the resources they are given, even their very lives, and use them to meet the needs of the valuable human beings God places in their lives. Because we believe the God of the Bible is the one true God who has a good plan revealed in his Word for all people to come into a relationship with him, the church offers a resounding "yes" to this key belief called stewardship.

In this chapter you will learn:

- God Is Owner
- God's People Are Managers
  ... of Their Children
  ... of Their Money
  ... of Their Homes
  ... of Their Bodies
  ... over All They Do!

## GOD IS OWNER

The psalms are filled with worship songs, beautiful poems and powerful stories about God's goodness and greatness. The psalmists were very aware that God is God, and we are not. Here are just two of the psalms that highlight how God is the owner of the earth and everything within it. This reality reminds us of our great responsibility to take good care of the good things God has made.

The earth is the LORD's, and everything in it,
　　the world, and all who live in it;
　for he founded it on the seas
　　and established it on the waters.　　PSALM 24:1–2

**"I have no need of a bull from your stall
or of goats from your pens,**

> for every animal of the forest is mine,
>     and the cattle on a thousand hills.
> I know every bird in the mountains,
>     and the insects in the fields are mine.
> If I were hungry I would not tell you,
>     for the world is mine, and all that is in it." PSALM 50:9–12

---

If God is self-sufficient and doesn't need anything
from us, why are we asked to give offerings? In other words,
why does God want "our" money?

---

## GOD'S PEOPLE ARE MANAGERS

*Since God created everything and owns everything, how do we as humans fit into the created order? What is our role in this reality? The parable below tells about the importance of seeing ourselves not as owners but as managers of our lives and gifts. The bags of gold represent any resource God, the master, gives us (our time, our money, our skills, etc.). He ultimately owns the resource, but we are charged with caring for it and investing it in ways that benefit his kingdom. Jesus said,*

"Again, it will be like a man going on a journey, who called his servants and entrusted his wealth to them. To one he gave five bags of gold, to another two bags, and to another one bag, each according to his ability. Then he went on his journey. The man who had received five bags of gold went at once and put his money to work and gained five bags more. So also, the one with two bags of gold gained two more. But the man who had received one bag went off, dug a hole in the ground and hid his master's money.

"After a long time the master of those servants returned and settled accounts with them. The man who had received five bags of gold brought the other five. 'Master,' he said, 'you entrusted me with five bags of gold. See, I have gained five more.'

**"His master replied, 'Well done, good and faithful servant! You have been faithful with a few things; I will put you in charge of many things. Come and share your master's happiness!'**

"The man with two bags of gold also came. 'Master,' he said, 'you entrusted me with two bags of gold; see, I have gained two more.'

"His master replied, 'Well done, good and faithful servant! You have been faithful with a few things; I will put you in charge of many things. Come and share your master's happiness!'

"Then the man who had received one bag of gold came. 'Master,' he said, 'I knew that you are a hard man, harvesting where you have not sown and gathering where you have not scattered seed. So I was afraid and went out and hid your gold in the ground. See, here is what belongs to you.'

"His master replied, 'You wicked, lazy servant! So you knew that I harvest where I have not sown and gather where I have not scattered seed? Well then, you should have put my money on deposit with the bankers, so that when I returned I would have received it back with interest.

"'So take the bag of gold from him and give it to the one who has ten bags. For whoever has will be given more, and they will have an abundance. Whoever does not have, even what they have will be taken from them. And throw that worthless servant outside, into the darkness, where there will be weeping and gnashing of teeth.'"

MATTHEW 25:14–30

### ... OF THEIR CHILDREN

*The book of 1 Samuel tells the story of a woman named Hannah who could not have children. She pleaded with the Lord for a child, and he granted her request. Hannah's story highlights that our children belong to the Lord. He gives them to us to raise according to his instructions, but ultimately they belong to him and exist for his purposes, not our own.*

Once when they had finished eating and drinking in Shiloh, Hannah stood up. Now Eli the priest was sitting on his chair by the doorpost of the LORD's house. In her deep anguish Hannah prayed to the LORD, weeping bitterly. And she made a vow, saying, "LORD Almighty, if you will only look on your servant's misery and remember me, and not forget your servant but give her a son, then I will give him to the LORD for all the days of his life, and no razor will ever be used on his head."

As she kept on praying to the LORD, Eli observed her mouth. Hannah was praying in her heart, and her lips were moving but her voice was not heard. Eli thought she was drunk and said to her, "How long are you going to stay drunk? Put away your wine."

"Not so, my lord," Hannah replied, "I am a woman who is deeply troubled. I have not been drinking wine or beer; I was pouring out my soul to the LORD. Do not take your servant for a wicked woman; I have been praying here out of my great anguish and grief."

Eli answered, "Go in peace, and may the God of Israel grant you what you have asked of him."

She said, "May your servant find favor in your eyes." Then she went her way and ate something, and her face was no longer downcast.

Early the next morning they arose and worshiped before the LORD and then went back to their home at Ramah. Elkanah made love to his wife Hannah, and the LORD remembered her. So in the course of time Hannah became pregnant and gave birth to a son. She named him Samuel, saying, "Because I asked the LORD for him."

When her husband Elkanah went up with all his family to offer the annual sacrifice to the LORD and to fulfill his vow, Hannah did not go. She said to her husband, "After the boy is weaned, I will take him and present him before the LORD, and he will live there always."

"Do what seems best to you," her husband Elkanah told her. "Stay here until you have weaned him; only may the LORD make good his word." So the woman stayed at home and nursed her son until she had weaned him.

After he was weaned, she took the boy with her, young as he was, along with a three-year-old bull, an ephah of flour and a skin of wine, and brought him to the house of the LORD at Shiloh. **When the bull had been sacrificed, they brought the boy to Eli, and she said to him, "Pardon me, my lord. As surely as you live, I am the woman who stood here beside you praying to the LORD. I prayed for this child, and the LORD has granted me what I asked of him. So now I give him to the LORD. For his whole life he will be given over to the LORD." And he worshiped the LORD there.** 1 SAMUEL 1:9–28

Samuel was ministering before the LORD — a boy wearing a linen ephod. Each year his mother made him a little robe and took it to him when she went up with her husband to offer the annual sacrifice. Eli would bless Elkanah and his wife, saying, "May the LORD give you children by this woman to take the place of the one she prayed for and gave to the LORD." Then they would go home. And the LORD was gracious to Hannah; she gave birth to three sons and two daughters. Meanwhile, the boy Samuel grew up in the presence of the LORD.                       1 SAMUEL 2:18–21 🔑

### ... OF THEIR MONEY

*For some people, money is the hardest thing to let go of. Holding tightly to what you have earned is not just a modern-day syndrome. During the prophet Malachi's day, at the end of the Old Testament era, the Israelites were failing to follow the requirements for offerings and gifts outlined for them. God issued a challenge — the only time in the Bible he told his people to test him. The test was this: give to God what he asked (since it was all from him anyway), and see what would happen.*

"I the LORD do not change. So you, the descendants of Jacob, are not destroyed. Ever since the time of your ancestors you have turned away from my decrees and have not kept them. Return to me, and I will return to you," says the LORD Almighty.

"But you ask, 'How are we to return?'

"Will a mere mortal rob God? Yet you rob me.

"But you ask, 'How are we robbing you?'

"In tithes and offerings. You are under a curse — your whole nation — because you are robbing me. **Bring the whole tithe into the storehouse, that there may be food in my house. Test me in this,"** says the LORD Almighty, **"and see if I will not throw open the floodgates of heaven and pour out so much blessing that there will not be room enough to store it.** I will prevent pests from devouring your crops, and the vines in your fields will not drop their fruit before it is ripe," says the LORD Almighty. "Then all the nations will call you blessed, for yours will be a delightful land," says the LORD Almighty.                       MALACHI 3:6–12

*Because everything we have is ultimately from the Lord, when we fail to return to him some of what he has given us, God says we are robbing him. Robbing him? Strong language is used often in the Bible when referring to money. Money has a lot of power that can be used for good or for evil. How we handle money is a gauge for how well we will manage everything else we have been given. Jesus said,*

"Whoever can be trusted with very little can also be trusted with much, and whoever is dishonest with very little will also be dishonest with much. So if you have not been trustworthy in handling worldly wealth, who will trust you with true riches? And if you have not been trustworthy with someone else's property, who will give you property of your own?

**"No one can serve two masters. Either you will hate the one and love the other, or you will be devoted to the one and despise the other. You cannot serve both God and money."**

The Pharisees, who loved money, heard all this and were sneering at Jesus. He said to them, "You are the ones who justify yourselves in the eyes of others, but God knows your hearts. What people value highly is detestable in God's sight."  LUKE 16:10–15

*In sharp contrast to the Pharisees, one poor widow Jesus encountered outside the temple used the money in her possession, though it was very little, not for herself but for God's kingdom. Unlike many others, she gave not to be noticed but to give back to God.*

⊙—🗝 Jesus sat down opposite the place where the offerings were put and watched the crowd putting their money into the temple treasury. Many rich people threw in large amounts. But a poor widow came and put in two very small copper coins, worth only a few cents.

Calling his disciples to him, Jesus said, **"Truly I tell you, this poor widow has put more into the treasury than all the others. They all gave out of their wealth; but she, out of her poverty, put in everything — all she had to live on."** MARK 12:41–44 ⊙—🗝

### ... OF THEIR HOMES

*Hospitality was a highly valued custom during Old Testament times, by the Israelites as well as by other peoples.*

*Elijah was living during a severe drought, and he along with everyone else in the region was running out of food. God sent Elijah outside Israel's borders, to the home of a poor Gentile widow, who seemed the least likely person to be able to provide hospitality. Their story shows the power of both human hospitality and divine provision.*

Some time later the brook dried up because there had been no rain in the land. Then the word of the LORD came to him [Elijah]: "Go at once to Zarephath in the region of Sidon and stay there. I have directed a widow there to supply you with food." So he went to Zarephath. When he came to the town gate, a widow was there gathering sticks. He called to her and asked, "Would you bring me a little water in a jar so I may have a drink?" As she was going to get it, he called, "And bring me, please, a piece of bread."

"As surely as the LORD your God lives," she replied, "I don't have any bread — only a handful of flour in a jar and a little olive oil in a jug. I am gathering a few sticks to take home and make a meal for myself and my son, that we may eat it — and die."

Elijah said to her, "Don't be afraid. Go home and do as you have said. But first make a small loaf of bread for me from what you have and bring it to me, and then make something for yourself and your son. For this is what the LORD, the God of Israel, says: 'The jar of flour will not be used up and the jug of oil will not run dry until the day the LORD sends rain on the land.'"

She went away and did as Elijah had told her. **So there was food every day for Elijah and for the woman and her family. For the jar of flour was not used up and the jug of oil did not run dry, in keeping with the word of the LORD spoken by Elijah.**

1 KINGS 17:7–16

*Our homes — no matter how large or small, no matter how simple or fancy — belong to God. Here are a few words of encouragement to practice hospitality.*

Share with the Lord's people who are in need. Practice hospitality.

ROMANS 12:13

Do not forget to show hospitality to strangers, for by so doing some people have shown hospitality to angels without knowing it.

HEBREWS 13:2

Offer hospitality to one another without grumbling.      1 PETER 4:9

Why are we encouraged to practice hospitality?
Why is hospitality important to God? When has
someone been welcoming and hospitable to you?

## ... OF THEIR BODIES

*Paul challenged the members of the church at Corinth to honor God with their bodies. Why? Because, like our other resources, our bodies belong to God. We are managers, not owners ... even of our own bodies.*

You say, "Food for the stomach and the stomach for food, and God will destroy them both." The body, however, is not meant for sexual immorality but for the Lord, and the Lord for the body. By his power God raised the Lord from the dead, and he will raise us also. Do you not know that your bodies are members of Christ himself? Shall I then take the members of Christ and unite them with a prostitute? Never! Do you not know that he who unites himself with a prostitute is one with her in body? For it is said,

"The two will become one flesh." But whoever is united with the Lord is one with him in spirit.

Flee from sexual immorality. All other sins a person commits are outside the body, but whoever sins sexually, sins against their own body. **Do you not know that your bodies are temples of the Holy Spirit, who is in you, whom you have received from God? You are not your own; you were bought at a price. Therefore honor God with your bodies.**                    1 CORINTHIANS 6:13–20

### ... OVER ALL THEY DO

*Paul brings us full circle by quoting from Psalm 24, which declares God's ownership over everything. We, on the other hand, are not owners, but managers—of our families, our money, our homes, and our bodies—even to the extent of everything we do, we are to do it all for his glory.*

"I have the right to do anything," you say—but not everything is beneficial. "I have the right to do anything"—but not everything is constructive. No one should seek their own good, but the good of others.                    1 CORINTHIANS 10:23–24

**So whether you eat or drink or whatever you do, do it all for the glory of God.** Do not cause anyone to stumble, whether Jews, Greeks or the church of God—even as I try to please everyone in every way. For I am not seeking my own good but the good of many, so that they may be saved. Follow my example, as I follow the example of Christ.                    1 CORINTHIANS 10:31—11:1

---

List some of the things God has entrusted to you
to manage. How are you doing in each of these areas?
How can you improve your stewardship of them?

---

## WHAT WE BELIEVE

*Stewardship can make a major difference in our lives when we move from simply understanding it in our heads to fully embracing it in our hearts. God is the owner of everything— everything we have and everything we are. When we come to faith in Christ, we turn over the "deed" of everything—our children, our money, our homes, our bodies, our very breath—to him. God then turns to us and invites us to manage all these things according to his purposes. When we do, we are freed from the hassles of ownership and enter into a life of reward and blessing.*

# THINK

## CHAPTER

## 10

# Eternity

──────── KEY QUESTION ────────

What happens next?

──────── KEY IDEA ────────

I believe there is a heaven and a hell and that Jesus will return
to judge all people and to establish his eternal kingdom.

──────── KEY VERSE ────────

Do not let your hearts be troubled. You believe in God;
believe also in me. My Father's house has many rooms;
if that were not so, would I have told you that
I am going there to prepare a place for you?
*John 14:1–2*

115

O U R  M A P

*Embracing the first nine beliefs of the Christian faith in our minds and hearts dramatically enhances our own quality of life, as well as the quality of life for the community around us. But there is something more—and it is huge. There is life after death. Eternal life with God. God wants to restore his original vision of life with us in the garden. The only way back into the garden (which can be called heaven or God's kingdom) is through faith in Jesus Christ. Those who embrace Christ in this life are reconciled to God and become a new creation with a new identity. For the Christian, not only can life be abundant today, but anticipating what is in store for us when we are reunited with God in the new heaven and new earth is simply breathtaking.*

*The Scripture in this chapter will unfold the journey to that place:*

- *The Ending of a Life*
- *The Intermediate State*
- *The Resurrection*
- *The Return of Christ*
- *A New Heaven and a New Earth*

## THE ENDING OF A LIFE

*While the Old Testament writers don't address the afterlife in as much detail as the New Testament writers, the Old Testament does contain the magnificent description of the prophet Elijah being taken up to heaven without dying. Elijah is one of only three people taken to heaven in bodily form, the other two being Enoch (you can read about him in Genesis 5:21–24) and, of course, Jesus. While our experience will be quite different at the end of our lives in these bodies, we bask in the promise of what awaits us on the other side.*

⚬🔑 The company of the prophets at Jericho went up to Elisha and asked him, "Do you know that the LORD is going to take your master from you today?"

"Yes, I know," he replied, "so be quiet."

Then Elijah said to him, "Stay here; the LORD has sent me to the Jordan."

And he replied, "As surely as the LORD lives and as you live, I will not leave you." So the two of them walked on.

Fifty men from the company of the prophets went and stood at a distance, facing the place where Elijah and Elisha had stopped at the Jordan. Elijah took his cloak, rolled it up and struck the water with it. The water divided to the right and to the left, and the two of them crossed over on dry ground.

When they had crossed, Elijah said to Elisha, "Tell me, what can I do for you before I am taken from you?"

"Let me inherit a double portion of your spirit," Elisha replied.

"You have asked a difficult thing," Elijah said, "yet if you see me when I am taken from you, it will be yours — otherwise, it will not."

**As they were walking along and talking together, suddenly a chariot of fire and horses of fire appeared and separated the two of them, and Elijah went up to heaven in a whirlwind.** Elisha saw this and cried out, "My father! My father! The chariots and horsemen of Israel!" And Elisha saw him no more. Then he took hold of his garment and tore it in two.

Elisha then picked up Elijah's cloak that had fallen from him and went back and stood on the bank of the Jordan. He took the cloak that had fallen from Elijah and struck the water with it. "Where now is the LORD, the God of Elijah?" he asked. When he struck the water, it divided to the right and to the left, and he crossed over.

The company of the prophets from Jericho, who were watching, said, "The spirit of Elijah is resting on Elisha." And they went to meet him and bowed to the ground before him. "Look," they said, "we your servants have fifty able men. Let them go and look for your master. Perhaps the Spirit of the LORD has picked him up and set him down on some mountain or in some valley."

"No," Elisha replied, "do not send them."

But they persisted until he was too embarrassed to refuse. So he said, "Send them." And they sent fifty men, who searched for three days but did not find him. When they returned to Elisha, who was staying in Jericho, he said to them, "Didn't I tell you not to go?"

2 KINGS 2:5–18

Given that the afterlife was not talked about
much in the Old Testament, why do you think
the prophets insisted on looking for Elijah? How would
you have responded if you were there?

## THE INTERMEDIATE STATE

*What happens when we die? The New Testament teaches that
people experience an "intermediate state," which refers to a person's existence between their time of death and the promised
resurrection of their new body. Their earthly body goes into the
grave; their spirit lives on in one of two places—either in God's
presence where they enjoy a time of peace until they receive their
resurrected bodies or in a place of torment where they await final
judgment. Jesus talked about this vividly in the story about a rich
man and Lazarus (not the Lazarus Jesus raised from the dead).
Jesus called the place of paradise for the righteous, "Abraham's
side" and the place of torment for the wicked, "Hades."*

"There was a rich man who was dressed in purple and fine
linen and lived in luxury every day. At his gate was laid a beggar
named Lazarus, covered with sores and longing to eat what fell
from the rich man's table. Even the dogs came and licked his sores.

"The time came when the beggar died and the angels carried
him to Abraham's side. The rich man also died and was buried. In
Hades, where he was in torment, he looked up and saw Abraham
far away, with Lazarus by his side. So he called to him, 'Father Abraham, have pity on me and send Lazarus to dip the tip of his finger in
water and cool my tongue, because I am in agony in this fire.'

"But Abraham replied, 'Son, remember that in your lifetime
you received your good things, while Lazarus received bad things,
but now he is comforted here and you are in agony. And besides
all this, between us and you a great chasm has been set in place, so
that those who want to go from here to you cannot, nor can anyone cross over from there to us.'

"He answered, 'Then I beg you, father, send Lazarus to my family, for I have five brothers. Let him warn them, so that they will
not also come to this place of torment.'

"Abraham replied, 'They have Moses and the Prophets; let them listen to them.'

"'No, father Abraham,' he said, 'but if someone from the dead goes to them, they will repent.'

"He said to him, 'If they do not listen to Moses and the Prophets, they will not be convinced even if someone rises from the dead.'"

LUKE 16:19–31

---

> Having a person come back from the dead
> to tell you what they experienced on the
> other side would seem rather convincing.
> Why did Abraham disagree?

---

## THE RESURRECTION

*There is more to come after we die than our spirits going to be with God while our bodies remain in the grave. The grand promise of God and the ultimate hope for all Christians is the resurrection. Just as Christ was raised from the dead and received a new body, so will all those who believe in Christ.*

But someone will ask, "How are the dead raised? With what kind of body will they come?" How foolish! What you sow does not come to life unless it dies. When you sow, you do not plant the body that will be, but just a seed, perhaps of wheat or of something else. But God gives it a body as he has determined, and to each kind of seed he gives its own body. Not all flesh is the same: People have one kind of flesh, animals have another, birds another and fish another. There are also heavenly bodies and there are earthly bodies; but the splendor of the heavenly bodies is one kind, and the splendor of the earthly bodies is another. The sun has one kind of splendor, the moon another and the stars another; and star differs from star in splendor.

**So will it be with the resurrection of the dead. The body that is sown is perishable, it is raised imperishable; it is sown in dishonor, it is raised in glory; it is sown in weakness, it is raised in power; it is sown a natural body, it is raised a spiritual body.**

1 CORINTHIANS 15:35–44A

How will our resurrected bodies be different from our earthly bodies? How does what the Bible says compare with some of our culture's popular notions of what we'll be like in heaven?

## THE RETURN OF CHRIST

*The event that will trigger this promised resurrection is the second coming of Christ. There are varied beliefs about the details leading up to this glorious day, but all followers of Jesus embrace its basic truth and biblical significance.*

*Paul addressed a misunderstanding he became aware of in the church at Thessalonica. Some of the believers thought all Christians would be alive at the return of Christ. This belief caused concern because some of their fellow believers had already died. Paul clarifies that on the great day of Christ's return, God will resurrect those who have died so that all believers, not just the living ones, will be brought together and will be with the Lord Jesus forever.*

As you read the writings of Paul and then Peter, look for ways we are encouraged to live our lives today considering Christ's imminent return.

For we believe that Jesus died and rose again, and so we believe that God will bring with Jesus those who have fallen asleep in him. According to the Lord's word, we tell you that we who are still alive, who are left until the coming of the Lord, will certainly not precede those who have fallen asleep. **For the Lord himself will come down from heaven, with a loud command, with the voice of the archangel and with the trumpet call of God, and the dead in Christ will rise first. After that, we who are still alive and are left will be caught up together with them in the clouds to meet the Lord in the air. And so we will be with the Lord forever. Therefore encourage one another with these words.**

1 THESSALONIANS 4:14–18

Since everything will be destroyed in this way, what kind of people ought you to be? You ought to live holy and godly lives as you look forward to the day of God and speed its coming. That day will bring about the destruction of the heavens by fire, and the elements will melt in the heat. But in keeping with his promise we are looking forward to a new heaven and a new earth, where righteousness dwells.

So then, dear friends, since you are looking forward to this, make every effort to be found spotless, blameless and at peace with him.                                              2 PETER 3:11–14

### A NEW HEAVEN AND A NEW EARTH

*After Jesus returns and we are resurrected into our eternal, imperishable bodies, there will be a final judgment by God where those who did not believe in God are sent to eternal punishment, and those who are children of God are brought into heaven.*

*John recorded a vision from God about how this would happen. Before his dazzling description of our future heavenly home, don't miss something special about the way we will be welcomed into heaven. A voice will announce that God will now live with us; we will be his people, and God will be our God. Amazingly, God used to say those exact words to the Israelites whenever he rescued them. He has wanted to be with his people for a long, long time, and our arrival in heaven will be the fulfillment of God's dream. What we read in the opening creation story of Genesis about the peace, innocence and unity God and humans had with each other, we see restored again in this chapter from the book of Revelation—but now a re-creation on a grander scale.*

Then I saw "a new heaven and a new earth," for the first heaven and the first earth had passed away, and there was no longer any sea. I saw the Holy City, the new Jerusalem, coming down out of heaven from God, prepared as a bride beautifully dressed for her husband. And I heard a loud voice from the throne saying, "Look! God's dwelling place is now among the people, and he will dwell with them. They will be his people, and God himself will be with them and be their God. 'He will wipe every tear from their eyes. There will be no more death' or mourning or crying or pain, for the old order of things has passed away."

He who was seated on the throne said, "I am making everything new!" Then he said, "Write this down, for these words are trustworthy and true."

He said to me: "It is done. I am the Alpha and the Omega, the Beginning and the End. To the thirsty I will give water without cost from the spring of the water of life. Those who are victorious will inherit all this, and I will be their God and they will be my children. But the cowardly, the unbelieving, the vile, the murderers, the sexually immoral, those who practice magic arts, the idolaters and all liars — they will be consigned to the fiery lake of burning sulfur. This is the second death."

One of the seven angels who had the seven bowls full of the seven last plagues came and said to me, "Come, I will show you the bride, the wife of the Lamb." And he carried me away in the Spirit to a mountain great and high, and showed me the Holy City, Jerusalem, coming down out of heaven from God. It shone with the glory of God, and its brilliance was like that of a very precious jewel, like a jasper, clear as crystal. It had a great, high wall with twelve gates, and with twelve angels at the gates. On the gates were written the names of the twelve tribes of Israel. There were three gates on the east, three on the north, three on the south and three on the west. The wall of the city had twelve foundations, and on them were the names of the twelve apostles of the Lamb.

The angel who talked with me had a measuring rod of gold to measure the city, its gates and its walls. The city was laid out like a square, as long as it was wide. He measured the city with the rod and found it to be 12,000 stadia in length, and as wide and high as it is long. The angel measured the wall using human measurement, and it was 144 cubits thick. The wall was made of jasper, and the city of pure gold, as pure as glass. The foundations of the city walls were decorated with every kind of precious stone. The first foundation was jasper, the second sapphire, the third agate, the fourth emerald, the fifth onyx, the sixth ruby, the seventh chrysolite, the eighth beryl, the ninth topaz, the tenth turquoise, the eleventh jacinth, and the twelfth amethyst. The twelve gates were twelve pearls, each gate made of a single pearl. The great street of the city was of gold, as pure as transparent glass.

I did not see a temple in the city, because the Lord God Almighty and the Lamb are its temple. The city does not need the sun or the moon to shine on it, for the glory of God gives it light, and the Lamb is its lamp. The nations will walk by its light, and the kings of the earth will bring their splendor into it. On no day will its gates ever be shut, for there will be no night there. The glory and honor of the nations will be brought into it. Nothing impure will ever enter it, nor will anyone who does what is shameful or deceitful, but only those whose names are written in the Lamb's book of life.

Then the angel showed me the river of the water of life, as clear as crystal, flowing from the throne of God and of the Lamb down the middle of the great street of the city. On each side of the river stood the tree of life, bearing twelve crops of fruit, yielding its fruit every month. And the leaves of the tree are for the healing of the nations. No longer will there be any curse. The throne of God and of the Lamb will be in the city, and his servants will serve him. They will see his face, and his name will be on their foreheads. There will be no more night. They will not need the light of a lamp or the light of the sun, for the Lord God will give them light. And they will reign for ever and ever.

The angel said to me, "These words are trustworthy and true. The Lord, the God who inspires the prophets, sent his angel to show his servants the things that must soon take place."

REVELATION 21:1—22:6

*In Jesus' last week on earth before he ascended to the Father in heaven, he comforted the disciples as they were worried about the future. He told them that he was leaving, but he also promised that he would be overseeing the construction of a place for each of them in heaven—the new Jerusalem that John described. As you read these words, please know that Jesus' message to the disciples applies to you as well. He has prepared an eternal home for all those who believe.*

"Do not let your hearts be troubled. You believe in God; believe also in me. My Father's house has many rooms; if that were not so, would I have told you that I am going there to prepare a place for you? **And if I go and prepare a place for you, I will come back**

**and take you to be with me that you also may be where I am.**
You know the way to the place where I am going."

Thomas said to him, "Lord, we don't know where you are going, so how can we know the way?"

Jesus answered, "I am the way and the truth and the life. No one comes to the Father except through me. If you really know me, you will know my Father as well. From now on, you do know him and have seen him."                                    JOHN 14:1–7

---

As you think about eternal life in the garden on the new earth without the presence of sin, hatred, problems, war or death, what do you most look forward to?

---

## WHAT WE BELIEVE

*When we die our bodies go into the ground and our spirits go to be with the Lord as we await the return of Christ. When he comes to establish the new heaven and the new earth, our spirits will receive the tent of a new, imperishable, resurrected body just as Jesus did. In these bodies we will live forever in the new garden with God and all those who believed in Jesus. And it is with this exciting reality that we conclude our journey through the ten key beliefs of the Christian life.*

*As followers of God we are invited to ponder and understand these profound concepts in our minds. Yet, to really think like Jesus and experience the full life Christ has given us, we must embrace these beliefs in our hearts—where real decisions are made. So how do we move these fantastic ideas from simply "being the right answer" to a way of life? We do so through the ten key practices of the Christian life, which are highlighted in the next section. Engaging in these activities (in partnership with God) will enable you to express your beliefs while reinforcing them in your heart. Turn the page with the anticipation of actually becoming more like Jesus!*

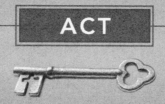

# What Should I Do?

Do you not know that in a race all the runners run, but
only one gets the prize? Run in such a way as to get the prize.
Everyone who competes in the games goes into strict training.
They do it to get a crown that will not last,
but we do it to get a crown that will last forever.
*1 Corinthians 9:24–25*

When you study the life of Jesus, you will notice a distinct pattern. Jesus faithfully lived in a purposeful way. Jesus was modeling the Christian life for us. All we have to do is simply follow his pattern — to *act* like Jesus.

The following ten chapters describe the key spiritual practices of the Christian life. You will encounter proverbs to guide you and real-life stories to inspire you.

As you read each chapter and come to understand what God wants you to do, prayerfully ask yourself, "Will I do what God is asking me to do?" In the passage above, the apostle Paul invites us to think of the Christian life in terms of athletics. If Olympic runners want to cross the finish line first, they must commit to a life of strict training. Essentially, Paul is saying that if we want to win at life, we need to be disciplined in the way we approach each day.

If you resolve to exercise what you are about to read, remember that you will not be alone. God's Spirit can give you the internal strength, silence the voices of dissenters and blow wind at your back.

These practices will not only help you in understanding the key beliefs, they will also enable you to fulfill your mission to love God and let his love flow through you to your neighbor. That way, all people will know God and know you are his disciple.

On your mark ... get set ... GO!

# ACT

## CHAPTER

## 11

# Worship

——— KEY QUESTION ———

How do I honor God in the way he deserves?

——— KEY IDEA ———

I worship God for who he is
and what he has done for me.

——— KEY VERSE ———

Come, let us sing for joy to the LORD;
let us shout aloud to the Rock of our salvation.
Let us come before him with thanksgiving
and extol him with music and song.
*Psalm 95:1–2*

O U R   M A P

*As we read in chapter 1, the first key belief in the Christian life begins with God. It is only logical that the first key practice in the Christian life is worshiping God. When we worship we are taking the revelation about the one true God—Father, Son and Holy Spirit—and reaffirming our belief that he is involved in our lives and wants to be in a relationship with us. As we do this, the amazing truths about God move from concepts in our heads to cries of our hearts. When we worship God for who he is and what he has done for us, it not only cements our confidence in God as we approach each day and each situation, but it also enables us to receive his love.*

*So read this chapter with great anticipation as we explore the different aspects of worship, including:*

- *The Heart's Intent*
- *Unashamed Worship*
- *Worshiping Together*

## THE HEART'S INTENT

*During Old Testament times, worship involved animal sacrifices. Instead of leaving his people with no remedy except to face their punishment for sin, God, in his mercy, allowed his people to sacrifice the best animals from their herd as a payment for their disobedience. The animal had to be without defect, since a defective sacrifice could not be a substitute for a defective people. This practice was intended to be accompanied by repentance. The worshiper confessed their sin and laid hands on the animal; then the sin was symbolically transferred away from the sinner to the sacrifice.*

*Unfortunately, over time the Israelites' sacrifices became meaningless rituals. God was angry and heartbroken. The people brought him an abundance of sacrifices, yet their character and conduct were anything but pleasing to him. God doesn't want us to simply go through the motions; he wants us to actually have a change in our hearts.*

---

What does the following psalm tell us about the kind
of worship God does not want? When our hearts are clean,
what is our behavior like?

---

"The multitude of your sacrifices —
  what are they to me?" says the LORD.
"I have more than enough of burnt offerings,
  of rams and the fat of fattened animals;
I have no pleasure
  in the blood of bulls and lambs and goats.
When you come to appear before me,
  who has asked this of you,
  this trampling of my courts?
Stop bringing meaningless offerings!
  Your incense is detestable to me.
New Moons, Sabbaths and convocations —
  I cannot bear your worthless assemblies.
Your New Moon feasts and your appointed festivals
  I hate with all my being.
They have become a burden to me;
  I am weary of bearing them.
When you spread out your hands in prayer,
  I hide my eyes from you;
even when you offer many prayers,
  I am not listening.

Your hands are full of blood!

Wash and make yourselves clean.
  Take your evil deeds out of my sight;
  stop doing wrong.
Learn to do right; seek justice.
  Defend the oppressed.
Take up the cause of the fatherless;
  plead the case of the widow.

**"Come now, let us settle the matter,"
  says the LORD.
"Though your sins are like scarlet,
  they shall be as white as snow;
though they are red as crimson,
  they shall be like wool.
If you are willing and obedient,
  you will eat the good things of the land;**

> **but if you resist and rebel,**
> **you will be devoured by the sword."**
> **For the mouth of the LORD has spoken.**
>
> ISAIAH 1:11–20

*In the New Testament, those who failed to worship God properly received some harsh words from Jesus. This was especially true for the religious leaders who hid their shallow, insincere faith by busying themselves with religious rituals and empty debates. As a crowd gathered to listen to Jesus' teachings, he warned them about the influence of these hypocritical religious leaders.*

---

As you read this passage, look for the behaviors and attitudes of the Pharisees with which Jesus took issue.

---

Then Jesus said to the crowds and to his disciples: "The teachers of the law and the Pharisees sit in Moses' seat. So you must be careful to do everything they tell you. But do not do what they do, for they do not practice what they preach. They tie up heavy, cumbersome loads and put them on other people's shoulders, but they themselves are not willing to lift a finger to move them.

"Everything they do is done for people to see: They make their phylacteries wide and the tassels on their garments long; they love the place of honor at banquets and the most important seats in the synagogues; they love to be greeted with respect in the marketplaces and to be called 'Rabbi' by others."     MATTHEW 23:1–7

"**Woe to you,** teachers of the law and Pharisees, you hypocrites! You give a tenth of your spices — mint, dill and cumin. But you have neglected the more important matters of the law — justice, mercy and faithfulness. You should have practiced the latter, without neglecting the former. You blind guides! You strain out a gnat but swallow a camel.

"**Woe to you,** teachers of the law and Pharisees, you hypocrites! You clean the outside of the cup and dish, but inside they are full of greed and self-indulgence. Blind Pharisee! First clean the inside of the cup and dish, and then the outside also will be clean.

"**Woe to you,** teachers of the law and Pharisees, you hypocrites! You are like whitewashed tombs, which look beautiful on the outside but on the inside are full of the bones of the dead and everything unclean. In the same way, on the outside you appear to people as righteous but on the inside you are full of hypocrisy and wickedness." MATTHEW 23:23–28

## UNASHAMED WORSHIP

*When you read "unashamed worship," you might think of someone who is singing and dancing before the Lord with wild abandon. But unashamed worship can also be displayed with very few words. Take Daniel, for example. His quiet refusal to worship anyone or anything but the one true God was bold because King Darius, the ruler of the Persian empire, dealt harshly with disobedience in his kingdom. Rather than fervent songs of praise, it was Daniel's actions that did all the talking.*

It pleased Darius to appoint 120 satraps to rule throughout the kingdom, with three administrators over them, one of whom was Daniel. The satraps were made accountable to them so that the king might not suffer loss. Now Daniel so distinguished himself among the administrators and the satraps by his exceptional qualities that the king planned to set him over the whole kingdom. At this, the administrators and the satraps tried to find grounds for charges against Daniel in his conduct of government affairs, but they were unable to do so. They could find no corruption in him, because he was trustworthy and neither corrupt nor negligent. Finally these men said, "We will never find any basis for charges against this man Daniel unless it has something to do with the law of his God."

So these administrators and satraps went as a group to the king and said: "May King Darius live forever! The royal administrators, prefects, satraps, advisers and governors have all agreed that the king should issue an edict and enforce the decree that anyone who prays to any god or human being during the next thirty days, except to you, Your Majesty, shall be thrown into the lions' den. Now, Your Majesty, issue the decree and put it in writing so that it cannot be altered — in accordance with the law of the Medes and Persians, which cannot be repealed." So King Darius put the decree in writing.

**Now when Daniel learned that the decree had been published, he went home to his upstairs room where the windows opened toward Jerusalem. Three times a day he got down on his knees and prayed, giving thanks to his God, just as he had done before.** Then these men went as a group and found Daniel praying and asking God for help. So they went to the king and spoke to him about his royal decree: "Did you not publish a decree that during the next thirty days anyone who prays to any god or human being except to you, Your Majesty, would be thrown into the lions' den?"

The king answered, "The decree stands — in accordance with the law of the Medes and Persians, which cannot be repealed."

Then they said to the king, "Daniel, who is one of the exiles from Judah, pays no attention to you, Your Majesty, or to the decree you put in writing. He still prays three times a day." When the king heard this, he was greatly distressed; he was determined to rescue Daniel and made every effort until sundown to save him.

Then the men went as a group to King Darius and said to him, "Remember, Your Majesty, that according to the law of the Medes and Persians no decree or edict that the king issues can be changed."

So the king gave the order, and they brought Daniel and threw him into the lions' den. The king said to Daniel, "May your God, whom you serve continually, rescue you!"

A stone was brought and placed over the mouth of the den, and the king sealed it with his own signet ring and with the rings of his nobles, so that Daniel's situation might not be changed. Then the king returned to his palace and spent the night without eating and without any entertainment being brought to him. And he could not sleep.

At the first light of dawn, the king got up and hurried to the lions' den. When he came near the den, he called to Daniel in an anguished voice, "Daniel, servant of the living God, has your God, whom you serve continually, been able to rescue you from the lions?"

Daniel answered, "May the king live forever! My God sent his angel, and he shut the mouths of the lions. They have not hurt me, because I was found innocent in his sight. Nor have I ever done any wrong before you, Your Majesty."

The king was overjoyed and gave orders to lift Daniel out of the den. And when Daniel was lifted from the den, no wound was found on him, because he had trusted in his God.

At the king's command, the men who had falsely accused Daniel were brought in and thrown into the lions' den, along with their wives and children. And before they reached the floor of the den, the lions overpowered them and crushed all their bones.

Then King Darius wrote to all the nations and peoples of every language in all the earth:

"May you prosper greatly!

"I issue a decree that in every part of my kingdom people must fear and reverence the God of Daniel.

> "For he is the living God
>     and he endures forever;
> his kingdom will not be destroyed,
>     his dominion will never end.
> He rescues and he saves;
>     he performs signs and wonders
>     in the heavens and on the earth.
> He has rescued Daniel
>     from the power of the lions."

DANIEL 6:1–27 🔑

---

What effect did Daniel's bold worship have
on the unbelieving King Darius? In what ways
do you think our modern-day worship
could have that same effect?

---

*God's miracles are awe-inspiring. In the book of Acts, Paul and Silas's boldness created an uproar in the town of Philippi, and they were thrown into jail. As they prayed and sang worship songs during the night, an earthquake led to their miraculous release from prison.*

The crowd joined in the attack against Paul and Silas, and the magistrates ordered them to be stripped and beaten with rods. After they had been severely flogged, they were thrown into prison, and the jailer was commanded to guard them carefully. When he received these orders, he put them in the inner cell and fastened their feet in the stocks.

**About midnight Paul and Silas were praying and singing hymns to God, and the other prisoners were listening to them. Suddenly there was such a violent earthquake that the foundations of the prison were shaken. At once all the prison doors flew open, and everyone's chains came loose.** The jailer woke up, and when he saw the prison doors open, he drew his sword and was about to kill himself because he thought the prisoners had escaped. But Paul shouted, "Don't harm yourself! We are all here!"

The jailer called for lights, rushed in and fell trembling before Paul and Silas. He then brought them out and asked, "Sirs, what must I do to be saved?"

They replied, "Believe in the Lord Jesus, and you will be saved — you and your household." Then they spoke the word of the Lord to him and to all the others in his house. At that hour of the night the jailer took them and washed their wounds; then immediately he and all his household were baptized. The jailer brought them into his house and set a meal before them; he was filled with joy because he had come to believe in God — he and his whole household.

When it was daylight, the magistrates sent their officers to the jailer with the order: "Release those men." ACTS 16:22–35

---

Why do you think God desires for us to worship him when we are in a difficult situation? When was the last time you worshiped God when it might not have immediately made sense to do so?

---

## WORSHIPING TOGETHER

*The Lord's Supper, or communion, essentially replaced the practice of animal sacrifice for sin in the New Testament church. When believers gather to pray, sing and learn, they break bread and share a cup of wine as a way of remembering Christ's love for them. Jesus introduced this new practice to his disciples the night before his crucifixion.*

When the hour came, Jesus and his apostles reclined at the table. And he said to them, "I have eagerly desired to eat this Passover with you before I suffer. For I tell you, I will not eat it again until it finds fulfillment in the kingdom of God."

**After taking the cup, he gave thanks and said, "Take this and divide it among you. For I tell you I will not drink again from the fruit of the vine until the kingdom of God comes."**

**And he took bread, gave thanks and broke it, and gave it to them, saying, "This is my body given for you; do this in remembrance of me."**

**In the same way, after the supper he took the cup, saying, "This cup is the new covenant in my blood, which is poured out for you.** But the hand of him who is going to betray me is with mine on the table. The Son of Man will go as it has been decreed. But woe to that man who betrays him!" They began to question among themselves which of them it might be who would do this.

A dispute also arose among them as to which of them was considered to be greatest. Jesus said to them, "The kings of the Gentiles lord it over them; and those who exercise authority over them call themselves Benefactors. But you are not to be like that. Instead, the greatest among you should be like the youngest, and the one who rules like the one who serves. For who is greater, the one who is at the table or the one who serves? Is it not the one who is at the table? But I am among you as one who serves. You are those who have stood by me in my trials. And I confer on you a kingdom, just as my Father conferred one on me, so that you may eat and drink at my table in my kingdom and sit on thrones, judging the twelve tribes of Israel." LUKE 22:14–30

*Of course, believers can also honor Jesus' sacrifice every day in the way that they choose to live. No one emphasized this more consistently than the apostle Paul. From under house arrest in Rome, Paul wrote to the Christians in the city of Colossae. He encouraged them to throw off their old, self-centered way of living and commit to live solely for the purpose of worshiping and serving God. Paul's instructions were not addressed to individual worshipers, but to the worship community as a whole.*

Since, then, you have been raised with Christ, set your hearts on things above, where Christ is, seated at the right hand of God. Set your minds on things above, not on earthly things. For you died, and your life is now hidden with Christ in God. When Christ, who is your life, appears, then you also will appear with him in glory.

Put to death, therefore, whatever belongs to your earthly nature: sexual immorality, impurity, lust, evil desires and greed, which is idolatry. Because of these, the wrath of God is coming. You used to walk in these ways, in the life you once lived. But now you must also rid yourselves of all such things as these: anger, rage, malice, slander, and filthy language from your lips. Do not lie to each other, since you have taken off your old self with its practices and have put on the new self, which is being renewed in knowledge in the image of its Creator. Here there is no Gentile or Jew, circumcised or uncircumcised, barbarian, Scythian, slave or free, but Christ is all, and is in all.

Therefore, as God's chosen people, holy and dearly loved, clothe yourselves with compassion, kindness, humility, gentleness and patience. Bear with each other and forgive one another if any of you has a grievance against someone. Forgive as the Lord forgave you. And over all these virtues put on love, which binds them all together in perfect unity.

**Let the peace of Christ rule in your hearts, since as members of one body you were called to peace. And be thankful. Let the message of Christ dwell among you richly as you teach and admonish one another with all wisdom through psalms, hymns, and songs from the Spirit, singing to God with gratitude in your hearts. And whatever you do, whether in word or deed, do it all in the name of the LORD Jesus, giving thanks to God the Father through him.** COLOSSIANS 3:1–17

---

According to the apostle Paul, what is the
centerpiece of New Testament worship? What attitudes
and actions are seen in proper worship?

---

## WHAT WE BELIEVE

*Throughout Scripture, believers in God are instructed to worship him. We are not called to merely go through the motions but instead we are encouraged to authentically worship God from our very hearts—as broken as they may be. While worshiping God for who he is and what he has done for us can be a private and personal practice, we can also feel free to share our worship of the one true God with the world. Finally, the practice of worship should be expressed in community with others. This pleases God and encourages us. We can worship God from our hearts through every single breath, expression, thought and activity of our lives. Doing this habitually will surely lead us closer to the great and gracious God of the universe. So, "Come, let us sing for joy to the LORD; let us shout aloud to the Rock of our salvation. Let us come before him with thanksgiving and extol him with music and song" (Psalm 95:1–2).*

# ACT

# CHAPTER

## 12

# Prayer

How do I grow by communicating with God?

I pray to God to know him, to find direction for my life
and to lay my requests before him.

If I had cherished sin in my heart, the LORD would not have
listened; but God has surely listened and has heard my prayer.
Praise be to God, who has not rejected my prayer
or withheld his love from me!
*Psalm 66:18–20*

OUR MAP

*The key beliefs of the Christian faith we studied in the first ten chapters emphasize that the one true God is a personal God who desires a real relationship with us. He provided the only way to this relationship through the sacrifice of his Son, Jesus Christ. When we embrace and receive Christ's forgiveness, we become children of God and gain access to him. He is not a distant, cosmic being but a good Father who longs to interact with his children. Prayer is the spiritual practice through which we take God up on his "open door" policy. Prayer is a conversation between God and his people. What an amazing privilege!*

*In this chapter you will find examples of those who model a vibrant prayer life, as well as information about how to use prayer to make the most of your relationship with God:*

- *The Model Prayer Life*
- *A Way to Find the Direction We Need*
- *A Way to Lay Our Requests before God*

## THE MODEL PRAYER LIFE

*There are lots of examples of men and women in the Bible who were prayer warriors—people who prayed to God honestly and consistently. Jesus, however, provides the perfect model of what prayer ought to look like. Through his times of prayer, he gained strength and guidance.*

---

Notice how Jesus prays before and after each major event in his life. What does Christ teach us by demonstrating this pattern of praying at these particular times?

---

*After ministry...*

That evening after sunset the people brought to Jesus all the sick and demon-possessed. The whole town gathered at the door, and Jesus healed many who had various diseases. He also drove out many demons, but he would not let the demons speak because they knew who he was.

**Very early in the morning, while it was still dark, Jesus got up, left the house and went off to a solitary place, where he prayed.**                                                            Mark 1:32–35

*Before a decision...*

**Jesus went out to a mountainside to pray, and spent the night praying to God.** When morning came, he called his disciples to him and chose twelve of them, whom he also designated apostles: Simon (whom he named Peter), his brother Andrew, James, John, Philip, Bartholomew, Matthew, Thomas, James son of Alphaeus, Simon who was called the Zealot, Judas son of James, and Judas Iscariot, who became a traitor.          Luke 6:12–16

*After a miracle...*

Jesus directed [the disciples] to have all the people sit down in groups on the green grass. So they sat down in groups of hundreds and fifties. Taking the five loaves and the two fish and looking up to heaven, he gave thanks and broke the loaves. Then he gave them to his disciples to distribute to the people. He also divided the two fish among them all. They all ate and were satisfied, and the disciples picked up twelve basketfuls of broken pieces of bread and fish. The number of the men who had eaten was five thousand. **Immediately Jesus made his disciples get into the boat and go on ahead of him to Bethsaida, while he dismissed the crowd. After leaving them, he went up on a mountainside to pray.**

                                                            Mark 6:39–46

*Prayer never ceased to be a part of Jesus' life. As Jesus approached the conclusion of his ministry, he knew it would culminate on a cross, which typically meant a slow and excruciatingly painful death. Knowing what he was about to endure, Jesus took refuge in an extended time of prayer. He appealed to God for a way around the torture, though he remained unflinching in his resolve to accomplish his Father's will.*

Jesus went with his disciples to a place called Gethsemane, and he said to them, "Sit here while I go over there and pray." He took Peter and the two sons of Zebedee along with him, and he began to be sorrowful and troubled. Then he said to them, "My soul is overwhelmed with sorrow to the point of death. Stay here and keep watch with me."

**Going a little farther, he fell with his face to the ground and prayed, "My Father, if it is possible, may this cup be taken from me. Yet not as I will, but as you will."**

Then he returned to his disciples and found them sleeping. "Couldn't you men keep watch with me for one hour?" he asked Peter. "Watch and pray so that you will not fall into temptation. The spirit is willing, but the flesh is weak."

He went away a second time and prayed, "My Father, if it is not possible for this cup to be taken away unless I drink it, may your will be done."

When he came back, he again found them sleeping, because their eyes were heavy. So he left them and went away once more and prayed the third time, saying the same thing.

Then he returned to the disciples and said to them, "Are you still sleeping and resting? Look, the hour has come, and the Son of Man is delivered into the hands of sinners. Rise! Let us go! Here comes my betrayer!" MATTHEW 26:36–46

---

Jesus had hoped for the prayer support of his friends,
not only for himself, but also to strengthen them
for what was to come. Notice what he specifically says to Peter.
In light of the fact that Peter was about to deny him three times,
how do you think Peter would have benefited if he
had stayed awake to pray for his friend?

---

## A WAY TO FIND THE DIRECTION WE NEED

*Like a needle on a compass, prayer helps us navigate life's toughest obstacles. Heroes of the faith from the beginning to the end of the Bible used prayer to determine their actions. Often the directions they received seemed a bit odd. For example, Gideon, who was by no means fearless, was asked to lead the Israelites into battle against an army that greatly outnumbered his own. God's clear directions allowed him to triumph. But before he set out, Gideon asked God to give him clarity on this overwhelming assignment. This is a good practice for all of us today. When we take our concerns and questions to God, he will provide the clarity we need.*

The angel of the LORD came and sat down under the oak in Ophrah that belonged to Joash the Abiezrite, where his son Gideon was threshing wheat in a winepress to keep it from the Midianites. When the angel of the LORD appeared to Gideon, he said, "The LORD is with you, mighty warrior."

"Pardon me, my lord," Gideon replied, "but if the LORD is with us, why has all this happened to us? Where are all his wonders that our ancestors told us about when they said, 'Did not the LORD bring us up out of Egypt?' But now the LORD has abandoned us and given us into the hand of Midian."

The LORD turned to him and said, "Go in the strength you have and save Israel out of Midian's hand. Am I not sending you?"

"Pardon me, my lord," Gideon replied, "but how can I save Israel? My clan is the weakest in Manasseh, and I am the least in my family."

The LORD answered, "I will be with you, and you will strike down all the Midianites, leaving none alive."

Gideon replied, "If now I have found favor in your eyes, give me a sign that it is really you talking to me. Please do not go away until I come back and bring my offering and set it before you."

And the LORD said, "I will wait until you return."

Gideon went inside, prepared a young goat, and from an ephah of flour he made bread without yeast. Putting the meat in a basket and its broth in a pot, he brought them out and offered them to him under the oak.

The angel of God said to him, "Take the meat and the unleavened bread, place them on this rock, and pour out the broth." And Gideon did so. Then the angel of the LORD touched the meat and the unleavened bread with the tip of the staff that was in his hand. Fire flared from the rock, consuming the meat and the bread. And the angel of the LORD disappeared. When Gideon realized that it was the angel of the LORD, he exclaimed, "Alas, Sovereign LORD! I have seen the angel of the LORD face to face!"

But the LORD said to him, "Peace! Do not be afraid. You are not going to die."

So Gideon built an altar to the LORD there and called it The LORD Is Peace. To this day it stands in Ophrah of the Abiezrites.

That same night the LORD said to him, "Take the second bull from your father's herd, the one seven years old. Tear down your father's altar to Baal and cut down the Asherah pole beside it. Then build a proper kind of altar to the LORD your God on the top of this height. Using the wood of the Asherah pole that you cut down, offer the second bull as a burnt offering."

So Gideon took ten of his servants and did as the LORD told him. But because he was afraid of his family and the townspeople, he did it at night rather than in the daytime.

In the morning when the people of the town got up, there was Baal's altar, demolished, with the Asherah pole beside it cut down and the second bull sacrificed on the newly built altar!

They asked each other, "Who did this?"

When they carefully investigated, they were told, "Gideon son of Joash did it."

The people of the town demanded of Joash, "Bring out your son. He must die, because he has broken down Baal's altar and cut down the Asherah pole beside it."

But Joash replied to the hostile crowd around him, "Are you going to plead Baal's cause? Are you trying to save him? Whoever fights for him shall be put to death by morning! If Baal really is a god, he can defend himself when someone breaks down his altar." So because Gideon broke down Baal's altar, they gave him the name Jerub-Baal that day, saying, "Let Baal contend with him."

Now all the Midianites, Amalekites and other eastern peoples joined forces and crossed over the Jordan and camped in the Valley of Jezreel. Then the Spirit of the LORD came on Gideon, and he blew a trumpet, summoning the Abiezrites to follow him. He sent messengers throughout Manasseh, calling them to arms, and also into Asher, Zebulun and Naphtali, so that they too went up to meet them.

**Gideon said to God, "If you will save Israel by my hand as**

you have promised — look, I will place a wool fleece on the threshing floor. If there is dew only on the fleece and all the ground is dry, then I will know that you will save Israel by my hand, as you said." And that is what happened. Gideon rose early the next day; he squeezed the fleece and wrung out the dew — a bowlful of water.

Then Gideon said to God, "Do not be angry with me. Let me make just one more request. Allow me one more test with the fleece, but this time make the fleece dry and let the ground be covered with dew." That night God did so. Only the fleece was dry; all the ground was covered with dew.

Early in the morning, Jerub-Baal (that is, Gideon) and all his men camped at the spring of Harod. The camp of Midian was north of them in the valley near the hill of Moreh. The LORD said to Gideon, "You have too many men. I cannot deliver Midian into their hands, or Israel would boast against me, 'My own strength has saved me.' Now announce to the army, 'Anyone who trembles with fear may turn back and leave Mount Gilead.'" So twenty-two thousand men left, while ten thousand remained.

But the LORD said to Gideon, "There are still too many men. Take them down to the water, and I will thin them out for you there. If I say, 'This one shall go with you,' he shall go; but if I say, 'This one shall not go with you,' he shall not go."

So Gideon took the men down to the water. There the LORD told him, "Separate those who lap the water with their tongues as a dog laps from those who kneel down to drink." Three hundred of them drank from cupped hands, lapping like dogs. All the rest got down on their knees to drink.

The LORD said to Gideon, "With the three hundred men that lapped I will save you and give the Midianites into your hands. Let all the others go home." So Gideon sent the rest of the Israelites home but kept the three hundred, who took over the provisions and trumpets of the others.

Now the camp of Midian lay below him in the valley. During that night the LORD said to Gideon, "Get up, go down against the camp, because I am going to give it into your hands. If you are afraid to attack, go down to the camp with your servant Purah and listen to what they are saying. Afterward, you will be encouraged to attack the camp." So he and Purah his servant went down to the outposts of the camp. The Midianites, the Amalekites and all the other eastern peoples had settled in the valley, thick as locusts. Their camels could no more be counted than the sand on the seashore.

Gideon arrived just as a man was telling a friend his dream. "I had a dream," he was saying. "A round loaf of barley bread came tumbling into the Midianite camp. It struck the tent with such force that the tent overturned and collapsed."

His friend responded, "This can be nothing other than the sword of Gideon son of Joash, the Israelite. God has given the Midianites and the whole camp into his hands."

When Gideon heard the dream and its interpretation, he bowed down and worshiped. He returned to the camp of Israel and called out, "Get up! The LORD has given the Midianite camp into your hands." Dividing the three hundred men into three companies, he placed trumpets and empty jars in the hands of all of them, with torches inside.

"Watch me," he told them. "Follow my lead. When I get to the edge of the camp, do exactly as I do. When I and all who are with me blow our trumpets, then from all around the camp blow yours and shout, 'For the LORD and for Gideon.'"

Gideon and the hundred men with him reached the edge of the camp at the beginning of the middle watch, just after they had changed the guard. They blew their trumpets and broke the jars that were in their hands. The three companies blew the trumpets and smashed the jars. Grasping the torches in their left hands and holding in their right hands the trumpets they were to blow, they shouted, "A sword for the LORD and for Gideon!" While each man held his position around the camp, all the Midianites ran, crying out as they fled.

When the three hundred trumpets sounded, the LORD caused the men throughout the camp to turn on each other with their swords. The army fled to Beth Shittah toward Zererah as far as the border of Abel Meholah near Tabbath. Israelites from Naphtali, Asher and all Manasseh were called out, and they pursued the Midianites. Gideon sent messengers throughout the hill country of Ephraim, saying, "Come down against the Midianites and seize the waters of the Jordan ahead of them as far as Beth Barah."

So all the men of Ephraim were called out and they seized the waters of the Jordan as far as Beth Barah.    JUDGES 6:11—7:24 ⚷

---

What do Gideon's interactions with God
teach us about God's character?

---

## A WAY TO LAY OUR REQUESTS BEFORE GOD

*In order to teach his followers how to be bold in prayer, Jesus used a simple model and tangible and relatable illustrations.*

---

In the following passage from Luke, what are
the main points of Jesus' teaching about prayer?

---

⚷ One day Jesus was praying in a certain place. When he finished, one of his disciples said to him, "Lord, teach us to pray, just as John taught his disciples."

**He said to them, "When you pray, say:**

> **" 'Father,**
> **hallowed be your name,**
> **your kingdom come.**
> **Give us each day our daily bread.**
> **Forgive us our sins,**
> **     for we also forgive everyone who sins against us.**
> **And lead us not into temptation.' "**

Then Jesus said to them, "Suppose you have a friend, and you go to him at midnight and say, 'Friend, lend me three loaves of bread; a friend of mine on a journey has come to me, and I have no food to offer him.' And suppose the one inside answers, 'Don't bother me. The door is already locked, and my children and I are in bed. I can't get up and give you anything.' I tell you, even though he will not get up and give you the bread because of friendship, yet because of your shameless audacity he will surely get up and give you as much as you need.

**"So I say to you: Ask and it will be given to you; seek and you will find; knock and the door will be opened to you. For every-**

**one who asks receives; the one who seeks finds; and to the one who knocks, the door will be opened.**

"Which of you fathers, if your son asks for a fish, will give him a snake instead? Or if he asks for an egg, will give him a scorpion? If you then, though you are evil, know how to give good gifts to your children, how much more will your Father in heaven give the Holy Spirit to those who ask him!"  LUKE 11:1–13 🔑

*The result of prayer is peace. The apostle Paul experienced this firsthand. He endured incredible hardships including religious persecution, wrongful imprisonment and a shipwreck that almost took his life. Yet in the letter he wrote to the Philippians, he encouraged them to do something he was obviously modeling himself: despite circumstances, find peace in God through prayer.*

**Do not be anxious about anything, but in every situation, by prayer and petition, with thanksgiving, present your requests to God. And the peace of God, which transcends all understanding, will guard your hearts and your minds in Christ Jesus.**

Finally, brothers and sisters, whatever is true, whatever is noble, whatever is right, whatever is pure, whatever is lovely, whatever is admirable — if anything is excellent or praiseworthy — think about such things. Whatever you have learned or received or heard from me, or seen in me — put it into practice. And the God of peace will be with you.  PHILIPPIANS 4:6–9

---

How do Paul's words about prayer encourage you?
How do they challenge you?

---

## WHAT WE BELIEVE

*Prayer is not only a practice; it is a privilege! To have direct access to the one true God 24/7 proves he is a personal God who wants to be in a relationship with us. Each time we pray we affirm our identity as children of God. He not only gives us the right to come to him, but he also longs for us to come to him. Jesus modeled the life of prayer during his stay on earth. Prayer (talking, listening and resting in God's presence) is an effective way to know him better and find direction for our lives. Why carry life's burdens alone when God invites us to lay them before him? When we do, we find a peace far above all understanding.*

CHAPTER

## 13

# Bible Study

—————— KEY QUESTION ——————

How do I study God's Word?

—————— KEY IDEA ——————

I study the Bible to know God and his truth
and to find direction for my daily life.

—————— KEY VERSE ——————

For the word of God is alive and active.
Sharper than any double-edged sword, it penetrates
even to dividing soul and spirit, joints and marrow;
it judges the thoughts and attitudes of the heart.

*Hebrews 4:12*

*The key idea highlighted in chapter four — the Bible is the Word of God and has the right to command our beliefs and actions — is a key belief for every Christian. Over many years God superintended the process to bring us his Word, his revelation. It is through the Bible that we learn how to think, act and become like Jesus. The ancient stories and words are "alive and active" and totally capable of leading us along the right path. But like a trustworthy map, we must use it for it to be effective. Making Bible study a key practice can help us get to where God wants to take us.*

*In this chapter you will be reading about:*

- *The First Scriptures*
- *The Road Map for Living*
- *Aids to Understanding*
- *A Transformed Life*

## THE FIRST SCRIPTURES

*Both Jews and Christians have traditionally regarded Moses as the author of the first five books of the Old Testament. Until the time of Moses, the words of God and the stories of his people were communicated orally from generation to generation. And even after Moses wrote these first portions of Scripture, the people didn't have access to their own complete copy.*

*Before Moses died, the Lord led him to deliver to the people farewell messages which are recorded in Deuteronomy. Parents were charged with the responsibility to share with their children God's principles and commandments. Moses also made a provision to ensure that everyone living in Israel would regularly and faithfully hear God's Word.*

In the future, when your son asks you, "What is the meaning of the stipulations, decrees and laws the LORD our God has commanded you?" tell him: "We were slaves of Pharaoh in Egypt, but the LORD brought us out of Egypt with a mighty hand. Before our eyes the LORD sent signs and wonders — great and terrible — on Egypt and Pharaoh and his whole household. But he brought us out from there to bring us in and give us the land he promised on oath to our ancestors. The Lord commanded us to obey all these decrees and to fear the Lord our God, so that we might always prosper and be kept alive, as is the case today. And if we are careful to obey all this law before the Lord our God, as he has commanded us, that will be our righteousness." Deuteronomy 6:20–25

So Moses wrote down this law and gave it to the Levitical priests, who carried the ark of the covenant of the Lord, and to all the elders of Israel. **Then Moses commanded them: "At the end of every seven years, in the year for canceling debts, during the Festival of Tabernacles, when all Israel comes to appear before the Lord your God at the place he will choose, you shall read this law before them in their hearing. Assemble the people — men, women and children, and the foreigners residing in your towns — so they can listen and learn to fear the Lord your God and follow carefully all the words of this law. Their children, who do not know this law, must hear it and learn to fear the Lord your God as long as you live in the land you are crossing the Jordan to possess."** Deuteronomy 31:9–13

*After Moses' death, the role of leadership was passed to Joshua. God spoke to Joshua to remind him of the importance of following God's laws and commands.*

After the death of Moses the servant of the Lord, the Lord said to Joshua son of Nun, Moses' aide: "Moses my servant is dead. Now then, you and all these people, get ready to cross the Jordan River into the land I am about to give to them — to the Israelites. I will give you every place where you set your foot, as I promised Moses. Your territory will extend from the desert to Lebanon, and from the great river, the Euphrates — all the Hittite country — to the Mediterranean Sea in the west. No one will be able to stand against you all the days of your life. As I was with Moses, so I will be with you; I will never leave you nor forsake you. Be strong and courageous, because you will lead these people to inherit the land I swore to their ancestors to give them.

"Be strong and very courageous. Be careful to obey all the law my servant Moses gave you; do not turn from it to the right or to the left, that you may be successful wherever you go. **Keep this Book of the Law always on your lips; meditate on it day and night, so that you may be careful to do everything written in it. Then you will be prosperous and successful.** Have I not commanded you? Be strong and courageous. Do not be afraid; do not be discouraged, for the LORD your God will be with you wherever you go." JOSHUA 1:1–9 ⚷

## THE ROAD MAP FOR LIVING

*It's interesting that the longest chapter in the Bible, Psalm 119, is entirely devoted to the subject of God's Word. This psalm is all about loving, knowing and following God's Word.*

---

See how many ways you can find to study and love the Bible in these portions of Psalm 119.

---

How can a young person stay on the path of purity?
    By living according to your word.
I seek you with all my heart;
    do not let me stray from your commands.
**I have hidden your word in my heart**
    **that I might not sin against you.**
Praise be to you, LORD;
    teach me your decrees.
With my lips I recount
    all the laws that come from your mouth.
I rejoice in following your statutes
    as one rejoices in great riches.
I meditate on your precepts
    and consider your ways.
I delight in your decrees;
    I will not neglect your word.

Be good to your servant while I live,
    that I may obey your word.
Open my eyes that I may see
    wonderful things in your law.

I am a stranger on earth;
    do not hide your commands from me.
My soul is consumed with longing
    for your laws at all times.
You rebuke the arrogant, who are accursed,
    those who stray from your commands.
Remove from me their scorn and contempt,
    for I keep your statutes.
Though rulers sit together and slander me,
    your servant will meditate on your decrees.
Your statutes are my delight;
    they are my counselors.         Psalm 119:9–24

Teach me, Lord, the way of your decrees,
    that I may follow it to the end.
Give me understanding, so that I may keep your law
    and obey it with all my heart.
Direct me in the path of your commands,
    for there I find delight.
Turn my heart toward your statutes
    and not toward selfish gain.
Turn my eyes away from worthless things;
    preserve my life according to your word.
Fulfill your promise to your servant,
    so that you may be feared.
Take away the disgrace I dread,
    for your laws are good.
How I long for your precepts!
    In your righteousness preserve my life.     Psalm 119:33–40

**Oh, how I love your law!**
    **I meditate on it all day long.**
Your commands are always with me
    and make me wiser than my enemies.
I have more insight than all my teachers,
    for I meditate on your statutes.
I have more understanding than the elders,
    for I obey your precepts.

I have kept my feet from every evil path
    so that I might obey your word.
I have not departed from your laws,
    for you yourself have taught me.
How sweet are your words to my taste,
    sweeter than honey to my mouth!
I gain understanding from your precepts;
    therefore I hate every wrong path.

**Your word is a lamp for my feet,**
    **a light on my path.**
I have taken an oath and confirmed it,
    that I will follow your righteous laws.
I have suffered much;
    preserve my life, LORD, according to your word.
Accept, LORD, the willing praise of my mouth,
    and teach me your laws.
Though I constantly take my life in my hands,
    I will not forget your law.
The wicked have set a snare for me,
    but I have not strayed from your precepts.
Your statutes are my heritage forever;
    they are the joy of my heart.
My heart is set on keeping your decrees
    to the very end.        PSALM 119:97–112

---

What is the difference between studying God's Word and
hiding it in our hearts? What is the difference between reading
God's Word and meditating on it day and night?

---

## AIDS TO UNDERSTANDING

*As you have probably observed, the Bible is unlike any other nar-*
*rative. It is God's story, chockful of amazing depth and application*
*for our lives. Jesus reminds us that the condition of our hearts is*
*important when we hear or read God's Word. Only when we are*
*open and receptive to God's words can they take root in our lives*
*and transform us.*

---

In the passage below, Jesus refers to four types of soil on which the
seed of his Word falls. Which type best describes you right now?
Was there a time when you would have answered differently?

---

Jesus went out of the house and sat by the lake. Such large
crowds gathered around him that he got into a boat and sat in it,
while all the people stood on the shore. Then he told them many
things in parables, saying: "A farmer went out to sow his seed. As
he was scattering the seed, some fell along the path, and the birds
came and ate it up. Some fell on rocky places, where it did not
have much soil. It sprang up quickly, because the soil was shallow.
But when the sun came up, the plants were scorched, and they
withered because they had no root. Other seed fell among thorns,
which grew up and choked the plants. Still other seed fell on good
soil, where it produced a crop—a hundred, sixty or thirty times
what was sown. Whoever has ears, let them hear."

The disciples came to him and asked, "Why do you speak to
the people in parables?"

He replied, "Because the knowledge of the secrets of the kingdom of heaven has been given to you, but not to them. Whoever
has will be given more, and they will have an abundance. Whoever
does not have, even what they have will be taken from them. This
is why I speak to them in parables:

"Though seeing, they do not see;
    though hearing, they do not hear or understand.

In them is fulfilled the prophecy of Isaiah:

"'You will be ever hearing but never understanding;
    you will be ever seeing but never perceiving.
For this people's heart has become calloused;
    they hardly hear with their ears,
    and they have closed their eyes.
Otherwise they might see with their eyes,
    hear with their ears,
    understand with their hearts
and turn, and I would heal them.'

But blessed are your eyes because they see, and your ears because they hear. For truly I tell you, many prophets and righteous people longed to see what you see but did not see it, and to hear what you hear but did not hear it.

"Listen then to what the parable of the sower means: When anyone hears the message about the kingdom and does not understand it, the evil one comes and snatches away what was sown in their heart. This is the seed sown along the path. The seed falling on rocky ground refers to someone who hears the word and at once receives it with joy. But since they have no root, they last only a short time. When trouble or persecution comes because of the word, they quickly fall away. The seed falling among the thorns refers to someone who hears the word, but the worries of this life and the deceitfulness of wealth choke the word, making it unfruitful. **But the seed falling on good soil refers to someone who hears the word and understands it. This is the one who produces a crop, yielding a hundred, sixty or thirty times what was sown."**

MATTHEW 13:1–23 🔑

*But how do we open our hearts to God? How can we receive his words? Before he ascended to heaven, Jesus taught his disciples that he would send the Holy Spirit into the hearts of those who believe. The Spirit of God now uses the Word of God to transform the people of God.*

---

As you read this message from Jesus and the
following passage from Paul's writings, look for ways
in which the Holy Spirit helps us understand Scripture.

---

"If you love me, keep my commands. And I will ask the Father, and he will give you another advocate to help you and be with you forever — the Spirit of truth. The world cannot accept him, because it neither sees him nor knows him. But you know him, for he lives with you and will be in you. I will not leave you as orphans; I will come to you. Before long, the world will not see me anymore, but you will see me. Because I live, you also will live. On that day you will realize that I am in my Father, and you are in me, and I am in you. Whoever has my commands and keeps them is the one who loves me. The one who loves me will be loved by my Father, and I too will love them and show myself to them."

Then Judas (not Judas Iscariot) said, "But, Lord, why do you intend to show yourself to us and not to the world?"

Jesus replied, "Anyone who loves me will obey my teaching. My Father will love them, and we will come to them and make our home with them. Anyone who does not love me will not obey my teaching. These words you hear are not my own; they belong to the Father who sent me.

"All this I have spoken while still with you. **But the Advocate, the Holy Spirit, whom the Father will send in my name, will teach you all things and will remind you of everything I have said to you.** Peace I leave with you; my peace I give you. I do not give to you as the world gives. Do not let your hearts be troubled and do not be afraid." JOHN 14:15–27

*One of the roles of the Holy Spirit is to shine light on the message of Scripture. It is through the Holy Spirit that we are able to understand the Bible's full meaning, accept it in our hearts and know how to apply it to our lives. The apostle Paul informed the church at Corinth of this truth.*

We do, however, speak a message of wisdom among the mature, but not the wisdom of this age or of the rulers of this age, who are coming to nothing. No, we declare God's wisdom, a mystery that has been hidden and that God destined for our glory before time began. None of the rulers of this age understood it, for if they had, they would not have crucified the Lord of glory. However, as it is written:

> "What no eye has seen,
>     what no ear has heard,
>   and what no human mind has conceived" —
>       the things God has prepared for those who love him —

these are the things God has revealed to us by his Spirit.

The Spirit searches all things, even the deep things of God. For who knows a person's thoughts except their own spirit within them? In the same way no one knows the thoughts of God except the Spirit of God. **What we have received is not the spirit of the world, but the Spirit who is from God, so that we may understand what God has freely given us.** This is what we speak, not in words taught us by human wisdom but in words taught by the Spirit, explaining spiritual realities with Spirit-taught words. The person without the Spirit does not accept the things that come from the Spirit of God but considers them foolishness, and cannot understand them because they are discerned only through the Spirit. The person with the Spirit makes judgments about all things, but such a person is not subject to merely human judgments, for,

> "Who has known the mind of the Lord
>     so as to instruct him?"

But we have the mind of Christ.                    1 CORINTHIANS 2:6–16

## A TRANSFORMED LIFE
*The purpose of studying God's truth is not just information but also transformation. It guides us along the path of maturity in Christ. We get into the Bible, and the Bible gets into us and changes us for the better.*

We have much to say about this, but it is hard to make it clear to you because you no longer try to understand. In fact, though by this time you ought to be teachers, you need someone to teach you the elementary truths of God's word all over again. You need milk, not solid food! Anyone who lives on milk, being still an infant, is not acquainted with the teaching about righteousness. **But solid food is for the mature, who by constant use have trained themselves to distinguish good from evil.**

**Therefore let us move beyond the elementary teachings about Christ and be taken forward to maturity,** not laying again the foundation of repentance from acts that lead to death, and of faith in God, instruction about cleansing rites, the laying on of hands, the resurrection of the dead, and eternal judgment. And God permitting, we will do so.                    HEBREWS 5:11—6:3

Take another look at the key verse at the beginning
of this chapter. According to the author,
the Word of God is like a double-edged sword;
it gets under our skins and speaks directly to our hearts.
In what ways have you experienced this?

## WHAT WE BELIEVE

*If we believe the Bible is the Word of God and can be trusted to guide us in the best and right direction, we must gain the skill and discipline to read, study, meditate on and apply it to our lives. God told Joshua that if he did this, he would be success-ful. God makes the same offer to us. When we open up God's Word, we learn more about the one true God who knows and loves us. The more we know about God's nature, character and movements, the easier it is to discern his will and direction for our lives. When we walk on the lighted path of God, it leads to peace and great blessing. But the Bible can be a bit over-whelming, can't it? Remember, you are not alone. You have the Spirit of God within you and a community of believers around you to help you. So please don't give up; keep reading!*

# ACT

## CHAPTER

### 14

# Single-Mindedness

———— KEY QUESTION ————

How do I keep my focus on Jesus
amidst distractions?

———— KEY IDEA ————

I focus on God and his priorities for my life.

———— KEY VERSE ————

But seek first his kingdom and his righteousness,
and all these things will be given to you as well.
*Matthew 6:33*

OUR MAP

*To be single-minded means to have one desire that trumps all others. One goal. One focus. From the beginning God made clear what his people's main focus should be — him. But this is challenging in a hectic, fast-paced world. It's easy for days, months and even years to get away from us. The spiritual practice of single-mindedness is all about determining our priorities to make sure we are practicing our faith, living out our beliefs and accomplishing God's will for our lives.*

*In this chapter you will be reading Scripture that addresses:*

- *Principles of Single-Mindedness*
- *Profiles of Single-Mindedness*
- *Product of Single-Mindedness*

## PRINCIPLES OF SINGLE-MINDEDNESS

*There is perhaps no better single statement of how to be single-minded than the first commandment.*

"You shall have no other gods before me."                EXODUS 20:3

---

Explain what the first commandment has to do
with single-mindedness. What are some of the gods in
our lives that could cause us to lose focus on God?

---

*God's people were given the first commandment because they needed to submit fully to his authority and look to him and him only to provide all they needed. In the New Testament, Jesus describes the "other gods" we might have in a way that hits close to home.*

**"Do not store up for yourselves treasures on earth, where moths and vermin destroy, and where thieves break in and steal. But store up for yourselves treasures in heaven, where moths and vermin do not destroy, and where thieves do not**

**break in and steal. For where your treasure is, there your heart will be also.**

"The eye is the lamp of the body. If your eyes are healthy, your whole body will be full of light. But if your eyes are unhealthy, your whole body will be full of darkness. If then the light within you is darkness, how great is that darkness!

**"No one can serve two masters. Either you will hate the one and love the other, or you will be devoted to the one and despise the other. You cannot serve both God and money."**

MATTHEW 6:19–24

---

What kind of "treasure" keeps us from being single-minded?
How can "unhealthy eyes" keep us from being single-minded?
Why isn't it possible to serve two masters?

---

## PROFILES OF SINGLE-MINDEDNESS

*King Jehoshaphat was a godly leader who faced a tremendous challenge. His land was threatened by a hostile army of enemies. Rather than being overcome by fear, or resorting to his own defense tactics, Jehoshaphat encouraged the people to turn to the Lord in single-minded trust. In fact, he even put the praise and worship team at the front of his battle formation!*

---

In the following passage, identify the key beliefs in which Jehoshaphat anchors his prayer. How can these key beliefs instill confidence in God's provision and guide our decisions?

---

The Moabites and Ammonites with some of the Meunites came to wage war against Jehoshaphat.

Some people came and told Jehoshaphat, "A vast army is coming against you from Edom, from the other side of the Dead Sea. It is already in Hazezon Tamar" (that is, En Gedi). Alarmed, Jehoshaphat resolved to inquire of the LORD, and he proclaimed a fast for all Judah. The people of Judah came together to seek help from the LORD; indeed, they came from every town in Judah to seek him.

Then Jehoshaphat stood up in the assembly of Judah and Jerusalem at the temple of the LORD in the front of the new courtyard and said:

"LORD, the God of our ancestors, are you not the God who is in heaven? You rule over all the kingdoms of the nations. Power and might are in your hand, and no one can withstand you. Our God, did you not drive out the inhabitants of this land before your people Israel and give it forever to the descendants of Abraham your friend? They have lived in it and have built in it a sanctuary for your Name, saying, 'If calamity comes upon us, whether the sword of judgment, or plague or famine, we will stand in your presence before this temple that bears your Name and will cry out to you in our distress, and you will hear us and save us.'

"But now here are men from Ammon, Moab and Mount Seir, whose territory you would not allow Israel to invade when they came from Egypt; so they turned away from them and did not destroy them. See how they are repaying us by coming to drive us out of the possession you gave us as an inheritance. Our God, will you not judge them? For we have no power to face this vast army that is attacking us. **We do not know what to do, but our eyes are on you.**"

All the men of Judah, with their wives and children and little ones, stood there before the LORD.

Then the Spirit of the LORD came on Jahaziel son of Zechariah, the son of Benaiah, the son of Jeiel, the son of Mattaniah, a Levite and descendant of Asaph, as he stood in the assembly.

He said: "Listen, King Jehoshaphat and all who live in Judah and Jerusalem! This is what the LORD says to you: 'Do not be afraid or discouraged because of this vast army. For the battle is not yours, but God's. Tomorrow march down against them. They will be climbing up by the Pass of Ziz, and you will find them at the end of the gorge in the Desert of Jeruel. **You will not have to fight this battle. Take up your positions; stand firm and see the deliverance the LORD will give you, Judah and Jerusalem. Do not be afraid; do not be discouraged. Go out to face them tomorrow, and the LORD will be with you.**'"

Jehoshaphat bowed down with his face to the ground, and all

the people of Judah and Jerusalem fell down in worship before the LORD. Then some Levites from the Kohathites and Korahites stood up and praised the LORD, the God of Israel, with a very loud voice.

Early in the morning they left for the Desert of Tekoa. As they set out, Jehoshaphat stood and said, "Listen to me, Judah and people of Jerusalem! Have faith in the LORD your God and you will be upheld; have faith in his prophets and you will be successful." After consulting the people, Jehoshaphat appointed men to sing to the LORD and to praise him for the splendor of his holiness as they went out at the head of the army, saying:

"Give thanks to the LORD,
for his love endures forever."

As they began to sing and praise, the LORD set ambushes against the men of Ammon and Moab and Mount Seir who were invading Judah, and they were defeated. The Ammonites and Moabites rose up against the men from Mount Seir to destroy and annihilate them. After they finished slaughtering the men from Seir, they helped to destroy one another.

When the men of Judah came to the place that overlooks the desert and looked toward the vast army, they saw only dead bodies lying on the ground; no one had escaped. So Jehoshaphat and his men went to carry off their plunder, and they found among them a great amount of equipment and clothing and also articles of value — more than they could take away. There was so much plunder that it took three days to collect it. On the fourth day they assembled in the Valley of Berakah, where they praised the LORD. This is why it is called the Valley of Berakah to this day.

Then, led by Jehoshaphat, all the men of Judah and Jerusalem returned joyfully to Jerusalem, for the LORD had given them cause to rejoice over their enemies. They entered Jerusalem and went to the temple of the LORD with harps and lyres and trumpets.

The fear of God came on all the surrounding kingdoms when they heard how the LORD had fought against the enemies of Israel. And the kingdom of Jehoshaphat was at peace, for his God had given him rest on every side.             2 CHRONICLES 20:1–30 🗝

*Unfortunately, Peter, Jesus' friend and disciple, had a bit more trouble maintaining his single-minded focus on God. Peter's experience is a good reminder of how we are to think about Jesus. We must keep our eyes on him, even when we get sidetracked or feel afraid.*

⚿ Jesus made the disciples get into the boat and go on ahead of him to the other side, while he dismissed the crowd. After he had dismissed them, he went up on a mountainside by himself to pray. Later that night, he was there alone, and the boat was already a considerable distance from land, buffeted by the waves because the wind was against it.

Shortly before dawn Jesus went out to them, walking on the lake. When the disciples saw him walking on the lake, they were terrified. "It's a ghost," they said, and cried out in fear.

But Jesus immediately said to them: "Take courage! It is I. Don't be afraid."

"Lord, if it's you," Peter replied, "tell me to come to you on the water."

"Come," he said.

**Then Peter got down out of the boat, walked on the water and came toward Jesus. But when he saw the wind, he was afraid and, beginning to sink, cried out, "Lord, save me!"**

Immediately Jesus reached out his hand and caught him. "You of little faith," he said, "why did you doubt?"

And when they climbed into the boat, the wind died down. Then those who were in the boat worshiped him, saying, "Truly you are the Son of God." MATTHEW 14:22–33 ⚿

*Ultimately, however, the disciples developed Jesus' single-minded devotion to God and his purposes.*

---

As you read the following story, identify what types
of pressure the apostles had to resist in order to stay focused
on their mission. What similar kinds of influences do
you face that threaten your devotion to God?

---

The apostles performed many signs and wonders among the people. And all the believers used to meet together in Solomon's Colonnade. No one else dared join them, even though they were highly regarded by the people. Nevertheless, more and more men and women believed in the Lord and were added to their number. As a result, people brought the sick into the streets and laid them on beds and mats so that at least Peter's shadow might fall on some of them as he passed by. Crowds gathered also from the towns around Jerusalem, bringing their sick and those tormented by impure spirits, and all of them were healed.

Then the high priest and all his associates, who were members of the party of the Sadducees, were filled with jealousy. They arrested the apostles and put them in the public jail. But during the night an angel of the Lord opened the doors of the jail and brought them out. "Go, stand in the temple courts," he said, "and tell the people all about this new life."

At daybreak they entered the temple courts, as they had been told, and began to teach the people.

When the high priest and his associates arrived, they called together the Sanhedrin — the full assembly of the elders of Israel — and sent to the jail for the apostles. But on arriving at the jail, the officers did not find them there. So they went back and reported, "We found the jail securely locked, with the guards standing at the doors; but when we opened them, we found no one inside." On hearing this report, the captain of the temple guard and the chief priests were at a loss, wondering what this might lead to.

Then someone came and said, "Look! The men you put in jail are standing in the temple courts teaching the people." At that, the captain went with his officers and brought the apostles. They did not use force, because they feared that the people would stone them.

The apostles were brought in and made to appear before the Sanhedrin to be questioned by the high priest. "We gave you strict orders not to teach in this name," he said. "Yet you have filled Jerusalem with your teaching and are determined to make us guilty of this man's blood."

**Peter and the other apostles replied: "We must obey God**

**rather than human beings!** The God of our ancestors raised Jesus from the dead — whom you killed by hanging him on a cross. God exalted him to his own right hand as Prince and Savior that he might bring Israel to repentance and forgive their sins. We are witnesses of these things, and so is the Holy Spirit, whom God has given to those who obey him."

When they heard this, they were furious and wanted to put them to death. But a Pharisee named Gamaliel, a teacher of the law, who was honored by all the people, stood up in the Sanhedrin and ordered that the men be put outside for a little while. Then he addressed the Sanhedrin: "Men of Israel, consider carefully what you intend to do to these men. Some time ago Theudas appeared, claiming to be somebody, and about four hundred men rallied to him. He was killed, all his followers were dispersed, and it all came to nothing. After him, Judas the Galilean appeared in the days of the census and led a band of people in revolt. He too was killed, and all his followers were scattered. **Therefore, in the present case I advise you: Leave these men alone! Let them go! For if their purpose or activity is of human origin, it will fail. But if it is from God, you will not be able to stop these men; you will only find yourselves fighting against God."**

His speech persuaded them. They called the apostles in and had them flogged. Then they ordered them not to speak in the name of Jesus, and let them go.

The apostles left the Sanhedrin, rejoicing because they had been counted worthy of suffering disgrace for the Name. **Day after day, in the temple courts and from house to house, they never stopped teaching and proclaiming the good news that Jesus is the Messiah.** Acts 5:12–42

## PRODUCT OF SINGLE-MINDEDNESS

*Near the end of the book of Deuteronomy — and Moses' life — the Lord called the Israelites to make a choice: trust and obey his commands or go their own way. Speaking through Moses, God gave this message to his people. And what was the result of the people's decision? Because they chose obedience, the following seven years were the most fruitful years in Israel's history — the glory days!*

See, I set before you today life and prosperity, death and destruction. For I command you today to love the LORD your God, to walk in obedience to him, and to keep his commands, decrees and laws; then you will live and increase, and the LORD your God will bless you in the land you are entering to possess.

But if your heart turns away and you are not obedient, and if you are drawn away to bow down to other gods and worship them, I declare to you this day that you will certainly be destroyed. You will not live long in the land you are crossing the Jordan to enter and possess.

**This day I call the heavens and the earth as witnesses against you that I have set before you life and death, blessings and curses. Now choose life, so that you and your children may live and that you may love the LORD your God, listen to his voice, and hold fast to him. For the LORD is your life, and he will give you many years in the land he swore to give to your fathers, Abraham, Isaac and Jacob.** DEUTERONOMY 30:15–20

*In the New Testament, the apostle Paul challenged believers to a single-minded commitment to God. He also gave them encouraging promises about the results of such devotion. As it was with Israel, so it is with us today: if we single-mindedly focus on Christ and his priorities for our lives, we will experience our own glory days!*

Therefore, I urge you, brothers and sisters, in view of God's mercy, to offer your bodies as a living sacrifice, holy and pleasing to God — this is your true and proper worship. **Do not conform to the pattern of this world, but be transformed by the renewing of your mind. Then you will be able to test and approve what God's will is — his good, pleasing and perfect will.** ROMANS 12:1–2

Since, then, you have been raised with Christ, set your hearts on things above, where Christ is, seated at the right hand of God. **Set your minds on things above, not on earthly things.** For you died, and your life is now hidden with Christ in God. When Christ, who is your life, appears, then you also will appear with him in glory. COLOSSIANS 3:1–4

Let the peace of Christ rule in your hearts, since as members of one body you were called to peace. And be thankful. Let the message of Christ dwell among you richly as you teach and admonish one another with all wisdom through psalms, hymns, and songs from the Spirit, singing to God with gratitude in your hearts. **And whatever you do, whether in word or deed, do it all in the name of the Lord Jesus, giving thanks to God the Father through him.** Colossians 3:15–17

---

Paul writes, "Whatever you do, whether in word or deed, do it all in the name of the Lord Jesus." Does he really mean "whatever"? How is it possible to really do what this verse says?

---

## WHAT WE BELIEVE

*The practice of single-mindedness is about setting priorities. This involves putting our past decisions and actions behind us and focusing on God's kingdom with help from the Holy Spirit. The Bible gives us many inspiring profiles of people who have displayed tremendous single-mindedness for God, including King Jehoshaphat in the Old Testament and Jesus in the New Testament. During his early years Peter struggled to "fix his eyes" on Jesus, but later he and the disciples declared with great conviction in the face of persecution, "We must obey God rather than human beings." The product of a life of single-minded determination and focus is an untouchable peace from the hand of the one true God who loves us deeply. Seek first God's kingdom!*

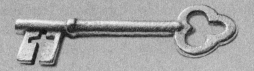

# ACT

## CHAPTER

### 15

# Total Surrender

---

KEY QUESTION

---

How do I cultivate a life of sacrificial service?

---

KEY IDEA

---

I dedicate my life to God's purposes.

---

KEY VERSE

---

I urge you, brothers and sisters, in view of God's mercy,
to offer your bodies as a living sacrifice,
holy and pleasing to God — this is
your true and proper worship.

*Romans 12:1*

OUR MAP

*A genuine decision to follow and obey God is a decision of total surrender. We leave nothing off the negotiation table. We are "all in" as a reasonable response to God being "all in" for us. When God the Father offered up his Son for our redemption, he revealed how valuable we are to him. The gift of salvation was an act of total surrender by our Savior. Are you willing to return the gesture? Are you prepared to surrender your life for his purposes?*

*Total surrender does not occur without some sacrifice, which is illustrated poignantly through these people and stories of the Bible:*

- *Profiles of Total Surrender*
- *The Cost of Total Surrender*
- *The Inspiration of Martyrs*

---

Reflect on the key verse. What do you think it means to offer yourself as a "living sacrifice"? Recalling our study of the practice of worship in chapter 11, why do you think offering yourself as a living sacrifice is the true and proper way to worship?

---

## PROFILES OF TOTAL SURRENDER

*Despite having God's expectations physically written in stone, the Israelites failed to remain faithful. After many years of disobedience, the people suffered when God removed his protection. Before the southern kingdom of Judah was conquered by the Babylonians, some of the people were carried off in deportations. Along with Daniel, a small group of bright young men—Shadrach, Meshach and Abednego—were selected from the captives to be trained to serve the king. While in captivity, they were forced to make a crucial choice: worship the one true God or compromise and save their lives. They chose total surrender.*

King Nebuchadnezzar made an image of gold, sixty cubits high and six cubits wide, and set it up on the plain of Dura in the province of Babylon. He then summoned the satraps, prefects, governors, advisers, treasurers, judges, magistrates and all the other provincial officials to come to the dedication of the image he had set up. So the satraps, prefects, governors, advisers, treasurers, judges, magistrates and all the other provincial officials assembled for the dedication of the image that King Nebuchadnezzar had set up, and they stood before it.

Then the herald loudly proclaimed, "Nations and peoples of every language, this is what you are commanded to do: As soon as you hear the sound of the horn, flute, zither, lyre, harp, pipe and all kinds of music, you must fall down and worship the image of gold that King Nebuchadnezzar has set up. Whoever does not fall down and worship will immediately be thrown into a blazing furnace."

Therefore, as soon as they heard the sound of the horn, flute, zither, lyre, harp and all kinds of music, all the nations and peoples of every language fell down and worshiped the image of gold that King Nebuchadnezzar had set up.

At this time some astrologers came forward and denounced the Jews. They said to King Nebuchadnezzar, "May the king live forever! Your Majesty has issued a decree that everyone who hears the sound of the horn, flute, zither, lyre, harp, pipe and all kinds of music must fall down and worship the image of gold, and that whoever does not fall down and worship will be thrown into a blazing furnace. But there are some Jews whom you have set over the affairs of the province of Babylon — Shadrach, Meshach and Abednego — who pay no attention to you, Your Majesty. They neither serve your gods nor worship the image of gold you have set up."

Furious with rage, Nebuchadnezzar summoned Shadrach, Meshach and Abednego. So these men were brought before the king, and Nebuchadnezzar said to them, "Is it true, Shadrach, Meshach and Abednego, that you do not serve my gods or worship the image of gold I have set up? Now when you hear the sound of the horn, flute, zither, lyre, harp, pipe and all kinds of music, if you are ready to fall down and worship the image I made, very good. But if you do not worship it, you will be thrown immediately into a blazing furnace. Then what god will be able to rescue you from my hand?"

**Shadrach, Meshach and Abednego replied to him, "King Nebuchadnezzar, we do not need to defend ourselves before you in this matter. If we are thrown into the blazing furnace, the God we serve is able to deliver us from it, and he will deliver us from Your Majesty's hand. But even if he does not, we want you to know, Your Majesty, that we will not serve your gods or worship the image of gold you have set up."**

Then Nebuchadnezzar was furious with Shadrach, Meshach and Abednego, and his attitude toward them changed. He ordered the furnace heated seven times hotter than usual and commanded some of the strongest soldiers in his army to tie up Shadrach, Meshach and Abednego and throw them into the blazing furnace. So these men, wearing their robes, trousers, turbans and other clothes, were bound and thrown into the blazing furnace. The king's command was so urgent and the furnace so hot that the flames of the fire killed the soldiers who took up Shadrach, Meshach and Abednego, and these three men, firmly tied, fell into the blazing furnace.

Then King Nebuchadnezzar leaped to his feet in amazement and asked his advisers, "Weren't there three men that we tied up and threw into the fire?"

They replied, "Certainly, Your Majesty."

He said, "Look! I see four men walking around in the fire, unbound and unharmed, and the fourth looks like a son of the gods."

Nebuchadnezzar then approached the opening of the blazing furnace and shouted, "Shadrach, Meshach and Abednego, servants of the Most High God, come out! Come here!"

So Shadrach, Meshach and Abednego came out of the fire, and the satraps, prefects, governors and royal advisers crowded around them. They saw that the fire had not harmed their bodies, nor was a hair of their heads singed; their robes were not scorched, and there was no smell of fire on them.

Then Nebuchadnezzar said, "Praise be to the God of Shadrach, Meshach and Abednego, who has sent his angel and rescued his servants! They trusted in him and defied the king's command and were willing to give up their lives rather than serve or worship any god except their own God." DANIEL 3:1–28

*Esther and her cousin Mordecai were living in Persia under the rule of King Xerxes. When the reigning queen was removed from power, Esther (who kept her Jewish heritage a secret) was selected to replace her. Haman, the king's highest official, hated Mordecai because Mordecai refused to bow down and honor him. As revenge, Haman made plans to kill Mordecai and all the rest of the Jews in the Persian kingdom. Like Shadrach, Meshach and Abednego, Esther had a difficult decision to make: protect her people or protect her position as queen—and perhaps her own life. She chose total surrender to God.*

When Haman saw that Mordecai would not kneel down or pay him honor, he was enraged. Yet having learned who Mordecai's people were, he scorned the idea of killing only Mordecai. Instead Haman looked for a way to destroy all Mordecai's people, the Jews, throughout the whole kingdom of Xerxes.

In the twelfth year of King Xerxes, in the first month, the month of Nisan, the *pur* (that is, the lot) was cast in the presence of Haman to select a day and month. And the lot fell on the twelfth month, the month of Adar.

Then Haman said to King Xerxes, "There is a certain people dispersed among the peoples in all the provinces of your kingdom who keep themselves separate. Their customs are different from those of all other people, and they do not obey the king's laws; it is not in the king's best interest to tolerate them. If it pleases the king, let a decree be issued to destroy them, and I will give ten thousand talents of silver to the king's administrators for the royal treasury."

So the king took his signet ring from his finger and gave it to Haman son of Hammedatha, the Agagite, the enemy of the Jews. "Keep the money," the king said to Haman, "and do with the people as you please."

Then on the thirteenth day of the first month the royal secretaries were summoned. They wrote out in the script of each province and in the language of each people all Haman's orders to the king's satraps, the governors of the various provinces and the nobles of the various peoples. These were written in the name of King Xerxes himself and sealed with his own ring. Dispatches were sent by couriers to all the king's provinces with the order to destroy, kill and annihilate all the Jews — young and old, women and children — on a single day, the thirteenth day of the twelfth month, the month of Adar, and to plunder their goods. A copy of the text of the edict was to be issued as law in every province and made known to the people of every nationality so they would be ready for that day.

The couriers went out, spurred on by the king's command, and the edict was issued in the citadel of Susa. The king and Haman sat down to drink, but the city of Susa was bewildered.

When Mordecai learned of all that had been done, he tore his clothes, put on sackcloth and ashes, and went out into the city, wailing loudly and bitterly. But he went only as far as the king's gate, because no one clothed in sackcloth was allowed to enter it. In every province to which the edict and order of the king came, there was great mourning among the Jews, with fasting, weeping and wailing. Many lay in sackcloth and ashes.

When Esther's eunuchs and female attendants came and told her about Mordecai, she was in great distress. She sent clothes for him to put on instead of his sackcloth, but he would not accept them. Then Esther summoned Hathak, one of the king's eunuchs assigned to attend her, and ordered him to find out what was troubling Mordecai and why.

So Hathak went out to Mordecai in the open square of the city in front of the king's gate. Mordecai told him everything that had happened to him, including the exact amount of money Haman had promised to pay into the royal treasury for the destruction of the Jews. He also gave him a copy of the text of the edict for their annihilation, which had been published in Susa, to show to Esther and explain it to her, and he told him to instruct her to go into the king's presence to beg for mercy and plead with him for her people.

Hathak went back and reported to Esther what Mordecai had said. Then she instructed him to say to Mordecai, "All the king's officials and the people of the royal provinces know that for any man or woman who approaches the king in the inner court without being summoned the king has but one law: that they be put to death unless the king extends the gold scepter to them and spares their lives. But thirty days have passed since I was called to go to the king."

When Esther's words were reported to Mordecai, he sent back this answer: "Do not think that because you are in the king's house you alone of all the Jews will escape. For if you remain silent at this time, relief and deliverance for the Jews will arise from another place, but you and your father's family will perish. And who knows but that you have come to your royal position for such a time as this?"

**Then Esther sent this reply to Mordecai: "Go, gather together all the Jews who are in Susa, and fast for me. Do not eat or drink for three days, night or day. I and my attendants will fast as you do. When this is done, I will go to the king, even though it is against the law. And if I perish, I perish."**

ESTHER 3:5—4:16

The two stories in the previous Profiles of Total Surrender section share several similarities. What similar action did the astrologers and Haman take? What did both the three young men and Mordecai choose to NOT do? What type of decree did both kings sign? To what degree did the three young men and Esther surrender?

## THE COST OF TOTAL SURRENDER

*Total surrender is easier said than done. Jesus was very clear about that. Aligning your life with God's purposes is exciting and meaningful, but it is not easy or cheap. Following God is going to cost you — emotionally, relationally, socially and even financially. Jesus explained this reality to his disciples.*

**Then [Jesus] said to them all: "Whoever wants to be my disciple must deny themselves and take up their cross daily and follow me. For whoever wants to save their life will lose it, but whoever loses their life for me will save it. What good is it for someone to gain the whole world, and yet lose or forfeit their very self? Whoever is ashamed of me and my words, the Son of Man will be ashamed of them when he comes in his glory and in the glory of the Father and of the holy angels."** LUKE 9:23—26

What did Jesus mean when he instructed the
disciples to "take up their cross daily"? Why does
Jesus say this is a wise decision to make?

## THE INSPIRATION OF MARTYRS

*Stephen was the first martyr of the Christian church. (A martyr is a
person who is killed for their beliefs.) He played an important role
in the early church by ministering to those in need and preaching
the gospel of Jesus. Stephen's death started a wave of persecution against other Christians. Stephen was brought before the
Jewish leaders where he put his total surrender on display.*

Now Stephen, a man full of God's grace and power, performed
great wonders and signs among the people. Opposition arose,
however, from members of the Synagogue of the Freedmen (as it
was called) — Jews of Cyrene and Alexandria as well as the provinces of Cilicia and Asia — who began to argue with Stephen. But
they could not stand up against the wisdom the Spirit gave him as
he spoke.

Then they secretly persuaded some men to say, "We have heard
Stephen speak blasphemous words against Moses and against God."

So they stirred up the people and the elders and the teachers
of the law. They seized Stephen and brought him before the Sanhedrin. They produced false witnesses, who testified, "This fellow
never stops speaking against this holy place and against the law.
For we have heard him say that this Jesus of Nazareth will destroy
this place and change the customs Moses handed down to us."

All who were sitting in the Sanhedrin looked intently at Stephen, and they saw that his face was like the face of an angel.

ACTS 6:8–15

*Stephen had one last chance to speak in his own defense. Instead
of trying to save himself, he spoke boldly about Jesus. He started
by recounting the history of the Jews, tracing their story up to the
current time when they had just witnessed the life, death and resurrection of Jesus. Read his daring words as he gets to the end
of his speech.*

"You stiff-necked people! Your hearts and ears are still uncir-cumcised. You are just like your ancestors: You always resist the Holy Spirit! Was there ever a prophet your ancestors did not per-secute? They even killed those who predicted the coming of the Righteous One. And now you have betrayed and murdered him — you who have received the law that was given through angels but have not obeyed it."

**When the members of the Sanhedrin heard this, they were furious and gnashed their teeth at him. But Stephen, full of the Holy Spirit, looked up to heaven and saw the glory of God, and Jesus standing at the right hand of God. "Look," he said, "I see heaven open and the Son of Man standing at the right hand of God."**

At this they covered their ears and, yelling at the top of their voices, they all rushed at him, dragged him out of the city and be-gan to stone him. Meanwhile, the witnesses laid their coats at the feet of a young man named Saul.

**While they were stoning him, Stephen prayed, "Lord Jesus, receive my spirit." Then he fell on his knees and cried out, "Lord, do not hold this sin against them." When he had said this, he fell asleep.** ACTS 7:51–60

*That "young man named Saul" became the apostle Paul, a great man of God. Once Paul gave his life to Jesus, he lived a life of total surrender. In fact, he eventually became a martyr himself. Knowing that painful hardship was in his future, he reassured his friends who feared for him and wanted to protect him more than he wished for protection for himself.*

**Then Paul answered, "Why are you weeping and breaking my heart? I am ready not only to be bound, but also to die in Jerusalem for the name of the Lord Jesus."** ACTS 21:13

*After being arrested in Jerusalem, Paul spent several years in prison or under house arrest in Rome. Jesus promised that when we lose our life we will truly find it. In other words, our life doesn't really make sense until we give God control of it. We find our deepest satisfaction not in pleasing ourselves but in pleasing*

*God. Surrendering his life for God's purposes was Paul's ultimate goal. Will you make it yours?*

---

Whose story in this chapter inspires you
the most? Shadrach, Meshach and Abednego,
Esther, Stephen, or Paul? Why?

---

Now I want you to know, brothers and sisters, that what has happened to me has actually served to advance the gospel. As a result, it has become clear throughout the whole palace guard and to everyone else that I am in chains for Christ. And because of my chains, most of the brothers and sisters have become confident in the Lord and dare all the more to proclaim the gospel without fear.

Philippians 1:12–14

I know that through your prayers and God's provision of the Spirit of Jesus Christ what has happened to me will turn out for my deliverance. **I eagerly expect and hope that I will in no way be ashamed, but will have sufficient courage so that now as always Christ will be exalted in my body, whether by life or by death. For to me, to live is Christ and to die is gain.** Philippians 1:19–21

---

Our key verse tells us to offer our bodies as a living
sacrifice, as our true and proper worship. In the stories
of Shadrach, Meshach and Abednego, and Esther,
we see people willing to sacrifice their lives to worship God.
With the stories of Stephen and Paul, we see men who actually
did die because of their beliefs. What do you think our key verse
means for us today when our lives might not necessarily be
threatened if we worship God?

---

## WHAT WE BELIEVE

*The decision to dedicate our lives to God's purposes is a daily practice. Jesus instructed his disciples to take up their cross daily and follow him. God expects this kind of dedication from us as well. Part of this dedication includes being a "living sacrifice," which requires a daily decision to crawl up on the altar. Thankfully we can find inspiration from the stories of many courageous and faithful followers of God, including Shadrach, Meshach, Abednego, Esther, Stephen and Paul.*

# ACT

## CHAPTER

### 16

# Biblical Community

—————— KEY QUESTION ——————

How do I develop healthy relationships with others?

—————— KEY IDEA ——————

I fellowship with Christians to accomplish God's purposes
in my life, in the lives of others and in the world.

—————— KEY VERSE ——————

All the believers were together and had everything in
common. They sold property and possessions to give to anyone
who had need. Every day they continued to meet together
in the temple courts. They broke bread in their homes and ate
together with glad and sincere hearts, praising God and
enjoying the favor of all the people. And the Lord added to
their number daily those who were being saved.

*Acts 2:44–47*

181

OUR MAP

*We are at the halfway point in our study of the ten practices. The first five were practices that deepen our relationship with God: worship, prayer, Bible study, single-mindedness, and total surrender. Now we shift to the practices that bless our relationships with people around us. The first of these is biblical community. We believe the one true God wants to be in a relationship with us for eternity. To make that possible, God provided the way to restore our relationship with him — through the sacrifice of his Son, Jesus Christ. All those who believe receive a new identity and come together to form a new community called the church. It is through the church that God will accomplish his primary purposes on earth.*

*Biblical community is essential to the Christian life and a vital aspect of the church. As we engage in this new family under God's leadership, we not only achieve God's purposes in our lives, in the lives of others and in the world, but we also reinforce our belief in God and his church.*

*Here are the big ideas we will be exploring in this chapter:*

- *Created for Community*
- *The Presence of God*
- *The New Community*
- *Marks of Biblical Community*

## CREATED FOR COMMUNITY

*Community is not a "nice-to-have" addition but an essential experience for living a godly and healthy life. God has always intended for humans to have rich, life-giving relationships with each other and with him. Adam and Eve experienced this perfect ideal in the garden. But their rejection of God's vision for life together caused them to be escorted from the garden and out of community with God. This separation from God and the presence of sin in every human being's nature makes it difficult, to this day, to create strong community. But it is clear from God's Word that people were not meant for isolation.*

Two are better than one,
    because they have a good return for their labor:

If either of them falls down,
>   one can help the other up.
But pity anyone who falls
>   and has no one to help them up.
Also, if two lie down together, they will keep warm.
>   But how can one keep warm alone?
Though one may be overpowered,
>   two can defend themselves.
A cord of three strands is not quickly broken.

ECCLESIASTES 4:9–12

---

This passage describes a relationship
between two people. Why, then, does it say
"a cord of three strands" is not quickly broken?

---

## THE PRESENCE OF GOD

*In order to keep true community alive, God must be at the center of it. But Adam and Eve rejected him in the garden, so community with God and with each other was difficult to recapture. Yet God never gave up on us, and the narrative of the Bible traces God's efforts to get back into community with us. After delivering the nation of Israel from bondage in Egypt, the Lord informed Moses of his intent to be with his people in a tent known as the tabernacle.*

The LORD said to Moses, "Tell the Israelites to bring me an offering. You are to receive the offering for me from everyone whose heart prompts them to give. These are the offerings you are to receive from them: gold, silver and bronze; blue, purple and scarlet yarn and fine linen; goat hair; ram skins dyed red and another type of durable leather; acacia wood; olive oil for the light; spices for the anointing oil and for the fragrant incense; and onyx stones and other gems to be mounted on the ephod and breastpiece.

**"Then have them make a sanctuary for me, and I will dwell among them. Make this tabernacle and all its furnishings exactly like the pattern I will show you."** EXODUS 25:1–9

*The cloud that had led the Israelites after their escape from Egypt covered and filled the newly established tabernacle. God's presence had arrived! About 500 years later, the Israelites built a temple in Jerusalem to replace the tabernacle with a permanent place where they could meet with God. And something very similar happened after King Solomon's prayer at the dedication of that temple.*

**When Solomon finished praying, fire came down from heaven and consumed the burnt offering and the sacrifices, and the glory of the LORD filled the temple.** The priests could not enter the temple of the LORD because the glory of the LORD filled it. When all the Israelites saw the fire coming down and the glory of the LORD above the temple, they knelt on the pavement with their faces to the ground, and they worshiped and gave thanks to the LORD, saying,

> "He is good;
>   his love endures forever." 2 CHRONICLES 7:1–3

*In the New Testament, God's presence among his people changed to a new location. At the moment of Jesus' death on the cross, the heavy curtain hanging in front of the Holy Place that separated God's people from God's presence was torn from top to bottom. God's presence was no longer isolated to this small room in the temple. Paul instructs us on how we were once separated from Christ, but now we ourselves are his temple.*

---

As you read the passage below, look for the differences between the two dwelling places for God: the temple and the New Testament church. What barriers are there in each of the two places? Who is allowed into each place? What is the cornerstone of each place?

---

Remember that formerly you who are Gentiles by birth and called "uncircumcised" by those who call themselves "the circumcision" (which is done in the body by human hands) — remember that at that time you were separate from Christ, excluded from citizenship in Israel and foreigners to the covenants of the promise, without hope and without God in the world. But now in Christ Jesus you who once were far away have been brought near by the blood of Christ.

For he himself is our peace, who has made the two groups one and has destroyed the barrier, the dividing wall of hostility, by setting aside in his flesh the law with its commands and regulations. His purpose was to create in himself one new humanity out of the two, thus making peace, and in one body to reconcile both of them to God through the cross, by which he put to death their hostility. He came and preached peace to you who were far away and peace to those who were near. For through him we both have access to the Father by one Spirit.

**Consequently, you are no longer foreigners and strangers, but fellow citizens with God's people and also members of his household, built on the foundation of the apostles and prophets, with Christ Jesus himself as the chief cornerstone. In him the whole building is joined together and rises to become a holy temple in the Lord. And in him you too are being built together to become a dwelling in which God lives by his Spirit.**

EPHESIANS 2:11–22

## THE NEW COMMUNITY

*During the time between Jesus' resurrection from the grave and his ascension to heaven, Jesus told the disciples to wait in Jerusalem for the coming of the Holy Spirit. As promised, the actual presence of God came into the new temple—into believers in Jesus Christ. We read about the arrival of the Holy Spirit on the day of Pentecost when we studied the birth of the church. Now, read further to discover that with God's presence dwelling in the hearts of believers, their ability to experience godly community was greatly enhanced.*

When the day of Pentecost came, they were all together in one place. Suddenly a sound like the blowing of a violent wind came from heaven and filled the whole house where they were sitting. They saw what seemed to be tongues of fire that separated and came to rest on each of them. All of them were filled with the Holy

Spirit and began to speak in other tongues as the Spirit enabled them.                                                                                    Acts 2:1–4

They devoted themselves to the apostles' teaching and to fellowship, to the breaking of bread and to prayer. Everyone was filled with awe at the many wonders and signs performed by the apostles. **All the believers were together and had everything in common.** They sold property and possessions to give to anyone who had need. Every day they continued to meet together in the temple courts. They broke bread in their homes and ate together with glad and sincere hearts, praising God and enjoying the favor of all the people. And the Lord added to their number daily those who were being saved.                                                   Acts 2:42–47

All the believers were one in heart and mind. No one claimed that any of their possessions was their own, but they shared everything they had. With great power the apostles continued to testify to the resurrection of the Lord Jesus. And God's grace was so powerfully at work in them all that there were no needy persons among them. For from time to time those who owned land or houses sold them, brought the money from the sales and put it at the apostles' feet, and it was distributed to anyone who had need.

Joseph, a Levite from Cyprus, whom the apostles called Barnabas (which means "son of encouragement"), sold a field he owned and brought the money and put it at the apostles' feet.
                                                                                    Acts 4:32–37

---

Imagine what it would have been like to be
a member of the early church after Pentecost.
Would you have wanted to be a part of that
community? Why or why not? In what ways should
our church today be like the early church?

---

## Marks of Biblical Community

*Biblical community encourages everyone to use their gifts, resources and time in order to accomplish the purposes of God. After the Israelites returned from captivity, they were rebuilding their lives. Nehemiah returned to lead the project of rebuild-ing the wall around Jerusalem to protect them from bullying by the surrounding nations. All the families—parents and chil-dren alike—were called to help with this massive and important project.*

I [Nehemiah] went to Jerusalem, and after staying there three days I set out during the night with a few others. I had not told anyone what my God had put in my heart to do for Jerusalem. There were no mounts with me except the one I was riding on.

By night I went out through the Valley Gate toward the Jackal Well and the Dung Gate, examining the walls of Jerusalem, which had been broken down, and its gates, which had been destroyed by fire. Then I moved on toward the Fountain Gate and the King's Pool, but there was not enough room for my mount to get through; so I went up the valley by night, examining the wall. Finally, I turned back and reentered through the Valley Gate. The officials did not know where I had gone or what I was doing, because as yet I had said nothing to the Jews or the priests or nobles or officials or any others who would be doing the work.

**Then I said to them, "You see the trouble we are in: Jeru-salem lies in ruins, and its gates have been burned with fire. Come, let us rebuild the wall of Jerusalem, and we will no lon-ger be in disgrace." I also told them about the gracious hand of my God on me and what the king had said to me.**

**They replied, "Let us start rebuilding." So they began this good work.**

But when Sanballat the Horonite, Tobiah the Ammonite official and Geshem the Arab heard about it, they mocked and ridiculed us. "What is this you are doing?" they asked. "Are you rebelling against the king?"

I answered them by saying, "The God of heaven will give us success. We his servants will start rebuilding, but as for you, you have no share in Jerusalem or any claim or historic right to it."

Eliashib the high priest and his fellow priests went to work and rebuilt the Sheep Gate. They dedicated it and set its doors in place, building as far as the Tower of the Hundred, which they dedicated, and as far as the Tower of Hananel. The men of Jericho built the adjoining section, and Zakkur son of Imri built next to them.

NEHEMIAH 2:11—3:2

*Nehemiah went on to describe how dozens of families worked together to rebuild the different sections of the wall.*

So the wall was completed on the twenty-fifth of Elul, in fifty-two days. NEHEMIAH 6:15 ⚷

*One of the main differences between the church and the rest of society is the call to live for others. Throughout the New Testament, Jesus' followers were urged to look out for one another. When the early Christians did this in faith, it irresistibly attracted outsiders to belong to the family of God. The practice of looking out for one another is a hallmark of true biblical community.*

For just as each of us has one body with many members, and these members do not all have the same function, so in Christ we, though many, form one body, and each member belongs to all the others. ROMANS 12:4–5

**Carry each other's burdens, and in this way you will fulfill the law of Christ.** GALATIANS 6:2

Be completely humble and gentle; be patient, **bearing with one another** in love. EPHESIANS 4:2

**Submit to one another** out of reverence for Christ.

EPHESIANS 5:21

*The calling among the early church to care for one another was also shown through simple hospitality—being welcoming. This way of showing love by having an open-door policy gave them a great sense of community and always left room for new people to belong, regardless of their station in life.*

As you read the remaining Scripture in this chapter, ponder
the emphasis and importance placed on hospitality.
Why do you think it was so important to the early church?
Is it still important today? Why or why not?

Keep on loving one another as brothers and sisters. **Do not forget to show hospitality to strangers, for by so doing some people have shown hospitality to angels without knowing it.** Continue to remember those in prison as if you were together with them in prison, and those who are mistreated as if you yourselves were suffering. HEBREWS 13:1–3

Through Jesus, therefore, let us continually offer to God a sacrifice of praise — the fruit of lips that openly profess his name. **And do not forget to do good and to share with others, for with such sacrifices God is pleased.** HEBREWS 13:15–16

That which was from the beginning, which we have heard, which we have seen with our eyes, which we have looked at and our hands have touched — this we proclaim concerning the Word of life. The life appeared; we have seen it and testify to it, and we proclaim to you the eternal life, which was with the Father and has appeared to us. We proclaim to you what we have seen and heard, so that you also may have fellowship with us. And our fellowship is with the Father and with his Son, Jesus Christ. We write this to make our joy complete.

This is the message we have heard from him and declare to you: God is light; in him there is no darkness at all. If we claim to have fellowship with him and yet walk in the darkness, we lie and do not live out the truth. **But if we walk in the light, as he is in the light, we have fellowship with one another, and the blood of Jesus, his Son, purifies us from all sin.** 1 JOHN 1:1–7

Dear friends, I am not writing you a new command but an old one, which you have had since the beginning. This old command is the message you have heard. Yet I am writing you a new command;

its truth is seen in him and in you, because the darkness is passing and the true light is already shining.

Anyone who claims to be in the light but hates a brother or sister is still in the darkness. Anyone who loves their brother and sister lives in the light, and there is nothing in them to make them stumble. But anyone who hates a brother or sister is in the darkness and walks around in the darkness. They do not know where they are going, because the darkness has blinded them.     1 JOHN 2:7–11

**This is how we know what love is: Jesus Christ laid down his life for us. And we ought to lay down our lives for our brothers and sisters. If anyone has material possessions and sees a brother or sister in need but has no pity on them, how can the love of God be in that person? Dear children, let us not love with words or speech but with actions and in truth.**  1 JOHN 3:16–18

---

The passages in this chapter from God's Word place a high value on Christian fellowship. How important is fellowship to you right now? What difference is it making in your life?

---

## WHAT WE BELIEVE

*We were created by God for community. Given our sinful nature, it is essential for God to be at the center of that community in order for us to have real fellowship. He was in the garden with Adam and Eve; he dwelled in the tabernacle and temple with Israel; he literally walked among the first disciples for more than 30 years. Since the inception of the church until now, God dwells not in a temple built by human hands, but in a new temple—the lives of his followers. As we welcome the presence of God's Spirit in and among us, we grow in true biblical community, marked by caring for one another and open hospitality. As we fellowship with other Christians, it not only becomes the rich experience we were created for, but it also sends out an "aroma" that draws others in. So make biblical community a priority in order to accomplish God's purposes in your life, in the lives of others and in the world.*

CHAPTER

## 17

# Spiritual Gifts

———— KEY QUESTION ————

What gifts and skills has God given me to serve others?

———— KEY IDEA ————

I know my spiritual gifts and
use them to fulfill God's purposes.

———— KEY VERSE ————

For just as each of us has one body with many members,
and these members do not all have the same function,
so in Christ we, though many, form one body, and each
member belongs to all the others. We have different gifts,
according to the grace given to each of us.

*Romans 12:4–6*

OUR MAP

*God has used two primary communities to accomplish his grand purpose to redeem humanity and restore his vision of being with them forever. In the Old Testament that community was Israel. In the New Testament that community was (and continues to be) the church. God equipped the individual members of these communities with the skills and gifts needed to accomplish his purpose and plan. It is up to each individual to acknowledge and use their gift for God's intended purposes. Then, collectively, the community must decide to work together in unity. When this happens, amazing things are accomplished.*

*In this chapter you will be reading Scripture that will help you understand more about spiritual gifts, including:*

- *Spiritual Gifts in the Old Testament*
- *The Purpose and Function of Spiritual Gifts*
- *Stewardship of Our Gifts*

## SPIRITUAL GIFTS IN THE OLD TESTAMENT

*Although the term "spiritual gift" isn't found in the Old Testament, we see clear evidence of the Holy Spirit working through people during this time. The unique empowering of the Spirit was given to individuals (oftentimes only temporarily) primarily to enable them to carry out the special responsibilities God had given them.*

*Occasionally in the Old Testament, spiritual gifts were used for the sake of outsiders (non-Israelites). In these situations, God used miraculous signs to reveal himself as the one true God. For example, while the Israelites were living in exile in Babylon, God empowered Daniel with the ability to interpret a complex dream for King Nebuchadnezzar.*

In the second year of his reign, Nebuchadnezzar had dreams; his mind was troubled and he could not sleep. So the king summoned the magicians, enchanters, sorcerers and astrologers to tell him what he had dreamed. When they came in and stood before the king, he said to them, "I have had a dream that troubles me and I want to know what it means."

Then the astrologers answered the king, "May the king live forever! Tell your servants the dream, and we will interpret it."

The king replied to the astrologers, "This is what I have firmly decided: If you do not tell me what my dream was and interpret it, I will have you cut into pieces and your houses turned into piles of rubble. But if you tell me the dream and explain it, you will receive from me gifts and rewards and great honor. So tell me the dream and interpret it for me."

Once more they replied, "Let the king tell his servants the dream, and we will interpret it."

Then the king answered, "I am certain that you are trying to gain time, because you realize that this is what I have firmly decided: If you do not tell me the dream, there is only one penalty for you. You have conspired to tell me misleading and wicked things, hoping the situation will change. So then, tell me the dream, and I will know that you can interpret it for me."

The astrologers answered the king, "There is no one on earth who can do what the king asks! No king, however great and mighty, has ever asked such a thing of any magician or enchanter or astrologer. What the king asks is too difficult. No one can reveal it to the king except the gods, and they do not live among humans."

This made the king so angry and furious that he ordered the execution of all the wise men of Babylon. So the decree was issued to put the wise men to death, and men were sent to look for Daniel and his friends to put them to death.

When Arioch, the commander of the king's guard, had gone out to put to death the wise men of Babylon, Daniel spoke to him with wisdom and tact. He asked the king's officer, "Why did the king issue such a harsh decree?" Arioch then explained the matter to Daniel. At this, Daniel went in to the king and asked for time, so that he might interpret the dream for him.

Then Daniel returned to his house and explained the matter to his friends Hananiah, Mishael and Azariah. He urged them to plead for mercy from the God of heaven concerning this mystery, so that he and his friends might not be executed with the rest of the wise men of Babylon. During the night the mystery was revealed to Daniel in a vision. Then Daniel praised the God of heaven and said:

"Praise be to the name of God for ever and ever;
   wisdom and power are his.
He changes times and seasons;
   he deposes kings and raises up others.
He gives wisdom to the wise
   and knowledge to the discerning.
He reveals deep and hidden things;
   he knows what lies in darkness,
   and light dwells with him.
I thank and praise you, God of my ancestors:
   You have given me wisdom and power,
you have made known to me what we asked of you,
   you have made known to us the dream of the king."

Then Daniel went to Arioch, whom the king had appointed to execute the wise men of Babylon, and said to him, "Do not execute the wise men of Babylon. Take me to the king, and I will interpret his dream for him."

Arioch took Daniel to the king at once and said, "I have found a man among the exiles from Judah who can tell the king what his dream means."

The king asked Daniel (also called Belteshazzar), "Are you able to tell me what I saw in my dream and interpret it?"

**Daniel replied, "No wise man, enchanter, magician or diviner can explain to the king the mystery he has asked about, but there is a God in heaven who reveals mysteries.** He has shown King Nebuchadnezzar what will happen in days to come. Your dream and the visions that passed through your mind as you were lying in bed are these:

"As Your Majesty was lying there, your mind turned to things to come, and the revealer of mysteries showed you what is going to happen. As for me, this mystery has been revealed to me, not because I have greater wisdom than anyone else alive, but so that Your Majesty may know the interpretation and that you may understand what went through your mind.

"Your Majesty looked, and there before you stood a large statue — an enormous, dazzling statue, awesome in appearance. The head of the statue was made of pure gold, its chest and arms of silver, its belly and thighs of bronze, its legs of iron, its feet partly of iron and partly of baked clay. While you were watching, a rock was cut out, but not by human hands. It struck the statue on its feet of iron and clay and smashed them. Then the iron, the clay, the bronze, the silver and the gold were all broken to pieces and became like chaff on a threshing floor in the summer. The wind swept them away without leaving a trace. But the rock that struck the statue became a huge mountain and filled the whole earth.

"This was the dream, and now we will interpret it to the king. Your Majesty, you are the king of kings. The God of heaven has given you dominion and power and might and glory; in your hands he has placed all mankind and the beasts of the field and the birds in the sky. Wherever they live, he has made you ruler over them all. You are that head of gold.

"After you, another kingdom will arise, inferior to yours. Next, a third kingdom, one of bronze, will rule over the whole earth. Finally, there will be a fourth kingdom, strong as iron — for iron breaks and smashes everything — and as iron breaks things to pieces, so it will crush and break all the others. Just as you saw that the feet and toes were partly of baked clay and partly of iron, so this will be a divided kingdom; yet it will have some of the strength of iron in it, even as you saw iron mixed with clay. As the toes were partly iron and partly clay, so this kingdom will be partly strong and partly brittle. And just as you saw the iron mixed with baked clay, so the people will be a mixture and will not remain united, any more than iron mixes with clay.

"In the time of those kings, the God of heaven will set up a kingdom that will never be destroyed, nor will it be left to another people. It will crush all those kingdoms and bring them to an end, but it will itself endure forever. This is the meaning of the vision of the rock cut out of a mountain, but not by human hands — a rock that broke the iron, the bronze, the clay, the silver and the gold to pieces.

"The great God has shown the king what will take place in the future. The dream is true and its interpretation is trustworthy."

Then King Nebuchadnezzar fell prostrate before Daniel and paid him honor and ordered that an offering and incense be presented to him. **The king said to Daniel, "Surely your God is the**

God of gods and the Lord of kings and a revealer of mysteries,
for you were able to reveal this mystery." DANIEL 2:1–47 ⚷

---

What was Daniel's spiritual gift? Why was it important
that Daniel acknowledge his gift was from the Lord?

---

## THE PURPOSE AND FUNCTION OF SPIRITUAL GIFTS

*Spiritual gifts are given with a purpose. God wants to redeem
this broken world, and he has chosen to use us, the church, to do
it. In the Old Testament, the Holy Spirit temporarily came upon
believers for specific tasks. In the New Testament, the Holy Spirit
permanently indwells believers and gives spiritual gifts to everyone. Since the New Testament refers to specific gifts, it seems
safe to assume that God wants us to identify our gifts in order to
best use them.*

---

As you read the following collection of New Testament letters
on spiritual gifts, highlight or write down which gift(s)
you believe you possess. Choose a family member or friend
and do the same for them. Let them know what you think their
gift is and how you have been positively impacted by it.

---

**For just as each of us has one body with many members, and
these members do not all have the same function, so in Christ
we, though many, form one body, and each member belongs to
all the others. We have different gifts, according to the grace
given to each of us.** If your gift is prophesying, then prophesy in
accordance with your faith; if it is serving, then serve; if it is teaching, then teach; if it is to encourage, then give encouragement; if it
is giving, then give generously; if it is to lead, do it diligently; if it is
to show mercy, do it cheerfully. ROMANS 12:4–8

⚷ **There are different kinds of gifts, but the same Spirit distributes them. There are different kinds of service, but the
same Lord. There are different kinds of working, but in all of
them and in everyone it is the same God at work.**

Now to each one the manifestation of the Spirit is given for the common good. To one there is given through the Spirit a message of wisdom, to another a message of knowledge by means of the same Spirit, to another faith by the same Spirit, to another gifts of healing by that one Spirit, to another miraculous powers, to another prophecy, to another distinguishing between spirits, to another speaking in different kinds of tongues, and to still another the interpretation of tongues. All these are the work of one and the same Spirit, and he distributes them to each one, just as he determines.

Just as a body, though one, has many parts, but all its many parts form one body, so it is with Christ. For we were all baptized by one Spirit so as to form one body — whether Jews or Gentiles, slave or free — and we were all given the one Spirit to drink. Even so the body is not made up of one part but of many.

Now if the foot should say, "Because I am not a hand, I do not belong to the body," it would not for that reason stop being part of the body. And if the ear should say, "Because I am not an eye, I do not belong to the body," it would not for that reason stop being part of the body. If the whole body were an eye, where would the sense of hearing be? If the whole body were an ear, where would the sense of smell be? But in fact God has placed the parts in the body, every one of them, just as he wanted them to be. If they were all one part, where would the body be? As it is, there are many parts, but one body.

The eye cannot say to the hand, "I don't need you!" And the head cannot say to the feet, "I don't need you!" On the contrary, those parts of the body that seem to be weaker are indispensable, and the parts that we think are less honorable we treat with special honor. And the parts that are unpresentable are treated with special modesty, while our presentable parts need no special treatment. But God has put the body together, giving greater honor to the parts that lacked it, so that there should be no division in the body, but that its parts should have equal concern for each other. If one part suffers, every part suffers with it; if one part is honored, every part rejoices with it.

Now you are the body of Christ, and each one of you is a part of it. And God has placed in the church first of all apostles, second prophets, third teachers, then miracles, then gifts of healing, of helping, of guidance, and of different kinds of tongues.

1 CORINTHIANS 12:4–28 🔑

---

Was there a time when you had an injury, even
a small one, and it affected your whole body? Thinking
about that, why does the body of Christ need you to use your
spiritual gift, even if you think it's not very important?

---

## STEWARDSHIP OF OUR GIFTS

*We are meant to use our spiritual gifts to benefit the body of Christ. Jesus used bags of gold to graphically illustrate this principle for his disciples. Like gold that should be invested, our spiritual gifts should be used for the good of others, multiplying the blessing as we share them according to God's purposes.*

"It will be like a man going on a journey, who called his servants and entrusted his wealth to them. To one he gave five bags of gold, to another two bags, and to another one bag, each according to his ability. Then he went on his journey. The man who had received five bags of gold went at once and put his money to work and gained five bags more. So also, the one with two bags of gold gained two more. But the man who had received one bag went off, dug a hole in the ground and hid his master's money.

"After a long time the master of those servants returned and settled accounts with them. The man who had received five bags of gold brought the other five. 'Master,' he said, 'you entrusted me with five bags of gold. See, I have gained five more.'

**"His master replied, 'Well done, good and faithful servant! You have been faithful with a few things; I will put you in charge of many things. Come and share your master's happiness!'**

"The man with two bags of gold also came. 'Master,' he said, 'you entrusted me with two bags of gold; see, I have gained two more.'

"His master replied, 'Well done, good and faithful servant! You have been faithful with a few things; I will put you in charge of many things. Come and share your master's happiness!'

"Then the man who had received one bag of gold came. 'Master,' he said, 'I knew that you are a hard man, harvesting where you have not sown and gathering where you have not scattered seed. So I was afraid and went out and hid your gold in the ground. See, here is what belongs to you.'

"His master replied, 'You wicked, lazy servant! So you knew that I harvest where I have not sown and gather where I have not scattered seed? Well then, you should have put my money on deposit with the bankers, so that when I returned I would have received it back with interest.

" 'So take the bag of gold from him and give it to the one who has ten bags. For whoever has will be given more, and they will have an abundance. Whoever does not have, even what they have will be taken from them. And throw that worthless servant outside, into the darkness, where there will be weeping and gnashing of teeth.'"                                         MATTHEW 25:14–30

---

If the Holy Spirit lives in you, you have received a spiritual gift. Have you been more like the faithful servant or the lazy servant in the way you have used your spiritual gift? What do you think this parable is saying will happen to people who let their spiritual gift go unused?

---

*Just as an engine requires clean gasoline to run smoothly, so also our gifts must be fueled with pure and loving intentions. Spiritual gifts that are powered by selfish ambition and pride will sputter and fail.*

The end of all things is near. Therefore be alert and of sober mind so that you may pray. Above all, love each other deeply, because love covers over a multitude of sins. Offer hospitality to one another without grumbling. **Each of you should use whatever gift you have received to serve others, as faithful stewards of God's grace in its various forms.** If anyone speaks, they should do so as one who speaks the very words of God. If anyone serves, they should do so with the strength God provides, so that in all things God may be praised through Jesus Christ. To him be the glory and the power for ever and ever. Amen.          1 PETER 4:7–11

What happens when spiritual gifts are exercised without love? (An example of hospitality without love is given by Peter.) Why is it so important to be driven by love when using your spiritual gifts?

## WHAT WE BELIEVE

*The one true God has partnered with his people to accomplish his purposes on earth. The third person of the Trinity, the Holy Spirit, is the driver of this initiative. In the Old Testament, the Holy Spirit only indwelled select individuals for a period of time to accomplish God's purposes. In the New Testament, Jesus promised the indwelling of the Holy Spirit for all believers. The Spirit deposits gifts in every believer for the express purpose of building God's kingdom on earth. We do not all have the same gift. In unity we are to celebrate the giftedness of others and work together to accomplish God's will in our lives together and in the world.*

CHAPTER

18

# Offering My Time

—————— KEY QUESTION ——————

How do I best use my time to serve God and others?

—————— KEY IDEA ——————

I offer my time to fulfill God's purposes.

—————— KEY VERSE ——————

Whatever you do, whether in word or deed,
do it all in the name of the Lord Jesus, giving
thanks to God the Father through him.
*Colossians 3:17*

*Believe is an action verb. Whatever we believe in our hearts will be expressed in the way we live. Beliefs such as the church, compassion and stewardship naturally lead to the practice of offering our time to God to accomplish his purposes. Every time we act on this key spiritual practice, even if our hearts are not totally committed, it helps to drive these beliefs from our heads to our hearts. So we act out our beliefs in faith.*

*In this chapter you will be reading Scripture centered on the following key topics:*

- *Offering God Our Time*
- *Serving God's Purposes*
- *Managing Our Time*
- *The Rewards of Offering Our Time to God*

## OFFERING GOD OUR TIME

*In reality, we cannot talk about "our" time since all time belongs to God. Every moment we have is a gift from him. Therefore, we are called to use that time to honor the Lord. The prophet Jonah learned this the hard way. God called him to redirect his time from the popular job of serving Israel to the unpopular assignment of traveling to Nineveh to give Israel's enemy a chance to repent and be saved by God. Needless to say, Jonah was not committed to the call.*

The word of the LORD came to Jonah son of Amittai: "Go to the great city of Nineveh and preach against it, because its wickedness has come up before me."

But Jonah ran away from the LORD and headed for Tarshish. He went down to Joppa, where he found a ship bound for that port. After paying the fare, he went aboard and sailed for Tarshish to flee from the LORD.

Then the LORD sent a great wind on the sea, and such a violent storm arose that the ship threatened to break up. All the sailors were afraid and each cried out to his own god. And they threw the cargo into the sea to lighten the ship.

But Jonah had gone below deck, where he lay down and fell into a deep sleep. The captain went to him and said, "How can you sleep? Get up and call on your god! Maybe he will take notice of us so that we will not perish."

Then the sailors said to each other, "Come, let us cast lots to find out who is responsible for this calamity." They cast lots and the lot fell on Jonah. So they asked him, "Tell us, who is responsible for making all this trouble for us? What kind of work do you do? Where do you come from? What is your country? From what people are you?"

He answered, "I am a Hebrew and I worship the LORD, the God of heaven, who made the sea and the dry land."

This terrified them and they asked, "What have you done?" (They knew he was running away from the LORD, because he had already told them so.)

The sea was getting rougher and rougher. So they asked him, "What should we do to you to make the sea calm down for us?"

"Pick me up and throw me into the sea," he replied, "and it will become calm. I know that it is my fault that this great storm has come upon you."

Instead, the men did their best to row back to land. But they could not, for the sea grew even wilder than before. Then they cried out to the LORD, "Please, LORD, do not let us die for taking this man's life. Do not hold us accountable for killing an innocent man, for you, LORD, have done as you pleased." Then they took Jonah and threw him overboard, and the raging sea grew calm. At this the men greatly feared the LORD, and they offered a sacrifice to the LORD and made vows to him.

Now the LORD provided a huge fish to swallow Jonah, and Jonah was in the belly of the fish three days and three nights.

From inside the fish Jonah prayed to the LORD his God. He said:

> "In my distress I called to the LORD,
>     and he answered me.
> From deep in the realm of the dead I called for help,
>     and you listened to my cry.
> You hurled me into the depths,
>     into the very heart of the seas,
>     and the currents swirled about me;

all your waves and breakers
    swept over me.
I said, 'I have been banished
    from your sight;
yet I will look again
    toward your holy temple.'
The engulfing waters threatened me,
    the deep surrounded me;
    seaweed was wrapped around my head.
To the roots of the mountains I sank down;
    the earth beneath barred me in forever.
But you, LORD my God,
    brought my life up from the pit.

"When my life was ebbing away,
    I remembered you, LORD,
and my prayer rose to you,
    to your holy temple.

**"Those who cling to worthless idols**
    **turn away from God's love for them.**
**But I, with shouts of grateful praise,**
    **will sacrifice to you.**
**What I have vowed I will make good.**
    **I will say, 'Salvation comes from the LORD.'"**

And the LORD commanded the fish, and it vomited Jonah onto dry land.                                              JONAH 1:1—2:10

---

Do you think God still puts people "in the
belly of a fish" when they ignore his call?

---

## SERVING GOD'S PURPOSES

*Not only are we to give our time to God, but we are also to use that time to serve his purposes, which can mean many different things. Like Jonah, God's people often needed reminders about this. When the first exiles returned to Judah from captivity in Babylon, one of their first priorities was to rebuild the temple and restore worship to the one true God. In 536 BC, under the leadership of Zerubbabel, the building project began. When opposition from the Samaritans and other neighbors intensified, the people became discouraged and the building came to a complete halt. For ten years the project laid dormant. The prophet Haggai delivered a chilling and effective message from God encouraging the people of God to reconsider how they prioritized their time.*

In the second year of King Darius, on the first day of the sixth month, the word of the LORD came through the prophet Haggai to Zerubbabel son of Shealtiel, governor of Judah, and to Joshua son of Jozadak, the high priest:

This is what the LORD Almighty says: "These people say, 'The time has not yet come to rebuild the LORD's house.'"

**Then the word of the LORD came through the prophet Haggai: "Is it a time for you yourselves to be living in your paneled houses, while this house remains a ruin?"**

**Now this is what the LORD Almighty says: "Give careful thought to your ways.** You have planted much, but harvested little. You eat, but never have enough. You drink, but never have your fill. You put on clothes, but are not warm. You earn wages, only to put them in a purse with holes in it."

This is what the LORD Almighty says: "Give careful thought to your ways. Go up into the mountains and bring down timber and build my house, so that I may take pleasure in it and be honored," says the LORD. "You expected much, but see, it turned out to be little. What you brought home, I blew away. Why?" declares the LORD Almighty. "Because of my house, which remains a ruin, while each of you is busy with your own house. Therefore, because of you the heavens have withheld their dew and the earth its crops. I called for a drought on the fields and the mountains, on the grain, the new wine, the olive oil and everything else the ground produces, on people and livestock, and on all the labor of your hands."

Then Zerubbabel son of Shealtiel, Joshua son of Jozadak, the high priest, and the whole remnant of the people obeyed the voice of the LORD their God and the message of the prophet Haggai, because the LORD their God had sent him. And the people feared the LORD.

Then Haggai, the LORD's messenger, gave this message of the LORD to the people: "I am with you," declares the LORD. So the LORD stirred up the spirit of Zerubbabel son of Shealtiel, governor of Judah, and the spirit of Joshua son of Jozadak, the high priest, and the spirit of the whole remnant of the people. They came and began to work on the house of the LORD Almighty, their God, on the twenty-fourth day of the sixth month.          HAGGAI 1:1–15A ⊙—ᴛᴛ

---

In light of what you have learned about the Old Testament temple from previous chapters, why did God want the returning captives to build his house before they built their own?

---

*One person who never needed reminding of the fact that his time was to be dedicated to God was God's Son, Jesus. After attending the Festival of Passover with his earthly parents, Jesus made the decision to stay a little longer and spend some time in the house of his heavenly Father. Even at the young age of twelve, Jesus understood how best to use his time.*

⊙—ᴛᴛ Every year Jesus' parents went to Jerusalem for the Festival of the Passover. When he was twelve years old, they went up to the festival, according to the custom. After the festival was over, while his parents were returning home, the boy Jesus stayed behind in Jerusalem, but they were unaware of it. Thinking he was in their company, they traveled on for a day. Then they began looking for him among their relatives and friends. When they did not find him, they went back to Jerusalem to look for him. After three days they found him in the temple courts, sitting among the teachers, listening to them and asking them questions. Everyone who heard him was amazed at his understanding and his answers. When his parents saw him, they were astonished. His mother said to him, "Son, why have you treated us like this? Your father and I have been anxiously searching for you."

**"Why were you searching for me?" he asked. "Didn't you know I had to be in my Father's house?"** But they did not understand what he was saying to them.

Then he went down to Nazareth with them and was obedient to them. But his mother treasured all these things in her heart. And Jesus grew in wisdom and stature, and in favor with God and man.                                                          Luke 2:41–52 🔑

## Managing Our Time

*God desires for us to be refreshed and renewed to best serve him and others. But in order to experience this, we must manage our time according to God's design for the rhythm and balance of life. God gave the Israelites a command and a lesson regarding the Sabbath day of rest and collecting manna. Although Christians today disagree concerning whether or not Sabbath-keeping is obligatory, God clearly designed people with the need for regular and deliberate rest.*

---

As you read the passages in this section, write down
any practical principles you find regarding managing time.

---

The Lord said to Moses, "I have heard the grumbling of the Israelites. Tell them, 'At twilight you will eat meat, and in the morning you will be filled with bread. Then you will know that I am the Lord your God.'"

That evening quail came and covered the camp, and in the morning there was a layer of dew around the camp. When the dew was gone, thin flakes like frost on the ground appeared on the desert floor. When the Israelites saw it, they said to each other, "What is it?" For they did not know what it was.

Moses said to them, "It is the bread the Lord has given you to eat. This is what the Lord has commanded: 'Everyone is to gather as much as they need. Take an omer for each person you have in your tent.'"

**The Israelites did as they were told; some gathered much, some little. And when they measured it by the omer, the one who gathered much did not have too much, and the one who**

gathered little did not have too little. Everyone had gathered just as much as they needed.

Then Moses said to them, "No one is to keep any of it until morning."

However, some of them paid no attention to Moses; they kept part of it until morning, but it was full of maggots and began to smell. So Moses was angry with them.

Each morning everyone gathered as much as they needed, and when the sun grew hot, it melted away. On the sixth day, they gathered twice as much — two omers for each person — and the leaders of the community came and reported this to Moses. He said to them, "This is what the LORD commanded: 'Tomorrow is to be a day of sabbath rest, a holy sabbath to the LORD. So bake what you want to bake and boil what you want to boil. Save whatever is left and keep it until morning.'"

So they saved it until morning, as Moses commanded, and it did not stink or get maggots in it. "Eat it today," Moses said, "because today is a sabbath to the LORD. You will not find any of it on the ground today. Six days you are to gather it, but on the seventh day, the Sabbath, there will not be any."

**Nevertheless, some of the people went out on the seventh day to gather it, but they found none. Then the LORD said to Moses, "How long will you refuse to keep my commands and my instructions? Bear in mind that the LORD has given you the Sabbath; that is why on the sixth day he gives you bread for two days. Everyone is to stay where they are on the seventh day; no one is to go out." So the people rested on the seventh day.**

EXODUS 16:11–30

*Jesus kept God as his focus in everything he did, including how he managed his time. When Jesus' ministry was in full swing, the demands on his schedule were intense. At this time in his journey, his brothers did not yet believe he was really the Messiah. They sarcastically suggested that Jesus should go to Judea for a major Jewish festival to unveil his "campaign." Jesus informed them of an important principle of his life—he managed his priorities according to the timing of God the Father.*

After this, Jesus went around in Galilee. He did not want to go about in Judea because the Jewish leaders there were looking for a way to kill him. But when the Jewish Festival of Tabernacles was near, Jesus' brothers said to him, "Leave Galilee and go to Judea, so that your disciples there may see the works you do. No one who wants to become a public figure acts in secret. Since you are doing these things, show yourself to the world." For even his own brothers did not believe in him.

**Therefore Jesus told them, "My time is not yet here; for you any time will do.** The world cannot hate you, but it hates me because I testify that its works are evil. You go to the festival. I am not going up to this festival, because my time has not yet fully come." After he had said this, he stayed in Galilee.

However, after his brothers had left for the festival, he went also, not publicly, but in secret. Now at the festival the Jewish leaders were watching for Jesus and asking, "Where is he?"

Among the crowds there was widespread whispering about him. Some said, "He is a good man."

Others replied, "No, he deceives the people." But no one would say anything publicly about him for fear of the leaders.

Not until halfway through the festival did Jesus go up to the temple courts and begin to teach. The Jews there were amazed and asked, "How did this man get such learning without having been taught?"

Jesus answered, "My teaching is not my own. It comes from the one who sent me." JOHN 7:1–16

## The Rewards of Offering Our Time to God

*When we give our time to others in order to serve the purposes of God, especially to help those who cannot pay us back, God not only takes notice but also may reward us greatly.*

---

As you read the rest of this chapter look
for the answer to this question: How does God
reward those who use their time to do what
he has asked them to do?

"Then the King will say to those on his right, 'Come, you who are blessed by my Father; take your inheritance, the kingdom prepared for you since the creation of the world. For I was hungry and you gave me something to eat, I was thirsty and you gave me something to drink, I was a stranger and you invited me in, I needed clothes and you clothed me, I was sick and you looked after me, I was in prison and you came to visit me.'

"Then the righteous will answer him, 'Lord, when did we see you hungry and feed you, or thirsty and give you something to drink? When did we see you a stranger and invite you in, or needing clothes and clothe you? When did we see you sick or in prison and go to visit you?'

**"The King will reply, 'Truly I tell you, whatever you did for one of the least of these brothers and sisters of mine, you did for me.'"** MATTHEW 25:34–40

**Be very careful, then, how you live — not as unwise but as wise, making the most of every opportunity, because the days are evil. Therefore do not be foolish, but understand what the Lord's will is.** EPHESIANS 5:15–17

Do not be deceived: God cannot be mocked. A man reaps what he sows. Whoever sows to please their flesh, from the flesh will reap destruction; whoever sows to please the Spirit, from the Spirit will reap eternal life. **Let us not become weary in doing good, for at the proper time we will reap a harvest if we do not give up.** Therefore, as we have opportunity, let us do good to all people, especially to those who belong to the family of believers. GALATIANS 6:7–10

---

Our key verse, found at the beginning of the chapter, says "whatever you do ... do it all in the name of the Lord Jesus." Can it really mean "whatever" and "all"? How?

---

## WHAT WE BELIEVE

*Jonah nailed it on the head when confronted by the sailors about the cause of the storm. He answered, "I am a Hebrew and I worship the LORD, the God of heaven, who made the sea and the dry land" (Jonah 1:9). Jonah worshiped the one true God and knew that God made everything and everything belonged to him. This belief drives our obedience in offering God our time to accomplish his purposes. As we seek to serve God, we would do well to keep on our minds God's words through the prophet Haggai: "Give careful thought to your ways" (Haggai 1:5). The goal, found in the key verse, Colossians 3:17, is not to offer more time to God but to repurpose everything we do for his glory and honor. The rewards from God make it worth the effort for those who give themselves faithfully to this spiritual practice.*

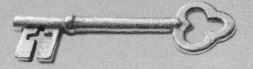

# ACT

## CHAPTER

### 19

# Giving My Resources

───── KEY QUESTION ─────

How do I best use my resources
to serve God and others?

───── KEY IDEA ─────

I give my resources to fulfill God's purposes.

───── KEY VERSE ─────

Since you excel in everything — in faith,
in speech, in knowledge, in complete earnestness
and in the love we have kindled in you — see that
you also excel in this grace of giving.

*2 Corinthians 8:7*

**OUR MAP**

*The beliefs that cause us to offer our time to God to fulfill his purposes—the church, compassion and stewardship—also drive us to give our resources. Everything we have belongs to God, and we have received clear instruction from the Bible to offer our time and give our resources to help those in need. We also recognize that our God is the one true God who loves us and has provided a way into a relationship with him as his children now and forever. Because of this, we surrender what rightfully belongs to him as an act of worship.*

*In this chapter you will be reading Scriptures from both the Old and New Testaments that address these topics:*

- *Giving Tithes and Offerings*
- *Advice from Wise Men*
- *Teachings from Jesus on Money and Giving*
- *Generosity in Action*

## GIVING TITHES AND OFFERINGS

*Throughout the Old Testament, God's people gave back to him one tenth (or 10 percent) of all their agricultural produce and personal income. This principle is called tithing. Giving a tithe started as a non-religious, political tradition in the ancient world where giving a 10 percent tax (a tithe) to the king was customary. This offering demonstrated allegiance to the king and his kingdom. When we give a tenth of our income to God's purposes, we declare our allegiance to God and his kingdom.*

*It is evident from many examples in the Bible that our offerings to God need not be confined to our money but can extend to our possessions, skills, labor, creativity and time. Remarkably, at a point in Israel's history when the Israelites were at their most vulnerable (wandering in the wilderness as nomads), they demonstrated their greatest generosity. God asked Moses to build a place called the tabernacle for him to dwell with his people. In order for this to happen, God's people needed to contribute their treasures and talents. Their generous response was so overwhelming that Moses had to tell them to stop bringing their gifts for the tabernacle.*

Find all the times the word "willing" is used in the story below.
Why is a willing heart so important to God?

Everyone who was willing and whose heart moved them came and brought an offering to the LORD for the work on the tent of meeting, for all its service, and for the sacred garments. All who were willing, men and women alike, came and brought gold jewelry of all kinds: brooches, earrings, rings and ornaments. They all presented their gold as a wave offering to the LORD. Everyone who had blue, purple or scarlet yarn or fine linen, or goat hair, ram skins dyed red or the other durable leather brought them. Those presenting an offering of silver or bronze brought it as an offering to the LORD, and everyone who had acacia wood for any part of the work brought it. Every skilled woman spun with her hands and brought what she had spun — blue, purple or scarlet yarn or fine linen. And all the women who were willing and had the skill spun the goat hair. The leaders brought onyx stones and other gems to be mounted on the ephod and breastpiece. They also brought spices and olive oil for the light and for the anointing oil and for the fragrant incense. All the Israelite men and women who were willing brought to the LORD freewill offerings for all the work the LORD through Moses had commanded them to do.

EXODUS 35:21–29

They received from Moses all the offerings the Israelites had brought to carry out the work of constructing the sanctuary. And the people continued to bring freewill offerings morning after morning. So all the skilled workers who were doing all the work on the sanctuary left what they were doing and said to Moses, "The people are bringing more than enough for doing the work the LORD commanded to be done."

**Then Moses gave an order and they sent this word throughout the camp: "No man or woman is to make anything else as an offering for the sanctuary." And so the people were restrained from bringing more, because what they already had was more than enough to do all the work.** EXODUS 36:3–7

## ADVICE FROM WISE MEN

*Giving away our money and resources is beneficial not only for the recipients but also for us. When giving to God's purposes becomes part of our regular spending habits, we honor God and deny personal greed. The writers of the book of Proverbs offered the following words of wisdom.*

---

As you read the Scripture in this section,
which piece of advice speaks most clearly
to you right now?

---

Honor the LORD with your wealth,
    with the firstfruits of all your crops;
then your barns will be filled to overflowing,
    and your vats will brim over with new wine.

PROVERBS 3:9–10

One person gives freely, yet gains even more;
    another withholds unduly, but comes to poverty.

**A generous person will prosper;**
    **whoever refreshes others will be refreshed.**

PROVERBS 11:24–25

Those who trust in their riches will fall,
    but the righteous will thrive like a green leaf.

PROVERBS 11:28

*Solomon, one of the writers of Proverbs and the son of King David, accumulated immense wealth during his lifetime. In the book of Ecclesiastes, traditionally considered to be written by Solomon, he reflects on his life and shares his words of wisdom with us regarding the dangers of wealth. Money itself is not evil, but the love of money can lead to sin. More wealth does not mean more satisfaction in life. To avoid falling victim to money's seductive lure, we are to use what we have for the Lord.*

Whoever loves money never has enough;
    whoever loves wealth is never satisfied with their
        income.
This too is meaningless.

As goods increase,
    so do those who consume them.
And what benefit are they to the owners
    except to feast their eyes on them?

The sleep of a laborer is sweet,
    whether they eat little or much,
but as for the rich, their abundance
    permits them no sleep.

I have seen a grievous evil under the sun:

wealth hoarded to the harm of its owners,
    or wealth lost through some misfortune,
so that when they have children
    there is nothing left for them to inherit.
Everyone comes naked from their mother's womb,
    and as everyone comes, so they depart.
They take nothing from their toil
    that they can carry in their hands.

This too is a grievous evil:

As everyone comes, so they depart,
    and what do they gain,
    since they toil for the wind?
All their days they eat in darkness,
    with great frustration, affliction and anger.

This is what I have observed to be good: that it is appropriate for a person to eat, to drink and to find satisfaction in their toilsome labor under the sun during the few days of life God has given them — for this is their lot. **Moreover, when God gives someone wealth and possessions, and the ability to enjoy them, to accept their lot and be happy in their toil — this is a gift of God. They seldom reflect on the days of their life, because God keeps them occupied with gladness of heart.** Ecclesiastes 5:10–20

*At the birth of Jesus, wise men (Magi) came to visit him with gifts. They were likely astrologers from Persia, southern Arabia or Mesopotamia who had been anticipating the arrival of the "king of the Jews" for some time. Their advice for us doesn't come from their lips as much as from their actions. They gave him months of their time as they traveled from a faraway land to see him. They were honored men, yet they humbled themselves and bowed their knees to give their worship to Jesus. And they gave him valuable treasures from their land, costly gifts that were the best they had to give.*

After Jesus was born in Bethlehem in Judea, during the time of King Herod, Magi from the east came to Jerusalem and asked, "Where is the one who has been born king of the Jews? We saw his star when it rose and have come to worship him."

When King Herod heard this he was disturbed, and all Jerusalem with him. When he had called together all the people's chief priests and teachers of the law, he asked them where the Messiah was to be born. "In Bethlehem in Judea," they replied, "for this is what the prophet has written:

> "'But you, Bethlehem, in the land of Judah,
>     are by no means least among the rulers of Judah;
> for out of you will come a ruler
>     who will shepherd my people Israel.'"

Then Herod called the Magi secretly and found out from them the exact time the star had appeared. He sent them to Bethlehem and said, "Go and search carefully for the child. As soon as you find him, report to me, so that I too may go and worship him."

After they had heard the king, they went on their way, and the star they had seen when it rose went ahead of them until it stopped over the place where the child was. When they saw the star, they were overjoyed. **On coming to the house, they saw the child with his mother Mary, and they bowed down and worshiped him. Then they opened their treasures and presented him with gifts of gold, frankincense and myrrh.** And having been warned in a dream not to go back to Herod, they returned to their country by another route. MATTHEW 2:1–12

## Teachings from Jesus on Money and Giving

*Jesus said more about money than about the topics of heaven and hell combined. Our attitudes toward money and personal resources say so much about our lives. There's a subtle trap to avoid in our giving—it should not be a way to draw attention to ourselves. It is also important to think beyond our earthly lives and ask, how can we share what we've been given in order to build God's kingdom?*

"Be careful not to practice your righteousness in front of others to be seen by them. If you do, you will have no reward from your Father in heaven.

"So when you give to the needy, do not announce it with trumpets, as the hypocrites do in the synagogues and on the streets, to be honored by others. Truly I tell you, they have received their reward in full. **But when you give to the needy, do not let your left hand know what your right hand is doing, so that your giving may be in secret. Then your Father, who sees what is done in secret, will reward you."** MATTHEW 6:1–4

"Do not store up for yourselves treasures on earth, where moths and vermin destroy, and where thieves break in and steal. But store up for yourselves treasures in heaven, where moths and vermin do not destroy, and where thieves do not break in and steal. For where your treasure is, there your heart will be also.

"The eye is the lamp of the body. If your eyes are healthy, your whole body will be full of light. But if your eyes are unhealthy, your whole body will be full of darkness. If then the light within you is darkness, how great is that darkness!

**"No one can serve two masters. Either you will hate the one and love the other, or you will be devoted to the one and despise the other. You cannot serve both God and money."** MATTHEW 6:19–24

Someone in the crowd said to him, "Teacher, tell my brother to divide the inheritance with me."

Jesus replied, "Man, who appointed me a judge or an arbiter between you?" Then he said to them, "Watch out! Be on your guard against all kinds of greed; life does not consist in an abundance of possessions."

And he told them this parable: "The ground of a certain rich man yielded an abundant harvest. He thought to himself, 'What shall I do? I have no place to store my crops.'

"Then he said, 'This is what I'll do. I will tear down my barns and build bigger ones, and there I will store my surplus grain. And I'll say to myself, "You have plenty of grain laid up for many years. Take life easy; eat, drink and be merry."'

**"But God said to him, 'You fool! This very night your life will be demanded from you. Then who will get what you have prepared for yourself?'**

**"This is how it will be with whoever stores up things for themselves but is not rich toward God."** Luke 12:13–21

*As you can see from the parable of the rich fool, Jesus had a knack for noticing teachable moments. Everyday encounters with fig trees, water wells and dinner parties provided illustrations for Jesus to explain what matters the most to God. In this next situation, Jesus was observing the daily activities at the temple when an opportunity arose for Jesus to teach his disciples what type of giving touches God's heart.*

Jesus sat down opposite the place where the offerings were put and watched the crowd putting their money into the temple treasury. Many rich people threw in large amounts. But a poor widow came and put in two very small copper coins, worth only a few cents.

Calling his disciples to him, Jesus said, **"Truly I tell you, this poor widow has put more into the treasury than all the others. They all gave out of their wealth; but she, out of her poverty, put in everything — all she had to live on."** Mark 12:41–44

---

How would you summarize what Jesus
taught about money and giving?

## GENEROSITY IN ACTION

*Evidence of the generosity of the early church can be seen in many circumstances. For instance, Paul encouraged the believers at Corinth to send an offering to their needy fellow believers in Jerusalem, something the Corinthians had intended to do but had not finished.*

---

According to the following passage, what is
the process believers should follow to determine
what they should give?

---

And now, brothers and sisters, we want you to know about the grace that God has given the Macedonian churches. In the midst of a very severe trial, their overflowing joy and their extreme poverty welled up in rich generosity. For I testify that they gave as much as they were able, and even beyond their ability. Entirely on their own, they urgently pleaded with us for the privilege of sharing in this service to the Lord's people. And they exceeded our expectations: They gave themselves first of all to the Lord, and then by the will of God also to us. So we urged Titus, just as he had earlier made a beginning, to bring also to completion this act of grace on your part. **But since you excel in everything — in faith, in speech, in knowledge, in complete earnestness and in the love we have kindled in you — see that you also excel in this grace of giving.**

I am not commanding you, but I want to test the sincerity of your love by comparing it with the earnestness of others. For you know the grace of our Lord Jesus Christ, that though he was rich, yet for your sake he became poor, so that you through his poverty might become rich.

And here is my judgment about what is best for you in this matter. Last year you were the first not only to give but also to have the desire to do so. Now finish the work, so that your eager willingness to do it may be matched by your completion of it, according to your means. For if the willingness is there, the gift is acceptable according to what one has, not according to what one does not have.

2 CORINTHIANS 8:1–12

**Remember this: Whoever sows sparingly will also reap sparingly, and whoever sows generously will also reap generously. Each of you should give what you have decided in your heart to give, not reluctantly or under compulsion, for God loves a cheerful giver.** And God is able to bless you abundantly, so that in all things at all times, having all that you need, you will abound in every good work. As it is written:

> "They have freely scattered their gifts to the poor;
>     their righteousness endures forever."

Now he who supplies seed to the sower and bread for food will also supply and increase your store of seed and will enlarge the harvest of your righteousness. You will be enriched in every way so that you can be generous on every occasion, and through us your generosity will result in thanksgiving to God.

This service that you perform is not only supplying the needs of the Lord's people but is also overflowing in many expressions of thanks to God. Because of the service by which you have proved yourselves, others will praise God for the obedience that accompanies your confession of the gospel of Christ, and for your generosity in sharing with them and with everyone else. And in their prayers for you their hearts will go out to you, because of the surpassing grace God has given you. Thanks be to God for his indescribable gift!                              2 CORINTHIANS 9:6–15

*Paul earned money as a tentmaker, though he was grateful for the financial support he received from some of the churches he served, such as the church at Philippi. He preached the gospel sincerely and freely, making sure he wasn't a financial burden to the local believers. In all of his circumstances, Paul learned a vital lesson: Contentment doesn't come from owning "things," but from knowing Christ.*

I am not saying this because I am in need, for I have learned to be content whatever the circumstances. I know what it is to be in need, and I know what it is to have plenty. I have learned the secret of being content in any and every situation, whether well fed or hungry, whether living in plenty or in want. I can do all this through him who gives me strength.                              PHILIPPIANS 4:11–13

On a scale of 1-10 evaluate your level of generosity.
What has helped you become more generous?
What still causes you to hold back?

## WHAT WE BELIEVE

*Many people see giving as an obligation, but it is really an act of worship from someone who has embraced in their heart the key beliefs of the Christian faith. The one true God is good and has provided the way to eternal salvation. When we accept this gift of life we are given a new identity and called to a new purpose to fulfill God's mission on earth until he returns. We give away our resources with that motivation and purpose in mind.*

*The people of the Old Testament gave the first 10 percent to God as a declaration of their allegiance to him. But they gave beyond the tithe out of a willing heart, because of God's great love for them. The words of the wisdom writers and the lives of the wise men who visited the baby Jesus illustrate the importance and benefits of being content and generous with our resources. Jesus reminds us that we should strive to think bigger than our earthly lives and use our resources to strengthen God's kingdom. As is evident in both the Old and New Testaments, God is more concerned about the reasons we give than about the size of our gift.*

CHAPTER

## 20

# Sharing My Faith

———— KEY QUESTION ————

How do I share my faith with those who don't know God?

———— KEY IDEA ————

I share my faith with others to fulfill God's purposes.

———— KEY VERSE ————

Pray also for me, that whenever I speak,
words may be given me so that I will fearlessly
make known the mystery of the gospel,
for which I am an ambassador in chains.
Pray that I may declare it fearlessly, as I should.
*Ephesians 6:19–20*

*We believe the one true God has unfolded his grand plan to provide salvation through Jesus Christ. We believe God loves all people and extends an invitation to everyone to receive eternal life. We believe there is a heaven and a hell and that Jesus will return to judge all people and establish his eternal kingdom. Only those who receive salvation by faith in Christ in this life will be a part of the eternal life to come. We believe God has designed the church to be the primary ambassador to spread this message, this good news to the world. Because of these beliefs we commit ourselves to the practice of sharing our faith. So how do we share our faith with those who don't know God?*

*In this chapter you will read Scripture that answers that question. The main topics of this chapter are:*

- *The Call to Share Our Faith*
- *Sharing Our Faith through Our Lives*
- *Sharing Our Faith through Our Words*
- *Sharing Our Faith with All*

## THE CALL TO SHARE OUR FAITH

*Israel was a living demonstration to the world of the lengths to which God would go to re-establish his relationship with his people. With the sacrifice of his Son, reconciliation with God became available to all humankind (not just to the Israelites). The exciting thing about being a part of God's story is that we can (and should) tell others about God's great rescue mission. By responding to the call to share our faith, we partner with God in his pursuit of broken people.*

For Christ's love compels us, because we are convinced that one died for all, and therefore all died. And he died for all, that those who live should no longer live for themselves but for him who died for them and was raised again.

So from now on we regard no one from a worldly point of view. Though we once regarded Christ in this way, we do so no longer. Therefore, if anyone is in Christ, the new creation has come: The old has gone, the new is here! All this is from God, who reconciled us to himself through Christ and gave us the ministry of reconciliation: that God was reconciling the world to himself in Christ, not counting people's sins against them. **And he has committed to us the message of reconciliation. We are therefore Christ's ambassadors, as though God were making his appeal through us.** We implore you on Christ's behalf: Be reconciled to God. God made him who had no sin to be sin for us, so that in him we might become the righteousness of God.                              2 Corinthians 5:14–21

---

What are some ways in which we can be God's "ambassadors" to the world?

---

### Sharing Our Faith through Our Lives

*The most powerful way to share our faith in God is through our lives—being a positive example in how we live every day. When others see the faith, hope and love in our lives, they are drawn to live the same way. After paying attention over time, they will notice our relationship with the one true God.*

*In 2 Kings we find a story in which a young girl from Israel speaks up because of her faith and her noble concern for her master, the commander of the army of Aram—Israel's enemy. The girl's words eventually led to the healing of this foreign soldier and inspired his belief in the one true God.*

Now Naaman was commander of the army of the king of Aram. He was a great man in the sight of his master and highly regarded, because through him the Lord had given victory to Aram. He was a valiant soldier, but he had leprosy. **Now bands of raiders from Aram had gone out and had taken captive a young girl from Israel, and she served Naaman's wife. She said to her mistress, "If only my master would see the prophet who is in Samaria! He would cure him of his leprosy."** Naaman went to his master and told him what the girl from Israel had said. "By all means, go," the king of Aram replied. "I will send a letter to the king of Israel." So Naaman left, taking with him ten talents of silver, six thousand shekels of gold and ten sets of clothing. The letter that he took to the king of Israel read: "With this letter I am sending my servant Naaman to you so that you may cure him of his leprosy."

As soon as the king of Israel read the letter, he tore his robes and said, "Am I God? Can I kill and bring back to life? Why does this fellow send someone to me to be cured of his leprosy? See how he is trying to pick a quarrel with me!"

When Elisha the man of God heard that the king of Israel had torn his robes, he sent him this message: "Why have you torn your robes? Have the man come to me and he will know that there is a prophet in Israel." So Naaman went with his horses and chariots and stopped at the door of Elisha's house. Elisha sent a messenger to say to him, "Go, wash yourself seven times in the Jordan, and your flesh will be restored and you will be cleansed."

But Naaman went away angry and said, "I thought that he would surely come out to me and stand and call on the name of the LORD his God, wave his hand over the spot and cure me of my leprosy. Are not Abana and Pharpar, the rivers of Damascus, better than all the waters of Israel? Couldn't I wash in them and be cleansed?" So he turned and went off in a rage.

Naaman's servants went to him and said, "My father, if the prophet had told you to do some great thing, would you not have done it? How much more, then, when he tells you, 'Wash and be cleansed'!" So he went down and dipped himself in the Jordan seven times, as the man of God had told him, and his flesh was restored and became clean like that of a young boy.

**Then Naaman and all his attendants went back to the man of God. He stood before him and said, "Now I know that there is no God in all the world except in Israel. So please accept a gift from your servant."** 2 KINGS 5:1–15

*God wants our lives to be centered on doing his will. In Jesus' famous Sermon on the Mount, he used the metaphors of salt and light to express the transforming power that comes from living by faith and obeying God's will.*

"You are the salt of the earth. But if the salt loses its saltiness, how can it be made salty again? It is no longer good for anything, except to be thrown out and trampled underfoot.

"You are the light of the world. A town built on a hill cannot be hidden. Neither do people light a lamp and put it under a bowl. Instead they put it on its stand, and it gives light to everyone in the house. **In the same way, let your light shine before others, that they may see your good deeds and glorify your Father in heaven.**"
MATTHEW 5:13–16

*The apostle Paul was very aware that his life was to be the light of Christ and the good flavor of salt to his world. He consciously did whatever it took to make sure he was putting others' needs before his own so they would have no reason to reject the good news.*

Though I am free and belong to no one, I have made myself a slave to everyone, to win as many as possible. To the Jews I became like a Jew, to win the Jews. To those under the law I became like one under the law (though I myself am not under the law), so as to win those under the law. To those not having the law I became like one not having the law (though I am not free from God's law but am under Christ's law), so as to win those not having the law. To the weak I became weak, to win the weak. **I have become all things to all people so that by all possible means I might save some. I do all this for the sake of the gospel, that I may share in its blessings.**
1 CORINTHIANS 9:19–23

---

What does Paul mean when he writes, "I have become all things to all people so that by all possible means I might save some"? What do you think this does not mean?

---

## SHARING OUR FAITH THROUGH OUR WORDS

*The entire early church had a mission to share the truth about God's love and faithfulness, which they accomplished by testifying about the resurrected Christ. But when it comes to actually using words, we could be afraid we won't know what to say. God promised us the Holy Spirit would give us words when we need them, just as Paul prays in our key verse at the beginning of the chapter. As we see with Philip, the Holy Spirit even makes sure we meet people at just the right time when they are ready to hear the good news.*

As you read about Philip's divine encounter
with the Ethiopian, identify Philip's strategies
for sharing his faith that you can imitate.

Now an angel of the Lord said to Philip, "Go south to the
road — the desert road — that goes down from Jerusalem to Gaza."
So he started out, and on his way he met an Ethiopian eunuch,
an important official in charge of all the treasury of the Kandake
(which means "queen of the Ethiopians"). This man had gone to Jerusalem to worship, and on his way home was sitting in his chariot
reading the Book of Isaiah the prophet. The Spirit told Philip, "Go
to that chariot and stay near it."

Then Philip ran up to the chariot and heard the man reading
Isaiah the prophet. "Do you understand what you are reading?"
Philip asked.

"How can I," he said, "unless someone explains it to me?" So he
invited Philip to come up and sit with him.

This is the passage of Scripture the eunuch was reading:

"He was led like a sheep to the slaughter,
    and as a lamb before its shearer is silent,
    so he did not open his mouth.
In his humiliation he was deprived of justice.
    Who can speak of his descendants?
    For his life was taken from the earth."

The eunuch asked Philip, "Tell me, please, who is the prophet talking about, himself or someone else?" **Then Philip began
with that very passage of Scripture and told him the good news
about Jesus.**

As they traveled along the road, they came to some water and
the eunuch said, "Look, here is water. What can stand in the way of
my being baptized?" And he gave orders to stop the chariot. Then
both Philip and the eunuch went down into the water and Philip
baptized him. When they came up out of the water, the Spirit of
the Lord suddenly took Philip away, and the eunuch did not see
him again, but went on his way rejoicing.              ACTS 8:26–39

## SHARING OUR FAITH WITH ALL

*Sometimes when you share your faith, people will reject it. This doesn't mean that you shouldn't have shared. Even if it doesn't feel like you are making a difference, you are. Remember Jonah? He avoided God's command to go to Nineveh, because he thought the people in Nineveh were beyond saving. Jews were traditionally very resistant to sharing their faith in God with outsiders. When we read the first part of Jonah's story (in Chapter 18), we left him when he had just been spit up on a beach by the big fish. Now we get to read the rest of the story. See what happened when Jonah finally obeyed God, even when he didn't think the people would respond.*

Then the word of the LORD came to Jonah a second time: "Go to the great city of Nineveh and proclaim to it the message I give you."

Jonah obeyed the word of the LORD and went to Nineveh. Now Nineveh was a very large city; it took three days to go through it. **Jonah began by going a day's journey into the city, proclaiming, "Forty more days and Nineveh will be overthrown." The Ninevites believed God.** A fast was proclaimed, and all of them, from the greatest to the least, put on sackcloth.

When Jonah's warning reached the king of Nineveh, he rose from his throne, took off his royal robes, covered himself with sackcloth and sat down in the dust. This is the proclamation he issued in Nineveh:

"By the decree of the king and his nobles:

Do not let people or animals, herds or flocks, taste anything; do not let them eat or drink. But let people and animals be covered with sackcloth. Let everyone call urgently on God. Let them give up their evil ways and their violence. Who knows? God may yet relent and with compassion turn from his fierce anger so that we will not perish."

When God saw what they did and how they turned from their evil ways, he relented and did not bring on them the destruction he had threatened. JONAH 3:1–10

*The unwillingness of the Jews to share their faith with outsiders carried over into the time of Jesus. The Samaritans were a mixed-blood race resulting from the intermarriage of Israelites with other nations. Hatred and discrimination existed between Jews and Samaritans in Jesus' day. Jews would often go out of their way to avoid any contact with the Samaritan people. To show his disciples the value of inclusivity, Jesus traveled directly through Samaria and went out of his way to talk to a Samaritan woman.*

---

As you read this story, look for how Jesus
treated the woman at the well that caused her
to respond positively to him and his message.

---

He came to a town in Samaria called Sychar, near the plot of ground Jacob had given to his son Joseph. Jacob's well was there, and Jesus, tired as he was from the journey, sat down by the well. It was about noon.

When a Samaritan woman came to draw water, Jesus said to her, "Will you give me a drink?" (His disciples had gone into the town to buy food.)

The Samaritan woman said to him, "You are a Jew and I am a Samaritan woman. How can you ask me for a drink?" (For Jews do not associate with Samaritans.)

Jesus answered her, "If you knew the gift of God and who it is that asks you for a drink, you would have asked him and he would have given you living water."

"Sir," the woman said, "you have nothing to draw with and the well is deep. Where can you get this living water? Are you greater than our father Jacob, who gave us the well and drank from it himself, as did also his sons and his livestock?"

Jesus answered, "Everyone who drinks this water will be thirsty again, but whoever drinks the water I give them will never thirst. Indeed, the water I give them will become in them a spring of water welling up to eternal life."

The woman said to him, "Sir, give me this water so that I won't get thirsty and have to keep coming here to draw water."

He told her, "Go, call your husband and come back."

"I have no husband," she replied.

Jesus said to her, "You are right when you say you have no husband. The fact is, you have had five husbands, and the man you now have is not your husband. What you have just said is quite true."

"Sir," the woman said, "I can see that you are a prophet. Our ancestors worshiped on this mountain, but you Jews claim that the place where we must worship is in Jerusalem."

"Woman," Jesus replied, "believe me, a time is coming when you will worship the Father neither on this mountain nor in Jerusalem. You Samaritans worship what you do not know; we worship what we do know, for salvation is from the Jews. Yet a time is coming and has now come when the true worshipers will worship the Father in the Spirit and in truth, for they are the kind of worshipers the Father seeks. God is spirit, and his worshipers must worship in the Spirit and in truth."

The woman said, "I know that Messiah" (called Christ) "is coming. When he comes, he will explain everything to us."

Then Jesus declared, "I, the one speaking to you — I am he."

Just then his disciples returned and were surprised to find him talking with a woman. But no one asked, "What do you want?" or "Why are you talking with her?"

Then, leaving her water jar, the woman went back to the town and said to the people, "Come, see a man who told me everything I ever did. Could this be the Messiah?" They came out of the town and made their way toward him.

Meanwhile his disciples urged him, "Rabbi, eat something."

But he said to them, "I have food to eat that you know nothing about."

Then his disciples said to each other, "Could someone have brought him food?"

"My food," said Jesus, "is to do the will of him who sent me and to finish his work. Don't you have a saying, 'It's still four months until harvest'? **I tell you, open your eyes and look at the fields! They are ripe for harvest. Even now the one who reaps draws a wage and harvests a crop for eternal life, so that the sower and the reaper may be glad together. Thus the saying 'One sows and another reaps' is true. I sent you to reap what you have**

**not worked for. Others have done the hard work, and you have reaped the benefits of their labor."**

Many of the Samaritans from that town believed in him because of the woman's testimony, "He told me everything I ever did." So when the Samaritans came to him, they urged him to stay with them, and he stayed two days. And because of his words many more became believers.

They said to the woman, "We no longer believe just because of what you said; now we have heard for ourselves, and we know that this man really is the Savior of the world." JOHN 4:5–42

---

In regard to sharing our faith, what did Jesus mean that some will "sow" the seed and others will "reap" the harvest? Why should we share our faith, even if we think our message could be rejected?

---

## WHAT WE BELIEVE

*All believers are called to share their faith with others. We have been given the "ministry of reconciliation"; we are God's "ambassadors" in the world. We are called to share our faith through the way we live our lives. We are to be "salt and light" to the people God has placed in our sphere of influence. The mere beauty of how Christians treat each other is an aroma that draws outsiders to want to know God and be in a relationship with him.*

*We are also called to share our faith through our words. Like Philip, we will look for divine appointments to share the gospel with people who are genuinely seeking. God's grace and love know no boundaries. He desires for all people to come into a saving relationship with him. Therefore, we will share our faith with our enemies, people of different races or religions, or sometimes even people in our own family. Let's pray, like Paul, that we "may declare it fearlessly."*

# Who Am I Becoming?

I am the vine; you are the branches.
If you remain in me and I in you, you will bear
much fruit; apart from me you can do nothing.
*John 15:5*

In the passage above, Jesus compares the Christian life to a grape-vine. He is the vine; we are the branches. If we are part of the vine of Christ, over time we will produce amazing fruit for all to see and taste.

People love ripe, delicious fruit, but no one likes to eat unripe, rotten or artificial fruit. Jesus wants to produce in us fruit that brings great joy to ourselves and to others. For this to happen, we must remain in Christ. To "remain" simply means to "stay put." Spiritual growth works like the growth of fruit. The longer we remain consistently with Christ, the better it gets.

Nurturing the passion and discipline to *think* and *act* like Jesus is our part in remaining in the vine of Christ, but we do not act alone. The Father is the Gardener. He waters us, tills our soil, prunes us and makes sure we have the proper exposure to the sun.

As we remain in Christ and the Gardener does his work, eventually buds appear on our branches. With time the fruit grows and ripens. Good-tasting fruit is evidence of the health of the branch on the inside. Mature fruit will help the people God has put in our lives. It attracts them to us; it cares for them and gives them refreshment. It pleases God when we give out the love he first put into us.

The final ten chapters lay out the ten key virtues or qualities God wants to see developed in your life. As you read, pray, "This is who I want to become!" And with God's help, you will.

I can do all this through him who gives me strength.
*Philippians 4:13*

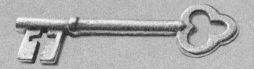

CHAPTER

21

# Love

--- KEY QUESTION ---

What does it mean to sacrificially
and unconditionally love others?

--- KEY IDEA ---

I am committed to loving God and loving others.

--- KEY VERSE ---

This is love: not that we loved God, but that he loved us and
sent his Son as an atoning sacrifice for our sins. Dear friends,
since God so loved us, we also ought to love one another.
No one has ever seen God; but if we love one another,
God lives in us and his love is made complete in us.

*1 John 4:10–12*

OUR MAP

*We believe to become. We believe the ten beliefs in our heads and move them into our hearts by doing the ten spiritual practices in order to become like Christ. And how do we become like Christ? By exhibiting the ten key virtues. They are a natural outflow of believing the beliefs and practicing the practices. As the beliefs are embraced and owned in our hearts, "buds" of the virtues, or the fruit of the Spirit, appear on the external branches of our lives for others to see and taste. The ultimate fruit, the most important expression of being like Jesus, is LOVE. What does it mean to sacrificially and unconditionally love and forgive others?*

*The Scripture included in this chapter will provide the answer under the following topics:*

- *Love Defined*
- *The Greatest Commandment*
- *The Power to Love*
- *A Loving Example: David and Jonathan*

## LOVE DEFINED

*The Bible is a long and sometimes complicated book. But what is the big—yet simple—idea behind all the stories and teachings contained in this ancient book? Love. Love dominates God's story. First Corinthians 13 provides us with an earnest description of love that echoes throughout Scripture.*

---

As you read this passage, make two lists: list the characteristics of love in the positive sense (all that love is), and list the characteristics love does not have.

---

If I speak in the tongues of men or of angels, but do not have love, I am only a resounding gong or a clanging cymbal. If I have the gift of prophecy and can fathom all mysteries and all knowledge, and if I have a faith that can move mountains, but do not have love, I am nothing. If I give all I possess to the poor and give over my body to hardship that I may boast, but do not have love, I gain nothing.

Love is patient, love is kind. It does not envy, it does not boast, it is not proud. It does not dishonor others, it is not self-seeking, it is not easily angered, it keeps no record of wrongs. Love does not delight in evil but rejoices with the truth. It always protects, always trusts, always hopes, always perseveres.

Love never fails. But where there are prophecies, they will cease; where there are tongues, they will be stilled; where there is knowledge, it will pass away. For we know in part and we prophesy in part, but when completeness comes, what is in part disappears. When I was a child, I talked like a child, I thought like a child, I reasoned like a child. When I became a man, I put the ways of childhood behind me. For now we see only a reflection as in a mirror; then we shall see face to face. Now I know in part; then I shall know fully, even as I am fully known.

**And now these three remain: faith, hope and love. But the greatest of these is love.** 1 Corinthians 13:1–13

## The Greatest Commandment

*Love as the greatest commandment can be found early in God's story with his people. For example, near the end of his life Moses gathered the Israelites together to remind them of what truly mattered as they readied themselves to enter the promised land. His words, recorded in the book of Deuteronomy, include a passage known as the Shema (Hebrew for "hear"), which later became the Jewish confession of faith, recited twice daily at the morning and evening prayer services. As the Shema beautifully articulates, the love between God and his people has always been the driver behind a life of faith.*

Hear, O Israel: The Lord our God, the Lord is one. **Love the Lord your God with all your heart and with all your soul and with all your strength.** These commandments that I give you today are to be on your hearts. Impress them on your children. Talk about them when you sit at home and when you walk along the road, when you lie down and when you get up. Tie them as symbols on your hands and bind them on your foreheads. Write them on the doorframes of your houses and on your gates.

Deuteronomy 6:4–9

*It is not possible to love God with all our hearts, souls and strength without also loving our neighbor (the people in our sphere of influence).*

" 'Do not hate a fellow Israelite in your heart. Rebuke your neighbor frankly so you will not share in their guilt.

" '**Do not seek revenge or bear a grudge against anyone among your people, but love your neighbor as yourself. I am the Lord.' "** LEVITICUS 19:17–18

*Jesus was often questioned by the religious leaders about his teachings. At one point, they asked him what the greatest commandment in all of Scripture was. His answer confirmed the Old Testament emphasis on love for God and for others.*

One of the teachers of the law came and heard them debating. Noticing that Jesus had given them a good answer, he asked him, "Of all the commandments, which is the most important?"

**"The most important one," answered Jesus, "is this: 'Hear, O Israel: The Lord our God, the Lord is one. Love the Lord your God with all your heart and with all your soul and with all your mind and with all your strength.' The second is this: 'Love your neighbor as yourself.' There is no commandment greater than these."**

"Well said, teacher," the man replied. "You are right in saying that God is one and there is no other but him. To love him with all your heart, with all your understanding and with all your strength, and to love your neighbor as yourself is more important than all burnt offerings and sacrifices."

When Jesus saw that he had answered wisely, he said to him, "You are not far from the kingdom of God." And from then on no one dared ask him any more questions. MARK 12:28–34

---

Using a scale of 1-10, how would you rank the amount of your heart, soul, mind and strength you love God with? How would you rank your love for yourself versus your love for others? Are you satisfied with the scores you have given yourself?

*With this increased capacity of God's love flowing in and through us comes increased expectation. The bar that Jesus set is higher than we could achieve on our own. But with God's love in us, it becomes possible.*

"You have heard that it was said, 'Love your neighbor and hate your enemy.' But I tell you, love your enemies and pray for those who persecute you, that you may be children of your Father in heaven. He causes his sun to rise on the evil and the good, and sends rain on the righteous and the unrighteous. If you love those who love you, what reward will you get? Are not even the tax collectors doing that? And if you greet only your own people, what are you doing more than others? Do not even pagans do that? Be perfect, therefore, as your heavenly Father is perfect."

MATTHEW 5:43–48

## THE POWER TO LOVE

*Left to ourselves, we naturally want to please ourselves rather than love others unconditionally. Love is a sacrifice. It is much easier to serve ourselves than to serve others. That's why we need God's help. When we experience God's love for us, we are able to love others the way he loves us. The commands of the Bible tell us how we should love others, but the Spirit of God in our hearts actually empowers us to do it.*

So I say, walk by the Spirit, and you will not gratify the desires of the flesh. For the flesh desires what is contrary to the Spirit, and the Spirit what is contrary to the flesh. They are in conflict with each other, so that you are not to do whatever you want. But if you are led by the Spirit, you are not under the law.

The acts of the flesh are obvious: sexual immorality, impurity and debauchery; idolatry and witchcraft; hatred, discord, jealousy, fits of rage, selfish ambition, dissensions, factions and envy; drunkenness, orgies, and the like. I warn you, as I did before, that those who live like this will not inherit the kingdom of God.

**But the fruit of the Spirit is love, joy, peace, forbearance, kindness, goodness, faithfulness, gentleness and self-control. Against such things there is no law.** Those who belong to Christ

Jesus have crucified the flesh with its passions and desires. Since
we live by the Spirit, let us keep in step with the Spirit.

GALATIANS 5:16–25

---

This passage contains two lists: the acts of the flesh,
and the fruit of the Spirit. After the list of the fruit of the Spirit
why does it say, "Against such things there is no law"?

---

*Jesus offers us a life of love, which he modeled perfectly. Notice
how he consistently referred to things flowing first from the Father
to him and then to us. This is the secret to loving others—being
loved by God and having his love to pass on.*

**"I am the good shepherd; I know my sheep and my sheep
know me — just as the Father knows me and I know the Father — and I lay down my life for the sheep.** I have other sheep
that are not of this sheep pen. I must bring them also. They too
will listen to my voice, and there shall be one flock and one shepherd. The reason my Father loves me is that I lay down my life —
only to take it up again. No one takes it from me, but I lay it down
of my own accord. I have authority to lay it down and authority to
take it up again. This command I received from my Father."

JOHN 10:14–18

---

Based on what Jesus said above combined with our key verse,
how does love work? In other words, where do we get
the love we need in order to love others the way Jesus does?

---

## A LOVING EXAMPLE: DAVID AND JONATHAN

*Now that we have a clear understanding of love as God intended
it to be, it's powerful to look at how that love has been exem-
plified by God's people in the Bible. One of the most beautiful
and inspiring stories of someone loving another as they would
themselves is Jonathan and David. Jonathan, the son of King
Saul, the first monarch of Israel, was next in line to reign. But
when young David emerged into the limelight after killing the*

*Philistine giant Goliath with only a slingshot, it was clear that God had other plans. Jonathan recognized God's hand on David and graciously stepped aside and even protected David. King Saul saw the same thing, but he instead became driven by jealousy and insecurity.*

---

As you read the story below, write down the ways you see Jonathan offering David unconditional and sacrificial love.

---

Jonathan became one in spirit with David, and he loved him as himself. From that day Saul kept David with him and did not let him return home to his family. And Jonathan made a covenant with David because he loved him as himself. Jonathan took off the robe he was wearing and gave it to David, along with his tunic, and even his sword, his bow and his belt. 1 SAMUEL 18:1B–4

Saul told his son Jonathan and all the attendants to kill David. But Jonathan had taken a great liking to David and warned him, "My father Saul is looking for a chance to kill you. Be on your guard tomorrow morning; go into hiding and stay there. I will go out and stand with my father in the field where you are. I'll speak to him about you and will tell you what I find out."

Jonathan spoke well of David to Saul his father and said to him, "Let not the king do wrong to his servant David; he has not wronged you, and what he has done has benefited you greatly. He took his life in his hands when he killed the Philistine. The LORD won a great victory for all Israel, and you saw it and were glad. Why then would you do wrong to an innocent man like David by killing him for no reason?"

Saul listened to Jonathan and took this oath: "As surely as the LORD lives, David will not be put to death."

So Jonathan called David and told him the whole conversation. He brought him to Saul, and David was with Saul as before.

1 SAMUEL 19:1–7

*Before long, Saul jealously turned against David again and threw a spear at David with the intent of killing him. David escaped and found himself on the run. Through this difficult season of life away from home, David learned to trust God in a deeper way. God often reveals himself more clearly during our trials. David eventually found his way safely to Jonathan. David apparently wanted to make one more attempt to come alongside Saul and serve him if Saul would accept him. David and Jonathan agreed on a plan to expose the intent of Saul's heart.*

Then Jonathan said to David, "I swear by the LORD, the God of Israel, that I will surely sound out my father by this time the day after tomorrow! If he is favorably disposed toward you, will I not send you word and let you know? But if my father intends to harm you, may the LORD deal with Jonathan, be it ever so severely, if I do not let you know and send you away in peace. May the LORD be with you as he has been with my father. But show me unfailing kindness like the LORD's kindness as long as I live, so that I may not be killed, and do not ever cut off your kindness from my family — not even when the LORD has cut off every one of David's enemies from the face of the earth."

So Jonathan made a covenant with the house of David, saying, "May the LORD call David's enemies to account." And Jonathan had David reaffirm his oath out of love for him, because he loved him as he loved himself.

Then Jonathan said to David, "Tomorrow is the New Moon feast. You will be missed, because your seat will be empty. The day after tomorrow, toward evening, go to the place where you hid when this trouble began, and wait by the stone Ezel. I will shoot three arrows to the side of it, as though I were shooting at a target. Then I will send a boy and say, 'Go, find the arrows.' If I say to him, 'Look, the arrows are on this side of you; bring them here,' then come, because, as surely as the LORD lives, you are safe; there is no danger. But if I say to the boy, 'Look, the arrows are beyond you,' then you must go, because the LORD has sent you away. And about the matter you and I discussed — remember, the LORD is witness between you and me forever."

So David hid in the field, and when the New Moon feast came, the king sat down to eat. He sat in his customary place by the wall, opposite Jonathan, and Abner sat next to Saul, but David's place was empty. Saul said nothing that day, for he thought, "Something must have happened to David to make him ceremonially unclean — surely he is unclean." But the next day, the second day of the month, David's place was empty again. Then Saul said to his son Jonathan, "Why hasn't the son of Jesse come to the meal, either yesterday or today?"

Jonathan answered, "David earnestly asked me for permission to go to Bethlehem. He said, 'Let me go, because our family is observing a sacrifice in the town and my brother has ordered me to be there. If I have found favor in your eyes, let me get away to see my brothers.' That is why he has not come to the king's table."

Saul's anger flared up at Jonathan and he said to him, "You son of a perverse and rebellious woman! Don't I know that you have sided with the son of Jesse to your own shame and to the shame of the mother who bore you? As long as the son of Jesse lives on this earth, neither you nor your kingdom will be established. Now send someone to bring him to me, for he must die!"

"Why should he be put to death? What has he done?" Jonathan asked his father. But Saul hurled his spear at him to kill him. Then Jonathan knew that his father intended to kill David.

Jonathan got up from the table in fierce anger; on that second day of the feast he did not eat, because he was grieved at his father's shameful treatment of David.

In the morning Jonathan went out to the field for his meeting with David. He had a small boy with him, and he said to the boy, "Run and find the arrows I shoot." As the boy ran, he shot an arrow beyond him. When the boy came to the place where Jonathan's arrow had fallen, Jonathan called out after him, "Isn't the arrow beyond you?" Then he shouted, "Hurry! Go quickly! Don't stop!" The boy picked up the arrow and returned to his master. (The boy knew nothing about all this; only Jonathan and David knew.) Then Jonathan gave his weapons to the boy and said, "Go, carry them back to town."

After the boy had gone, David got up from the south side of the stone and bowed down before Jonathan three times, with his face to the ground. Then they kissed each other and wept together — but David wept the most.

Jonathan said to David, "Go in peace, for we have sworn friendship with each other in the name of the LORD, saying, 'The LORD is witness between you and me, and between your descendants and my descendants forever.'" Then David left, and Jonathan went back to the town.    1 SAMUEL 20:12–42

## WHAT WE BELIEVE

*Love is the ultimate expression of becoming like Jesus. God the Father desires for us to unconditionally and sacrificially love others. Biblical love is defined in 1 Corinthians 13 and declared the greatest commandment in Mark 12. The greatest commandment to love God and love our neighbor is the standard of God, which on our own we cannot achieve. God has to pour his presence and love within us first. Then, as we receive it, we let his love pass through us to others. Jonathan provides a beautiful example of love in his relationship with David. With God's love and presence in us, we can become more and more like Jesus.*

**BE**

# CHAPTER

## 22

# Joy

───── KEY QUESTION ─────

What gives us true happiness
and contentment in life?

───── KEY IDEA ─────

Despite my circumstances,
I feel inner contentment and understand
my purpose in life.

───── KEY VERSE ─────

I have told you this so that my joy may be in you
and that your joy may be complete.
*John 15:11*

OUR MAP

*A person can have money, all the possessions they desire, health, and even good looks, but if they don't have joy, life can be rather challenging. It is easier to find joy when things are going well. Yet some people struggle to experience this virtue even amidst life's most favorable situations. Here is some amazing news! Christ offers us joy, no matter what our circumstances are. True joy is rooted in the belief that the one true God is a personal God who is involved in and cares about our daily lives. He loves us and is working out a good plan for us. When we confidently believe this in our hearts, we can rise above our circumstances and find joy in Christ alone. How can this be? This is what you will be exploring in this chapter.*

*As you read you will learn about the following biblical concepts:*

- *Source of Joy*
- *Joyful Celebrations*
- *Joy Despite Our Circumstances*

## SOURCE OF JOY

*God may shower us with blessings and circumstances that bring joy to our lives, but true joy is found not in those things themselves but in their source—God himself. Joy can also be fueled and found in living out God's Word and trusting in the promises God makes to us in his Word. The psalmist declared this truth with great confidence in this song:*

Keep me safe, my God,
　　for in you I take refuge.

I say to the LORD, "You are my Lord;
　　apart from you I have no good thing."
I say of the holy people who are in the land,
　　"They are the noble ones in whom is all my delight."
Those who run after other gods will suffer more and more.
　　I will not pour out libations of blood to such gods
　　or take up their names on my lips.

Lord, you alone are my portion and my cup;
　　you make my lot secure.
The boundary lines have fallen for me in pleasant places;
　　surely I have a delightful inheritance.
I will praise the Lord, who counsels me;
　　even at night my heart instructs me.
I keep my eyes always on the Lord.
　　With him at my right hand, I will not be shaken.

Therefore my heart is glad and my tongue rejoices;
　　my body also will rest secure,
because you will not abandon me to the realm of the dead,
　　nor will you let your faithful one see decay.
**You make known to me the path of life;**
　　**you will fill me with joy in your presence,**
　　**with eternal pleasures at your right hand.**　Psalm 16:1–11

*God's promises find their ultimate fulfillment in his Son Jesus. Note how his arrival into our world brought joy to everyone present.*

While they were there, the time came for the baby to be born, and she gave birth to her firstborn, a son. [Mary] wrapped him in cloths and placed him in a manger, because there was no guest room available for them.

And there were shepherds living out in the fields nearby, keeping watch over their flocks at night. An angel of the Lord appeared to them, and the glory of the Lord shone around them, and they were terrified. **But the angel said to them, "Do not be afraid. I bring you good news that will cause great joy for all the people. Today in the town of David a Savior has been born to you; he is the Messiah, the Lord.** This will be a sign to you: You will find a baby wrapped in cloths and lying in a manger."

Suddenly a great company of the heavenly host appeared with the angel, praising God and saying,

"Glory to God in the highest heaven,
　　and on earth peace to those on whom his favor rests."

When the angels had left them and gone into heaven, the

shepherds said to one another, "Let's go to Bethlehem and see this thing that has happened, which the Lord has told us about."

So they hurried off and found Mary and Joseph, and the baby, who was lying in the manger. When they had seen him, they spread the word concerning what had been told them about this child, and all who heard it were amazed at what the shepherds said to them. But Mary treasured up all these things and pondered them in her heart. The shepherds returned, glorifying and praising God for all the things they had heard and seen, which were just as they had been told.                                    LUKE 2:6–20 ⌐━

> *Jesus taught us that spiritual growth is much like the development of fruit on a vine. He is the vine and we become the branches when we place our faith in him. As we abide in the vine of Christ through obedience to his commands, his nutrients of joy run through our spiritual veins from the inside out and produce the ripe, juicy fruit of joy in and through our lives.*

"I am the true vine, and my Father is the gardener. He cuts off every branch in me that bears no fruit, while every branch that does bear fruit he prunes so that it will be even more fruitful. You are already clean because of the word I have spoken to you. Remain in me, as I also remain in you. No branch can bear fruit by itself; it must remain in the vine. Neither can you bear fruit unless you remain in me.

"I am the vine; you are the branches. If you remain in me and I in you, you will bear much fruit; apart from me you can do nothing. If you do not remain in me, you are like a branch that is thrown away and withers; such branches are picked up, thrown into the fire and burned. If you remain in me and my words remain in you, ask whatever you wish, and it will be done for you. This is to my Father's glory, that you bear much fruit, showing yourselves to be my disciples.

**"As the Father has loved me, so have I loved you. Now remain in my love. If you keep my commands, you will remain in my love, just as I have kept my Father's commands and remain in his love. I have told you this so that my joy may be in you and that your joy may be complete."** JOHN 15:1–11

How does keeping God's commands produce joy in our lives?

## JOYFUL CELEBRATIONS

*In the Old Testament, people often responded to God's blessings with joyful celebrations. Coming together to remember God put joy in the hearts of the people. The annual Festival of Tabernacles especially provided an opportunity for the Israelites to celebrate God's goodness, since the focus was on reminding them that God provided food and shelter during their days in the wilderness. When the people returned from captivity, it had been years since they gathered for this joy-filled celebration. With great passion they reinstated this tradition, and the results speak for themselves.*

On the second day of the month, the heads of all the families, along with the priests and the Levites, gathered around Ezra the teacher to give attention to the words of the Law. They found written in the Law, which the LORD had commanded through Moses, that the Israelites were to live in temporary shelters during the festival of the seventh month and that they should proclaim this word and spread it throughout their towns and in Jerusalem: "Go out into the hill country and bring back branches from olive and wild olive trees, and from myrtles, palms and shade trees, to make temporary shelters" — as it is written.

So the people went out and brought back branches and built themselves temporary shelters on their own roofs, in their courtyards, in the courts of the house of God and in the square by the Water Gate and the one by the Gate of Ephraim. The whole company that had returned from exile built temporary shelters and lived in them. **From the days of Joshua son of Nun until that day, the Israelites had not celebrated it like this. And their joy was very great.** NEHEMIAH 8:13–17

How does acknowledging God's involvement in our lives give us joy? Israel held annual festivals and traditions to celebrate God's blessings. How do Christians accomplish this today?

## Joy Despite Our Circumstances

*James introduces the book bearing his name with a thought-provoking declaration: not only can we have joy despite our difficult circumstances, but joy can grow through our difficult circumstances.*

**Consider it pure joy, my brothers and sisters, whenever you face trials of many kinds, because you know that the testing of your faith produces perseverance.** Let perseverance finish its work so that you may be mature and complete, not lacking anything. If any of you lacks wisdom, you should ask God, who gives generously to all without finding fault, and it will be given to you. But when you ask, you must believe and not doubt, because the one who doubts is like a wave of the sea, blown and tossed by the wind. That person should not expect to receive anything from the Lord. Such a person is double-minded and unstable in all they do.

Believers in humble circumstances ought to take pride in their high position. But the rich should take pride in their humiliation — since they will pass away like a wild flower. For the sun rises with scorching heat and withers the plant; its blossom falls and its beauty is destroyed. In the same way, the rich will fade away even while they go about their business.

Blessed is the one who perseveres under trial because, having stood the test, that person will receive the crown of life that the Lord has promised to those who love him.

When tempted, no one should say, "God is tempting me." For God cannot be tempted by evil, nor does he tempt anyone; but each person is tempted when they are dragged away by their own evil desire and enticed. Then, after desire has conceived, it gives birth to sin; and sin, when it is full-grown, gives birth to death.

Don't be deceived, my dear brothers and sisters. Every good and perfect gift is from above, coming down from the Father of the heavenly lights, who does not change like shifting shadows.

JAMES 1:2–17

How can difficult circumstances actually produce joy?
What role do our attitudes play in being able to experience joy?

*One person whose joy seemed to grow despite his circumstances was the apostle Paul who wrote a joyful treatise of sorts while under house arrest and chained to a Roman guard. In a passionate letter to the church at Philippi, Paul fervently expressed his joy in Christ. At the letter's opening, notice how he found joy in the people God had placed in his life.*

**I thank my God every time I remember you. In all my prayers for all of you, I always pray with joy because of your partnership in the gospel from the first day until now, being confident of this, that he who began a good work in you will carry it on to completion until the day of Christ Jesus.**

It is right for me to feel this way about all of you, since I have you in my heart and, whether I am in chains or defending and confirming the gospel, all of you share in God's grace with me. God can testify how I long for all of you with the affection of Christ Jesus.
PHILIPPIANS 1:3–8

*Then we learn that Paul even saw his imprisonment as a blessing, for it helped bring attention to the gospel message.*

Now I want you to know, brothers and sisters, that what has happened to me has actually served to advance the gospel. As a result, it has become clear throughout the whole palace guard and to everyone else that I am in chains for Christ. And because of my chains, most of the brothers and sisters have become confident in the Lord and dare all the more to proclaim the gospel without fear.

It is true that some preach Christ out of envy and rivalry, but others out of goodwill. The latter do so out of love, knowing that I am put here for the defense of the gospel. The former preach Christ out of selfish ambition, not sincerely, supposing that they can stir up trouble for me while I am in chains. But what does it matter? **The important thing is that in every way, whether from false motives or true, Christ is preached. And because of this I rejoice.**

**Yes, and I will continue to rejoice, for I know that through your prayers and God's provision of the Spirit of Jesus Christ what has happened to me will turn out for my deliverance.**
PHILIPPIANS 1:12–19

*Paul wrapped up his letter by revealing the secret to contentment in any and every circumstance.*

I rejoiced greatly in the Lord that at last you renewed your concern for me. Indeed, you were concerned, but you had no opportunity to show it. I am not saying this because I am in need, for I have learned to be content whatever the circumstances. I know what it is to be in need, and I know what it is to have plenty. **I have learned the secret of being content in any and every situation, whether well fed or hungry, whether living in plenty or in want. I can do all this through him who gives me strength.**

PHILIPPIANS 4:10–13

---

Paul said he had learned how to be content even
when he had plenty. Why is it sometimes difficult for
people who have plenty to be content?

---

*Like Paul, the apostle Peter also taught the early Christians that believers can experience joy in spite of and because of their difficult circumstances. God used trials in their lives to bless them. The same is true for followers of Jesus today.*

Praise be to the God and Father of our Lord Jesus Christ! In his great mercy he has given us new birth into a living hope through the resurrection of Jesus Christ from the dead, and into an inheritance that can never perish, spoil or fade. This inheritance is kept in heaven for you, who through faith are shielded by God's power until the coming of the salvation that is ready to be revealed in the last time. In all this you greatly rejoice, though now for a little while you may have had to suffer grief in all kinds of trials. These have come so that the proven genuineness of your faith — of greater worth than gold, which perishes even though refined by fire — may result in praise, glory and honor when Jesus Christ is revealed. **Though you have not seen him, you love him; and even though you do not see him now, you believe in him and are filled with an inexpressible and glorious joy, for you are receiving the end result of your faith, the salvation of your souls.** 1 PETER 1:3–9

Dear friends, do not be surprised at the fiery ordeal that has come on you to test you, as though something strange were happening to you. **But rejoice inasmuch as you participate in the sufferings of Christ, so that you may be overjoyed when his glory is revealed.** If you are insulted because of the name of Christ, you are blessed, for the Spirit of glory and of God rests on you. If you suffer, it should not be as a murderer or thief or any other kind of criminal, or even as a meddler. However, if you suffer as a Christian, do not be ashamed, but praise God that you bear that name.

1 PETER 4:12–16

**Humble yourselves, therefore, under God's mighty hand, that he may lift you up in due time. Cast all your anxiety on him because he cares for you.**

Be alert and of sober mind. Your enemy the devil prowls around like a roaring lion looking for someone to devour. Resist him, standing firm in the faith, because you know that the family of believers throughout the world is undergoing the same kind of sufferings.

And the God of all grace, who called you to his eternal glory in Christ, after you have suffered a little while, will himself restore you and make you strong, firm and steadfast. To him be the power for ever and ever. Amen.

1 PETER 5:6–11

---

How often do you joyfully acknowledge
God's goodness in your life? Identify
one good thing God has given to you or
done for you in the past week and take a moment
to celebrate that with someone else.

---

## WHAT WE BELIEVE

If we want to experience true joy, we must anchor our lives in the source of that joy—God himself. Saturating our minds in the key beliefs and practices of the Christian faith can help draw us closer to God. The closer we are to him, the more confidence we will have as we face each day. Like the Israelites did, we can celebrate even God's smallest blessings in our lives.

Christ offers contentment and happiness not limited by circumstances. Because of God's integrity, faithfulness and promises, we can overcome any circumstance with true joy in our hearts. As Christians, we share the knowledge of this virtue with those God places in our lives so that they too can experience the deep and never-ending well of God's joy.

# CHAPTER

## 23

# Peace

─────── KEY QUESTION ───────

Where do I find strength to battle anxiety and fear?

─────── KEY IDEA ───────

I am free from anxiety because I have found peace with God,
peace with others and peace with myself.

─────── KEY VERSE ───────

Do not be anxious about anything, but in every situation,
by prayer and petition, with thanksgiving, present
your requests to God. And the peace of God,
which transcends all understanding, will guard
your hearts and your minds in Christ Jesus.
*Philippians 4:6–7*

**OUR MAP**

Most of us think of peace as a feeling. We want to trade our anxiety, depression and fear for calm tranquility. There are many harmful and temporary ways people attempt to achieve this feeling, most notoriously by using alcohol or drugs. Biblical peace, however, starts not with the feeling of peace but with the source of peace, namely a strong and healthy relationship with God and with others. Where does one find the strength to battle anxiety and fear? In right relationships.

In this chapter you will discover how to find:

- Peace with God
- Peace with Others
- Peace with Yourself (Inner Peace)

## PEACE WITH GOD

Peace with God is made possible only through the Prince of Peace. When Christ returns to earth to establish his eternal kingdom, there will be worldwide peace. Around 700 years before Jesus was born, Isaiah foretold of Jesus' arrival on earth and the far-reaching impact of his reign.

> **For to us a child is born,**
> **to us a son is given,**
> **and the government will be on his shoulders.**
> **And he will be called**
> **Wonderful Counselor, Mighty God,**
> **Everlasting Father, Prince of Peace.**
> Of the greatness of his government and peace
> there will be no end.
> He will reign on David's throne
> and over his kingdom,
> establishing and upholding it
> with justice and righteousness
> from that time on and forever.
> The zeal of the LORD Almighty
> will accomplish this. ISAIAH 9:6–7

## PEACE WITH OTHERS

*While the Bible is full of examples of hostility and fighting, it also contains many inspiring examples of people striving for peace. For instance, in the Old Testament Abram (later named Abraham) and his wife, Sarai (Sarah), and nephew, Lot, moved to Canaan where they lived as nomadic shepherds. When conflict arose between Abram and Lot regarding available pastures and water for their livestock, Abram took the initiative to settle the dispute. Although Abram would normally have first pick of the land since he was older, he put the peace of the family above his individual wishes.*

So Abram went up from Egypt to the Negev, with his wife and everything he had, and Lot went with him. Abram had become very wealthy in livestock and in silver and gold.

From the Negev he went from place to place until he came to Bethel, to the place between Bethel and Ai where his tent had been earlier and where he had first built an altar. There Abram called on the name of the LORD.

Now Lot, who was moving about with Abram, also had flocks and herds and tents. But the land could not support them while they stayed together, for their possessions were so great that they were not able to stay together. And quarreling arose between Abram's herders and Lot's. The Canaanites and Perizzites were also living in the land at that time.

**So Abram said to Lot, "Let's not have any quarreling between you and me, or between your herders and mine, for we are close relatives. Is not the whole land before you? Let's part company. If you go to the left, I'll go to the right; if you go to the right, I'll go to the left."**

Lot looked around and saw that the whole plain of the Jordan toward Zoar was well watered, like the garden of the LORD, like the land of Egypt. (This was before the LORD destroyed Sodom and Gomorrah.) So Lot chose for himself the whole plain of the Jordan and set out toward the east. The two men parted company: Abram lived in the land of Canaan, while Lot lived among the cities of the plain and pitched his tents near Sodom. Now the people of Sodom were wicked and were sinning greatly against the LORD.

The LORD said to Abram after Lot had parted from him, "Look around from where you are, to the north and south, to the east and west. All the land that you see I will give to you and your offspring forever. I will make your offspring like the dust of the earth, so that if anyone could count the dust, then your offspring could be counted. Go, walk through the length and breadth of the land, for I am giving it to you."

So Abram went to live near the great trees of Mamre at Hebron, where he pitched his tents. There he built an altar to the LORD.

GENESIS 13:1–18

---

When Abram wanted to make peace with Lot, he let him choose first. How did God reward Abram for putting others first and giving up what appeared to be the best land? When is it hard for you to let others go first?

---

*During the early part of his reign, King Solomon had a special encounter with God. His response to that encounter led to greater peace with God and a greater ability to know right from wrong as he led his kingdom. Wise and just ruling resolves conflicts properly and leads to greater peace with others in the long run. The same principles apply to our lives today. (Note: Solomon's obedience to God is found in the shift from his sacrifices on the high places of Gibeon to his sacrifice in front of the ark of the Lord's covenant in Jerusalem after his dream.)*

Solomon showed his love for the LORD by walking according to the instructions given him by his father David, except that he offered sacrifices and burned incense on the high places.

The king went to Gibeon to offer sacrifices, for that was the most important high place, and Solomon offered a thousand burnt offerings on that altar. At Gibeon the LORD appeared to Solomon during the night in a dream, and God said, "Ask for whatever you want me to give you."

Solomon answered, "You have shown great kindness to your servant, my father David, because he was faithful to you and righteous and upright in heart. You have continued this great kindness to him and have given him a son to sit on his throne this very day.

"Now, LORD my God, you have made your servant king in place of my father David. But I am only a little child and do not know how to carry out my duties. Your servant is here among the people you have chosen, a great people, too numerous to count or number. So give your servant a discerning heart to govern your people and to distinguish between right and wrong. For who is able to govern this great people of yours?"

The LORD was pleased that Solomon had asked for this. So God said to him, "Since you have asked for this and not for long life or wealth for yourself, nor have asked for the death of your enemies but for discernment in administering justice, I will do what you have asked. I will give you a wise and discerning heart, so that there will never have been anyone like you, nor will there ever be. Moreover, I will give you what you have not asked for — both wealth and honor — so that in your lifetime you will have no equal among kings. And if you walk in obedience to me and keep my decrees and commands as David your father did, I will give you a long life." Then Solomon awoke — and he realized it had been a dream.

He returned to Jerusalem, stood before the ark of the LORD's covenant and sacrificed burnt offerings and fellowship offerings. Then he gave a feast for all his court.                    1 KINGS 3:3–15

*The outcome of Solomon's decision is recorded below. If we want greater peace in our lives, we should first seek to live in obedience to God and then apply his wisdom to find peace in our relationships with others.*

The people of Judah and Israel were as numerous as the sand on the seashore; they ate, they drank and they were happy. And Solomon ruled over all the kingdoms from the Euphrates River to the land of the Philistines, as far as the border of Egypt. These countries brought tribute and were Solomon's subjects all his life.

Solomon's daily provisions were thirty cors of the finest flour and sixty cors of meal, ten head of stall-fed cattle, twenty of pasture-fed cattle and a hundred sheep and goats, as well as deer, gazelles, roebucks and choice fowl. **For he ruled over all the kingdoms west of the Euphrates River, from Tiphsah to Gaza, and**

**had peace on all sides. During Solomon's lifetime Judah and Israel, from Dan to Beersheba, lived in safety, everyone under their own vine and under their own fig tree.** 1 KINGS 4:20–25 🔑

*Living at peace with one another can be a challenge. We each think and feel differently. Naturally there are bound to be conflicts among us. The church in New Testament times was made up of both Jews and Gentiles. Many Jewish converts to Christianity held on to the rituals of the Old Testament Law regarding diets and festivals. Other Jews gladly left these rules behind in favor of their new freedom in Christ. Because the Gentiles had little concern for these traditions, it often created tension in their church communities. Paul instructed the church in Rome how to experience peace even amid their intense disagreements.*

Accept the one whose faith is weak, without quarreling over disputable matters. One person's faith allows them to eat anything, but another, whose faith is weak, eats only vegetables. The one who eats everything must not treat with contempt the one who does not, and the one who does not eat everything must not judge the one who does, for God has accepted them. Who are you to judge someone else's servant? To their own master, servants stand or fall. And they will stand, for the Lord is able to make them stand.

One person considers one day more sacred than another; another considers every day alike. Each of them should be fully convinced in their own mind. Whoever regards one day as special does so to the Lord. Whoever eats meat does so to the Lord, for they give thanks to God; and whoever abstains does so to the Lord and gives thanks to God. For none of us lives for ourselves alone, and none of us dies for ourselves alone. If we live, we live for the Lord; and if we die, we die for the Lord. So, whether we live or die, we belong to the Lord. For this very reason, Christ died and returned to life so that he might be the Lord of both the dead and the living.

You, then, why do you judge your brother or sister? Or why do you treat them with contempt? For we will all stand before God's judgment seat. It is written:

> "'As surely as I live,' says the Lord,
> 'every knee will bow before me;
>     every tongue will acknowledge God.'"

So then, each of us will give an account of ourselves to God.

Therefore let us stop passing judgment on one another. Instead, make up your mind not to put any stumbling block or obstacle in the way of a brother or sister. I am convinced, being fully persuaded in the Lord Jesus, that nothing is unclean in itself. But if anyone regards something as unclean, then for that person it is unclean. If your brother or sister is distressed because of what you eat, you are no longer acting in love. Do not by your eating destroy someone for whom Christ died. Therefore do not let what you know is good be spoken of as evil. For the kingdom of God is not a matter of eating and drinking, but of righteousness, peace and joy in the Holy Spirit, because anyone who serves Christ in this way is pleasing to God and receives human approval.

**Let us therefore make every effort to do what leads to peace and to mutual edification.** Do not destroy the work of God for the sake of food. All food is clean, but it is wrong for a person to eat anything that causes someone else to stumble. It is better not to eat meat or drink wine or to do anything else that will cause your brother or sister to fall.

So whatever you believe about these things keep between yourself and God. Blessed is the one who does not condemn himself by what he approves. But whoever has doubts is condemned if they eat, because their eating is not from faith; and everything that does not come from faith is sin.

We who are strong ought to bear with the failings of the weak and not to please ourselves. Each of us should please our neighbors for their good, to build them up. For even Christ did not please himself but, as it is written: "The insults of those who insult you have fallen on me." For everything that was written in the past was written to teach us, so that through the endurance taught in the Scriptures and the encouragement they provide we might have hope.

May the God who gives endurance and encouragement give you the same attitude of mind toward each other that Christ Jesus had, so that with one mind and one voice you may glorify the God and Father of our Lord Jesus Christ.

Accept one another, then, just as Christ accepted you, in order to bring praise to God. For I tell you that Christ has become a servant of the Jews on behalf of God's truth, so that the promises made to the patriarchs might be confirmed and, moreover, that the Gentiles might glorify God for his mercy. As it is written:

> "Therefore I will praise you among the Gentiles;
>     I will sing the praises of your name."

Again, it says,

> "Rejoice, you Gentiles, with his people."

And again,

> "Praise the Lord, all you Gentiles;
>     let all the peoples extol him."

And again, Isaiah says,

> "The Root of Jesse will spring up,
>     one who will arise to rule over the nations;
>     in him the Gentiles will hope."

May the God of hope fill you with all joy and peace as you trust in him, so that you may overflow with hope by the power of the Holy Spirit.                                    ROMANS 14:1—15:13

---

"Disputable matters" are areas where there is more than
one acceptable option or opinion, so we must each decide
with conviction and yet respect others who choose differently.
What are "disputable matters" for Christians today?

---

## PEACE WITH YOURSELF (INNER PEACE)

*As followers of Christ, we must be prepared to deal with the troubles that come our way in the strength God provides. It might be tempting to give in to the stress, but as Jesus clearly illustrated to his disciples, through our faith we can find peace and remain in control.*

⊶ That day when evening came, he said to his disciples, "Let us go over to the other side." Leaving the crowd behind, they took him along, just as he was, in the boat. There were also other boats with him. A furious squall came up, and the waves broke over the boat, so that it was nearly swamped. Jesus was in the stern, sleeping on a cushion. The disciples woke him and said to him, "Teacher, don't you care if we drown?"

He got up, rebuked the wind and said to the waves, "Quiet! Be still!" Then the wind died down and it was completely calm.

**He said to his disciples, "Why are you so afraid? Do you still have no faith?"**

They were terrified and asked each other, "Who is this? Even the wind and the waves obey him!"                    Mark 4:35–41 ⊶

---

When have you seen Jesus calm a "storm"
(a stressful situation) in your life? How did he do it?

---

*Worry is the thief of peace in our lives. Worry not only prevents us from sleeping well at night, but it also keeps us on edge during the day. Our Prince of Peace, Jesus, emphasized the Father's ability to care for his people individually before they let the worries of this life overwhelm them.*

"Therefore I tell you, do not worry about your life, what you will eat or drink; or about your body, what you will wear. Is not life more than food, and the body more than clothes? Look at the birds of the air; they do not sow or reap or store away in barns, and yet your heavenly Father feeds them. Are you not much more valuable than they? Can any one of you by worrying add a single hour to your life?

"And why do you worry about clothes? See how the flowers of the field grow. They do not labor or spin. Yet I tell you that not even Solomon in all his splendor was dressed like one of these. If that is how God clothes the grass of the field, which is here today and tomorrow is thrown into the fire, will he not much more clothe you — you of little faith? **So do not worry, saying, 'What shall we eat?' or 'What shall we drink?' or 'What shall we wear?' For** the pagans run after all these things, and your heavenly Father knows that you need them. **But seek first his kingdom and his righteousness, and all these things will be given to you as well.** Therefore do not worry about tomorrow, for tomorrow will worry about itself. Each day has enough trouble of its own."

Matthew 6:25–34

---

What is Jesus' prescription for anxiety and worry?

---

*As Paul wrapped up his personal letter to the believers at Philippi, he spoke to them directly on how to obtain a peace that goes beyond human understanding.*

Rejoice in the Lord always. I will say it again: Rejoice! Let your gentleness be evident to all. The Lord is near. **Do not be anxious about anything, but in every situation, by prayer and petition, with thanksgiving, present your requests to God. And the peace of God, which transcends all understanding, will guard your hearts and your minds in Christ Jesus.**

Finally, brothers and sisters, whatever is true, whatever is noble, whatever is right, whatever is pure, whatever is lovely, whatever is admirable — if anything is excellent or praiseworthy — think about such things. Whatever you have learned or received or heard from me, or seen in me — put it into practice. And the God of peace will be with you.

Philippians 4:4–9

---

From this passage containing our key verse,
what is Paul's prescription for anxiety and worry?
How do the prescriptions of Paul
and Jesus work together?

---

## WHAT WE BELIEVE

*The feeling of peace we long for will flow naturally when things are right in our relationships. Of greatest importance is a reconciled relationship with God, made possible through Jesus Christ. When we accept his offer of salvation, the conflict between God and us is forever eliminated. A reconciled relationship with God now becomes the source of peace in our relationships with others.*

*The Scripture in this chapter lays out how we do our part to promote peace in our relationships. God's Spirit within enables us to achieve this. We are also called to live at peace with ourselves by accepting God's love and forgiveness in our lives. It requires that we take the things that burden and trouble us and give them to God. When we do this we declare that God is bigger than any of our problems and that the "peace of God, which transcends all understanding, will guard [our] hearts and [our] minds in Christ Jesus" (Philippians 4:7).*

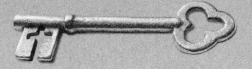

# CHAPTER

## 24

# Self-Control

---

### KEY QUESTION

How does God free me from addictions and sinful habits?

---

### KEY IDEA

I have the power through Christ to control myself.

---

### KEY VERSE

For the grace of God has appeared that offers salvation
to all people. It teaches us to say "No" to ungodliness
and worldly passions, and to live self-controlled,
upright and godly lives in this present age, while we wait
for the blessed hope — the appearing of the glory
of our great God and Savior, Jesus Christ.

*Titus 2:11–13*

OUR MAP

*Self-control refers to the ability to control one's emotions and behavior. Everyone at some point struggles with self-control—it's the presence of the sin nature within us. So how does God help us when we have lost control and have let our sinful nature take over? How does he free us from addictions and sinful habits? God's Word contains the answer.*

*In this chapter we will be reading about:*

- *The Call and the Challenge*
- *Models of Self-Control: Bad and Good*
- *The How-To's*

## THE CALL AND THE CHALLENGE

*God desires for all of us to have self-control. However, in the face of pressure, the battle to keep our sinful nature in check is easier said than done. The writer of Proverbs places options before us, clearly showing the benefits of a self-controlled life and the pain of a reckless one.*

Better a patient person than a warrior,
   one with self-control than one who takes a city.

PROVERBS 16:32

The one who has knowledge uses words with restraint,
   and whoever has understanding is even-tempered.

PROVERBS 17:27

**Like a city whose walls are broken through
is a person who lacks self-control.** PROVERBS 25:28

Fools give full vent to their rage,
   but the wise bring calm in the end. PROVERBS 29:11

*Self-control means having power over one's own impulses, reactions and desires. Paul wrote a personal letter to his ministry partner Titus instructing him to appoint elders in the church in Crete. Self-control was a prominent characteristic Titus was to look for in these spiritual leaders. Paul also instructed Titus to call believers of all ages to this virtue, which was obviously much needed in Crete.*

To Titus, my true son in our common faith:

Grace and peace from God the Father and Christ Jesus our Savior.

The reason I left you in Crete was that you might put in order what was left unfinished and appoint elders in every town, as I directed you. An elder must be blameless, faithful to his wife, a man whose children believe and are not open to the charge of being wild and disobedient. **Since an overseer manages God's household, he must be blameless — not overbearing, not quick-tempered, not given to drunkenness, not violent, not pursuing dishonest gain. Rather, he must be hospitable, one who loves what is good, who is self-controlled, upright, holy and disciplined.** He must hold firmly to the trustworthy message as it has been taught, so that he can encourage others by sound doctrine and refute those who oppose it.                    Titus 1:4–9

Likewise, teach the older women to be reverent in the way they live, not to be slanderers or addicted to much wine, but to teach what is good. Then they can urge the younger women to love their husbands and children, to be self-controlled and pure, to be busy at home, to be kind, and to be subject to their husbands, so that no one will malign the word of God.

Similarly, encourage the young men to be self-controlled. In everything set them an example by doing what is good. In your teaching show integrity, seriousness and soundness of speech that cannot be condemned, so that those who oppose you may be ashamed because they have nothing bad to say about us.

                                                        Titus 2:3–8

For the grace of God has appeared that offers salvation to all people. It teaches us to say "No" to ungodliness and worldly passions, and to live self-controlled, upright and godly lives in this present age, while we wait for the blessed hope — the appearing of the glory of our great God and Savior, Jesus Christ, who gave himself for us to redeem us from all wickedness and to purify for himself a people that are his very own, eager to do what is good.

These, then, are the things you should teach. Encourage and rebuke with all authority. Do not let anyone despise you.

TITUS 2:11–15

---

Underline or highlight every time the word "self-control" was used in the previous passages. Why do you think self-control is a key virtue required for church leaders?

---

## MODELS OF SELF-CONTROL: BAD AND GOOD

*During the days of the judges, the Philistines bullied Israel for forty years. But time after time, God raised up a special person, a judge, to deliver Israel from this oppression. God intervened in the life of a childless Israelite couple and enabled the wife to conceive and give birth to Samson, who would be used by God to set Israel free from this bondage. From conception Samson was a Nazirite—which comes from the Hebrew word meaning "separated"—and God blessed him with supernatural strength. As a spiritual and physical sign of this vow, Samson was never to cut his hair. Interestingly, this special man, one of the last judges of Israel, struggled mightily with self-control over his sexual passions; and ironically, he was particularly attracted to Philistine women. Eventually Samson let his lack of self-control get the best of him.*

[Samson] fell in love with a woman in the Valley of Sorek whose name was Delilah. The rulers of the Philistines went to her and said, "See if you can lure him into showing you the secret of his great strength and how we can overpower him so we may tie him up and subdue him. Each one of us will give you eleven hundred shekels of silver."

So Delilah said to Samson, "Tell me the secret of your great strength and how you can be tied up and subdued."

Samson answered her, "If anyone ties me with seven fresh bowstrings that have not been dried, I'll become as weak as any other man."

Then the rulers of the Philistines brought her seven fresh bow-strings that had not been dried, and she tied him with them. With men hidden in the room, she called to him, "Samson, the Philistines are upon you!" But he snapped the bowstrings as easily as a piece of string snaps when it comes close to a flame. So the secret of his strength was not discovered.

Then Delilah said to Samson, "You have made a fool of me; you lied to me. Come now, tell me how you can be tied."

He said, "If anyone ties me securely with new ropes that have never been used, I'll become as weak as any other man."

So Delilah took new ropes and tied him with them. Then, with men hidden in the room, she called to him, "Samson, the Philistines are upon you!" But he snapped the ropes off his arms as if they were threads.

Delilah then said to Samson, "All this time you have been making a fool of me and lying to me. Tell me how you can be tied."

He replied, "If you weave the seven braids of my head into the fabric on the loom and tighten it with the pin, I'll become as weak as any other man." So while he was sleeping, Delilah took the seven braids of his head, wove them into the fabric and tightened it with the pin.

Again she called to him, "Samson, the Philistines are upon you!" He awoke from his sleep and pulled up the pin and the loom, with the fabric.

Then she said to him, "How can you say, 'I love you,' when you won't confide in me? This is the third time you have made a fool of me and haven't told me the secret of your great strength." With such nagging she prodded him day after day until he was sick to death of it.

**So he told her everything. "No razor has ever been used on my head," he said, "because I have been a Nazirite dedicated to God from my mother's womb. If my head were shaved, my strength would leave me, and I would become as weak as any other man."**

When Delilah saw that he had told her everything, she sent word to the rulers of the Philistines, "Come back once more; he has told me everything." So the rulers of the Philistines returned with the silver in their hands. After putting him to sleep on her lap, she called for someone to shave off the seven braids of his hair, and so began to subdue him. And his strength left him.

Then she called, "Samson, the Philistines are upon you!"

He awoke from his sleep and thought, "I'll go out as before and shake myself free." But he did not know that the LORD had left him.

Then the Philistines seized him, gouged out his eyes and took him down to Gaza. Binding him with bronze shackles, they set him to grinding grain in the prison.          JUDGES 16:4–21 ⚷

## THE HOW-TO'S

*The Bible offers practical instruction on how to grow in the virtue of self-control. One of the best pieces of advice is to "flee"—flee from the person, environment or situation that tempts us to lose control. This was especially needed in the ancient city of Corinth. It was a tough place to live a pure life because the people were known for sinful living. In Paul's letter to the Christians there, he reminded them how to fight against impurity.*

**Flee from sexual immorality.** All other sins a person commits are outside the body, but whoever sins sexually, sins against their own body. Do you not know that your bodies are temples of the Holy Spirit, who is in you, whom you have received from God? You are not your own; you were bought at a price. Therefore honor God with your bodies.          1 CORINTHIANS 6:18–20

*Paul wrote two letters to a man named Timothy, who was a young church leader. In these letters, he gave him instructions on how to live a holy life and also guide others to do the same. Paul encouraged Timothy to avoid false teachers and the love of money. Again we see the word "flee." There are times when it is best to avoid people who may draw you into ungodly behaviors.*

But godliness with contentment is great gain. For we brought nothing into the world, and we can take nothing out of it. But if we have food and clothing, we will be content with that. Those who want to get rich fall into temptation and a trap and into many foolish and harmful desires that plunge people into ruin and destruction. For the love of money is a root of all kinds of evil. Some people, eager for money, have wandered from the faith and pierced themselves with many griefs.

**But you, man of God, flee from all this,** and pursue righteousness, godliness, faith, love, endurance and gentleness.

1 TIMOTHY 6:6–11

**Flee the evil desires of youth** and pursue righteousness, faith, love and peace, along with those who call on the Lord out of a pure heart. Don't have anything to do with foolish and stupid arguments, because you know they produce quarrels. And the Lord's servant must not be quarrelsome but must be kind to everyone, able to teach, not resentful. Opponents must be gently instructed, in the hope that God will grant them repentance leading them to a knowledge of the truth, and that they will come to their senses and escape from the trap of the devil, who has taken them captive to do his will.

2 TIMOTHY 2:22–26

---

What does the company we keep have to do
with our ability to be self-controlled?

---

*The answer to temptation isn't always to "flee." Sometimes God calls us not to run away but to resist. This is what we see in the letter written by James. He reminds us that it is hard work to hold your tongue when you're angry or to forgive someone when they've offended you. In those times, it often seems like "self-control" isn't enough, and in one sense, it isn't. We need not only self-control but "God-control"—we need to let God take over our lives and guide our actions. The only way we can continually fight against sin and impurity is to remember that God is within us and has the power to help us overcome any temptation.*

When we put bits into the mouths of horses to make them obey us, we can turn the whole animal. Or take ships as an example. Although they are so large and are driven by strong winds, they are steered by a very small rudder wherever the pilot wants to go. Likewise, the tongue is a small part of the body, but it makes great boasts. Consider what a great forest is set on fire by a small spark. The tongue also is a fire, a world of evil among the parts of the body. It corrupts the whole body, sets the whole course of one's life on fire, and is itself set on fire by hell.

All kinds of animals, birds, reptiles and sea creatures are being tamed and have been tamed by mankind, but no human being can tame the tongue. It is a restless evil, full of deadly poison.

With the tongue we praise our Lord and Father, and with it we curse human beings, who have been made in God's likeness. Out of the same mouth come praise and cursing. My brothers and sisters, this should not be. Can both fresh water and salt water flow from the same spring?                    JAMES 3:3–11

What causes fights and quarrels among you? Don't they come from your desires that battle within you? You desire but do not have, so you kill. You covet but you cannot get what you want, so you quarrel and fight. You do not have because you do not ask God. When you ask, you do not receive, because you ask with wrong motives, that you may spend what you get on your pleasures.

You adulterous people, don't you know that friendship with the world means enmity against God? Therefore, anyone who chooses to be a friend of the world becomes an enemy of God. Or do you think Scripture says without reason that he jealously longs for the spirit he has caused to dwell in us? But he gives us more grace. That is why Scripture says:

> "God opposes the proud
>    but shows favor to the humble."

**Submit yourselves, then, to God. Resist the devil, and he will flee from you. Come near to God and he will come near to you.** Wash your hands, you sinners, and purify your hearts, you double-minded. Grieve, mourn and wail. Change your laughter to mourning and your joy to gloom. Humble yourselves before the Lord, and he will lift you up.                    JAMES 4:1–10

---

Why is our tongue so difficult to control?

*The best solution for "self-control" is to learn "God-control." Paul reminds us to rely on God's grace, walk with the Holy Spirit's power, and follow the example of Jesus.*

So I say, walk by the Spirit, and you will not gratify the desires of the flesh. For the flesh desires what is contrary to the Spirit, and the Spirit what is contrary to the flesh. They are in conflict with each other, so that you are not to do whatever you want. But if you are led by the Spirit, you are not under the law.

The acts of the flesh are obvious: sexual immorality, impurity and debauchery; idolatry and witchcraft; hatred, discord, jealousy, fits of rage, selfish ambition, dissensions, factions and envy; drunkenness, orgies, and the like. I warn you, as I did before, that those who live like this will not inherit the kingdom of God.

But the fruit of the Spirit is love, joy, peace, forbearance, kindness, goodness, faithfulness, gentleness and self-control. Against such things there is no law. Those who belong to Christ Jesus have crucified the flesh with its passions and desires. Since we live by the Spirit, let us keep in step with the Spirit.     GALATIANS 5:16–25

Describe in your own words how "God-control" works to bring about "self-control" in our lives.

*Bottom line, we all struggle and fall. This failure can leave us drowning in a pile of guilt that causes us to hide from God out of embarrassment. God knows we struggle. He sent his only Son to make up the difference in the gap of righteousness in our lives. He wants for us to "come home" to him no matter our condition. This is demonstrated in the most beautiful way in the story below from the lips of Jesus himself.*

Jesus continued: "There was a man who had two sons. The younger one said to his father, 'Father, give me my share of the estate.' So he divided his property between them.

"Not long after that, the younger son got together all he had, set off for a distant country and there squandered his wealth in wild living. After he had spent everything, there was a severe famine in that whole country, and he began to be in need. So he went and hired himself out to a citizen of that country, who sent him to his fields to feed pigs. He longed to fill his stomach with the pods that the pigs were eating, but no one gave him anything.

"When he came to his senses, he said, 'How many of my father's hired servants have food to spare, and here I am starving to death! I will set out and go back to my father and say to him: Father, I have sinned against heaven and against you. I am no longer worthy to be called your son; make me like one of your hired servants.' So he got up and went to his father.

"But while he was still a long way off, his father saw him and was filled with compassion for him; he ran to his son, threw his arms around him and kissed him.

"The son said to him, 'Father, I have sinned against heaven and against you. I am no longer worthy to be called your son.'

**"But the father said to his servants, 'Quick! Bring the best robe and put it on him. Put a ring on his finger and sandals on his feet. Bring the fattened calf and kill it. Let's have a feast and celebrate. For this son of mine was dead and is alive again; he was lost and is found.' So they began to celebrate."**

LUKE 15:11–24

---

In what areas of your life do you struggle
with self-control? How do these readings
challenge you? How does the knowledge
of God's grace comfort you?

---

## WHAT WE BELIEVE

*If we truly desire to become like Jesus for the sake of others, we will receive the call and challenge to be self-controlled. As we read the true stories found in the pages of the Bible we see evidence of the wreckage in our lives when we lack self-control, as in the case with Samson. How do we free ourselves from addictions and sinful habits? We must learn how to "flee" and how to resist the temptation before us. But the ultimate producer of self-control is "God-control." As we yield our lives to God's plan, his divine power gives us the strength to say no to ungodliness and yes to his will. We have the power, through Christ, to control ourselves. Yet, when we fall, we can remember God's grace and run back to him. He will be waiting every time with welcoming arms.*

CHAPTER

## 25

# Hope

---

### KEY QUESTION

How do I deal with the hardships and struggles of life?

---

### KEY IDEA

I can deal with the hardships of life
because of the hope I have in Jesus Christ.

---

### KEY VERSE

We have this hope as an anchor for the soul,
firm and secure. It enters the inner sanctuary
behind the curtain, where our forerunner,
Jesus, has entered on our behalf.
*Hebrews 6:19–20*

*We simply cannot live without hope. As our key verse above states, Christian hope is an anchor for our souls. It stabilizes us during difficult seasons because we know this is not how our story ends. It is rooted in our belief and trust in God, our personal God, and the salvation and eternity he offers. If we believe these truths in our hearts, it will produce a hope that doesn't disappoint.*

*This chapter addresses:*

- *Sources of False Hope*
- *The Source of True Hope*
- *The Effect of Hope*

*and how...*

- *Hope Activates Faith, Faith Deepens Hope*

## SOURCES OF FALSE HOPE

*Our deep need for hope sometimes leads us to falsely put our hope in unhealthy things. False hope causes people to plan, build and risk for something that is not likely to happen. The Bible identifies several things humans unfortunately place their hope in, only to be disappointed in the end.*

---

As you read about the four sources of false hope, which one are you most susceptible to? What made you pick the one you did?

---

*False hope ... in riches.*

*Paul tells Timothy to instruct believers about the false hope of trusting in riches.*

**Command those who are rich in this present world not to be arrogant nor to put their hope in wealth, which is so uncertain, but to put their hope in God, who richly provides us with everything for our enjoyment.** 1 TIMOTHY 6:17

*False hope ... in people.*

*The Bible tells us that we will be disappointed if we place our hope in people rather than God.*

**It is better to take refuge in the Lord
than to trust in humans.**
It is better to take refuge in the Lord
than to trust in princes. PSALM 118:8–9

**"Cursed is the one who trusts in man,
who draws strength from mere flesh
and whose heart turns away from the Lord.**
That person will be like a bush in the wastelands;
they will not see prosperity when it comes.
They will dwell in the parched places of the desert,
in a salt land where no one lives." JEREMIAH 17:5B–6

*False hope ... in idols.*
*An idol is anything we place above God. The prophet Habakkuk reminds us how foolish it is to place our hope in such manmade inventions.*

**"Of what value is an idol carved by a craftsman?**
Or an image that teaches lies?
For the one who makes it trusts in his own creation;
he makes idols that cannot speak.
Woe to him who says to wood, 'Come to life!'
Or to lifeless stone, 'Wake up!'
Can it give guidance?
It is covered with gold and silver;
there is no breath in it." HABAKKUK 2:18–19

*False hope ... in human government.*
*It is easy for people to place their hope in nations and government. Isaiah warns the people of Judah to avoid such a mistake, even with a strong nation like Egypt.*

**But the Egyptians are mere mortals and not God;**
their horses are flesh and not spirit.
When the Lord stretches out his hand,
those who help will stumble,
those who are helped will fall;
all will perish together. ISAIAH 31:3

## THE SOURCE OF TRUE HOPE

*True hope is found only in God.*

*Hope is only as good as the power and character of the one who guarantees it. Our hope is not in the temporary things of this world but in the eternal God who has promised to give us eternal life. The ultimate promise of God is our future resurrection. The hope of this promise trumps all our present difficulties.*

---

What promises of God can you find
in the Scripture in this section?

---

Peter, an apostle of Jesus Christ,

To God's elect, exiles scattered throughout the provinces of Pontus, Galatia, Cappadocia, Asia and Bithynia, who have been chosen according to the foreknowledge of God the Father, through the sanctifying work of the Spirit, to be obedient to Jesus Christ and sprinkled with his blood:

Grace and peace be yours in abundance.

Praise be to the God and Father of our Lord Jesus Christ! **In his great mercy he has given us new birth into a living hope through the resurrection of Jesus Christ from the dead, and into an inheritance that can never perish, spoil or fade.** This inheritance is kept in heaven for you, who through faith are shielded by God's power until the coming of the salvation that is ready to be revealed in the last time. In all this you greatly rejoice, though now for a little while you may have had to suffer grief in all kinds of trials. These have come so that the proven genuineness of your faith — of greater worth than gold, which perishes even though refined by fire — may result in praise, glory and honor when Jesus Christ is revealed. Though you have not seen him, you love him; and even though you do not see him now, you believe in him and are filled with an inexpressible and glorious joy, for you are receiving the end result of your faith, the salvation of your souls.                1 PETER 1:1–9

**Therefore, with minds that are alert and fully sober, set your hope on the grace to be brought to you when Jesus Christ**

**is revealed at his coming.** As obedient children, do not conform to the evil desires you had when you lived in ignorance. But just as he who called you is holy, so be holy in all you do; for it is written: "Be holy, because I am holy."

Since you call on a Father who judges each person's work impartially, live out your time as foreigners here in reverent fear. For you know that it was not with perishable things such as silver or gold that you were redeemed from the empty way of life handed down to you from your ancestors, but with the precious blood of Christ, a lamb without blemish or defect. He was chosen before the creation of the world, but was revealed in these last times for your sake. Through him you believe in God, who raised him from the dead and glorified him, and so your faith and hope are in God.

1 PETER 1:13–21

## THE EFFECT OF HOPE

*When we hope in God's promises, the effect on our lives is profound. Even if we are going through difficulties, hope gives us the strength to endure. Isaiah prophesied that the people of Judah were about to go through 70 years of difficulty as captives of the Babylonians. Despite such suffering, Isaiah was able to confidently give the people hope because God promised to bring them home. The exiles could live full, happy lives in a painful situation because they knew God would keep his promise.*

"To whom will you compare me?
    Or who is my equal?" says the Holy One.
Lift up your eyes and look to the heavens:
    Who created all these?
He who brings out the starry host one by one
    and calls forth each of them by name.
Because of his great power and mighty strength,
    not one of them is missing.

Why do you complain, Jacob?
    Why do you say, Israel,
"My way is hidden from the LORD;
    my cause is disregarded by my God"?

282 | BELIEVE: Student Edition

Do you not know?
  Have you not heard?
The LORD is the everlasting God,
  the Creator of the ends of the earth.
He will not grow tired or weary,
  and his understanding no one can fathom.
He gives strength to the weary
  and increases the power of the weak.
**Even youths grow tired and weary,**
  **and young men stumble and fall;**
**but those who hope in the LORD**
  **will renew their strength.**
**They will soar on wings like eagles;**
  **they will run and not grow weary,**
  **they will walk and not be faint.**          ISAIAH 40:25–31 ⌥

---

What situations do you encounter that make you grow
tired and weary, or stumble and fall? How do you
think hoping in the Lord works to re-energize you?

---

*The positive effect of hope on our lives is more powerful than
we realize. Simeon waited many long years without seeing the
fulfillment of his hope, but he carried on, letting hope give him
strength for each new day. God and his promises are the reason for our hope. When we embrace this hope, it has a dramatic
effect on our daily lives. Simeon's story helps us realize what a
great impact our hope in Christ has on our ability to get through
our days, to persevere.*

⌥ Now there was a man in Jerusalem called Simeon, who was
righteous and devout. He was waiting for the consolation of Israel,
and the Holy Spirit was on him. It had been revealed to him by
the Holy Spirit that he would not die before he had seen the Lord's
Messiah. Moved by the Spirit, he went into the temple courts.
When the parents brought in the child Jesus to do for him what
the custom of the Law required, Simeon took him in his arms and
praised God, saying:

"Sovereign Lord, as you have promised,
    you may now dismiss your servant in peace.
For my eyes have seen your salvation,
    which you have prepared in the sight of all nations:
a light for revelation to the Gentiles,
    and the glory of your people Israel."

The child's father and mother marveled at what was said about him. Then Simeon blessed them and said to Mary, his mother: "This child is destined to cause the falling and rising of many in Israel, and to be a sign that will be spoken against, so that the thoughts of many hearts will be revealed. And a sword will pierce your own soul too."
LUKE 2:25–35 ⚷

---

What effect did God's promise to Simeon that he would
see the first arrival of Christ have on his life?
What effect should God's promise to us that we will see
the second arrival of Christ have on our lives?

---

## HOPE ACTIVATES FAITH, FAITH DEEPENS HOPE

*Hope is available to all followers of God, but not everyone takes hold of it. It can be hard for us to trust in a God we cannot see and hold fast to fantastic promises yet to come. To activate the power of hope in our lives, we need to have faith in God and his promises. The writer of Hebrews preached this message to his readers. He then listed people from the past who placed their faith in God and experienced amazing results in their lives. God offers this same opportunity to us today. In fact, God has "something better" planned for those who know Jesus.*

**Now faith is confidence in what we hope for and assurance about what we do not see. This is what the ancients were commended for.**

By faith we understand that the universe was formed at God's command, so that what is seen was not made out of what is visible.

By faith Abel brought God a better offering than Cain did. By faith he was commended as righteous, when God spoke well of his offerings. And by faith Abel still speaks, even though he is dead.

By faith Enoch was taken from this life, so that he did not experience death: "He could not be found, because God had taken him away." For before he was taken, he was commended as one who pleased God. And without faith it is impossible to please God, because anyone who comes to him must believe that he exists and that he rewards those who earnestly seek him.

By faith Noah, when warned about things not yet seen, in holy fear built an ark to save his family. By his faith he condemned the world and became heir of the righteousness that is in keeping with faith.

By faith Abraham, when called to go to a place he would later receive as his inheritance, obeyed and went, even though he did not know where he was going. By faith he made his home in the promised land like a stranger in a foreign country; he lived in tents, as did Isaac and Jacob, who were heirs with him of the same promise. For he was looking forward to the city with foundations, whose architect and builder is God. And by faith even Sarah, who was past childbearing age, was enabled to bear children because she considered him faithful who had made the promise. And so from this one man, and he as good as dead, came descendants as numerous as the stars in the sky and as countless as the sand on the seashore.

All these people were still living by faith when they died. They did not receive the things promised; they only saw them and welcomed them from a distance, admitting that they were foreigners and strangers on earth. People who say such things show that they are looking for a country of their own. If they had been thinking of the country they had left, they would have had opportunity to return. Instead, they were longing for a better country — a heavenly one. Therefore God is not ashamed to be called their God, for he has prepared a city for them.

By faith Abraham, when God tested him, offered Isaac as a sacrifice. He who had embraced the promises was about to sacrifice his one and only son, even though God had said to him, "It is through Isaac that your offspring will be reckoned." Abraham reasoned that God could even raise the dead, and so in a manner of speaking he did receive Isaac back from death.

By faith Isaac blessed Jacob and Esau in regard to their future.

By faith Jacob, when he was dying, blessed each of Joseph's sons, and worshiped as he leaned on the top of his staff.

By faith Joseph, when his end was near, spoke about the exodus of the Israelites from Egypt and gave instructions concerning the burial of his bones.

By faith Moses' parents hid him for three months after he was born, because they saw he was no ordinary child, and they were not afraid of the king's edict.

By faith Moses, when he had grown up, refused to be known as the son of Pharaoh's daughter. He chose to be mistreated along with the people of God rather than to enjoy the fleeting pleasures of sin. He regarded disgrace for the sake of Christ as of greater value than the treasures of Egypt, because he was looking ahead to his reward. By faith he left Egypt, not fearing the king's anger; he persevered because he saw him who is invisible. By faith he kept the Passover and the application of blood, so that the destroyer of the firstborn would not touch the firstborn of Israel.

By faith the people passed through the Red Sea as on dry land; but when the Egyptians tried to do so, they were drowned.

By faith the walls of Jericho fell, after the army had marched around them for seven days.

By faith the prostitute Rahab, because she welcomed the spies, was not killed with those who were disobedient.

And what more shall I say? I do not have time to tell about Gideon, Barak, Samson and Jephthah, about David and Samuel and the prophets, who through faith conquered kingdoms, administered justice, and gained what was promised; who shut the mouths of lions, quenched the fury of the flames, and escaped the edge of the sword; whose weakness was turned to strength; and who became powerful in battle and routed foreign armies. Women received back their dead, raised to life again. There were others who were tortured, refusing to be released so that they might gain an even better resurrection. Some faced jeers and flogging, and even chains and imprisonment. They were put to death by stoning; they were sawed in two; they were killed by the sword. They went about in sheepskins and goatskins, destitute, persecuted and mistreated — the world was not worthy of them. They wandered in deserts and mountains, living in caves and in holes in the ground.

These were all commended for their faith, yet none of them received what had been promised, since God had planned something better for us so that only together with us would they be made perfect.

**Therefore, since we are surrounded by such a great cloud of witnesses, let us throw off everything that hinders and the sin that so easily entangles. And let us run with perseverance the race marked out for us, fixing our eyes on Jesus, the pioneer and perfecter of faith. For the joy set before him he endured the cross, scorning its shame, and sat down at the right hand of the throne of God. Consider him who endured such opposition from sinners, so that you will not grow weary and lose heart.**

HEBREWS 11:1—12:3

According to the writer of Hebrews, what did the biblical heroes endure because they had hope in God? What is the "race marked out for us"? How is hope dependent on faith?

## WHAT WE BELIEVE

*We can cope when we have hope, but that hope must be true. Unfortunately, too often humans put their hope in things that overpromise and underdeliver—riches, people, idols, government. The only true source of hope is found in Jesus Christ. Christ and his promises become an anchor for our souls and the reason we can persevere. Of all the promises Jesus has made to us, the promise of eternal life with God is the most significant. No matter what we may be going through today, we know what happens in this life is not how our story ends. Our story ends, or really only begins, in the presence of God in his eternal kingdom. The more faith we have in God and his promises, the deeper the hope. The effect of hope? We can cope with the hardships and struggles of life through the hope we have in Jesus Christ.*

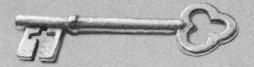

CHAPTER

## 26

# Patience

---

**KEY QUESTION**

How does God provide the help
I need to deal with stress?

---

**KEY IDEA**

I am slow to anger and endure patiently
under the unavoidable pressures of life.

---

**KEY VERSE**

Whoever is patient has great understanding,
but one who is quick-tempered displays folly.
*Proverbs 14:29*

287

As with the beliefs and the practices, the first half of the virtues are more vertical or inward in nature—God plants within us his heart of love, joy, peace, self-control and hope. Now we turn more outward and consider virtues that are felt by others when we exhibit them.

One of the virtues that is most evident when it is missing is patience. We all have stress triggers—proverbial buttons that when pushed cause us to lose our patience. Some of these triggers are other people. The way they act, move, talk, or even look can set us off. Then there are those triggers of circumstances. We are too busy; we have a family member who is making bad choices; we suffer from a physical condition or a lingering illness. Under these stressful circumstances it is hard not to "lose our cool." But, if we long to be like Jesus, becoming a more patient person is nonnegotiable. So, how does God provide the help we need to deal with stress? That is the focus of the passages of Scripture you are about to read.

In this chapter you will learn:

- God Is Patient with Us
- Being Slow to Become Angry
- Waiting for an Answer to Prayer

## GOD IS PATIENT WITH US

As you might suspect, God models the virtue he desires to see in us.

**But you, Lord, are a compassionate and gracious God, slow to anger, abounding in love and faithfulness.**

PSALM 86:15

God's patience with us is clear throughout Scripture. In Peter's second letter he tells his readers about "the day of the Lord" when Christ will return and bring all things to consummation. This will be the day of judgment for unbelievers but the day of redemption for believers. God demonstrates his patience towards all humanity by delaying this ultimate and final judgment *to give more people an opportunity to reach out and take hold of his forgiveness.*

Above all, you must understand that in the last days scoffers will come, scoffing and following their own evil desires. They will say, "Where is this 'coming' he promised? Ever since our ancestors died, everything goes on as it has since the beginning of creation." But they deliberately forget that long ago by God's word the heavens came into being and the earth was formed out of water and by water. By these waters also the world of that time was deluged and destroyed. By the same word the present heavens and earth are reserved for fire, being kept for the day of judgment and destruction of the ungodly.

But do not forget this one thing, dear friends: With the Lord a day is like a thousand years, and a thousand years are like a day. **The Lord is not slow in keeping his promise, as some understand slowness. Instead he is patient with you, not wanting anyone to perish, but everyone to come to repentance.**

But the day of the Lord will come like a thief. The heavens will disappear with a roar; the elements will be destroyed by fire, and the earth and everything done in it will be laid bare.

Since everything will be destroyed in this way, what kind of people ought you to be? You ought to live holy and godly lives as you look forward to the day of God and speed its coming. That day will bring about the destruction of the heavens by fire, and the elements will melt in the heat. But in keeping with his promise we are looking forward to a new heaven and a new earth, where righteousness dwells.

So then, dear friends, since you are looking forward to this, make every effort to be found spotless, blameless and at peace with him. **Bear in mind that our Lord's patience means salvation.**

2 PETER 3:3–15A

---

While God is demonstrating patience by waiting
until everyone has an opportunity to repent,
how should we be living our lives? Why?

---

## BEING SLOW TO BECOME ANGRY

*One of the primary ideas behind the virtue of patience is taking a long time to become angry—to overheat. The Greek word carries the idea of a thermometer. If a spiritual thermometer were placed in our mouths as we faced a difficult situation, how long would it take for our temperature to rise? As we mature, we learn to control our anger and practice patience in all circumstances.*

*Young David was a threat to King Saul. While popularity was not David's goal, he was loved by the people of Israel. King Saul burned with anger and jealousy towards David. For the next several years he pursued David, hoping to capture and kill him. David, forced to become a fugitive, proved he was a "man after God's own heart" when he waited on God's timing instead of taking matters into his own hands. David trusted God and never retaliated with vengeance or violence toward Saul. This patience showcased David's strong character and faith in God.*

---

As you read this true account, look for examples
of how David waited on God's timing.
Why is this so difficult for many people to do?

---

After Saul returned from pursuing the Philistines, he was told, "David is in the Desert of En Gedi." So Saul took three thousand able young men from all Israel and set out to look for David and his men near the Crags of the Wild Goats.

He came to the sheep pens along the way; a cave was there, and Saul went in to relieve himself. David and his men were far back in the cave. The men said, "This is the day the LORD spoke of when he said to you, 'I will give your enemy into your hands for you to deal with as you wish.'" Then David crept up unnoticed and cut off a corner of Saul's robe.

Afterward, David was conscience-stricken for having cut off a corner of his robe. He said to his men, "The LORD forbid that I should do such a thing to my master, the LORD's anointed, or lay my hand on him; for he is the anointed of the LORD." With these words David sharply rebuked his men and did not allow them to attack Saul. And Saul left the cave and went his way.

Then David went out of the cave and called out to Saul, "My lord the king!" When Saul looked behind him, David bowed down and prostrated himself with his face to the ground. He said to Saul, "Why do you listen when men say, 'David is bent on harming you'? This day you have seen with your own eyes how the LORD delivered you into my hands in the cave. Some urged me to kill you, but I spared you; I said, 'I will not lay my hand on my lord, because he is the LORD's anointed.' See, my father, look at this piece of your robe in my hand! I cut off the corner of your robe but did not kill you. See that there is nothing in my hand to indicate that I am guilty of wrongdoing or rebellion. I have not wronged you, but you are hunting me down to take my life. May the LORD judge between you and me. And may the LORD avenge the wrongs you have done to me, but my hand will not touch you. As the old saying goes, 'From evildoers come evil deeds,' so my hand will not touch you.

"Against whom has the king of Israel come out? Who are you pursuing? A dead dog? A flea? May the LORD be our judge and decide between us. May he consider my cause and uphold it; may he vindicate me by delivering me from your hand." 1 SAMUEL 24:1–15

*Saul returned home, but his jealousy remained. As the days passed, Saul allowed his anger against David to fester and grow. Once again Saul led three thousand troops on a mission to capture and kill David.*

The Ziphites went to Saul at Gibeah and said, "Is not David hiding on the hill of Hakilah, which faces Jeshimon?"

So Saul went down to the Desert of Ziph, with his three thousand select Israelite troops, to search there for David. Saul made his camp beside the road on the hill of Hakilah facing Jeshimon, but David stayed in the wilderness. When he saw that Saul had followed him there, he sent out scouts and learned that Saul had definitely arrived.

Then David set out and went to the place where Saul had camped. He saw where Saul and Abner son of Ner, the commander of the army, had lain down. Saul was lying inside the camp, with the army encamped around him.

David then asked Ahimelek the Hittite and Abishai son of Zeruiah, Joab's brother, "Who will go down into the camp with me to Saul?"

"I'll go with you," said Abishai.

So David and Abishai went to the army by night, and there was Saul, lying asleep inside the camp with his spear stuck in the ground near his head. Abner and the soldiers were lying around him.

Abishai said to David, "Today God has delivered your enemy into your hands. Now let me pin him to the ground with one thrust of the spear; I won't strike him twice."

**But David said to Abishai, "Don't destroy him! Who can lay a hand on the LORD's anointed and be guiltless? As surely as the LORD lives," he said, "the LORD himself will strike him, or his time will come and he will die, or he will go into battle and perish. But the LORD forbid that I should lay a hand on the LORD's anointed.** Now get the spear and water jug that are near his head, and let's go."

So David took the spear and water jug near Saul's head, and they left. No one saw or knew about it, nor did anyone wake up. They were all sleeping, because the LORD had put them into a deep sleep.

Then David crossed over to the other side and stood on top of the hill some distance away; there was a wide space between them. He called out to the army and to Abner son of Ner, "Aren't you going to answer me, Abner?"

Abner replied, "Who are you who calls to the king?"

David said, "You're a man, aren't you? And who is like you in Israel? Why didn't you guard your lord the king? Someone came to destroy your lord the king. What you have done is not good. As surely as the LORD lives, you and your men must die, because you did not guard your master, the LORD's anointed. Look around you. Where are the king's spear and water jug that were near his head?"

Saul recognized David's voice and said, "Is that your voice, David my son?"

David replied, "Yes it is, my lord the king." And he added, "Why is my lord pursuing his servant? What have I done, and what wrong am I guilty of? Now let my lord the king listen to his servant's words. If the LORD has incited you against me, then may he accept an offering. If, however, people have done it, may they be cursed before the LORD! They have driven me today from my share in the LORD's inheritance and have said, 'Go, serve other gods.' Now do not let my blood fall to the ground far from the presence of the LORD. The king of Israel has come out to look for a flea — as one hunts a partridge in the mountains."

Then Saul said, "I have sinned. Come back, David my son. Because you considered my life precious today, I will not try to harm you again. Surely I have acted like a fool and have been terribly wrong."

"Here is the king's spear," David answered. "Let one of your young men come over and get it. The LORD rewards everyone for their righteousness and faithfulness. The LORD delivered you into my hands today, but I would not lay a hand on the LORD's anointed. **As surely as I valued your life today, so may the LORD value my life and deliver me from all trouble."**

Then Saul said to David, "May you be blessed, David my son; you will do great things and surely triumph."

So David went on his way, and Saul returned home.

1 SAMUEL 26:1–25 ⚷

*Saul was critically wounded in a battle against the Philistines and eventually died after falling on his own sword. When David got word of the deaths of Saul and his son Jonathan, he refused to celebrate victory for himself but grieved the loss of Israel's king. In the course of time, David became king of his own tribe, Judah; seven years later he was crowned king of all Israel. All through those long years from when he was chosen to be the next king at age fifteen to the day of his coronation fifteen years later, David patiently waited for God to work out his plan.*

*David's son Solomon took the throne of Israel after David's death. In Proverbs, Solomon shares from his amazing reservoir of God-instilled wisdom. Listen to and learn from what he wrote about the virtue of patience.*

As you read the selected Proverbs below, ponder these two questions: How does patience calm a conflict? How do impatience and rashness escalate it?

Whoever is patient has great understanding,
  but one who is quick-tempered displays folly.

PROVERBS 14:29

**A hot-tempered person stirs up conflict,**
  **but the one who is patient calms a quarrel.**

PROVERBS 15:18

Better a patient person than a warrior,
  one with self-control than one who takes a city.

PROVERBS 16:32

A person's wisdom yields patience;
  it is to one's glory to overlook an offense.     PROVERBS 19:11

Through patience a ruler can be persuaded,
  and a gentle tongue can break a bone.     PROVERBS 25:15

*In the New Testament, James offered this advice in our relation-ships with others—particularly those who "push our buttons."*

**My dear brothers and sisters, take note of this: Everyone should be quick to listen, slow to speak and slow to become angry, because human anger does not produce the righteousness that God desires.**     JAMES 1:19–20

## WAITING FOR AN ANSWER TO PRAYER

*It also takes patience to wait for answers to prayer. Sometimes we don't know why God takes so long to respond to our request, especially when we need help badly. Living through a bad situation can make life hard to endure. It can make it difficult to be patient and wait for God's answer to our prayer. When things are not going well, we just want God to help us immediately! But being patient pays off, as it did for the lame man waiting at the pool of Bethesda.*

Some time later, Jesus went up to Jerusalem for one of the Jewish festivals. Now there is in Jerusalem near the Sheep Gate a pool, which in Aramaic is called Bethesda and which is surrounded by five covered colonnades. Here a great number of disabled people used to lie — the blind, the lame, the paralyzed. One who was there had been an invalid for thirty-eight years. When Jesus saw him lying there and learned that he had been in this condition for a long time, he asked him, "Do you want to get well?"

"Sir," the invalid replied, "I have no one to help me into the pool when the water is stirred. While I am trying to get in, someone else goes down ahead of me."

Then Jesus said to him, "Get up! Pick up your mat and walk." At once the man was cured; he picked up his mat and walked.

The day on which this took place was a Sabbath, and so the Jewish leaders said to the man who had been healed, "It is the Sabbath; the law forbids you to carry your mat."

But he replied, "The man who made me well said to me, 'Pick up your mat and walk.' "

So they asked him, "Who is this fellow who told you to pick it up and walk?"

The man who was healed had no idea who it was, for Jesus had slipped away into the crowd that was there.

Later Jesus found him at the temple and said to him, "See, you are well again. Stop sinning or something worse may happen to you." The man went away and told the Jewish leaders that it was Jesus who had made him well.                    JOHN 5:1–15 ⊙━ᴙ

*Sometimes the Lord's answer to prayer is physical healing and sometimes it is not. The apostle Paul discovered a different plan from God and came to terms with its good purpose in his life. (Note: Paul does not say what his chronic problem is. Some believe it was some sort of eye disease.)*

In order to keep me from becoming conceited, I was given a thorn in my flesh, a messenger of Satan, to torment me. Three times I pleaded with the Lord to take it away from me. But he said to me, "My grace is sufficient for you, for my power is made perfect in weakness." Therefore I will boast all the more gladly about my weaknesses, so that Christ's power may rest on me. That is why, for Christ's sake, I delight in weaknesses, in insults, in hardships,

296 | BELIEVE: Student Edition

in persecutions, in difficulties. For when I am weak, then I am strong.           2 CORINTHIANS 12:7B–10

---

Can you discern why God healed the lame man and not Paul?
How does believing in God's goodness give us
the strength to live patiently with our suffering?

---

On a scale of 1-10, rate yourself in patience. Do you
struggle more with being patient with other people or dealing
with unavoidable pressures in your life? What is one thing
you learned from this chapter that might help you?

---

## WHAT WE BELIEVE

*Not all our stories are the same, yet we are all called to respond with patience. Patience is a virtue that we must work to develop. Our cultivation of patience pleases God, who is patient with us. Showing patience positively affects our relationships and brings great joy to our lives and community. If we trust God and have a passion to treat others the way God treats us, we will try to learn more each day how to be slow to anger and endure patiently under the unavoidable pressures of life.*

# BE

# CHAPTER

## 27

# Kindness/Goodness

―――― KEY QUESTION ――――

What does it mean to do the right thing?
How do I know?

―――― KEY IDEA ――――

I choose to be kind and good
in my relationships with others.

―――― KEY VERSE ――――

Make sure that nobody pays back wrong
for wrong, but always strive to do what is good
for each other and for everyone else.
*1 Thessalonians 5:15*

OUR MAP

*The virtues of kindness and goodness found in the list of the fruit of the Spirit in Galatians 5:22 are almost always spoken of together—and rightfully so. While the meaning behind these two words in the original Greek is similar, they are less like twins and more like cousins. Both indicate how to respond to others from a deep moral inner conviction of what is the right thing to do for the sake of the other person.*

*Our conviction flows from the ten key beliefs (see chapters 1–10) embraced and owned in our hearts. Kindness always involves doing something deemed positive by the recipient. Goodness, however, sometimes entails tough love for the benefit of another because it will genuinely help them. This could involve speaking the truth in love or even withholding something that would ultimately harm them. But at the end of the day both virtues seek the best for others. How do you know the right thing to do?*

*This chapter will help you as you read Scriptures about:*

- *Our Kind and Good God*
- *A Story of Kindness: David*
- *A Story of Kindness: The Dinner Guest*
- *A Story of Kindness: Paul, Onesimus and Philemon*
- *Teachings on Goodness*

## OUR KIND AND GOOD GOD

*As with all the virtues, our God is the perfect example of kindness and goodness. This psalm was likely written after the Israelites returned from captivity in Babylon and was recited each year at one of the annual religious festivals. Throughout their history the Israelites cried out to God for mercy and help. Each time God responded from a tender and kind heart. Look for the cycle of rebellion, suffering, crying out to God, and God's kindness as you read this psalm.*

**Give thanks to the LORD, for he is good;**
**his love endures forever.**

**Let the redeemed of the LORD tell their story —**
  those he redeemed from the hand of the foe,
those he gathered from the lands,
  from east and west, from north and south.

Some wandered in desert wastelands,
  finding no way to a city where they could settle.
They were hungry and thirsty,
  and their lives ebbed away.
Then they cried out to the LORD in their trouble,
  and he delivered them from their distress.
He led them by a straight way
  to a city where they could settle.
Let them give thanks to the LORD for his unfailing love
  and his wonderful deeds for mankind,
for he satisfies the thirsty
  and fills the hungry with good things.

Some sat in darkness, in utter darkness,
  prisoners suffering in iron chains,
because they rebelled against God's commands
  and despised the plans of the Most High.
So he subjected them to bitter labor;
  they stumbled, and there was no one to help.
Then they cried to the LORD in their trouble,
  and he saved them from their distress.
He brought them out of darkness, the utter darkness,
  and broke away their chains.
Let them give thanks to the LORD for his unfailing love
  and his wonderful deeds for mankind,
for he breaks down gates of bronze
  and cuts through bars of iron.

Some became fools through their rebellious ways
  and suffered affliction because of their iniquities.
They loathed all food
  and drew near the gates of death.
Then they cried to the LORD in their trouble,
  and he saved them from their distress.

He sent out his word and healed them;
he rescued them from the grave.
**Let them give thanks to the LORD for his unfailing love
and his wonderful deeds for mankind.
Let them sacrifice thank offerings
and tell of his works with songs of joy.**   PSALM 107:1–22

---

Write your own short psalm. Start with the same opening words
of this psalm — "Give thanks to the LORD, for he is good;
his love endures forever. Let the redeemed of the LORD tell
their story." Then write out the story of an act of God's kindness
and goodness that God has shown towards you.

---

## A STORY OF KINDNESS: DAVID

*The prophet Samuel anointed David when he was just a teenager
to be Israel's next king. His coronation, however, was a number
of years away. Over the next several years God would use the
rebellious heart of King Saul to grow David's trust in God. Before
David took off running from King Saul, Jonathan, Saul's son and
successor to the throne, had a sobering conversation with David.
Jonathan acknowledged and accepted God's plan for David, not
himself, to be the next king. However, he made one request of
the future king of Israel.*

**"Show me unfailing kindness like the LORD's kindness as
long as I live, so that I may not be killed, and do not ever cut off
your kindness from my family — not even when the LORD has
cut off every one of David's enemies from the face of the earth."**

1 SAMUEL 20:14–15

*Fast-forward many years. Saul and Jonathan were both dead, and
David was king. All potential threats from the old royal house of
Saul had been removed, and David remembered his promise to
Jonathan.*

**David asked, "Is there anyone still left of the house of Saul
to whom I can show kindness for Jonathan's sake?"**

Now there was a servant of Saul's household named Ziba. They summoned him to appear before David, and the king said to him, "Are you Ziba?"

"At your service," he replied.

The king asked, "Is there no one still alive from the house of Saul to whom I can show God's kindness?"

Ziba answered the king, "There is still a son of Jonathan; he is lame in both feet."

"Where is he?" the king asked.

Ziba answered, "He is at the house of Makir son of Ammiel in Lo Debar."

So King David had him brought from Lo Debar, from the house of Makir son of Ammiel.

When Mephibosheth son of Jonathan, the son of Saul, came to David, he bowed down to pay him honor.

David said, "Mephibosheth!"

"At your service," he replied.

"Don't be afraid," David said to him, "for I will surely show you kindness for the sake of your father Jonathan. I will restore to you all the land that belonged to your grandfather Saul, and you will always eat at my table."

Mephibosheth bowed down and said, "What is your servant, that you should notice a dead dog like me?"

**Then the king summoned Ziba, Saul's steward, and said to him, "I have given your master's grandson everything that belonged to Saul and his family. You and your sons and your servants are to farm the land for him and bring in the crops, so that your master's grandson may be provided for. And Mephibosheth, grandson of your master, will always eat at my table."** (Now Ziba had fifteen sons and twenty servants.)

Then Ziba said to the king, "Your servant will do whatever my lord the king commands his servant to do." So Mephibosheth ate at David's table like one of the king's sons.

Mephibosheth had a young son named Mika, and all the members of Ziba's household were servants of Mephibosheth. And Mephibosheth lived in Jerusalem, because he always ate at the king's table; he was lame in both feet. 2 SAMUEL 9:1–13

## A Story of Kindness: The Dinner Guest

*The Jewish religious leaders in Jesus' day held exclusive dinner parties. Only invited guests of significant public standing were allowed to attend. Upon arrival, the host would seat guests in order of importance. On one occasion when Jesus was invited to eat at the table of a well-known Pharisee, he took advantage of the opportunity to teach a lesson first about humility and then about the kind of people who should be on the guest list of such occasions.*

When [Jesus] noticed how the guests picked the places of honor at the table, he told them this parable: "When someone invites you to a wedding feast, do not take the place of honor, for a person more distinguished than you may have been invited. If so, the host who invited both of you will come and say to you, 'Give this person your seat.' Then, humiliated, you will have to take the least important place. But when you are invited, take the lowest place, so that when your host comes, he will say to you, 'Friend, move up to a better place.' Then you will be honored in the presence of all the other guests. For all those who exalt themselves will be humbled, and those who humble themselves will be exalted."

Then Jesus said to his host, "When you give a luncheon or dinner, do not invite your friends, your brothers or sisters, your relatives, or your rich neighbors; if you do, they may invite you back and so you will be repaid. **But when you give a banquet, invite the poor, the crippled, the lame, the blind, and you will be blessed. Although they cannot repay you, you will be repaid at the resurrection of the righteous."** Luke 14:7–14

---

Jesus was teaching us to do what David did for Mephibosheth. Why does it matter that we invite people into our lives who cannot give back in return? Can you think of a way to include someone in your activities who is usually left out?

---

## A Story of Kindness: Paul, Onesimus and Philemon

*While Paul was in prison he met a slave named Onesimus, who evidently stole from his master before running away. Through Paul's ministry, Onesimus became a Christian and eventually decided he would return to his master. As it turned out, the master, a man name Philemon, was a Christian and Paul's close friend. Paul sent Onesimus home with a personal letter he had written to give to Philemon. The letter encouraged Philemon to exercise kindness toward his slave and accept Onesimus as a Christian brother.*

---

As you read, note the ways Paul shows kindness
in the way he makes his appeal to Philemon.

---

Paul, a prisoner of Christ Jesus, and Timothy our brother,

To Philemon our dear friend and fellow worker.     Philemon 1

**Although in Christ I could be bold and order you to do what you ought to do, yet I prefer to appeal to you on the basis of love.** It is as none other than Paul — an old man and now also a prisoner of Christ Jesus — that I appeal to you for my son Onesimus, who became my son while I was in chains. Formerly he was useless to you, but now he has become useful both to you and to me.

I am sending him — who is my very heart — back to you. I would have liked to keep him with me so that he could take your place in helping me while I am in chains for the gospel. But I did not want to do anything without your consent, so that any favor you do would not seem forced but would be voluntary. Perhaps the reason he was separated from you for a little while was that you might have him back forever — no longer as a slave, but better than a slave, as a dear brother. He is very dear to me but even dearer to you, both as a fellow man and as a brother in the Lord.

So if you consider me a partner, welcome him as you would welcome me. If he has done you any wrong or owes you anything, charge it to me. I, Paul, am writing this with my own hand. I will pay it back — not to mention that you owe me your very self. I do wish, brother, that I may have some benefit from you in the Lord; refresh my heart in Christ. Confident of your obedience, I write to you, knowing that you will do even more than I ask.     Philemon 8–21

If you were giving advice to Philemon, how could you use our key verse to encourage Philemon to show kindness?

## Teachings on Goodness

*Jesus left us instructions for being good to others that are both practical and radical. Remember that kindness is doing something that the recipient feels positively about, but goodness does the right thing for a person, even when it may not necessarily feel good. Goodness is sometimes called "tough love," because it speaks the truth or withholds something harmful for the ultimate benefit of the recipient.*

Write down a list of every principle you discover from the teachings of Jesus, Peter and Paul on how to not only do the kind thing but also the right thing in our relationships. Which principle speaks to you the most? Why?

"But to you who are listening I say: Love your enemies, do good to those who hate you, bless those who curse you, pray for those who mistreat you. If someone slaps you on one cheek, turn to them the other also. If someone takes your coat, do not withhold your shirt from them. Give to everyone who asks you, and if anyone takes what belongs to you, do not demand it back. **Do to others as you would have them do to you.**

"If you love those who love you, what credit is that to you? Even sinners love those who love them. And if you do good to those who are good to you, what credit is that to you? Even sinners do that. And if you lend to those from whom you expect repayment, what credit is that to you? Even sinners lend to sinners, expecting to be repaid in full. But love your enemies, do good to them, and lend to them without expecting to get anything back. Then your reward will be great, and you will be children of the Most High, because he is kind to the ungrateful and wicked. Be merciful, just as your Father is merciful.

"Do not judge, and you will not be judged. Do not condemn, and you will not be condemned. Forgive, and you will be forgiven.

Give, and it will be given to you. A good measure, pressed down, shaken together and running over, will be poured into your lap. For with the measure you use, it will be measured to you."

He also told them this parable: "Can the blind lead the blind? Will they not both fall into a pit? The student is not above the teacher, but everyone who is fully trained will be like their teacher.

"Why do you look at the speck of sawdust in your brother's eye and pay no attention to the plank in your own eye? How can you say to your brother, 'Brother, let me take the speck out of your eye,' when you yourself fail to see the plank in your own eye? You hypocrite, first take the plank out of your eye, and then you will see clearly to remove the speck from your brother's eye.

"No good tree bears bad fruit, nor does a bad tree bear good fruit. Each tree is recognized by its own fruit. People do not pick figs from thornbushes, or grapes from briers. **A good man brings good things out of the good stored up in his heart, and an evil man brings evil things out of the evil stored up in his heart. For the mouth speaks what the heart is full of."** LUKE 6:27–45

*Two good men who were followers of Jesus—the apostles Peter and Paul—offered instruction to the early believers on living a life of kindness and goodness. In the Scriptures below, they remind us how our goodness to others can show the world about our good God. In other words, the way we treat people is a reflection of our relationship with God.*

Finally, all of you, be like-minded, be sympathetic, love one another, be compassionate and humble. Do not repay evil with evil or insult with insult. On the contrary, repay evil with blessing, because to this you were called so that you may inherit a blessing. For,

> "Whoever would love life
>     and see good days
> must keep their tongue from evil
>     and their lips from deceitful speech.
> They must turn from evil and do good;
>     they must seek peace and pursue it.

> For the eyes of the Lord are on the righteous
> and his ears are attentive to their prayer,
> but the face of the Lord is against those who do evil."
>
> 1 PETER 3:8–12

We who are strong ought to bear with the failings of the weak and not to please ourselves. Each of us should please our neighbors for their good, to build them up. ROMANS 15:1–2

Let us not become weary in doing good, for at the proper time we will reap a harvest if we do not give up. **Therefore, as we have opportunity, let us do good to all people, especially to those who belong to the family of believers.** GALATIANS 6:9–10

Get rid of all bitterness, rage and anger, brawling and slander, along with every form of malice. **Be kind and compassionate to one another, forgiving each other, just as in Christ God forgave you.** Follow God's example, therefore, as dearly loved children and walk in the way of love, just as Christ loved us and gave himself up for us as a fragrant offering and sacrifice to God. EPHESIANS 4:31—5:2

**Make sure that nobody pays back wrong for wrong, but always strive to do what is good for each other and for everyone else.** 1 THESSALONIANS 5:15

In everything set them an example by doing what is good. TITUS 2:7A

Remind the people to be subject to rulers and authorities, to be obedient, to be ready to do whatever is good, to slander no one, to be peaceable and considerate, and always to be gentle toward everyone. TITUS 3:1–2

**Our people must learn to devote themselves to doing what is good, in order to provide for urgent needs and not live unproductive lives.** TITUS 3:14

## WHAT WE BELIEVE

*Throughout history God has consistently showed his kindness and goodness to all people. If God's love is in us, we will seek to show that love to the people in our lives. Most often we will engage in positive acts of kindness toward others. However, occasionally we can help someone by issuing some tough love—a confrontation, a rebuke, a refusal. We have many great examples in the Bible to look to, including David, Jesus, and Paul. We have also been given practical principles to guide our demonstration of both random and intentional acts of goodness and kindness. Pick one principle and one person in your life with the most need and give it a try!*

# CHAPTER

## 28

# Faithfulness

--- KEY QUESTION ---

Why is it important to be loyal
and committed to God and others?

--- KEY IDEA ---

I have established a good name with God
and others based on my loyalty to those relationships.

--- KEY VERSE ---

Let love and faithfulness never leave you; bind them around
your neck, write them on the tablet of your heart. Then you will
win favor and a good name in the sight of God and man.

*Proverbs 3:3–4*

OUR MAP

*As with all the other virtues, faithfulness benefits the people in our lives. When we are faithful to them, they are blessed. And over time, as our key verse expresses, our faithfulness to others also has a reciprocal benefit. First, we win favor. As needs emerge in our lives, people will be inclined to help us. Second, we establish a good name. When our name is mentioned, even when we are not present, it is spoken with high regard. A good name established through a life of faithfulness is a boundless gift to pass on to our children. Most of all, faithfulness pleases God, who is always loyal and committed to us. Our loyalty and commitment to others reflects the love God has shown us. Yet because of our sinful nature, we struggle to be faithful. That is where God and his presence in our lives come into play.*

*In this chapter you will read Scripture that addresses the following subjects to instruct and inspire you:*

- *God's Faithfulness*
- *Called to Faithfulness*
- *A Story of Faithfulness: Joseph*
- *A Story of Faithfulness: Mary*

## God's Faithfulness

*The ultimate example of faithfulness is God's faithfulness to us. Many biblical authors wrote about this topic. Here in Deuteronomy, Moses wrote a song about the promise-keeping God he worshiped.*

As you read the Scriptures in this section, highlight
the phrases that best express God's faithfulness to you.

Listen, you heavens, and I will speak;
    hear, you earth, the words of my mouth.
Let my teaching fall like rain
    and my words descend like dew,
like showers on new grass,
    like abundant rain on tender plants.

I will proclaim the name of the LORD.
   Oh, praise the greatness of our God!
He is the Rock, his works are perfect,
   and all his ways are just.
**A faithful God who does no wrong,
   upright and just is he.**       DEUTERONOMY 32:1–4

*While living in a world with so much uncertainty, the psalmist took great comfort in the extent of God's devotion and faithfulness to us.*

**Your love, LORD, reaches to the heavens,
   your faithfulness to the skies.**
Your righteousness is like the highest mountains,
   your justice like the great deep.
   You, LORD, preserve both people and animals.
How priceless is your unfailing love, O God!
   People take refuge in the shadow of your wings.
They feast on the abundance of your house;
   you give them drink from your river of delights.
For with you is the fountain of life;
   in your light we see light.       PSALM 36:5–9

*While God was always faithful to his people, his people were not always faithful to him. God had to discipline them often for their unfaithfulness. The following passage, likely penned by Jeremiah, was written after Jerusalem had been destroyed and the people of Judah had been exiled to Babylon. In addition to lamenting what he saw and felt, Jeremiah also reminds the people of the consistent faithfulness and mercy of God.*

I remember my affliction and my wandering,
   the bitterness and the gall.
I well remember them,
   and my soul is downcast within me.
Yet this I call to mind
   and therefore I have hope:

**Because of the LORD's great love we are not**
**consumed,**
    **for his compassions never fail.**
**They are new every morning;**
    **great is your faithfulness.**
I say to myself, "The LORD is my portion;
    therefore I will wait for him."     LAMENTATIONS 3:19–24

## CALLED TO FAITHFULNESS

*The book of Proverbs calls us to be faithful and reminds us of the great rewards of a faithful life:*

My son, do not forget my teaching,
    but keep my commands in your heart,
for they will prolong your life many years
    and bring you peace and prosperity.

**Let love and faithfulness never leave you;**
    **bind them around your neck,**
    **write them on the tablet of your heart.**
**Then you will win favor and a good name**
    **in the sight of God and man.**

Trust in the LORD with all your heart
    and lean not on your own understanding;
in all your ways submit to him,
    and he will make your paths straight.     PROVERBS 3:1–6

Many claim to have unfailing love,
    but a faithful person who can find?     PROVERBS 20:6

A faithful person will be richly blessed,
    but one eager to get rich will not go unpunished.

                        PROVERBS 28:20

---

Why will a faithful person be richly blessed and
one eager to get rich be punished eventually?

## A STORY OF FAITHFULNESS: JOSEPH

*God built Israel from scratch, starting with Abraham, to reveal his plan to provide a way for people to come back into a relationship with him. Israel's faithfulness to God over the next 2,000 years was sketchy at best. However, a few Israelites, such as Joseph, did display devoted faithfulness both to God and to others.*

*At the age of seventeen, Joseph, one of the twelve sons of Jacob, had two dreams in which his brothers bowed down to him. The brothers were furious with their younger brother, whom their dad already favored. So they plotted together one day and sold Joseph to a caravan of Ishmaelites who sold him into slavery in Egypt. The brothers returned home and lied to their father, telling him that Joseph had been killed by a ferocious animal. Jacob was crushed. Joseph, however, prospered despite his brothers' jealous attempts to destroy him.*

---

As you read Joseph's story, look back at our key verse from Proverbs 3:3–4. How did Joseph live out the truth of this verse?

---

Now Joseph had been taken down to Egypt. Potiphar, an Egyptian who was one of Pharaoh's officials, the captain of the guard, bought him from the Ishmaelites who had taken him there.

The LORD was with Joseph so that he prospered, and he lived in the house of his Egyptian master. When his master saw that the LORD was with him and that the LORD gave him success in everything he did, Joseph found favor in his eyes and became his attendant. Potiphar put him in charge of his household, and he entrusted to his care everything he owned. From the time he put him in charge of his household and of all that he owned, the LORD blessed the household of the Egyptian because of Joseph. The blessing of the LORD was on everything Potiphar had, both in the house and in the field. So Potiphar left everything he had in Joseph's care; with Joseph in charge, he did not concern himself with anything except the food he ate. GENESIS 39:1–6A

*As part of God's master plan, Joseph rose again only to be cast into another "pit." Potiphar's wife tried to seduce Joseph, but*

*Joseph maintained his integrity and faithfulness to both Potiphar and God by resisting the temptation. Because he rejected her, Potiphar's wife made false accusations against Joseph, and he was thrown into prison. But God was with him there too and he eventually lifted him up yet again.*

*For over two years everyone forgot about Joseph until the Pharaoh had a dream that no one could interpret. Pharaoh's cupbearer, who had been in prison with Joseph, remembered that Joseph was a man who could interpret dreams. So they brought him out of prison to see if he could explain the meaning of the dream. Joseph remained faithful to God as he stood before Pharaoh.*

Pharaoh said to Joseph, "I had a dream, and no one can interpret it. But I have heard it said of you that when you hear a dream you can interpret it."

"I cannot do it," Joseph replied to Pharaoh, "but God will give Pharaoh the answer he desires."

Then Pharaoh said to Joseph, "In my dream I was standing on the bank of the Nile, when out of the river there came up seven cows, fat and sleek, and they grazed among the reeds. After them, seven other cows came up — scrawny and very ugly and lean. I had never seen such ugly cows in all the land of Egypt. The lean, ugly cows ate up the seven fat cows that came up first. But even after they ate them, no one could tell that they had done so; they looked just as ugly as before. Then I woke up.

"In my dream I saw seven heads of grain, full and good, growing on a single stalk. After them, seven other heads sprouted — withered and thin and scorched by the east wind. The thin heads of grain swallowed up the seven good heads. I told this to the magicians, but none of them could explain it to me."

Then Joseph said to Pharaoh, "The dreams of Pharaoh are one and the same. God has revealed to Pharaoh what he is about to do. The seven good cows are seven years, and the seven good heads of grain are seven years; it is one and the same dream. The seven lean, ugly cows that came up afterward are seven years, and so are the seven worthless heads of grain scorched by the east wind: They are seven years of famine.

"It is just as I said to Pharaoh: God has shown Pharaoh what he is about to do. Seven years of great abundance are coming throughout the land of Egypt, but seven years of famine will follow them. Then all the abundance in Egypt will be forgotten, and the famine will ravage the land. The abundance in the land will not be remembered, because the famine that follows it will be so severe. The reason the dream was given to Pharaoh in two forms is that the matter has been firmly decided by God, and God will do it soon.

"And now let Pharaoh look for a discerning and wise man and put him in charge of the land of Egypt. Let Pharaoh appoint commissioners over the land to take a fifth of the harvest of Egypt during the seven years of abundance. They should collect all the food of these good years that are coming and store up the grain under the authority of Pharaoh, to be kept in the cities for food. This food should be held in reserve for the country, to be used during the seven years of famine that will come upon Egypt, so that the country may not be ruined by the famine."

The plan seemed good to Pharaoh and to all his officials. So Pharaoh asked them, "Can we find anyone like this man, one in whom is the spirit of God?"

Then Pharaoh said to Joseph, "Since God has made all this known to you, there is no one so discerning and wise as you. You shall be in charge of my palace, and all my people are to submit to your orders. Only with respect to the throne will I be greater than you."

So Pharaoh said to Joseph, "I hereby put you in charge of the whole land of Egypt." Then Pharaoh took his signet ring from his finger and put it on Joseph's finger. He dressed him in robes of fine linen and put a gold chain around his neck. He had him ride in a chariot as his second-in-command, and people shouted before him, "Make way!" Thus he put him in charge of the whole land of Egypt.

Then Pharaoh said to Joseph, "I am Pharaoh, but without your word no one will lift hand or foot in all Egypt." Pharaoh gave Joseph the name Zaphenath-Paneah and gave him Asenath daughter of Potiphera, priest of On, to be his wife. And Joseph went throughout the land of Egypt.

Joseph was thirty years old when he entered the service of Pharaoh king of Egypt. GENESIS 41:15–46A

*Just as Joseph had predicted, seven years of bumper crops were followed by seven years of famine throughout the land. Joseph made sure Egypt saved up enough food during the good years to survive the hard years. Although he was now a rich and influential man, Joseph stayed faithful to his promise to help Egypt survive the famine. Meanwhile, back in Joseph's homeland, his father and brothers began to talk about where they might be able to find more food for their families. Joseph's long-ago dream was about to come true.*

When Jacob learned that there was grain in Egypt, he said to his sons, "Why do you just keep looking at each other?" He continued, "I have heard that there is grain in Egypt. Go down there and buy some for us, so that we may live and not die."

Then ten of Joseph's brothers went down to buy grain from Egypt. But Jacob did not send Benjamin, Joseph's brother, with the others, because he was afraid that harm might come to him. So Israel's sons were among those who went to buy grain, for there was famine in the land of Canaan also.

**Now Joseph was the governor of the land, the person who sold grain to all its people. So when Joseph's brothers arrived, they bowed down to him with their faces to the ground.**

GENESIS 42:1–6

*Twenty-one years had passed, during which time Joseph went from the bottom to the top, more than once. But in all of his circumstances, whether terribly unjust or tremendously prosperous, Joseph remained faithful to God and to the people he served. Because of his lifelong faithfulness, Joseph was able to help the emerging nation of Israel (his family) survive through the famine.*

---

Throughout the Bible, God never calls us to be successful but to be faithful. As we saw in Joseph's life, sometimes success follows faithfulness, sometimes it doesn't. What do you think about this? How are you doing at being faithful?

---

## A STORY OF FAITHFULNESS: MARY

*In the New Testament, God chose a faithful girl for an assignment that would lead to a blessing for the whole world. Young Mary got quite a shock when an angel appeared to tell her she would be the mother of God's Son. But her response shows us her heart of faithfulness.*

God sent the angel Gabriel to Nazareth, a town in Galilee, to a virgin pledged to be married to a man named Joseph, a descendant of David. The virgin's name was Mary. The angel went to her and said, "Greetings, you who are highly favored! The Lord is with you."

Mary was greatly troubled at his words and wondered what kind of greeting this might be. **But the angel said to her, "Do not be afraid, Mary; you have found favor with God. You will conceive and give birth to a son, and you are to call him Jesus. He will be great and will be called the Son of the Most High. The Lord God will give him the throne of his father David, and he will reign over Jacob's descendants forever; his kingdom will never end."**

"How will this be," Mary asked the angel, "since I am a virgin?"

The angel answered, "The Holy Spirit will come on you, and the power of the Most High will overshadow you. So the holy one to be born will be called the Son of God. Even Elizabeth your relative is going to have a child in her old age, and she who was said to be unable to conceive is in her sixth month. For no word from God will ever fail."

**"I am the Lord's servant," Mary answered. "May your word to me be fulfilled."** Then the angel left her.

At that time Mary got ready and hurried to a town in the hill country of Judea, where she entered Zechariah's home and greeted Elizabeth. When Elizabeth heard Mary's greeting, the baby leaped in her womb, and Elizabeth was filled with the Holy Spirit. In a loud voice she exclaimed: "Blessed are you among women, and blessed is the child you will bear! But why am I so favored, that the mother of my Lord should come to me? As soon as the sound of your greeting reached my ears, the baby in my womb leaped for joy. Blessed is she who has believed that the Lord would fulfill his promises to her!"

And Mary said:

> "My soul glorifies the Lord
>> and my spirit rejoices in God my Savior,
> for he has been mindful
>> of the humble state of his servant.
> From now on all generations will call me blessed,
>> for the Mighty One has done great things for me —
>> holy is his name.
> His mercy extends to those who fear him,
>> from generation to generation.
> He has performed mighty deeds with his arm;
>> he has scattered those who are proud in their inmost
>>> thoughts.
> He has brought down rulers from their thrones
>> but has lifted up the humble.
> He has filled the hungry with good things
>> but has sent the rich away empty.
> He has helped his servant Israel,
>> remembering to be merciful
> to Abraham and his descendants forever,
>> just as he promised our ancestors."   LUKE 1:26B–55

---

Based on what you have learned about faithfulness,
who are some of the most faithful people you know?
How have they found honor and a good name in your sight?
In the sight of others? If it is possible, let them know.

---

## WHAT WE BELIEVE

*Throughout the Bible, God asked his followers to be faithful to his assignments for them, no matter how difficult. In fact, it was often amid the difficult seasons that they discovered the trustworthiness of God the most. When they aligned their lives to God's story, he was with them and accomplished great things through them. All believers have the opportunity to open their lives to God's will and demonstrate their faithfulness. The results of such faithfulness can be both great and beautiful as God works through those who believe.*

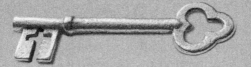

CHAPTER

29

# Gentleness

KEY QUESTION

How do I demonstrate thoughtfulness
and consideration?

KEY IDEA

I am thoughtful, considerate and calm
in my dealings with others.

KEY VERSE

Let your gentleness be evident to all.
The Lord is near.
*Philippians 4:5*

OUR MAP

Nothing kills a family, a friendship, a neighborhood or even a church like pride, arrogance, anger, closed ears and raised voices. Since God is all about community, he calls his followers to be gentle. The New Testament word for "gentleness" comes from a medical word and is associated with a mild medication. Essentially, we might say a gentle person is someone who is easy on your stomach. The person who lacks gentleness causes our stomach to double up in knots. God wants us to be healing agents in the lives of those around us. So, how do we learn how to demonstrate thoughtfulness and consideration to others?

That is the focus of this chapter, with Scripture about:

- Gentle Jesus
- Nuggets on Gentleness
- A Story of Gentleness: Abigail

Look at the key verse again. Why do you think
Paul put these two sentences together?

## GENTLE JESUS

*Throughout the Bible we find stories and people who reinforce the fact that gentleness is a character trait that God has intended for us. Jesus, of course, is our greatest example of someone who displayed gentleness in his dealings with others. This is particularly true in his relationship with Peter. At the Last Supper on the night before Jesus was crucified, Peter told Jesus he would die for him. Jesus, predicting Peter's future betrayal, corrected him. Peter could not imagine betraying his master, teacher and friend. He had given up so much to follow him already. But when Jesus was arrested later that night, Peter's fear overcame his faith.*

Then the detachment of soldiers with its commander and the Jewish officials arrested Jesus. They bound him and brought him first to Annas, who was the father-in-law of Caiaphas, the high priest that year. Caiaphas was the one who had advised the Jewish leaders that it would be good if one man died for the people.

Simon Peter and another disciple were following Jesus. Because this disciple was known to the high priest, he went with Jesus into the high priest's courtyard, but Peter had to wait outside at the door. The other disciple, who was known to the high priest, came back, spoke to the servant girl on duty there and brought Peter in.

**"You aren't one of this man's disciples too, are you?" she asked Peter.**

**He replied, "I am not."**

It was cold, and the servants and officials stood around a fire they had made to keep warm. Peter also was standing with them, warming himself.

Meanwhile, the high priest questioned Jesus about his disciples and his teaching.

"I have spoken openly to the world," Jesus replied. "I always taught in synagogues or at the temple, where all the Jews come together. I said nothing in secret. Why question me? Ask those who heard me. Surely they know what I said."

When Jesus said this, one of the officials nearby slapped him in the face. "Is this the way you answer the high priest?" he demanded.

"If I said something wrong," Jesus replied, "testify as to what is wrong. But if I spoke the truth, why did you strike me?" Then Annas sent him bound to Caiaphas the high priest.

**Meanwhile, Simon Peter was still standing there warming himself. So they asked him, "You aren't one of his disciples too, are you?"**

**He denied it, saying, "I am not."**

**One of the high priest's servants, a relative of the man whose ear Peter had cut off, challenged him, "Didn't I see you with him in the garden?" Again Peter denied it, and at that moment a rooster began to crow.**                                    JOHN 18:12–27

*Sometime between Jesus' resurrection and his ascension into heaven, he appeared to Peter and several of the disciples while they were fishing. In a memorable display of gentleness, Jesus restored Peter's relationship with him and reinstated Peter to a position of special responsibility in the church.*

⚷ Afterward Jesus appeared again to his disciples, by the Sea of Galilee. It happened this way: Simon Peter, Thomas (also known as Didymus), Nathanael from Cana in Galilee, the sons of Zebedee, and two other disciples were together. "I'm going out to fish," Simon Peter told them, and they said, "We'll go with you." So they went out and got into the boat, but that night they caught nothing.

Early in the morning, Jesus stood on the shore, but the disciples did not realize that it was Jesus.

He called out to them, "Friends, haven't you any fish?"

"No," they answered.

He said, "Throw your net on the right side of the boat and you will find some." When they did, they were unable to haul the net in because of the large number of fish.

Then the disciple whom Jesus loved said to Peter, "It is the Lord!" As soon as Simon Peter heard him say, "It is the Lord," he wrapped his outer garment around him (for he had taken it off) and jumped into the water. The other disciples followed in the boat, towing the net full of fish, for they were not far from shore, about a hundred yards. When they landed, they saw a fire of burning coals there with fish on it, and some bread.

Jesus said to them, "Bring some of the fish you have just caught." So Simon Peter climbed back into the boat and dragged the net ashore. It was full of large fish, 153, but even with so many the net was not torn. Jesus said to them, "Come and have breakfast." None of the disciples dared ask him, "Who are you?" They knew it was the Lord. Jesus came, took the bread and gave it to them, and did the same with the fish. This was now the third time Jesus appeared to his disciples after he was raised from the dead.

When they had finished eating, Jesus said to Simon Peter, **"Simon son of John, do you love me more than these?"**

"Yes, Lord," he said, "you know that I love you."

Jesus said, "Feed my lambs."

**Again Jesus said, "Simon son of John, do you love me?"**

He answered, "Yes, Lord, you know that I love you."

Jesus said, "Take care of my sheep."

**The third time he said to him, "Simon son of John, do you love me?"**

Peter was hurt because Jesus asked him the third time, "Do you love me?" He said, "Lord, you know all things; you know that I love you."

Jesus said, "Feed my sheep. Very truly I tell you, when you were younger you dressed yourself and went where you wanted; but when you are old you will stretch out your hands, and someone else will dress you and lead you where you do not want to go." Jesus said this to indicate the kind of death by which Peter would glorify God. Then he said to him, "Follow me!"      JOHN 21:1–19

---

Some have suggested that Jesus asked Simon Peter
if he loved him three times to help restore Peter
from the three times he had denied Jesus. Do you
think this was Jesus' intent? Do you think this would have
helped you if you were in Peter's sandals?

---

*Peter's relationship was fully restored by Jesus' gentle invitation. The rest of the New Testament tells us how Peter fulfilled this life-mission given to him by Jesus. He spoke the Word of God boldly and provided leadership to God's people. Peter isn't the only one Jesus spoke to with gentleness. He calls all of us to follow him with gentle words like these:*

**"Come to me, all you who are weary and burdened, and I will give you rest. Take my yoke upon you and learn from me, for I am gentle and humble in heart, and you will find rest for your souls. For my yoke is easy and my burden is light."**

MATTHEW 11:28–30

### NUGGETS ON GENTLENESS

*The New Testament offers a lot of practical instruction on how to be gentle, thoughtful, considerate and calm. In one of Jesus' teachings called the Sermon on the Mount, he offered powerful insights on how to be gentle.*

---

As you read these pieces of advice on gentleness, identify
one that speaks most to you. Why did you choose that one?

"Blessed are the meek,
   for they will inherit the earth."                MATTHEW 5:5

"You have heard that it was said, 'Eye for eye, and tooth for tooth.' But I tell you, do not resist an evil person. **If anyone slaps you on the right cheek, turn to them the other cheek also.** And if anyone wants to sue you and take your shirt, hand over your coat as well. If anyone forces you to go one mile, go with them two miles. Give to the one who asks you, and do not turn away from the one who wants to borrow from you."        MATTHEW 5:38–42

**"Do not judge, or you too will be judged.** For in the same way you judge others, you will be judged, and with the measure you use, it will be measured to you.

"Why do you look at the speck of sawdust in your brother's eye and pay no attention to the plank in your own eye? How can you say to your brother, 'Let me take the speck out of your eye,' when all the time there is a plank in your own eye? You hypocrite, first take the plank out of your own eye, and then you will see clearly to remove the speck from your brother's eye."        MATTHEW 7:1–5

*Jesus wasn't the only one to teach about gentleness. Many of the apostles followed Jesus' lead and also wrote about this important virtue.*

The fruit of the Spirit is love, joy, peace, forbearance, kindness, goodness, faithfulness, gentleness and self-control. Against such things there is no law.        GALATIANS 5:22–23

Be completely humble and gentle; be patient, bearing with one another in love.        EPHESIANS 4:2

**"In your anger do not sin":** Do not let the sun go down while you are still angry, and do not give the devil a foothold.** Anyone who has been stealing must steal no longer, but must work, doing something useful with their own hands, that they may have something to share with those in need.

**Do not let any unwholesome talk come out of your mouths,**

**but only what is helpful for building others up according to their needs, that it may benefit those who listen.** And do not grieve the Holy Spirit of God, with whom you were sealed for the day of redemption. Get rid of all bitterness, rage and anger, brawling and slander, along with every form of malice. Be kind and compassionate to one another, forgiving each other, just as in Christ God forgave you. EPHESIANS 4:26–32

Therefore, as God's chosen people, holy and dearly loved, clothe yourselves with compassion, kindness, humility, gentleness and patience. COLOSSIANS 3:12

**The Lord's servant must not be quarrelsome but must be kind to everyone, able to teach, not resentful.** Opponents must be gently instructed, in the hope that God will grant them repentance leading them to a knowledge of the truth, and that they will come to their senses and escape from the trap of the devil, who has taken them captive to do his will. 2 TIMOTHY 2:24–26

Remind the people to be subject to rulers and authorities, to be obedient, to be ready to do whatever is good, to slander no one, to be peaceable and considerate, and always to be gentle toward everyone. TITUS 3:1–2

**The wisdom that comes from heaven is first of all pure; then peace-loving, considerate, submissive, full of mercy and good fruit, impartial and sincere.** Peacemakers who sow in peace reap a harvest of righteousness. JAMES 3:17–18

---

Look at Ephesians 4:26–32 again.
How do we give the devil a foothold in our lives when
we let the sun go down while we are still angry?

---

## A STORY OF GENTLENESS: ABIGAIL

*We find an example of gentleness in the Old Testament story where David encounters Nabal and Abigail, a husband who was cruel and his wife who was gentle. David, before he was king, spent years running and hiding from King Saul, who wanted to kill him. While he was on the run, David got food and supplies for his men as payment for protecting people's flocks, including flocks belonging to Nabal and Abigail. David and his men had done a good job keeping Nabal's flocks safe, but when David's men asked Nabal for some food, they got a cruel answer.*

As you read this story, look for the ways anger is stirred up, and look for how gentleness affects a tense situation.

While David was in the wilderness, he heard that Nabal was shearing sheep. So he sent ten young men and said to them, "Go up to Nabal at Carmel and greet him in my name. Say to him: 'Long life to you! Good health to you and your household! And good health to all that is yours!

"'Now I hear that it is sheep-shearing time. When your shepherds were with us, we did not mistreat them, and the whole time they were at Carmel nothing of theirs was missing. Ask your own servants and they will tell you. Therefore be favorable toward my men, since we come at a festive time. Please give your servants and your son David whatever you can find for them.'"

When David's men arrived, they gave Nabal this message in David's name. Then they waited.

Nabal answered David's servants, "Who is this David? Who is this son of Jesse? Many servants are breaking away from their masters these days. Why should I take my bread and water, and the meat I have slaughtered for my shearers, and give it to men coming from who knows where?"

David's men turned around and went back. When they arrived, they reported every word. David said to his men, "Each of you strap on your sword!" So they did, and David strapped his on as well. About four hundred men went up with David, while two hundred stayed with the supplies. 1 SAMUEL 25:4–13

*David was angry! He was determined to get revenge on Nabal. As he was marching towards Nabal's home, Nabal's wife Abigail was warned and she moved into action.*

One of the servants told Abigail, Nabal's wife, "David sent messengers from the wilderness to give our master his greetings, but he hurled insults at them. Yet these men were very good to us. They did not mistreat us, and the whole time we were out in the fields near them nothing was missing. Night and day they were a wall around us the whole time we were herding our sheep near them. Now think it over and see what you can do, because disaster is hanging over our master and his whole household. He is such a wicked man that no one can talk to him."

Abigail acted quickly. She took two hundred loaves of bread, two skins of wine, five dressed sheep, five seahs of roasted grain, a hundred cakes of raisins and two hundred cakes of pressed figs, and loaded them on donkeys. Then she told her servants, "Go on ahead; I'll follow you." But she did not tell her husband Nabal.

1 SAMUEL 25:14–19

*One of the most dramatic meetings in the Bible was about to take place. An angry David with four hundred of his men were out to get revenge, and gentle Abigail, loaded down with food, ran to intercept him. If Abigail had met David with force and anger, David could have gotten even angrier and may have even killed Abigail on the spot. But Abigail saved the day by calming David down with her gentle approach. She was an example of the proverb that says, "A gentle answer turns away wrath, but a harsh word stirs up anger" (Proverbs 15:1). Read how Abigail gently convinced David not to sin.*

When Abigail saw David, she quickly got off her donkey and bowed down before David with her face to the ground. She fell at his feet and said: "Pardon your servant, my lord, and let me speak to you; hear what your servant has to say. Please pay no attention, my lord, to that wicked man Nabal. He is just like his name — his name means Fool, and folly goes with him. And as for me, your servant, I did not see the men my lord sent. And now, my lord, as surely as the LORD your God lives and as you live, since the LORD has kept you from bloodshed and from avenging yourself with your own hands, may your enemies and all who are intent on harming my lord be like Nabal. And let this gift, which your servant has brought to my lord, be given to the men who follow you." 1 SAMUEL 25:23–27

David said to Abigail, "Praise be to the Lord, the God of Israel, who has sent you today to meet me. May you be blessed for your good judgment and for keeping me from bloodshed this day and from avenging myself with my own hands. Otherwise, as surely as the Lord, the God of Israel, lives, who has kept me from harming you, if you had not come quickly to meet me, not one male belonging to Nabal would have been left alive by daybreak."

Then David accepted from her hand what she had brought him and said, "Go home in peace. I have heard your words and granted your request."

When Abigail went to Nabal, he was in the house holding a banquet like that of a king. He was in high spirits and very drunk. So she told him nothing at all until daybreak. Then in the morning, when Nabal was sober, his wife told him all these things, and his heart failed him and he became like a stone. About ten days later, the Lord struck Nabal and he died.

When David heard that Nabal was dead, he said, "Praise be to the Lord, who has upheld my cause against Nabal for treating me with contempt. He has kept his servant from doing wrong and has brought Nabal's wrongdoing down on his own head."

Then David sent word to Abigail, asking her to become his wife. His servants went to Carmel and said to Abigail, "David has sent us to you to take you to become his wife."

She bowed down with her face to the ground and said, "I am your servant and am ready to serve you and wash the feet of my lord's servants." Abigail quickly got on a donkey and, attended by her five female servants, went with David's messengers and became his wife.                    1 Samuel 25:32–42

## WHAT WE BELIEVE

*Gentleness is rooted in our belief in humanity. When we see people the way God sees them, we are compelled to treat them well. A gentle person, according to God's vision, is thoughtful. They think before they talk or act. A gentle person is considerate. They consistently put themselves in other people's shoes and act accordingly. A gentle person is calm. They are known for their even temper and positive energy. Jesus modeled this for us in so many of his relationships. We also see gentleness on display in Abigail. Pay attention to the lives of men like Nabal. Sometimes looking at a negative example can be eye-opening. Go back to the nuggets on gentleness you read earlier in the chapter. Pick just one suggestion and try it for seven days and see if it doesn't make a difference in your life and the lives of those God has placed around you.*

CHAPTER

## 30

# Humility

---

KEY QUESTION

What does it mean to value others before myself?

---

KEY IDEA

I choose to esteem others above myself.

---

KEY VERSE

Do nothing out of selfish ambition or vain conceit.
Rather, in humility value others above yourselves,
not looking to your own interests
but each of you to the interests of the others.
*Philippians 2:3–4*

OUR MAP

*Humility is a driving virtue in the Christian life and community. Choosing to value others above oneself encourages harmony and love. The opposite of humility is pride. Prideful people typically believe they are better than others. They try to get their way at the expense of others or boast as a way of boosting low self-esteem. When a person possesses biblical humility they draw from internal "God-esteem." They have received God's unconditional love and embraced their inherent worth as God's child—their identity in Christ. From this belief they are capable of lifting others up.*

*Do you want this virtue? This chapter will give you God's Word on the matter.*

- *Christ As Our Example*
- *God Opposes the Proud, Grants Favor to the Humble*
- *The Paradox of Humility*

## CHRIST AS OUR EXAMPLE

*Jesus is our supreme example of humility. The God of the universe could have ridden into our world on a white horse with a serious entourage and fanfare. Instead he came to us as a baby born in a stable to poor parents.*

In those days Caesar Augustus issued a decree that a census should be taken of the entire Roman world. (This was the first census that took place while Quirinius was governor of Syria.) And everyone went to their own town to register.

So Joseph also went up from the town of Nazareth in Galilee to Judea, to Bethlehem the town of David, because he belonged to the house and line of David. He went there to register with Mary, who was pledged to be married to him and was expecting a child. While they were there, the time came for the baby to be born, and she gave birth to her firstborn, a son. **She wrapped him in cloths and placed him in a manger, because there was no guest room available for them.**

And there were shepherds living out in the fields nearby, keeping watch over their flocks at night. An angel of the Lord appeared to them, and the glory of the Lord shone around them, and they were terrified. But the angel said to them, "Do not be afraid. I bring you good news that will cause great joy for all the people. Today in the town of David a Savior has been born to you; he is the Messiah, the Lord. This will be a sign to you: You will find a baby wrapped in cloths and lying in a manger."

Suddenly a great company of the heavenly host appeared with the angel, praising God and saying,

> "Glory to God in the highest heaven,
>    and on earth peace to those on whom his favor rests."

LUKE 2:1–14

*As his time on earth was coming to a close, Jesus wanted to give his disciples an unforgettable lesson about the importance of humility. This is what he did:*

It was just before the Passover Festival. Jesus knew that the hour had come for him to leave this world and go to the Father. Having loved his own who were in the world, he loved them to the end.

The evening meal was in progress, and the devil had already prompted Judas, the son of Simon Iscariot, to betray Jesus. **Jesus knew that the Father had put all things under his power, and that he had come from God and was returning to God; so he got up from the meal, took off his outer clothing, and wrapped a towel around his waist. After that, he poured water into a basin and began to wash his disciples' feet, drying them with the towel that was wrapped around him.**

He came to Simon Peter, who said to him, "Lord, are you going to wash my feet?"

Jesus replied, "You do not realize now what I am doing, but later you will understand."

"No," said Peter, "you shall never wash my feet."

Jesus answered, "Unless I wash you, you have no part with me."

"Then, Lord," Simon Peter replied, "not just my feet but my hands and my head as well!"

Jesus answered, "Those who have had a bath need only to wash their feet; their whole body is clean. And you are clean, though not every one of you." For he knew who was going to betray him, and that was why he said not every one was clean.

When he had finished washing their feet, he put on his clothes and returned to his place. "Do you understand what I have done for you?" he asked them. "You call me 'Teacher' and 'Lord,' and rightly so, for that is what I am. Now that I, your Lord and Teacher, have washed your feet, you also should wash one another's feet. I have set you an example that you should do as I have done for you. Very truly I tell you, no servant is greater than his master, nor is a messenger greater than the one who sent him. Now that you know these things, you will be blessed if you do them."

JOHN 13:1–17 🗝

Servant leadership is what Jesus modeled while on earth. What other ways can we demonstrate this principle besides washing someone's feet?

*Following in the steps of his Savior, the apostle Paul wrote a tender letter to the church at Philippi instructing them to practice humility. He cited Jesus as the perfect example.*

Do nothing out of selfish ambition or vain conceit. Rather, in humility value others above yourselves, not looking to your own interests but each of you to the interests of the others.

In your relationships with one another, have the same mindset as Christ Jesus:

> **Who, being in very nature God,**
> **did not consider equality with God something to be**
> **used to his own advantage;**
> **rather, he made himself nothing**
> **by taking the very nature of a servant,**
> **being made in human likeness.**
> **And being found in appearance as a man,**
> **he humbled himself**
> **by becoming obedient to death —**
> **even death on a cross!**

Therefore God exalted him to the highest place
  and gave him the name that is above every name,
that at the name of Jesus every knee should bow,
  in heaven and on earth and under the earth.

PHILIPPIANS 2:3–10

---

What do you think was involved when Jesus
"made himself nothing?" What was he before
he made himself nothing? Why did he do this?

---

## GOD OPPOSES THE PROUD, GRANTS FAVOR TO THE HUMBLE

*There is a very clear pattern in the Bible — God opposes the proud but grants favor to the humble. The following passages from the books of Psalms and Proverbs tell us more about what humility and pride look like practically. As you read the Scripture in this section, write down all the ways God opposes the proud and grants favor to the humble.*

The LORD's curse is on the house of the wicked,
  but he blesses the home of the righteous.
He mocks proud mockers
  but shows favor to the humble and oppressed.

PROVERBS 3:33–34

When pride comes, then comes disgrace,
  but with humility comes wisdom.  PROVERBS 11:2

**Pride goes before destruction,
  a haughty spirit before a fall.**

Better to be lowly in spirit along with the oppressed
  than to share plunder with the proud.  PROVERBS 16:18–19

Before a downfall the heart is haughty,
  but humility comes before honor.  PROVERBS 18:12

**Humility is the fear of the LORD;
  its wages are riches and honor and life.**  PROVERBS 22:4

> Pride brings a person low,
> but the lowly in spirit gain honor. PROVERBS 29:23

*One example of God opposing the proud and granting favor to the humble can be found in the story of a young Hebrew man named Daniel, who was taken captive in Babylon. After three years of training, Daniel was given an important job in King Nebuchadnezzar's service. With God's help, Daniel was able to interpret dreams, and he soon became one of the most important people in the royal court. God used Daniel to teach Nebuchadnezzar a memorable lesson in humility.*

*King Nebuchadnezzar had a dream he asked Daniel to interpret. When Daniel heard the dream, it terrified him. He reluctantly told the king what his dream meant. It was God's warning about what would happen to King Nebuchadnezzar if he did not change his ways. When the king showed pride by taking credit for the blessings that God had given him, his terrifying dream immediately came true.*

Daniel (also called Belteshazzar) was greatly perplexed for a time, and his thoughts terrified him. So the king said, "Belteshazzar, do not let the dream or its meaning alarm you."

Belteshazzar answered, "My lord, if only the dream applied to your enemies and its meaning to your adversaries! The tree you saw, which grew large and strong, with its top touching the sky, visible to the whole earth, with beautiful leaves and abundant fruit, providing food for all, giving shelter to the wild animals, and having nesting places in its branches for the birds — Your Majesty, you are that tree! You have become great and strong; your greatness has grown until it reaches the sky, and your dominion extends to distant parts of the earth.

"Your Majesty saw a holy one, a messenger, coming down from heaven and saying, 'Cut down the tree and destroy it, but leave the stump, bound with iron and bronze, in the grass of the field, while its roots remain in the ground. Let him be drenched with the dew of heaven; let him live with the wild animals, until seven times pass by for him.'

**"This is the interpretation, Your Majesty, and this is the de-**

cree the Most High has issued against my lord the king: You will be driven away from people and will live with the wild animals; you will eat grass like the ox and be drenched with the dew of heaven. Seven times will pass by for you until you acknowledge that the Most High is sovereign over all kingdoms on earth and gives them to anyone he wishes. The command to leave the stump of the tree with its roots means that your kingdom will be restored to you when you acknowledge that Heaven rules. Therefore, Your Majesty, be pleased to accept my advice: Renounce your sins by doing what is right, and your wickedness by being kind to the oppressed. It may be that then your prosperity will continue."

All this happened to King Nebuchadnezzar. Twelve months later, as the king was walking on the roof of the royal palace of Babylon, he said, "Is not this the great Babylon I have built as the royal residence, by my mighty power and for the glory of my majesty?"

Even as the words were on his lips, a voice came from heaven, "This is what is decreed for you, King Nebuchadnezzar: Your royal authority has been taken from you. You will be driven away from people and will live with the wild animals; you will eat grass like the ox. Seven times will pass by for you until you acknowledge that the Most High is sovereign over all kingdoms on earth and gives them to anyone he wishes."

Immediately what had been said about Nebuchadnezzar was fulfilled. He was driven away from people and ate grass like the ox. His body was drenched with the dew of heaven until his hair grew like the feathers of an eagle and his nails like the claws of a bird.

At the end of that time, I, Nebuchadnezzar, raised my eyes toward heaven, and my sanity was restored. Then I praised the Most High; I honored and glorified him who lives forever.

> His dominion is an eternal dominion;
>> his kingdom endures from generation to generation.
> All the peoples of the earth
>> are regarded as nothing.

He does as he pleases
  with the powers of heaven
  and the peoples of the earth.
No one can hold back his hand
  or say to him: "What have you done?"

At the same time that my sanity was restored, my honor and splendor were returned to me for the glory of my kingdom. My advisers and nobles sought me out, and I was restored to my throne and became even greater than before. Now I, Nebuchadnezzar, praise and exalt and glorify the King of heaven, because everything he does is right and all his ways are just. **And those who walk in pride he is able to humble.**      Daniel 4:19–37 ⌐┰

---

What was King Nebuchadnezzar's opinion about himself
before his dream came true? What was his opinion
about himself after his mind cleared? What does a humble
person think about themselves in relation to God?

---

## The Paradox of Humility

*A "paradox" is a statement that seems contrary to common sense and yet is true. Some might believe that a humble person always loses out, gets overlooked and comes in dead last, while someone with less humility always wins, gets noticed and comes in first. But the Bible teaches the opposite. There are great blessings in store for people who demonstrate humility. It doesn't mean humble people will always "win" or "come in first" in a worldly sense, but it does mean that they will experience true contentment and joy.*

---

As you read the Scriptures in this section, identify all of
God's paradoxes (such as, "rejoice when people persecute you,"
or "the last shall be first"). Have you seen the truth
in any of these paradoxes in your own experience?

---

Now when Jesus saw the crowds, he went up on a mountainside and sat down. His disciples came to him, and he began to teach them.

He said:

"Blessed are the poor in spirit,
  for theirs is the kingdom of heaven.
Blessed are those who mourn,
  for they will be comforted.
**Blessed are the meek,**
  **for they will inherit the earth.**
Blessed are those who hunger and thirst for righteousness,
  for they will be filled.
Blessed are the merciful,
  for they will be shown mercy.
Blessed are the pure in heart,
  for they will see God.
Blessed are the peacemakers,
  for they will be called children of God.
Blessed are those who are persecuted because of
      righteousness,
  for theirs is the kingdom of heaven.

"Blessed are you when people insult you, persecute you and falsely say all kinds of evil against you because of me. Rejoice and be glad, because great is your reward in heaven, for in the same way they persecuted the prophets who were before you."   MATTHEW 5:1–12

*This question of which of Jesus' disciples would be the greatest arose on a number of occasions. You would think the message would have eventually sunk in, but because of their pride, they kept asking. As Jesus was on his way to Jerusalem for the last time, the brothers James and John—two of Jesus' inner circle of disciples—approached him with a request.*

James and John, the sons of Zebedee, came to him. "Teacher," they said, "we want you to do for us whatever we ask."
"What do you want me to do for you?" he asked.
They replied, "Let one of us sit at your right and the other at your left in your glory."
"You don't know what you are asking," Jesus said. "Can you drink the cup I drink or be baptized with the baptism I am baptized with?"

"We can," they answered.

Jesus said to them, "You will drink the cup I drink and be baptized with the baptism I am baptized with, but to sit at my right or left is not for me to grant. These places belong to those for whom they have been prepared."

When the ten heard about this, they became indignant with James and John. Jesus called them together and said, "You know that those who are regarded as rulers of the Gentiles lord it over them, and their high officials exercise authority over them. Not so with you. **Instead, whoever wants to become great among you must be your servant, and whoever wants to be first must be slave of all. For even the Son of Man did not come to be served, but to serve, and to give his life as a ransom for many."**

MARK 10:35–45

*John the Baptist gave perhaps the most succinct recipe for humility when he was asked about the fact that people were leaving him to follow Jesus.*

To this John replied, "A person can receive only what is given them from heaven. You yourselves can testify that I said, 'I am not the Messiah but am sent ahead of him.' The bride belongs to the bridegroom. The friend who attends the bridegroom waits and listens for him, and is full of joy when he hears the bridegroom's voice. That joy is mine, and it is now complete. **He must become greater; I must become less."** JOHN 3:27–30

---

What are some ways we can follow John's recipe
for becoming more humble?

---

*Because of his humility, Jesus called John the Baptist the greatest of all men, but what he said next was in keeping with the paradox of humility.*

"Truly I tell you, among those born of women there has not risen anyone greater than John the Baptist; yet whoever is least in the kingdom of heaven is greater than he." MATTHEW 11:11

*Someone we typically look to as an example of humility is the apostle Paul, but he wasn't always a humble servant of Jesus. Before his conversion, he was an arrogant and violent persecutor of Christians. In his first letter to Timothy, he wrote about this past life. God can transform angry and prideful people into loving and humble servants of Jesus.*

I thank Christ Jesus our Lord, who has given me strength, that he considered me trustworthy, appointing me to his service. Even though I was once a blasphemer and a persecutor and a violent man, I was shown mercy because I acted in ignorance and unbelief. The grace of our Lord was poured out on me abundantly, along with the faith and love that are in Christ Jesus.

Here is a trustworthy saying that deserves full acceptance: Christ Jesus came into the world to save sinners — of whom I am the worst. **But for that very reason I was shown mercy so that in me, the worst of sinners, Christ Jesus might display his immense patience as an example for those who would believe in him and receive eternal life.** Now to the King eternal, immortal, invisible, the only God, be honor and glory for ever and ever. Amen.

1 TIMOTHY 1:12–17

## WHAT WE BELIEVE

*One of the most amazing pieces of evidence that we are becoming more and more like Jesus is the virtue of humility. Believers do not lift others up because they think lowly of themselves. No, they are able to esteem others above themselves because they have accepted the high esteem they have found through faith in Christ. Because we are freed from the struggle to prove we are somebody special, we can humble ourselves and look instead to build up others. When we do, it signals God's presence within us. Remember, God opposes the proud but grants favor to the humble. Don't let the world fool you; a humble person wins out at the end of the day and in eternity. God requires his followers to act justly, love mercy and walk humbly before him. It's a requirement that leads to great blessing. Remember, "I can do all this through [Christ] who gives me strength" (Philippians 4:13).*

# Epilogue

You have just finished reading the stories of real people in ancient times who encountered the one true God. They were invited to be a positive character in the unfolding of God's Grand Love Story.

Many believed; many did not. But for all it was a journey.

We see this in one of the stories contained in the Bible. A man brought his boy to Jesus to heal him of seizures caused by an evil spirit. Jesus asked the father how long his son had been like this. The father replied, "From childhood ... It has often thrown him into fire or water to kill him. But if you can do anything, take pity on us and help us."

"If you can?" said Jesus. "Everything is possible for one who believes."

Immediately the boy's father exclaimed, "I do believe; help me overcome my unbelief!"

Right now, Jesus invites you to believe—to believe in him and to believe the truths taught in the pages of Scripture that guide our lives daily and into eternity. Be honest like this boy's father and tell Jesus where you are at with all your doubts, and then invite him to help you with your unbelief—and he will. He doesn't want you to stop at believing these truths only in your head. He wants you to take them into your heart, the place where you decide how you will live.

Here is the promise: what you once thought was impossible will now be possible. The more you believe, the more you see and discover the power of God. The more you believe, the more he changes you from the inside out to become the kind of person you have only dreamed about—filled with love, joy, peace, patience, kindness, goodness, faithfulness, self-control, gentleness, humility and hope. These virtues are displayed in your life like fruit on a tree for others to enjoy. When we *think* and *act* like Jesus, empowered by his presence within us, little by little we *become* like Jesus. This is not only the most wonderful and abundant way to live, but it is truly the best gift we can give to our family and other people God places in our lives.

So spiritual pilgrim, BELIEVE. "Taste and see that the LORD is good."

# Chart of References

## CHAPTER 1: GOD

Genesis 1:1
Psalm 19:1–4
Romans 1:20
Deuteronomy 6:1–9
Joshua 24:2
Joshua 24:6–14

1 Kings 18:21–39
Genesis 2:15–24
John 1:1–5
Luke 3:15–18
Luke 3:21–22
Acts 17:16–34

## CHAPTER 2: PERSONAL GOD

Genesis 16:1–16
Genesis 21:1–21
Psalm 23:1–6
2 Kings 20:1–7
Jeremiah 1:4–10
Jeremiah 1:17–19
Jeremiah 29:1

Jeremiah 29:10–14
Matthew 6:25–34
Romans 8:26–28
Romans 8:38–39
James 1:2–5
James 1:13–18

## CHAPTER 3: SALVATION

Genesis 2:8–9
Genesis 2:15–17
Genesis 3:1–6
Genesis 3:13–15
Genesis 3:21–24
Exodus 12:21–31
Isaiah 53:2–9

Matthew 27:39–54
Matthew 28:1–10
John 3:1–18
Romans 5:12
Romans 5:15–19
Romans 10:9–10

## CHAPTER 4: THE BIBLE

Exodus 3:1–14
Luke 24:27–49
2 Peter 1:1–21
Exodus 20:1–17
Matthew 4:1–11

2 Timothy 3:14–17
Hebrews 4:12
Deuteronomy 4:1–2
Proverbs 30:5–6
Revelation 22:18–19

## CHAPTER 5: IDENTITY IN CHRIST

Genesis 17:1–7
Jeremiah 31:31–34
John 1:9–13
Luke 19:1–9
Romans 3:10–26

Romans 5:6–11
Romans 6:1–7
Romans 8:1–2
Romans 8:10–25
Ephesians 2:1–22

## CHAPTER 6: CHURCH

Genesis 12:1–4
Genesis 15:1–6
Matthew 16:13–18
Acts 1:4–5
Acts 1:8–9
Acts 2:1–24
Acts 2:36–41
Acts 13:38–39
Acts 13:44–48
Acts 20:17–31
Ephesians 4:1–6
Ephesians 4:11–16

## CHAPTER 7: HUMANITY

Genesis 1:26–31
Genesis 4:1–5
Genesis 4:6–16
Hosea 11:1–11
John 1:4
John 1:7
John 3:16
John 3:36
John 4:14
John 5:24
John 6:37
John 6:51
John 8:12
John 8:51
John 10:9
John 11:26a
Matthew 18:12–14
Luke 6:27–36
Philemon 1–25

## CHAPTER 8: COMPASSION

Nehemiah 9:25–28
Romans 3:23–26
1 John 4:9–10
Deuteronomy 24:10–15
Deuteronomy 24:17–22
Ruth 2:1–13
Ruth 2:19–20
Ruth 4:9–17
Luke 10:25–37
Matthew 25:34–40
James 1:22—2:4
James 2:12–13

## CHAPTER 9: STEWARDSHIP

Psalm 24:1–2
Psalm 50:9–12
Matthew 25:14–30
1 Samuel 1:9–28
1 Samuel 2:18–21
Malachi 3:6–12
Luke 16:10–15
Mark 12:41–44
1 Kings 17:7–16
Romans 12:13
Hebrews 13:2
1 Peter 4:9
1 Corinthians 6:13–20
1 Corinthians 10:23–24
1 Corinthians 10:31—11:1

## CHAPTER 10: ETERNITY

2 Kings 2:5–18
Luke 16:19–31
1 Corinthians 15:35–44a
1 Thessalonians 4:14–18
2 Peter 3:11–14
Revelation 21:1—22:6
John 14:1–7

## Chapter 11: Worship

Isaiah 1:11–20
Matthew 23:1–7
Matthew 23:23–28
Daniel 6:1–27

Acts 16:22–35
Luke 22:14–30
Colossians 3:1–17

## Chapter 12: Prayer

Mark 1:32–35
Luke 6:12–16
Mark 6:39–46
Matthew 26:36–46

Judges 6:11—7:24
Luke 11:1–13
Philippians 4:6–9

## Chapter 13: Bible Study

Deuteronomy 6:20–25
Deuteronomy 31:9–13
Joshua 1:1–9
Psalm 119:9–24
Psalm 119:33–40

Psalm 119:97–112
Matthew 13:1–23
John 14:15–27
1 Corinthians 2:6–16
Hebrews 5:11—6:3

## Chapter 14: Single-Mindedness

Exodus 20:3
Matthew 6:19–24
2 Chronicles 20:1–30
Matthew 14:22–33
Acts 5:12–42

Deuteronomy 30:15–20
Romans 12:1–2
Colossians 3:1–4
Colossians 3:15–17

## Chapter 15: Total Surrender

Daniel 3:1–28
Esther 3:5—4:16
Luke 9:23–26
Acts 6:8–15

Acts 7:51–60
Acts 21:13
Philippians 1:12–14
Philippians 1:19–21

## Chapter 16: Biblical Community

Ecclesiastes 4:9–12
Exodus 25:1–9
2 Chronicles 7:1–3
Ephesians 2:11–22
Acts 2:1–4
Acts 2:42–47
Acts 4:32–37
Nehemiah 2:11—3:2
Nehemiah 6:15

Romans 12:4–5
Galatians 6:2
Ephesians 4:2
Ephesians 5:21
Hebrews 13:1–3
Hebrews 13:15–16
1 John 1:1–7
1 John 2:7–11
1 John 3:16–18

## CHAPTER 17: SPIRITUAL GIFTS

Daniel 2:1–47
Romans 12:4–8
1 Corinthians 12:4–28

Matthew 25:14–30
1 Peter 4:7–11

## CHAPTER 18: OFFERING MY TIME

Jonah 1:1—2:10
Haggai 1:1–15a
Luke 2:41–52
Exodus 16:11–30

John 7:1–16
Matthew 25:34–40
Ephesians 5:15–17
Galatians 6:7–10

## CHAPTER 19: GIVING MY RESOURCES

Exodus 35:21–29
Exodus 36:3–7
Proverbs 3:9–10
Proverbs 11:24–25
Proverbs 11:28
Ecclesiastes 5:10–20
Matthew 2:1–12

Matthew 6:1–4
Matthew 6:19–24
Luke 12:13–21
Mark 12:41–44
2 Corinthians 8:1–12
2 Corinthians 9:6–15
Philippians 4:11–13

## CHAPTER 20: SHARING MY FAITH

2 Corinthians 5:14–21
2 Kings 5:1–15
Matthew 5:13–16
1 Corinthians 9:19–23

Acts 8:26–39
Jonah 3:1–10
John 4:5–42

## CHAPTER 21: LOVE

1 Corinthians 13:1–13
Deuteronomy 6:4–9
Leviticus 19:17–18
Mark 12:28–34
Matthew 5:43–48

Galatians 5:16–25
John 10:14–18
1 Samuel 18:1b–4
1 Samuel 19:1–7
1 Samuel 20:12–42

## CHAPTER 22: JOY

Psalm 16:1–11
Luke 2:6–20
John 15:1–11
Nehemiah 8:13–17
James 1:2–17
Philippians 1:3–8

Philippians 1:12–19
Philippians 4:10–13
1 Peter 1:3–9
1 Peter 4:12–16
1 Peter 5:6–11

## CHAPTER 23: PEACE

Isaiah 9:6–7
Genesis 13:1–18
1 Kings 3:3–15
1 Kings 4:20–25

Romans 14:1—15:13
Mark 4:35–41
Matthew 6:25–34
Philippians 4:4–9

## CHAPTER 24: SELF-CONTROL

Proverbs 16:32
Proverbs 17:27
Proverbs 25:28
Proverbs 29:11
Titus 1:4–9
Titus 2:3–8
Titus 2:11–15
Judges 16:4–21

1 Corinthians 6:18–20
1 Timothy 6:6–11
2 Timothy 2:22–26
James 3:3–11
James 4:1–10
Galatians 5:16–25
Luke 15:11–24

## CHAPTER 25: HOPE

1 Timothy 6:17
Psalm 118:8–9
Jeremiah 17:5b–6
Habakkuk 2:18–19
Isaiah 31:3

1 Peter 1:1–9
1 Peter 1:13–21
Isaiah 40:25–31
Luke 2:25–35
Hebrews 11:1—12:3

## CHAPTER 26: PATIENCE

Psalm 86:15
2 Peter 3:3–15a
1 Samuel 24:1–15
1 Samuel 26:1–25
Proverbs 14:29
Proverbs 15:18

Proverbs 16:32
Proverbs 19:11
Proverbs 25:15
James 1:19–20
John 5:1–15
2 Corinthians 12:7b–10

## CHAPTER 27: KINDNESS/GOODNESS

Psalm 107:1–22
1 Samuel 20:14–15
2 Samuel 9:1–13
Luke 14:7–14
Philemon 1
Philemon 8–21
Luke 6:27–45
1 Peter 3:8–12

Romans 15:1–2
Galatians 6:9–10
Ephesians 4:31—5:2
1 Thessalonians 5:15
Titus 2:7a
Titus 3:1–2
Titus 3:14

346 | BELIEVE: Student Edition

## CHAPTER 28: FAITHFULNESS

Deuteronomy 32:1–4

Psalm 36:5–9

Lamentations 3:19–24

Proverbs 3:1–6

Proverbs 20:6

Proverbs 28:20

Genesis 39:1–6a

Genesis 41:15–46a

Genesis 42:1–6

Luke 1:26b–55

## CHAPTER 29: GENTLENESS

John 18:12–27

John 21:1–19

Matthew 11:28–30

Matthew 5:5

Matthew 5:38–42

Matthew 7:1–5

Galatians 5:22–23

Ephesians 4:2

Ephesians 4:26–32

Colossians 3:12

2 Timothy 2:24–26

Titus 3:1–2

James 3:17–18

1 Samuel 25:4–13

1 Samuel 25:14–19

1 Samuel 25:23–27

1 Samuel 25:32–42

## CHAPTER 30: HUMILITY

Luke 2:1–14

John 13:1–17

Philippians 2:3–10

Proverbs 3:33–34

Proverbs 11:2

Proverbs 16:18–19

Proverbs 18:12

Proverbs 22:4

Proverbs 29:23

Daniel 4:19–37

Matthew 5:1–12

Mark 10:35–45

John 3:27–30

Matthew 11:11

1 Timothy 1:12–17

# BELIEVE

POWERED BY ⚡ZONDERVAN®

Dear Reader,

Notable researcher George Gallup Jr. summarized his findings on the state of American Christianity with this startling revelation: "Churches face no greater challenge…than overcoming biblical illiteracy, and the prospects for doing so are formidable because **the stark fact is, many Christians don't know what they believe or why.**"

The problem is not that people lack a hunger for God's Word. Research tells us that the number one thing people want from their church is for it to help them understand the Bible, and that Bible engagement is the number one catalyst for spiritual growth. Nothing else comes close.

This is why I am passionate about the book you're holding in your hands: *Believe* — a Bible engagement experience to anchor every member of your family in the key teachings of Scripture.

The *Believe* experience helps you answer three significant questions: Can you clearly articulate the essentials of the faith? Would your neighbors or coworkers identify you as a Christian based on their interactions with you and your family? Is the kingdom of God expanding in your corner of the world?

Grounded in Scripture, *Believe* is a spiritual growth experience for all ages, taking each person on a journey toward becoming more like Jesus in their beliefs, actions, and character. There is one edition for adults, one for students, and two versions for children. All four age-appropriate editions of *Believe* unpack the 10 key beliefs, 10 key practices, and 10 key virtues of a Christian, so that everyone in your family and your church can learn together to be more like Jesus.

When these timeless truths are understood, believed in the heart, and applied to our daily living, they will transform a life, a family, a church, a city, a nation, and even our world.

Imagine thousands of churches and hundreds of thousands of individuals all over the world who will finally be able to declare— **"I know what I believe and why, and in God's strength I will seek to live it out all the days of my life."** It could change the world. It has in the past; it could happen again.

In Him,

Randy Frazee
General Editor, *Believe*

LIVING THE STORY OF THE BIBLE TO BECOME LIKE JESUS

# Teach your whole family how to live the story of the Bible!

- **Adults** – Unlocks the 10 key beliefs, 10 key practices, and 10 key virtues that help people live the story of the Bible. Bible Study DVD and Study Guide also available.
- *Think, Act, Be Like Jesus* – A companion to *Believe*, this fresh resource by pastor Randy Frazee will help readers develop a personal vision for spiritual growth and a simple plan for getting started on the *Believe* journey.
- **Students** – This edition contains fewer Scriptures than the adult edition, but with transitions and fun features to engage teens and students. Bible Study DVD also available.
- **Children** – With a Kids' Edition for ages 8-12, a Storybook for ages 4-8, a coloring book for toddlers, and four levels of curriculum for toddlers, preschool, early elementary, and later elementary, children of all ages will learn how to think, act, and be like Jesus.
- **Churches** – *Believe* is flexible, affordable, and easy to use with your whole church.
- **Spanish** – All *Believe* resources are also available in Spanish.

## FOR ADULTS

9780310443834

9780310250173

## FOR STUDENTS

9780310745617

## FOR CHILDREN

Ages 8–12
9780310746010

Ages 4–8
9780310745907

Ages 2–5
9780310752226

## FOR CHURCHES

Campaign Kit  9780310681717

# BELIEVE
POWERED BY ZONDERVAN

# THE STORY

POWERED BY ■ ZONDERVAN®

READ THE STORY. EXPERIENCE THE BIBLE.

Here I am, 50 years old. I have been to college, seminary, engaged in ministry my whole life, my dad is in ministry, my grandfather was in ministry, and **The Story has been one of the most unique experiences of my life**. The Bible has been made fresh for me. It has made God's redemptive plan come alive for me once again.
—Seth Buckley, Youth Pastor,
Spartanburg Baptist Church, Spartanburg, SC

As my family and I went through *The Story* together, the more I began to believe and the more real [the Bible] became to me, and **it rubbed off on my children and helped them with their walk with the Lord.** *The Story* inspired conversations we might not normally have had.
—Kelly Leonard, Parent, Shepherd of the Hills Christian Church, Porter Ranch, CA

**We have people reading** *The Story*—**some devour it and can't wait for the next week.** Some have never really read the Bible much, so it's exciting to see a lot of adults reading the Word of God for the first time. I've heard wonderful things from people who are long-time readers of Scripture. They're excited about how it's all being tied together for them. It just seems to make more sense.
—Lynnette Schulz,
Director of Worship
Peace Lutheran Church,
Eau Claire, WI

## FOR ADULTS

9780310950974

## FOR TEENS

Ages 13+
9780310722809

## FOR KIDS

Ages 8–12
9780310719250

# Dive into the Bible in a whole new way!

*The Story* is changing lives, making it easy for any person, regardless of age or biblical literacy level, to understand the Bible.

*The Story* comes in five editions, one for each age group from toddlers to adults. All five editions are organized chronologically into 31 chapters with selected Scripture from Genesis to Revelation. The additional resources create an engaging group Bible-reading experience, whether you read *The Story* with your whole church, in small groups, or with your family.

- **Adults** – Read the Bible as one compelling story, from Genesis to Revelation. Available in NIV, KJV, NKJV, large print, imitation leather, and audio editions. Curriculum DVD and Participant's Guide also available.
- **Teens** – Teen edition of *The Story*, with special study helps and features designed with teens in mind. Curriculum DVD also available.
- **Children** – With a Kids' Edition for ages 8-12, a Storybook Bible for ages 4-8, a Storybook Bible for toddlers, fun trading cards, and three levels of curriculum for preschool, early elementary, and later elementary, children of all ages will learn how their story fits into God's story.
- **Churches** – *The Story* is flexible, affordable, and easy to use with your church, in any ministry, from nursery to adult Sunday school, small groups to youth group…and even the whole church.
- **Spanish** – *The Story* resources are also available in Spanish.

## FOR CHILDREN

Ages 4–8
9780310719755

Ages 2–5
9780310719274

## FOR CHURCHES

Campaign Kit   9780310941538

THE STORY
POWERED BY ZONDERVAN